Also by J. R. Ward

LOVER
REVEALED

J. R. WARD

piatkus

PIATKUS

First published in the US in 2007 by New American Library,
A division of Penguin Group (USA) Inc.
First published in Great Britain in 2007 by Piatkus Books
This paperback edition published in 2010 by Piatkus Books
Reprinted 2010 (twice)

A CIP catalogue record for this book
is available from the British Library.

ISBN 978-0-7499-3822-2

Typeset in Garamond by Palimpsest Book Production Limited,
Grangemouth, Stirlingshire
Printed in the UK by CPI Mackays, Chatham ME5 8TD

Papers used by Piatkus are natural, renewable and
recyclable products sourced from well-managed forests and certified
in accordance with the rules of the Forest Stewardship Council.

Mixed Sources
Product group from well-managed
forests and other controlled sources
www.fsc.org Cert no. SGS-COC-004081
© 1996 Forest Stewardship Council

Piatkus
An imprint of
Little, Brown Book Group
100 Victoria Embankment
London EC4Y 0DY

An Hachette UK Company
www.hachette.co.uk
www.piatkus.co.uk

DEDICATED TO: *YOU*.

Man, you had me at *Hard-ass*, you really did.
But then there was your *Here's looking at you, kid* . . .
Mad love to you.

With immense gratitude to the readers
of the Black Dagger Brotherhood
and a shout out to the Cellies—
what couch are we on now?

Thank you so very much:
Karen Solem, Kara Cesare, Claire Zion, Kara Welsh.

Thank you, Cap'n Bunny a.k.a the Pink Beast and
PythAngie the Pitbull Mod—
seriously, Dorine and Angie, you take such good
care of me.

Thank you to the Party of Four: MFN hugs . . .
M-F-N hugs.
Don't know what I would do without you.

To DLB: Remember ya mummy loves you. Always.
To NTM: The thing I love most about you-know-where
is . . . you. I'm just so lucky to know you.

As always, with thanks to my Executive Committee:
Sue Grafton, Dr. Jessica Andersen, Betsey Vaughan.
And with much respect to the incomparable
Suzanne Brockmann.

With love to my Boat, my family, and my
writer friends.

GLOSSARY OF TERMS
AND PROPER NOUNS

ahvenge v. Act of mortal retribution, carried out typically by a male loved one.

Black Dagger Brotherhood pr n. Highly trained vampire warriors who protect their species against the Lessening Society. As a result of selective breeding within the race, Brothers possess immense physical and mental strength as well as rapid healing capabilities. They are not siblings for the most part, and are inducted into the Brotherhood upon nomination by the Brothers. Aggressive, self-reliant, and secretive by nature, they exist apart from civilians, having little contact with members of the other classes except when they need to feed. They are the subjects of legend and the objects of reverence within the vampire world. They may be killed only by the most serious of wounds, e.g., a gunshot or stab to the heart, etc.

blood slave n. Male or female vampire who has been subjugated to serve the blood needs of another. The practice of keeping blood slaves has largely been discontinued, though it has not been outlawed.

the Chosen pr n. Female vampires who have been bred to serve the Scribe Virgin. They are considered members of the aristocracy, though they are spiritually rather than temporally focused. They have little or no interaction with males but can be mated to Brothers at the Scribe Virgin's direction to propagate their class. They have the ability to prognosticate. In the past, they were used to meet the blood needs of unmated members of the Brotherhood, but that practice has been abandoned by the Brothers.

cohntehst n. Conflict between two males competing for the right to be a female's mate.

Dhunhd pr n. Hell.

doggen n. Member of the servant class within the vampire world. *Doggen* have old, conservative traditions about service to their superiors, following a formal code of dress and behavior. They are able to go out during the day, but they age relatively quickly. Life expectancy is approximately five hundred years.

the Fade pr n. Nontemporal realm where the dead reunite with their loved ones and pass eternity.

First Family pr n. The king and queen of the vampires and any children they may have.

ghardian n. Custodian of an individual. There are varying degrees of *ghardians*, with the most powerful being that of a *sehcluded* female, known as a *whard*.

glymera n. The social core of the aristocracy, roughly equivalent to Regency England's *ton*.

hellren n. Male vampire who has been mated to a female. Males may take more than one female as mate.

leahdyre n. A person of power and influence.

leelan adj.; n. A term of endearment loosely translated as "dearest one."

Lessening Society pr n. Order of slayers convened by the Omega for the purpose of eradicating the vampire species.

lesser n. De-souled human who targets vampires for extermination as a member of the Lessening Society. *Lessers* must be stabbed through the chest in order to be killed; otherwise they are ageless. They do not eat or drink and are impotent. Over time, their hair, skin, and irises lose pigmentation until they are blond, blushless, and pale-eyed. They smell like baby powder. Inducted into the society by the Omega, they retain a ceramic jar thereafter, into which their heart was placed after it was removed.

lheage n. A term of respect used by a sexual submissive to refer to her dominant.

mahmen n. Mother. Used both as an identifier and a term of affection.

mhis n. The masking of a given physical environment; the creation of a field of illusion.

nalla (f.) or *nallum* (m.) n. Beloved.

needing period n. Female vampire's time of fertility, generally lasting for two days and accompanied by intense sexual cravings. Occurs approximately five years after a female's transition and then once a decade thereafter. All males respond to some degree if they are around a female in her need. It can be a dangerous time, with conflicts and fights breaking out between competing males, particularly if the female is not mated.

newling n. A virgin.

the Omega pr n. Malevolent, mystical figure who has targeted the vampires for extinction out of resentment directed toward the Scribe Virgin. Exists in a nontemporal realm and has extensive powers, though not the power of creation.

phearsom adj. Term referring to the potency of a male's sexual organs. Literal translation something close to "worthy of entering a female."

princeps n. Highest level of the vampire aristocracy, second only to members of the First Family or the Scribe Virgin's Chosen. Must be born to the title; it may not be conferred.

pyrocant n. Refers to a critical weakness in an individual. The weakness can be internal, such as an addiction, or external, such as a lover.

rythe n. Ritual manner of assuaging honor granted by one who has offended another. If accepted, the offended chooses a weapon and strikes the offender, who presents him- or herself without defenses.

the Scribe Virgin pr n. Mystical force who is counselor to the king as well as the keeper of vampire archives and the dispenser of privileges. Exists in a nontemporal realm and has extensive powers. Capable of a single act of creation, which she expended to bring the vampires into existence.

sehclusion n. Status conferred by the king upon a female as a result of a petition by the female's family. Places the female under the sole direction of her *whard*, typically the eldest male in her household. Her *whard* then has the legal right to determine all manner of her life, restricting at will any and all interactions she has with the world.

shellan n. Female vampire who has been mated to a male. Females generally do not take more than one mate due to the highly territorial nature of bonded males.

symphath n. Subspecies within the vampire world characterized by the ability and desire to manipulate emotions in others (for the purposes of an energy exchange), among other traits. Historically, they have been discriminated against and during certain eras hunted by vampires. They are near to extinction.

the Tomb pr n. Sacred vault of the Black Dagger Brotherhood. Used as a ceremonial site as well as a storage facility for the jars of *lessers*. Ceremonies performed there include inductions, funerals, and disciplinary actions against Brothers. No one may enter except for members of the Brotherhood, the Scribe Virgin, or candidates for induction.

trahyner n. Word used between males of mutual respect and affection. Translated loosely as "beloved friend."

transition n. Critical moment in a vampire's life when he or she transforms into an adult. Thereafter, they must drink the blood of the opposite sex to survive and are unable to withstand sunlight. Occurs generally in the mid-twenties. Some vampires do not survive their transitions, males in particular. Prior to their transitions, vampires are physically weak, sexually unaware and unresponsive, and unable to dematerialize.

vampire n. Member of a species separate from that of Homo sapiens. Vampires must drink the blood of the opposite sex to survive. Human blood will keep them alive, though the strength does not last long. Following their transitions, which occur in their mid-twenties, they are unable to go out into sunlight and must feed from the vein regularly. Vampires cannot "convert" humans through a bite or transfer of blood, though they are in rare cases able to breed with the other species. Vampires can dematerialize at will, though they must be able to calm themselves and concentrate to do so and may not carry anything heavy with them. They are able to strip the memories of humans, provided such memories are short term. Some vampires are able to read minds. Life expectancy is upward of a thousand years or in some cases even longer.

wahlker n. An individual who has died and returned to the living from the Fade. They are accorded great respect and are revered for their travails.

whard n. Custodian of a *sehcluded* female.

ONE

"What if I told you I had a fantasy?"

Butch O'Neal put his Scotch down and eyed the blonde who'd spoken to him. Against the backdrop of ZeroSum's VIP area, she was something else, dressed in white patent leather strips, a cross between Barbie and Barbarella. It was hard to know if she was one of the club's professionals or not. The Reverend only trafficked in the best, but maybe she was a model for *FHM* or *Maxim*.

She planted her hands on the marble tabletop and leaned in toward him. Her breasts were perfect, the very best money could buy. And her smile was radiant, a promise of acts done with knee pads. Paid or not, this was a woman who got plenty of vitamin D and liked it.

"Well, daddy?" she said over the trippy techno music. "Want to make my dream come true?"

He shot her a hard smile. Sure as hell, she was going to make someone very happy tonight. Probably a busload of someones. But he wasn't going to be riding that double-decker.

"Sorry, you need to go taste the rainbow somewhere else."

Her total lack of reaction sealed the deal on her professional status. With a vacant smile, she floated over to the next table and pulled the same lean and gleam.

Butch tilted his head back and swallowed the inch of Lagavulin left in his glass. His next move was to flag down a waitress. She didn't come over, just nodded and beat feet for the bar to get him another.

It was almost three a.m., so the rest of the troika were going to show up in a half hour. Vishous and Rhage were out hunting *lessers*, those soulless bastards that killed their kind, but the two vampires were probably going to come in for a landing disappointed. The secret war between their species and the Lessening Society had been quiet all January and February, with few slayers out and around. This was good news for the race's civilian population. Cause for concern for the Black Dagger Brotherhood.

"Hello, cop." The low male voice came from right behind Butch's head.

Butch smiled. That sound always made him think of night fog, the kind that hides what's going to kill you. Good thing he liked the dark side.

"Evening, Reverend," he said without turning around.

"I knew you were going to turn her down."

"You a mind reader?"

"Sometimes."

Butch glanced over his shoulder. The Reverend was poised in the shadows, amethyst eyes glowing, mohawk trimmed tight to his skull. His black suit was sweet: Valentino. Butch had one just like it.

Although in the Reverend's case the worsted wool had been bought with the guy's own money. The Reverend, a.k.a. Rehvenge, a.k.a. brother of Z's *shellan*, Bella, owned ZeroSum and took a cut of everything that went down. Hell, with all the depravity for sale in the club, he had a forest worth of green funneling into his piggy bank at the end of every night.

"Nah, she just wasn't for you." The Reverend slid into the booth, smoothing his perfectly knotted Versace necktie. "And I know why you said no."

"Oh, yeah?"

"You don't like blondes."

Not anymore he didn't. "Maybe I just wasn't into her."

"I know what you want."

As Butch's newest Scotch arrived, he gave it a quick vertical workout. "Do you now?"

"It's my job. Trust me."

"No offense, but I'd rather not about this."

"Tell you what, cop." The Reverend leaned in close and he smelled fantastic. Then again, Cool Water by Davidoff was an oldie but goodie. "I'll help you anyway."

Butch clapped a hand on the male's heavy shoulder. "Only interested in bartenders, buddy. Good Samaritans give me the scratch."

"Sometimes only the opposite will do."

"Then we're SOL." Butch nodded out at the half-naked crowd writhing on hits of X and coke. "Everyone looks the same around here."

Funny, during his years in the Caldwell Police Department, ZeroSum had been an enigma to him. Everyone knew the place was a drug hole and a sex pool. But no one at the CPD had been able to pin down enough probable cause to get a search warrant—even though you could walk in any night of the week and see dozens of legal infractions, most of them happening in tandem.

But now that Butch was hanging with the Brotherhood, he knew why. The Reverend had lots of little tricks in his bag when it came to changing people's perceptions of events and circumstances. As a vampire, he could scrub clean the memories of any human, manipulate security cameras, dematerialize at will. The guy and his biz were a moving target that never moved.

"Tell me something," Butch said, "how have you managed to keep your aristocratic family from knowing about this little night job you got going on?"

The Reverend smiled so that only the tips of his fangs showed. "Tell me something, how did a human get so tight with the Brotherhood?"

Butch tipped his glass in deference. "Sometimes fate takes you in fucked-up directions."

"So true, human. So very true." As Butch's cell phone went off, the Reverend got up. "I'll send you over something."

"Unless it's Scotch I don't want it, my man."

"You're going to take that back."

"Doubt it." Butch took out his Motorola Razr and flipped it open. "What up, V? Where are you?"

Vishous was breathing like a racehorse with the dull roar of wind distortion backing him up: a symphony of ass hauling. "Shit, cop. We got problems."

Butch's adrenaline kicked in, lighting him up like a Christmas tree. "Where are you?"

"Out in the burbs with a situation. The damn slayers have started hunting civilians in their homes."

Butch leaped to his feet. "I'm coming—"

"The hell you are. You stay put. I only called so you wouldn't think we were dead when we didn't show. Later."

The connection cut off.

Butch sank back down in the booth. From the table next to him, a group of people let out a loud, happy burst, some shared joke teeing their laughter off like birds flushed into the open air.

Butch looked into his glass. Six months ago he'd had nothing in his life. No woman. No family he was close to. No home to speak of. And his job as a homicide detective had been eating him alive. Then he'd gotten canned for police brutality. Fallen in with the Brotherhood through a bizarre series of events. Met the one and only woman who'd ever awed him stupid. Also had a total wardrobe makeover.

At least that last one was in the good category and had stayed there.

For a while the change had been a great mask of reality, but lately he'd noticed that for all the differences, he was right where he'd always been: no more alive than when he'd been rotting in his old life. Still on the outside looking in.

Sucking back his Lag, he thought of Marissa and pictured her hip-length blond hair. Her pale skin. Her light blue eyes. Her fangs.

Yeah, no blondes for him. He couldn't go even remotely sexual with the pale-haired types.

Ah, hell, screw the Clairol chart. It wasn't like any woman in this club or on the face of the planet could come close to Marissa. She had been pure in the manner of a crystal, refracting the light, and life around her improved, enlivened, colored with her grace.

Shit. He was such a sap.

Except, man, she'd been so lovely. For the short time when she'd seemed to be attracted to him, he'd hoped they might get something off the ground. But then she'd up and disappeared. Which of course proved she was smart. He didn't have much to offer a female like her and not because he was just a human. He was treading water on the fringes of the Brotherhood's world, unable to fight at their side because of what he was, unable to go back to the human world because he knew too much. And the only way out of this deserted middle ground was with a toe tag.

Now was he a real eHarmony contender or what?

With another rush of happy-happy-joy-joy, the group next door let off a fresh buckshot of hilarity and Butch glanced over. At the center of the party was a little blond guy in a slick suit. He looked fifteen, but he'd been a

5

regular in the VIP section for the past month, throwing cash around like it was confetti.

Obviously, the guy made up for his physical deficiencies through the use of his wallet. Another example of green being golden.

Butch finished his Scotch, fingered for the waitress, then looked at the bottom of his glass. Shit. After four doubles, he didn't feel buzzed at all, which told him how well his tolerance was faring. Clearly, he was a varsity alcoholic now, no more of that training at the junior levels thing.

And when the realization didn't bother him, he realized he'd stopped treading water. Now he was sinking.

Well, wasn't he a party tonight.

"The Reverend says you need a friend."

Butch didn't bother glancing up at the woman. "No, thanks."

"Why don't you look at me first?"

"Tell your boss I appreciate his—" Butch glanced up and clapped his mouth shut.

He recognized the woman immediately, but then again, ZeroSum's head of security was pretty damn unforgettable. Six feet tall, easy. Hair jet-black and cut like a man's. Eyes the dark gray color of a shotgun barrel. With the wife-beater she had on, she was popping the upper body of an athlete, all muscles, veins, and no fat. The vibe she gave off was that she could break bones and enjoy it, and absently he looked at her hands. Long-fingered. Strong. The kind that could do damage.

Holy hell . . . he would like to be hurt. Tonight he would like to hurt on the outside for a change.

The woman smiled a little, like she knew what he was thinking, and he caught a glimpse of fangs. Ah . . . so she was not woman. She was female. She was vampire.

6

The Reverend had been right, that bastard. This one would do, because she was everything Marissa wasn't. And because she was the kind of anonymous sex Butch had had all his adult life. And because she was just the sort of pain he was looking for and hadn't known it.

As he slipped a hand into his Ralph Lauren Black Label suit, the female shook her head. "I don't work it for cash. Ever. Consider it a favor for a friend."

"I don't know you."

"You're not the friend I'm talking about."

Butch looked over her shoulder and saw Revenge staring across the VIP section. The male shot back a very self-satisfied smile, then disappeared into his private office.

"He's a very good friend of mine," the female murmured.

"Oh, really. What's your name?"

"Not important." She held out her hand. "Come on, Butch, a.k.a. Brian, last name O'Neal. Come back with me. Forget for a while whatever makes you hammer those shots of Lagavulin. I promise you, all that self-destruction will be waiting for you when you get back."

Man, he really wasn't psyched about how much she had on him. "Why don't you tell me your name first."

"Tonight you can call me Sympathy. How 'bout that."

He eyed her from bangs to boots. She was wearing leather pants. No surprise. "You happen to have two heads there, Sympathy?"

She laughed, a low, rich sound. "No, and I'm not a shemale, either. Yours isn't the only sex that can be strong."

He stared hard into her cast-iron eyes. Then looked back at the private bathrooms. God . . . this was so familiar. A quickie with a stranger, a meaningless crash between two bodies. This shit had been the cash-and-carry of his sex life since he could remember—except he didn't recall ever feeling this kind of sick despair before.

7

Whatever. Was he really going to stay celibate until he kicked it when his liver corroded? Just because a female he didn't deserve didn't want him?

He glanced down at his pants. His body was willing. At least that part of the math added up.

Butch slid out of the booth, his chest as cold as winter pavement. "Let's go."

On a lovely tremble of violins, the chamber orchestra glided into a waltz and Marissa watched the glittering crowd coalesce in the ballroom. All around her, males and females came together, hands linking, bodies meeting, stares locking. The mingling of dozens of different variations on the bonding scent filled the air with a rich spice.

She breathed in through her lips, trying not to smell so much of it.

Escape proved futile, however, which was the way things worked. Though the aristocracy prided itself on its manners and style, the *glymera* was, after all, still subject to the race's biological truths: When males bonded, their possessiveness carried a scent. When females accepted their mates, they bore that dark fragrance on their skin with pride.

Or at least Marissa assumed it was with pride.

Of the hundred twenty-five vampires in her brother's ball-room, she was the only unmated female. There were a number of unmated males, but it wasn't as if they would ever ask her to dance. Better that those *princeps* sit out the waltzing or take their mothers or sisters to the floor than get anywhere near her.

No, she was forever unwanted, and as a couple twirled by right in front of her, she glanced down to be polite. Last thing she needed was for them to trip all over each other as they avoided looking her in the eye.

While her skin shriveled, she wasn't sure why tonight

8

her status as shunned spectator seemed a special burden. For God's sake, no member of the *glymera* had met her stare for four hundred years and she was used to it: First she had been the Blind King's unwanted *shellan*. Now she was his *former* unwanted *shellan*, who had been passed over for his beloved half-breed queen.

Maybe she was finally exhausted with being on the outside.

Hands shaking, lips tight, she picked up the heavy skirt of her gown and made for the ballroom's grand archway. Salvation was just outside in the hall, and she pushed open the door to the mistresses' lounge with a prayer. The air that greeted her smelled of freesia and perfume and within the arms of its invisible embrace there was . . . only silence.

Thank the Scribe Virgin.

Her tension eased marginally as she went in and looked around. She'd always thought of this particular bathroom in her brother's mansion as a luxurious locker room for debutantes. Decorated in a vivid Russian czarist motif, the bloodred sitting and primping area was kitted out with ten matching vanities, each makeup station holding everything a female could want to improve her appearance. Extending out the back of the lounge were the private lavatory chambers, all of which were done in the scheme of a different Fabergé egg from her brother's extensive collection.

Perfectly feminine. Perfectly lovely.

Standing in the middle of it all, she wanted to scream.

Instead, she bit her lip and bent down to check her hair in one of the mirrors. The blond weight, which reached the small of her back when down, was arranged with watchmaker precision on the top of her head and the chignon was holding up well. Even after several hours, everything was still in place, the pearl strands woven in by her *doggen* exactly where they'd been when she'd come down to the ball.

Then again, standing on the fringes hadn't really given the Marie Antoinette job a workout.

But her necklace was out of whack again. She jogged the multitiered pearl collar back into position so that its lowest drop, a Tahitian twenty-three-millimeter, pointed directly down into what little cleavage she had.

Her dove gray gown was vintage Balmain, one that she'd bought in Manhattan in the 1940s. Shoes were Stuart Weitzman and brand-new, not that anyone saw them under the floor-length skirt. Necklace, earrings, and cuffs were Tiffany, as always: When her father had discovered the great Louis Comfort in the late 1800s, the family had become loyal customers of the company and had stayed that way.

Which was the hallmark of the aristocracy, wasn't it? Constancy and quality in all things, change and defects to be greeted with glaring disapproval.

She straightened and backed up until she could see her whole self from across the room. The image staring back at her was ironic: Her reflection was of utter female flawlessness, an improbable beauty that seemed sculpted, not born. Tall and thin, her body was made up of delicate angles, and her face was absolutely sublime, a perfect combination of lips and eyes and cheeks and nose. The skin over it all was alabaster. The eyes were silver blue. The blood in her veins was among the very purest in the species.

Yet here she was. The forsaken female. The one left behind. The unwanted, defective, spinster virgin who not even a purebred warrior like Wrath had been able to bear sexually even *once*, if only to rid her of being a *newling*. And thanks to his repulsion, she was ever unmated, though she'd been with Wrath for what had seemed like forever. You had to have been taken to be considered someone's *shellan*.

Their end had been a surprise and no surprise at all. To anyone. Despite Wrath declaring that she had left him, the *glymera* knew the truth. She'd been untouched for centuries, never carrying the bonding scent from him, never spending a day alone with him. More to the point, no female would have left Wrath voluntarily. He was the Blind King, the last purebred vampire on the planet, a great warrior and a member of the Black Dagger Brotherhood. There was no higher than he.

The conclusion among the aristocracy? Something had to be wrong with her, most likely hidden beneath her clothes, and the deficiency was probably sexual in nature. Why else would a full-blooded warrior have no erotic impulse toward her?

She took a deep breath. Then another. And another.

The scent of the fresh-cut flowers invaded her nose, the sweetness swelling, taking over, replacing the air . . . until it was only fragrance going down into her lungs. Her throat seemed to close up, as if to fight the onslaught, and she pulled at her necklace. Tight . . . it was so tight on her neck. And heavy . . . like hands choking her . . . She opened her mouth to breathe, but it didn't help. Her lungs were clogged with the flower stench, coated by it . . . she was suffocating, drowning, though she was not in water . . .

On loose legs, she walked to the door, but she couldn't face those dancing couples, those people who defined who they were by ostracizing her. No, she couldn't let them see her . . . they would know how upset she was. They would see how hard this was for her. Then they would despise her even more.

Her eyes shot around the mistresses' lounge, skipping

11

over everything, bouncing off all the mirrors. Frantically she tried to . . . what was she doing? Where could she . . . go—bedroom, upstairs . . . She had to . . . oh, God . . . *she couldn't breathe*. She was going to die here, right here and now, from her throat closing up tight as a fist.

Havers . . . her brother . . . she needed to reach him. He was a doctor . . . He would come and help her—but his birthday would be ruined. *Ruined* . . . because of her. Everything ruined because of her . . . It was all her fault . . . everything. All the disgrace she bore was her fault . . . Thank God her parents had been dead for centuries and hadn't seen her for what . . . she was . . .

Going to throw up. She was definitely going to throw up.

Hands shaking, legs like pudding, she lurched into one of the bathrooms and locked herself inside. On the way to the toilet, she fumbled with the sink, turning the water on to drown out her rasping breath in case someone came in. Then she fell to her knees and bent over the porcelain bowl.

She gagged and wretched, her throat working through the dry heaves, nothing coming up but air. Sweat broke out on her forehead and under her armpits and between her breasts. Head spinning, mouth gaping, she struggled for breath as thoughts of dying and having no one to help her, of ruining her brother's party, of being an abhorred object swarmed like bees . . . bees in her head, buzzing, stinging . . . causing the death . . . thoughts like bees . . .

Marissa started to cry, not because she thought she was going to die but because she knew she wasn't.

God, the panic attacks had been brutal these last few months, her anxiety a stalker with no solid form, whose persistence knew no exhaustion. And every time she had a meltdown, the experience was a fresh and horrible revelation.

Propping her head on her hand, she wept hoarsely, tears running down her face and getting trapped in the pearls and diamonds at her throat. She was so alone. Caged in a beautiful, wealthy, fancy nightmare where the bogeymen wore tuxedos and smoking jackets and the vultures swooped down on wings of satin and silk to peck out her eyes.

Taking a deep breath, she tried to get some control over her respiration. *Easy . . . easy now. You're okay. You've done this before.*

After a while, she looked down into the toilet. The bowl was solid gold and her tears made the surface of the water ripple as if sunlight shined within it. She became abruptly aware that the tile was hard beneath her knees. And her corset was biting into her rib cage. And her skin was clammy.

She lifted her head and glanced around. Well, what do you know. She'd picked her favorite private chamber to fall apart in, the one based on the Lilies of the Valley egg. As she sat draped over the toilet, she was surrounded by blush-pink walls hand-painted with bright green vines and little white flowers. The floor and counter and sink were pink marble veined with white and cream. The sconces were gold.

Very nice. Perfect background for an anxiety attack, really. But then, lately panic went with everything, didn't it? The new black.

Marissa pushed herself up from the floor, turned off the faucet, and collapsed into the little silk-covered chair in the corner. Her gown settled around her as if it were an animal stretching out now that the drama was over.

She looked at herself in the mirror. Her face was blotchy, her nose red. Her makeup was ruined. Her hair was a ragged mess.

See, this was what she looked like on the inside, so no

wonder the *glymera* despised her. Somehow they knew this was the truth of her.

God . . . maybe that was why Butch hadn't wanted her—

Oh, hell no. The last thing she needed was to think about him right now. What she had to do was straighten herself up as best she could and then scoot up to her bedroom. Sure, hiding was unattractive, but so was she.

Just as she reached up to her hair, she heard the outside door to the lounge open, the chamber music swelling, then easing off as it closed.

Great. Now she was trapped. But maybe it was only one female so she didn't have to worry about being an eavesdropper.

"I can't believe I spilled on my shawl, Sanima."

Okay, so now she was an eavesdropper as well as a coward.

"It's barely noticeable," Sanima said. "Although thank the Virgin you caught it before anyone else did. We'll go in here together and use some water."

Marissa shook herself into focus. *Don't worry about them, just fix your hair. And for the Virgin's sake do something about that mascara. You look like a raccoon.*

She grabbed a washcloth and wet it quietly while the two females went into the little room across the way. Obviously, they left the door open—their voices were undimmed.

"But what if someone saw?"

"Shh . . . let's take the shawl off—oh, my Lord." There was a short laugh. "Your neck."

The younger female's voice dropped to an ecstatic hush. "It's Marlus. Ever since we were mated last month, he's been . . ."

Now the laughter was shared.

14

"Does he come to you often during the day?" Sanima's secretive tone was delighted.

"Oh, yes. When he said he wanted our bedrooms connected, I didn't know why. Now, I do. He's . . . insatiable. And he . . . he doesn't just want to feed."

Marissa stopped with the washcloth under her eye. Only once had she known a male's hunger for her. One kiss, only one . . . and she held the memory with care. She was going to her grave a virgin, and that brief meeting of mouths was all she would ever have of anything sexual.

Butch O'Neal. Butch had kissed her with— *Stop it.*

She went to work on the other side of her face.

"To be newly mated, how marvelous. Though you mustn't let anyone see these marks. Your skin is marred."

"That's why I rushed in here. What if someone told me to take off the wrap because of the wine I spilled?" This was said with the kind of horror usually reserved for accidents involving knives.

Although, given the *glymera,* Marissa could understand all too well wanting to avoid their attention.

Tossing the washcloth aside, she tried to rework her hair . . . and gave up not thinking about Butch.

God, she would have loved having to hide his teeth marks from the eyes of the *glymera.* Would have loved to hold the delicious secret that under the civilized gowns she wore, her body had known his raw sex. And she would have loved to bear the scent of his bonding for her on her skin, emphasizing it, as mated females did, by choosing the perfect complementary perfume.

But none of that was going to happen. For one thing, humans didn't bond, from what she'd heard. And even if they did, Butch O'Neal had walked away from her the last time she'd seen him, so he wasn't interested in her anymore.

Probably because he'd heard about her deficiencies. As he was close with the Brotherhood, no doubt he knew all kinds of things about her now.

"Is there someone in here?" Sanima said sharply.

Marissa cursed under her breath and figured she'd just sighed out loud. Giving up on her hair and her face, she opened the door. When she stepped out, both females looked down, which in this instance was a good thing. Her hair was a train wreck.

"Worry not. I will say nothing," she murmured. Because sex was never to be discussed in a public place. Or any private ones, really.

The two curtsied dutifully and did not reply while Marissa left.

As soon as she walked out of the lounge, she felt more glances sliding away from her, all eyes going elsewhere . . . especially those of the unmated males smoking cigars over in the corner.

Just before she turned her back on the ball, she caught Havers's stare through the crowd. He nodded and smiled sadly, as if he knew she couldn't stay a moment longer.

Dearest brother, she thought. He had always supported her, had never given any indication he was ashamed of how she had turned out. She would have loved him for their shared parents, but she adored him for his loyalty most of all.

With a last look at the *glymera* in all its glory, she went to her room. After a quick shower, she changed into a simpler floor-length dress and lower-heeled shoes, then went down the mansion's back stairs.

Untouched and unwanted she could deal with. If that was the fate the Scribe Virgin laid upon her, so be it. There were far worse lives to be led, and bemoaning what she lacked, considering all she had, was boring and selfish.

What she couldn't handle was being purposeless. Thank God that she had her position on the *Princeps* Council and that her seat was secure by virtue of her bloodline. But there was also another way to leave a positive mark on her world.

As she keyed in a code and unlocked a steel door, she envied the couples dancing at the other end of the mansion and probably always would. Except that was not her destiny. She had other paths to walk.

TWO

Butch left ZeroSum at three forty-five, and though the Escalade was parked in the back, he headed in the opposite direction. He needed air. Jesus . . . he needed air.

The middle of March was still winter so far as upstate New York was concerned, and the night was meat-locker cold. As he walked alone down Trade Street, his breath left his mouth in white clouds and drifted over his shoulder. The chill and the isolation suited him: He was hot and crowded even though he'd left the club's crush of sweaty people behind.

As he went along, his Ferragamos hit hard against the side-walk, the heels grinding the salt and sand on the little concrete strip between dirty snowbanks. In the background, muffled music thumped out of the other bars on Trade, though business hours were soon going to be over.

When he came up to McGrider's, he popped his collar and up'd his pace. He avoided the blues bar because the boys on the force hung out there and he didn't want to see them. Far as his former colleagues in the CPD knew, he'd up and disappeared, and that was the way he wanted to keep it.

Screamer's was next and hard-core rap pounded, turning the whole damn building into a bass extender. When he got to the far side of the club, he paused and looked down the alley that ran the length of the place.

It had all started here. His weird trip into the vampire world had started right here the previous July, with a car bomb he'd investigated at this site: a BMW blown to shit.

A man ashed. No material evidence left behind except a couple of martial-arts throwing stars. The hit had been very professional, the kind of thing that sent a message, and shortly thereafter the bodies of the prostitutes had appeared in the alleys. Throats cut. Blood levels sky high with heroin. With more martial-arts weapons around.

He and his partner, José de la Cruz, had assumed the blast was a pimp-related turf toaster and the dead women payback, but soon enough he'd learned the whole story. Darius, a member of the Black Dagger Brotherhood, had been taken out by his race's enemies, the *lessers*. And the murders of those prostitutes were part of a strategy by the Lessening Society to capture civilian vampires for questioning.

Man, back then he'd never have even guessed vampires existed. Much less drove $90,000 BMWs. Or had sophisticated enemies.

Butch walked down the alley, right to the spot where the 650i had been blown to high heaven. There was still a black soot ring on the building from the bomb's heat and he reached out, putting fingertips on the cold brick.

It had all started here.

A gust of wind came up and flashed under his coat, lifting the fine cashmere, getting to the fancy suit underneath. Dropping his hand, he looked down at his clothes. Overcoat was Missoni, about five grand. Suit underneath, an RL Black Label, about three grand. Shoes were amateur night at a mere seven hundred bucks. Cuff links were Cartier and into the five-digit category. Watch was Patek Philippe. Twenty-five grand.

The two forty-millimeter Glocks under his pits were two grand a piece.

So he was sporting . . . Jesus Christ, about $44,000 worth of Saks Fifth and Army/Navy. And this wasn't even the tip of the iceberg for his threads. He had two closets worth of the shit back at the compound . . . none of which he'd bought with his own cash. All of which had been purchased with Brotherhood green.

Shit . . . he dressed in clothes that weren't his. Lived in a house and ate food and watched a plasma screen TV . . . none of which were his. Drank Scotch he didn't pay for. Drove a sweet ride he didn't own. And what did he do in return? Not a whole hell of a lot. Every time action went down, the brothers kept him on the sidelines—

Footsteps rang out at the far end of the alley, pounding, pounding, getting closer. And there was more than one set.

Butch eased back into the shadows, slipping free the buttons on his coat and his suit jacket so he could get at his heat if he needed it. He had no intention of mixing up someone else's biz, but he wasn't the type to hang back if an innocent was getting cracked.

Guess the cop in him wasn't dead yet.

As the alley had only one open end, the track-and-fielders heading this way were going to pass by him. Hoping to avoid any crossfire, he got tight with a Dumpster and waited to see what turned up.

Young guy flew by, terror on his face, his body all jerky panic. And then . . . well, what do you know, the two thugs in his trunk were pale haired. Big as houses. Smelling like baby powder.

Lessers. Going after a civilian.

Butch palmed one of his Glocks, speed-dialed V's cell phone, and took off in pursuit. As he ran, the call dumped into voice mail, so he just shoved his Razr back into his pocket.

When he caught up with the drama, the three were at the base of the alley, a loose knot of bad news. Now that

20

the slayers had the civilian cornered, they were moving all lazy, closing in, backing off, smiling, toying. The civilian was shaking, eyes so wide the whites glowed in the dark.

Butch leveled his gun at the scene. "Hey, Blondies, how 'bout you show me your hands?"

The *lessers* stopped and looked at him. Man, it was like getting pegged with headlights, assuming you were a deer and the thing coming at you was a Peterbilt. Those undead bastards were pure power backed up by cold logic—a nasty combination, especially in duplicate.

"This isn't your business," the one on the left said.

"Yeah, that's what my roommate keeps telling me. But, see, I don't take direction real well."

He had to give the *lessers* credit; they were smart. One focused on him. The other closed in on the civilian, who looked as if he was way too scared to be able to dematerialize.

This is quickly going to become a hostage situation, Butch thought.

"Why don't you head out?" the bastard on the right said. "Better for you."

"Probably, but worse for him." Butch nodded toward the civilian.

An ice cube breeze shot down the alley, ruffling orphaned newspaper pages and empty plastic shopping bags. Butch's nose tingled and he shook his head, hating the smell.

"You know," he said, "this whole baby powder thing— how do you *lessers* stand it?"

The slayers' pale eyes traveled up and down him as if they couldn't figure out why he even knew the word. And then they both flipped into action. The *lesser* closest to the civilian made a grab and hauled the vampire against its chest, turning the hostage potential into a reality. At the same moment, the other one lunged at Butch, moving quick as a blink.

Butch wasn't into getting rattled, though. He calmly angled the muzzle of the Glock and shot the steamrolling sonofabitch right in the chest. The second his bullet penetrated, a screech worthy of a banshee exploded out of the slayer's throat and the thing hit the ground like a bag of sand, immobilized.

Which was not the normal *lesser* response to getting plugged. Usually they could throw it off, but Butch was packing something special in his clip, thanks to the Brotherhood.

"What the fuck," the upright slayer breathed.

"Surprise, surprise, cocksucker. Got me some fancy lead."

The *lesser* snapped back to reality and hauled the civilian off the ground in a one-arm waist hold, using the vampire as a body shield.

Butch leveled the gun at the twosome. *Goddamn it. No shot. No shot at all.* "Let him go."

A muzzle emerged from under the civilian's armpit.

Butch dove for a shallow doorway as the first bullet ricocheted off the asphalt. Just as he took shelter, a second shot ripped through his thigh.

Fuuuuuck, welcome to roadkill-ville. His leg felt like it had a red-hot roofing spike drilled into it, the niche he was jammed into offered about as much protection as a lamppost and the *lesser* was moving into better shooting position.

Butch grabbed an empty Coors bottle and tossed it across the alley. As the *lesser*'s head popped around the civilian's shoulder to track the sound, Butch lit off four precisely targeted shots in a semicircle around the pair. The vampire panicked, just as expected, and became an unstable load. As he fell loose from the slayer's grip, Butch put a slug into the *lesser*'s shoulder, spinning the bastard away, landing him facefirst on the ground.

Great shot, but the undead was still moving, and sure as shit he was going to be on his feet in another minute and a half. Those special bullets were good, but the stun didn't last forever and it helped if you nailed a chest rather than an arm.

And what do you know. More problems.

Now that the civilian vampire was free, he'd caught his breath and started to scream.

Butch limped over, cursing through the pain in his leg. Jesus Christ, this male was making enough racket to bring in an entire police force—all the way from goddamned Manhattan.

Butch got up in the guy's face, pegging him with hard eyes. "I need you to stop yelling, okay? Listen to me. Stop. Yelling. Now." The vampire sputtered, then clammed up like his voice box's engine had run out of gas. "Good. I got two things I need from you. First, I want you to calm yourself so you can dematerialize. Do you understand what I'm saying? Breathe slow and deep—that's right. Nice. And I want you to cover your eyes now. Go on, cover them."

"How do you know—"

"Talking wasn't on your to-do list. Close your eyes and cover them. And keep breathing. Everything's going to be okay provided you get yourself out of this alley."

As the male clamped trembling hands over his eyes, Butch went over to the second slayer, who was lying face-down on the pavement. The thing had black blood oozing from its shoulder and little moans coming out of its mouth.

Butch grabbed a fistful of the *lesser*'s hair, tilted the thing's head off the asphalt, and put the Glock's muzzle in tight to the base of the skull. He pulled the trigger.

As the top half of the bastard's face vaporized, its arms and legs twitched. Fell still.

But the job wasn't done. Both slayers needed to be stabbed in the chest to truly be dead. And Butch didn't have anything sharp and shiny on him.

He got out his cell phone and hit speed dial again as he rolled the slayer over with his foot. While V's cell started to ring, Butch went through the *lesser*'s pockets. He lifted a BlackBerry as well as a wallet—

"Fuck me," Butch breathed. The slayer had activated his phone, obviously calling for an assist. And through the open line, the sounds of heavy breathing and flapping clothes were a loud and clear sign that the backup brigade was coming fast.

Butch glanced at the vampire as V's phone continued to ring. "How we doin'? You look good. You look really calm and in control."

V, pick up the damn phone. V—

The vampire dropped his hands, and his eyes fell upon the slayer, whose forehead was now all over the brick wall on the right. "Oh . . . my God—"

Butch stood up, putting his body in the way. "You don't think about that."

The civilian's hand came out and pointed downward. "And you—you're shot."

"Yeah, you don't worry about me, either. I need you to cool out and leave, my man." *Like right fucking now.*

Just as V's voice mail kicked in, the sound of boots pounding the pavement drifted down the alley. Butch shoved his phone in the vicinity of his pocket and ditched the clip out of the Glock. As he slammed in a fresh one, he was through with the hand-holding. "Dematerialize. Dematerialize *now*."

"But—but—"

"*Now!* For fuck's sake, get your ass out of here or you're going home in a box."

"Why are you doing this? You're just a human—"

"I am *so* sick of hearing that. *Leave!*"

The vampire closed his eyes, breathed a word in the Old Language, and disappeared.

As the hellfire beat of the slayers got louder, Butch looked around for shelter, aware that his left shoe was soaking wet from his own blood. The shallow doorway was his only bet. Cursing again, he flattened himself in it and looked at what was coming at him.

"Oh, shit . . ." *Jesus God in heaven* . . . there were six of them.

Vishous knew what was about to happen next, and it was nothing he needed to be a part of. As a flash of brilliant white light turned the night to noontime, he spun away, shoving his shitkickers into the ground. And there was no reason to glance back when the great roar of the beast rumbled through the night. V knew the drill: Rhage had turned, the creature was loose, and the *lessers* they'd been fighting were about to be lunch. Pretty much business as usual . . . except for their current location: Caldwell High School's football field.

Go, Bulldogs! Rah!

V pounded over to the bleachers and StairMastered them, taking himself to the top of CHS's cheering section. Down below, on the fifty-yard line, the beast snatched a *lesser*, tossed the thing up into the air, and caught the undead between its teeth.

Vishous glanced around. The moon wasn't out, which was great, but there were maybe twenty-five frickin' houses around the high school. And the humans inside those split-levels and ranches and Middle America colonials had just woken up to a flare as bright as a nuclear explosion.

V cursed and whipped off the lead-lined driving glove that covered his right hand. As he put his arm out, the glow from his godforsaken palm's inner core illuminated the tattoos that ran from his fingertips to his wrist on both sides. Staring at the field, V concentrated on the beat of his heart, feeling the pump in his veins and getting into the pulse, the pulse, the pulse . . .

Buffering waves came out of his palm, something like heat waves rising off asphalt. Just as a couple of porch lights came on and front doors were opened and fathers of the household poked their heads out of their castles, the masking of *mhis* took over: The sights and the sounds of the fighting on the field were replaced with the nothing special illusion that all was well and as it should be.

From the bleachers, V used his night vision to watch the human men look around and wave to each other. When one smiled and shrugged, V could imagine the conversation.

Hey, Bob, you see that too?

Yeah, Gary. Big light. Huge.

Should we call the police?

Everything looks okay.

Yeah. Weird. Hey, you and Marilyn and the kids free this Saturday? We could do a mall crawl, maybe hit pizza afterward?

Great idea. I'll talk to Sue. 'Night.

'Night.

While the doors were shut and those men no doubt shuffled to the refridge for a night bite, Vishous kept up the masking.

The beast didn't take long. And didn't leave much uneaten. When it was finished, the scaled dragon looked around and as the thing spotted V, a growl rippled up to the bleachers, then ended in a snort.

"You finished, big guy?" V called down. "FYI, goal-post over there would work righteous as a toothpick."

Another snort. Then the creature lay down and Rhage appeared naked in its place on the black-soaked ground. As soon as the change was complete, V hauled it down the bleachers and jogged across the field.

"My brother?" Rhage groaned as he shivered in the snow.

"Yeah, Hollywood, it's me. I'm gonna get you home to Mary."

"Not as bad as it used to be."

"Good."

V whipped off his leather jacket and stretched it across Rhage's chest; then he snagged his cell phone from a pocket. Two calls had come through from Butch's number and he hit back at the cop, needing a pickup fast. When there was no answer, V called the Pit and got voice mail.

Holy hell . . . Phury was at Havers's getting his prosthesis adjusted again. Wrath couldn't drive because of his blindness. No one had seen Tohrment for months. That left . . . Zsadist.

After a hundred years of dealing with that male, it was hard not to curse as the call went out. Z was not lifeboat material, not by a long shot; he was more like the sharks in the water. But what was the other option? Besides, at least the brother had been a little better since he'd gotten mated.

"Yeah," came the sharp answer.

"Hollywood expressed his inner Godzilla again. I need a car."

"Where are you?"

"Weston Road. Caldwell High School football field."

"I'll be there in ten. First aid?"

"No, we're both intact."

"Got it. Hang tight."

The connection ended and V looked at his phone. The idea that that scary-ass bastard could be relied upon was a surprise. Never would have seen that one coming . . . not that he saw anything anymore.

V put his good hand on Rhage's shoulder and looked up at the sky. An infinite, unknowable universe loomed above him, above them all, and for the first time, the vastness terrified him. But then, for the first time in his life he was flying without a net.

His visions were gone. Those snapshots of the future, those bullshit, invasive telecasts of what was coming, those pictures without dates that had kept him on edge ever since he could remember, were just gone. And so were the intrusions of other people's thoughts.

He'd always wanted to be alone in his head. How ironic that he found the silence deafening.

"V? We okay?"

He looked down at Rhage. The brother's perfect blond beauty was still blinding, even with all the *lesser* blood on his face. "Ride's coming soon. We'll get you home to your Mary."

Rhage started to mumble and V just let him go. Poor miserable guy. Curses were never a party.

Ten minutes later, Zsadist pulled right up onto the football field in his twin's BMW, busting through a shrinking, dirty snowbank and mud-tracking it in. As the M5 came through the snow, V knew they were going to trash the leather in the back-seat, but then Fritz, butler extraordinaire, could get stains out like you wouldn't believe.

Zsadist got out of the car and came around the hood. After a century of being half-starved by choice, he was now packing a good two hundred eighty-five pounds on his six-foot-six frame. The scar on his face remained obvious, and so did his tattooed slave bands, but thanks to his *shellan*, Bella, his eyes were no longer black pits of hatred. For the most part.

Without saying anything, the two of them manhandled Rhage over to the car and stuffed his massive body into the backseat.

"You poofing it home?" Z said as he got behind the wheel.

"Yeah, but I need to clear the scene." Which meant using his hand to fry-clean the *lesser* blood that was splattered everywhere.

"You want me to wait?"

"No, get our boy home. Mary's going to want to see him ASAP."

Zsadist scanned the vicinity with a quick head twist. "I'll wait."

"Z, it's cool. I won't stay here alone long."

That ruined lip lifted into a snarl. "If you're not at the compound by the time I get there, I'm coming for you."

The Beemer took off, back tires kicking up mud and snow.

Jesus, Z really was backup.

Ten minutes later V dematerialized to the compound, just as Zsadist was pulling in with Rhage. As Z took Hollywood inside, Vishous looked around at the cars parked in the courtyard. Where the hell was the Escalade? Butch should be back by now.

V took out his phone and hit speed dial. When he got voice mail, he said, "Hey, buddy, I'm home. Where are you, cop?"

As the two of them called each other constantly, he knew Butch would check in soon enough. Hell, maybe the guy was getting busy for the first time in recorded history. It was about time the sorry SOB shelved his obsession with Marissa and got a little sexual relief.

And speaking of relief . . . V measured the light in the sky. He figured he had about an hour and a half of darkness left, and man, he was twitchy as shit. There was something going on tonight, something bad in the air, but with his visions gone, he didn't know what it was. And the blank slate was making him mental.

He fired up his cell again and hit a number. When the ringing stopped, he didn't wait for a hello. "You will get ready for me now. You will wear what I bought for you. Your hair will be bound and off your neck."

He waited to hear the only three words he cared about and they came right away, the female voice saying, "Yes, my *lheage*."

V hung up and dematerialized.

THREE

ZeroSum was doing excellent business lately, Rehvenge thought as he looked at the tallies. Cash flow was strong. There was growth in the sports booking receipts. Attendance was up. God, he'd owned the club for how long now? Five? Six years? And it was finally cranking enough income that he could take a deep breath.

It was a despicable way of making money, of course, what with the sex and the drugs and the booze and the betting. But he needed to support his *mahmen* and, up until recently, his sister, Bella. Then there was the blackmail overhead he had to cover.

Secrets could be so expensive to keep.

Rehv looked up as the door to his office opened. As his chief security officer came in, he could smell the lingering scent of O'Neal on her and he smiled a little. He liked being right. "Thanks for taking care of Butch."

Xhex's gray eyes were direct as always. "I wouldn't have if I hadn't wanted him."

"And I wouldn't have asked if I hadn't known that. Now, where are we?"

She sat down opposite his desk, her powerful body as hard as the marble he was resting his elbows on. "Nonconsensual sex in the mezzanine men's room. I took care of it. The woman is pressing charges."

"Was the guy walking after you were through with him?"

"Yeah, but he was wearing a new pair of earrings, if you know what I mean. I also found two minors on the premises and kicked them out. And one of the bouncers was taking kickbacks from the line, so I fired him."

"Anything else?"

"We had another OD."

"*Shit*. Not our product, though, right?"

"Nope. Outside junk." She pulled a small cellophane bag out of the back pocket of her leathers and tossed it on his desk. "I managed to snag this before the EMTs arrived. I'm hiring some extra staff to deal with the situation."

"Good. You find that freelancer, you bring his ass to me. I want to take care of him personally."

"Will do."

"You got anything more for me?"

In the silence that followed, Xhex leaned forward and linked her hands together. Her body was all tight muscle, nothing but hard angles except for her high, small breasts. She was deliciously hermaphroditic, although fully a female so far as he'd heard.

The cop should feel lucky, he thought. Xhex didn't have sex that often, and then only when she found the male worthy.

She also didn't waste time. Usually. "Xhex, talk."

"I want to know something."

Rehv eased back in his chair. "Is this going to piss me off?"

"Yup. Are you looking for a mate?"

As his eyes started to glow purple, he tilted his chin down and stared at her from under his brows. "Who said I was? And I want the name."

"Deduction, not gossip. According to GPS records, your Bentley's been by Havers's a lot lately. I happen to know Marissa is unattached. She's beautiful. Complicated. But you've never cared about the *glymera*. You thinking about mating her?"

"Not at all," he lied.

"Good." As Xhex's eyes nailed into him, it was obvious she knew the truth. "Because it would be crazy for you to give it a shot. She'd find out about you—and I'm not talking about what goes down here. She's a member of the *Princeps* Council, for chrissakes. If she knew you were a *symphath*, that would compromise both of us."

Rehv rose to his feet and palmed his cane. "The Brotherhood already knows about me."

"How?" Xhex breathed.

He thought about the little lip/fang thing he and the Brother, Phury, had shared and decided to keep that on the down-low. "They just do. And now that my sister's mated to a Brother, I'm a member of the frickin' family. So even if the *Princeps* Council found out, those warriors would keep them at bay."

Too bad his blackmailer was unaffected by the ways of the Normals. *Symphaths*, he was learning, made very bad enemies. No wonder his kind were hated.

"You sure about that?" Xhex said.

"It would kill Bella if I were sent to one of those colonies. You think that *hellren* of hers would stand for her being upset like that, especially as she's *pregnant*? Z's one mean-ass motherfucker and he is very protective of her. So, yeah, I'm sure."

"She ever guessed about you?"

"No." And though Zsadist knew, he wasn't going to tell his mate. No way he'd put Bella in that position. Laws read that if you knew of a *symphath* you had to report him or her or face prosecution.

Rehv came around the desk, relying on his cane now that Xhex was the only one around. The dopamine he shot himself up with regularly kept the worst of the *symphath* urges at bay, enabling him to pass for a Normal. He wasn't sure how Xhex managed it. Wasn't sure he wanted to know. But the thing was, with his sense of touch gone, he had to use a cane or he was liable to fall. After all, depth perception got you only so far when you couldn't feel your feet or legs.

"You don't worry," he said. "No one knows what either one of us are. And it's going to stay that way."

Gray eyes stared up at him. "Are you feeding her, Rehv." Not a question. A demand. "Are you feeding Marissa?"

"That's my business, not yours."

She shot to her feet. "*Goddamn you*—we agreed. Twenty-five years ago when I had my little problem, we agreed. No mates. No feeding with Normals. What the *hell* are you doing?"

"I'm in control and this conversation is over." He checked his watch. "And what do you know, it's closing time and you need a break. The Moors can lock up."

She glared at him for a moment. "I don't leave until the job is done—"

"I'm telling you to go home, not being nice, I'll see you tomorrow night."

"No offense, but fuck you, Rehvenge."

She stalked over to the door, moving like the killer she was. As he watched her go, he was reminded that this security stuff for him was nothing compared to what she was capable of.

"Xhex," he said, "maybe we were wrong about the mating."

She sent an *are-you-stupid?* frown over her shoulder. "You shoot yourself up twice a day. You think Marissa wouldn't notice that eventually? How about the fact that you have to go to her brother the good doctor for the neuromodulator you rely on? Besides, what would an aris-tocrat like her say about all . . . this?" She swept her arm

34

around his office. "We weren't wrong. You're just forgetting the *whys* of it all."

The door eased shut behind her and Rehv looked down at his numb body. He pictured Marissa, so pure and beautiful, so different from the other females he was around, so different from Xhex . . . who he fed from.

He wanted Marissa, was half in love with her at this point. And the male in him wanted to claim what was his even though his drugs made him impotent. Except surely he wouldn't hurt what he loved, even if his dark parts were out? Right?

He thought of her, wearing her lovely haute couture gowns, so properly dressed, so genteel, so . . . clean. The *glymera* was wrong about her. She wasn't defective; she was perfect.

He smiled, his body flushing up with a burn that only hardcore orgasms could douse. It was getting to be that time of the month, so she would be calling him soon. Yeah, she would need him again . . . soon. As his blood was diluted, she had to feed with gratifying frequency, and the last time had been almost three weeks ago.

She would be calling him within days. And he couldn't wait to be of service to her.

V got back to the Brotherhood's compound with minutes to spare, materializing just outside the gatehouse's front door. He'd hoped his kind of sex would have taken the edge off of him, but no, he was still bladed as shit.

He went through the Pit's vestibule and disarmed along the way, all tensed up and *so* ready for a shower to get the smell of the female off him. He should have been hungry; instead, all he wanted was some Grey Goose.

"Butch, my man!" he called out.

Silence.

V walked down the hall to the cop's bedroom. "You crashed?"

He pushed open the door. The king-sized bed was empty. So maybe the cop was up at the main house?

V jogged through the Pit and put his head out through the vestibule's door. A quick glance around at the cars parked in the courtyard and his heart went snare drum on him. No Escalade. So Butch wasn't at the compound.

With the sky beginning to lighten off to the east, the glow of day stung V's eyes, so he ducked back into the house and sat down behind his bank of computers. Firing up the coordinates on the Escalade, he saw that the SUV was parked behind Screamer's.

Which was good. At least Butch wasn't wrapped around a tree—

V froze. Slowly, he pushed his hand into the back pocket of his leathers, a horrible feeling coming over him, hot and prickly like a rash. Flipping open the Razr, he accessed his voice mail. First message was a hang-up from Butch's number.

As the second message clicked on, the Pit's steel shutters started to come down for the day.

V frowned. There was only a hissing sound coming from the voice mail. But then a clatter had him yanking the phone away from his ear.

Now Butch's voice, hard, loud: *"Dematerialize. Dematerialize now."*

A scared male: *"But—but—"*

"Now! For fuck's sake, get your ass out of here . . ." Sounds of muffled flapping.

"Why are you doing this? You're just a human—"

"I am so sick of hearing that. Leave!"

There was a metallic shifting, a gun being reloaded.

Butch's voice: *"Oh, shit . . ."*

Then all hell broke loose. Gunshots, grunts, thuds.

V leaped up from his desk so fast he knocked his chair over. Only to realize he was trapped inside by daylight.

FOUR

The first thing Butch thought when he came around was that someone needed to turn that faucet off. The drip, drip, drip was annoying.

Then he cracked an eyelid and realized his own blood was pulling the Kohler routine. *Oh . . . right.* He'd been beaten and he was leaking.

This had been a long, long, very bad day. How many hours had he been interrogated? Twelve? Felt like a thousand.

He tried to take a deep breath, but some of his ribs were broken, so he picked hypoxia over more pain. Man, thanks to his captor's attentions, everything hurt like a motherfucker, but at least the *lesser* had sealed up that gunshot wound.

Just to keep the questioning going longer.

The only saving grace to the nightmare was that not one thing about the Brotherhood had passed his lips. Not a thing. Even when the slayer went to work on his fingernails and between his legs. Butch was going to die soon, but at least he could look Saint Peter in the eye and know he wasn't a squealer when he got to heaven.

Or had he died and gone to hell? Was that what all this was about? Given some of the shit he'd pulled on earth, he could see why he'd ended up in the devil's guesthouse. But then wouldn't his torturer have horns, like demons did?

Okay, he was flirting with Looney Tunes here.

He opened his eyes a little farther, figuring it was time

to try to separate reality from mind-grinding nonsense. He had a feeling this was probably his last shot at consciousness, so he should make it count.

Vision was blurry. Hands . . . feet . . . yup, chained down. And he was still lying on something hard, a table. Room was . . . dark. Dirt smell meant he was probably in a basement. Bald lightbulb revealed . . . yeah, the torture tool kit. He looked away from the spread of sharp things, shuddering.

What was that sound? A dim roar. Getting louder. Louder.

As soon as it was cut off, a door opened upstairs and Butch heard a man say in a muffled voice, "Master."

Soft reply. Indistinct. Then a conversation, with one set of footsteps pacing around, causing dust to filter down from the floorboards. Eventually, another door squeaked open, and the stairs next to him started to creak.

Butch broke out in a cold sweat and lowered his eyelids. Through the cracks between his lashes, he watched what came at him.

First guy was the *lesser* who'd been working him out, the guy from over the summer, from the Caldwell Martial Arts Academy—Joseph Xavier was his name, if Butch remembered correctly. The other was draped from head to foot in a brilliant white robe, his face and hands completely covered. Looked like some kind of monk or priest.

Except that was no man of God under there. As Butch absorbed the person's vibe, he couldn't breathe from his repulsion. Whatever was hidden by that robe was distilled evil, the kind that mobilized serial killers and rapists and murderers and people who enjoyed beating their children: hatred and malevolence in an upright, solid form.

Butch's fear level shot through the roof. He could handle being knocked around; the pain was bitch, but there was a definable end point marked by when his heart stopped beating. But whatever was hiding under that robe held mysteries of suffering the likes of which were biblical. And how did he know? His whole body was revolting, his instincts firing off to run, save himself . . . *pray*.

Words came to him, marching through his mind. *The Lord is my shepherd, I shall not want . . .*

The robed figure's hood turned toward Butch with the boneless swivel of an owl's head.

Butch slammed his lids shut and hurried through the Twenty-third Psalm. Faster . . . needed to get the words into his mind, faster. *He maketh me to lie down in green pastures; He leadeth me beside the still waters . . . He restoreth my soul; He leadeth me in the paths of righteousness for his name's sake . . .*

"This man is the one?" The voice that reverberated through the basement tripped Butch up, making him lose his rhythm: It was resonant and carried an echo, something out of a sci-fi movie with all that eerie distortion.

"His gun had the Brotherhood's bullets in it."

Get back to the Psalm. And do it faster. *Yea, though I walk through the valley of the shadow of death, I will fear no evil—*

"I know you wake, human." The echoing voice shot right into Butch's ear. "Look upon me and know your captor's master."

Butch opened his eyes, turned his head, and swallowed compulsively. The face staring down into his was condensed blackness, a shadow come to life.

The Omega.

The Evil laughed a little. "So you know what I am, do you?" It straightened. "Given you anything, has he, *Forelesser*?"

"I'm not finished."

"Ah, so that is no. And you have worked him well, given how close to death he is. Yes, I can feel it coming to him. So close." The Omega bent down again and inhaled the air over Butch's body. "Yes, within the hour. Maybe less."

"He'll last as long as I want him to."

"No, he won't." The Omega started to circle the table and Butch tracked the movement, terror getting tighter and tighter, strengthening in the centrifugal force of the Evil's pacing. Around, around, around . . . Butch trembled so badly his teeth clapped together.

The shaking dried up the second the Omega came to a halt at the far end of the table. Shadowy hands lifted up, grasped the white robe's hood, and pulled it off. Overhead, the bald light-bulb flickered as if its illumination were sucked in by the black form.

"You are letting him go," the Omega said, that voice like a wave, filtered and enhanced by the air in turns. "You are leaving him out in the woods. You are telling the others to stay away from him."

What? Butch thought.

"What?" the *Fore-lesser* said.

"The Brotherhood has among its weaknesses a paralyzing loyalty, do they not? Yes, paralyzing fidelity. They claim what is theirs. It is the animal in them." The Omega held out its hand. "A knife, please. I am of a mind to make this human useful."

"You just said he was going to die."

"But I'm going to give him a little life, as it were. As well as a gift. *Knife.*"

Butch's eyes cracked wide open as an eight-inch hunting number was exchanged.

The Omega placed one hand on the table, put the blade to the tip of its finger, and bore down. There was a crack, like a carrot had been cut.

41

The Omega leaned over Butch. "Where to hide, where to hide . . ."

As the knife came up and hovered over Butch's abdomen, Butch screamed. And he was still screaming as a shallow slice was made into his belly. Then the Omega picked up the little part of itself, the black digit.

Butch fought, yanking against the binds. Horror had his eyes bulging until the pressure on his optic nerves blinded him.

The Omega inserted its fingertip into Butch's gut, then bent low and blew over the fresh cut. The skin sealed up, the flesh knitting together. Immediately, Butch felt the rotting inside him, sensed the evil worming around, moving. He lifted his head. The skin around the cut was already turning gray.

Tears raced to his eyes. Seeped down his raw cheeks.

"Release him."

The *Fore-lesser* went to work on the chains, but when they were off, Butch realized he couldn't move. He was paralyzed.

"I will take him," the Omega said. "And he will survive and find his way back to the Brotherhood."

"They'll sense you."

"Perhaps, but they will take him."

"He'll tell them."

"No, because he won't remember me." The Omega's face tilted toward Butch. "You won't remember a thing."

As their stares met, Butch could feel the affinity between them, could sense the bond, the sameness. He wept for the violation of himself, but more for the Brotherhood. They would take him in. They would try to help him in whatever way they could.

And sure as the evil in him, he would end up betraying them.

42

Except maybe Vishous or the brothers wouldn't find him. How could they? And with no clothes on, surely he would die from exposure fast.

The Omega reached out and wiped the tears from one of Butch's cheeks. The shimmer of wetness was iridescent against those translucent black fingers, and Butch wanted what had come out of him back. Not to be. Lifting the hand to its mouth, the Evil savored Butch's pain and fear, licking . . . sucking.

Despair scrambled Butch's memory, but the faith he'd thought he'd foresworn spit out another line of the Psalm: *Surely goodness and mercy shall follow me all the days of my life and I will dwell in the house of the Lord for ever.*

But that was no longer possible now, was it? He had evil inside him, under his skin.

The Omega smiled, though Butch didn't know how he knew it. "Pity we don't have more time, as you are in a fragile state. But there will be opportunities for you and me in the future. What I claim as my own always comes back to me. Now, sleep."

And like a lamp being clicked off, Butch did.

"Answer the fucking question, Vishous."

V looked away from his king just as the grandfather clock in the corner of the study started to go off. It stopped at four chimes, so it was four in the afternoon. The Brotherhood had been in Wrath's command central all day long, prowling around the ridiculously elegant Louis XIV salon, saturating the delicate air of the place with their anger.

"Vishous," Wrath growled, "I'm waiting. How will you know how to find the cop? And why didn't you mention this before now?"

Because he'd known it was going to create problems, and their shopping cart of shit was already full.

As V tried to think of what he could say, he looked at his brothers. Phury was on the pale blue silk couch in front of the fireplace, his body dwarfing the piece of furniture, his multicolored hair now back down past his jawline. Z was behind his twin, up against the mantel, his eyes back to black because he was enraged. Rhage was by the door, his beautiful face set in a nasty expression, his shoulders twitching as if his inner beast was likewise rip shit pissed.

And then there was Wrath. Behind a dainty desk, the Blind King was all menace, his cruel visage set hard, his weak eyes hidden behind black-framed wraparounds. His heavy forearms, marked on the insides with tattoos of his pure-blooded lineage, were planted on a gold-embossed blotter.

That Tohr was not with the group was a gaping wound to all of them.

"V? Answer the question or so help me God I'll beat it out of you."

"I just know how to find him."

"What are you hiding?"

V went over to the bar, poured himself a couple fingers of Grey Goose, and hammered the shot. He swallowed a number of times and then let the words fly.

"I fed him."

A chorus of inhales floated around the room. As Wrath rose in disbelief, V poured himself another hit of Goose.

"You did *what*?" The last word was bellowed.

"I had him drink some of me."

"Vishous . . ." Wrath stalked around the desk, shitkickers hitting the floor like boulders. The king got face-to-face close. "He's a male. He's *human*. What the fuck were you thinking?"

More vodka. Definitely time for more Goose.

V swallowed the shot and poured number four. "With my blood in him, I can find him and that's why I had him drink. I saw . . . that I was supposed to. So I did it, and I would do it again."

Wrath wheeled away and paced around the room, hands cranked into fists. As the boss man walked off frustration, the rest of the Brotherhood looked over with curiosity.

"I did what I had to," V snapped, throwing his glass back.

Wrath stopped by one of the floor-to-ceiling windows. The thing was shuttered for the day, no light coming through. "Did he take your vein?"

"No."

A couple of the brothers cleared their throats, like they were urging him to be honest.

V cursed and poured some more. "Oh, for God's sake, it's not like that with him. I gave him some in a glass. He didn't know what he was drinking."

"Shit, V," Wrath muttered, "you could have killed him outright—"

"It was three months ago. He got through it, so there's no harm done—"

Wrath's voice rang out loud as an air strike. "You violated the law! Feeding a *human*? Christ! What am I supposed to do with this?"

"You want to serve me up to the Scribe Virgin, I'll go willingly. But I want to be clear. First, I find Butch and bring him home, dead or alive."

Wrath popped up his sunglasses and rubbed his eyes, a habit he'd developed lately when he got tired of the king shit. "If he was interrogated, he may have talked. We could be compromised."

V looked down into his glass and slowly shook his head. "He'd die before giving us up. I guarantee it." He swallowed the vodka and felt it slide down his throat. "My man is good like that."

FIVE

Rehvenge had not seemed at all surprised when she called him, Marissa thought. But then, he'd always had this uncanny way of reading her.

Gathering up her black cloak, she stepped out the back of her brother's mansion. Night had just fallen, and she shivered, though not because of the cold. It was that horrible dream she'd had during the day. She'd been flying, flying across the landscape, flying over a frozen pond with pines on its far side, going farther past a ring of trees, until she'd slowed and peered downward. On the snowy ground, curled up and bleeding, she saw . . . *Butch*.

The urge to call the Brotherhood lingered as much as the images of the nightmare did. Except how stupid would she feel when the warriors called back all annoyed, just to tell her he was perfectly fine? They'd probably think she was stalking him. Except, God . . . that vision of him bleeding into the white-covered earth, that picture of him, helpless in the fetal position, haunted her.

It was only a dream, though. Merely . . . a dream.

Closing her eyes, she forced herself into a semblance of calm and dematerialized downtown to the terrace of a pent-house apartment some thirty stories up. As soon as she took form, Rehvenge slid open one of six glass doors.

He immediately frowned. "You're upset."

She forced a smile as she went over to him. "You know I'm always a little uncomfortable."

He pointed his gold engraved cane at her. "No, this is different."

God, she'd never known anyone so in tune with her emotions. "I'll be fine."

As he took her elbow and pulled her inside, a tropical warmth embraced her. Rehv always had the temperature this high, and his floor length sable coat always stayed on until they got to the couch. She had no idea how he could stand the heat, but he seemed to crave it.

He shut the slider. "Marissa, I want to know what's doing."

"Nothing, really."

With a twist, she took off her cloak and draped it on a chrome-and-black chair. Three sides of the penthouse were made up of sheets of glass, and the sprawling view of Caldwell's two halves included the shimmering lights of downtown, the dark curve of the Hudson River, the stars over it all. Unlike the twinkling landscape, though, the decor was minimalist, all ebony and cream elegance . . . rather like Rehv, with his black mohawk and his golden skin and his perfect clothes.

Under different circumstances, she would have adored the penthouse.

Under different circumstances, she might have adored him.

Rehv's violet eyes narrowed as he leaned on his cane and came to her. He was a huge male, built like a Brother, and he had looming down pat, his handsome face hard. "Don't lie to me."

She smiled slightly. Males like him tended to be very protective, and though the two of them were not mated, she wasn't surprised he seemed ready to hunt something down on her behalf. "I had a disturbing dream this morning and haven't shaken it off yet. That's all."

As he measured her, she had the oddest sense he was sifting through her emotions, examining how they interconnected from the inside.

48

"Give me your hand," he said.

She reached out with no hesitation. He always observed the *glymera*'s formalities, and he hadn't yet greeted her as custom required. Except when their palms met, he didn't brush his lips across her knuckles. He put his thumb over her wrist and pushed down a little. Then even harder. Suddenly, as if he'd opened up some kind of drain, her feelings of fear and worry tunneled down her arm and out to him, pulled through by the contact.

"Rehvenge?" she whispered weakly.

The instant he let her go, the emotions came back, a wellspring no longer tapped.

"You won't be able to be with me tonight."

She flushed and rubbed the skin where he'd touched her. "Of course I will. It's . . . time."

To get them started, she went to the black leather couch they usually used and stood beside it. After a moment, Rehvenge came over to her and took off his sable coat, slinging the fur out flat for them to lie on. Then he unbuttoned his black suit coat and removed it as well. His fine silk shirt, which seemed so very white, parted down the middle at his fingertips and then the heavy, hairless expense of his chest was revealed. Tattoos marked his pecs, two five-pointed stars in red ink, and there were more designs on his ribbed stomach.

As he sat down and eased back into the couch's arms, his muscles flexed. Looking up at her, his glowing amethyst stare drew her in, and so did his hand as he extended his arm and crooked his forefinger at her. "Come here, *tahlly*. I've got what you need."

She lifted the skirt of her gown and climbed between his legs. Rehv always insisted she take from his throat, but in the three times they had done this, he had never once been aroused. Which was a relief as well as a reminder.

Wrath had never had an erection when he was near her either.

As she glanced down at Rehv's smooth-skinned male glory, the low-level hunger she had been feeling for the past few days hit hard. She put her palms on his pecs and arched over him, watching as he closed his eyes, tilted his chin to the side, and ran his hands up her arms. A soft groan left his lips, which was something he always did right before she struck. In another situation, she would have said it was anticipation, but she knew that wasn't true. His body was always flaccid, and she couldn't believe he liked being used that much.

She opened her mouth, her fangs elongating, extending downward from her upper jaw. Leaning into Rehv, she—

The image of Butch in the snow froze her, and she had to shake her head to refocus on Rehv's throat and her hunger.

Feed, she told herself. *Take what he offers.*

She tried again, only to stop with her mouth on his neck. As she squeezed her eyes shut in frustration, Rehv put his hand under her chin and lifted her head up.

"Who is he, *tahlly*?" Rehv's thumb stroked her bottom lip. "Who is this male you love who won't feed you? And I'm going to be totally insulted if you don't tell me."

"Oh, Rehvenge . . . it's no one you know."

"He is a fool."

"No. I am the fool."

With an unexpected surge, Rehv pulled her down to his mouth. She was so shocked, she gasped, and in an erotic rush, his tongue entered her. He kissed her with skill, all smooth moves and sliding penetrations. She felt no arousal but could tell what kind of lover he would be: dominant, powerful . . . thorough.

When she pushed against his chest, he let her break the contact.

As Rehv eased back, his amethyst eyes glowed, a beautiful purple light pouring out of them, pouring into her. Though she felt no erection at his hips, the trembling that ran throughout his big, muscular body told her he was a male with sex on his mind and in his blood—and that he wanted to penetrate her.

"You look so surprised," he drawled.

Considering the way most males regarded her, she was. "That was unexpected. Especially as I didn't think you could—"

"I am capable of mating with a female." His lids dropped, and for a moment he looked frightening. "Under certain circumstances."

From out of nowhere, a shocking image shot into her brain: her naked on a bed with a sable blanket beneath her, Rehv naked and fully aroused, spreading her legs with his hips. On the inside of her thigh, she saw a bite mark, as if he'd fed from the vein there.

As she inhaled sharply and covered her eyes, the vision disappeared and he murmured, "My apologies, *tahlly.* I fear my fantasies are rather well developed. But don't worry, we can just keep them in my head."

"Dear God, Rehvenge, I never would have guessed. And maybe if things were different . . ."

"Fair enough." He stared into her face and then shook his head. "I really want to meet this male of yours."

"That's the problem. He's not mine."

"Then like I said, he's a fool." Rehv touched her hair. "And hungry as you are, we're going to have to do this another time, *tahlly.* That heart of yours isn't going to allow it tonight."

She pushed away from him and stood up, her eyes

51

going to the windows and the glowing city. She wondered where Butch was and what he was doing, then looked back over at Rehv and wanted to know why in the hell she wasn't attracted to him. He was beautiful in the ways of a warrior—potent, thick-blooded, strong . . . especially now, with his massive body sprawled on the sable-covered couch, his legs spread in blatant sexual invitation.

"I wish I wanted you, Rehv."

He laughed dryly. "Funny, I know just what you mean."

V pushed out through the mansion's vestibule and stood in the courtyard. In the lee of the looming stone manse, he cast his mind out into the night, radar looking for a signal.

"You do *not* go in alone," Rhage snarled at his ear. "You find the place they're keeping him and you call us."

When V didn't reply, he was grabbed by the back of the neck and shaken like a rag doll. In spite of the fact that he was a jacked six-foot-six.

Rhage's face pushed into his, all *no-fooling-around*. "Vishous. You hear me?"

"Yeah, whatever." He shoved the male off him, only to become very aware that they were not alone. The rest of the Brotherhood was waiting, armed and angry, a cannon ready to be fired. Except . . . in the midst of all their aggression, they were looking over at him with worry. As the concern drove him nuts, he turned away.

V marshaled his mind and sifted through the night, trying to find the small echo of himself inside Butch. Penetrating the darkness, he searched across fields and mountains and frozen lakes and rushing streams . . . out . . . out . . . out—

Oh, God.

Butch was alive. Barely. And he was . . . north and east. Twelve, maybe fifteen miles away.

As V took out his Glock, an iron hand grabbed his arm. Rhage was back with a hard-on. "You do *not* take those *lessers* on alone."

"I got it."

"Swear to me," Rhage snapped. Like he knew damn well V was thinking of rushing whoever held Butch and only calling for cleanup.

Except this was personal, not just about the war between the vampires and the Lessening Society. Those undead bastards had taken his—well, he didn't know what Butch was to him specifically. But it ran deeper than anything he'd felt in a long time.

"Vishous—"

"I'll call you when I'm good and fucking ready." V dematerialized free of his brother's hold.

Traveling in a loose scramble of molecules, he misted out into Caldwell's rural farmland to a grove of woods beyond a pond that was still frozen. He triangulated his reappearance about a hundred yards away from the signal he got from Butch, coming together crouched and ready for a fight.

Which was a good plan because, holy hell, he could feel *lessers* everywhere—

V frowned and held his breath. Moving slowly, he turned in a semicircle, searching with his eyes and his ears, not his instincts. There were no slayers around. There was *nothing* around. Not even a shack or a hunting lodge—

Abruptly, he shuddered. No, there was something in these woods, all right—a big-ass something, a condensed mark of malevolence, an evil that made him twitchy.

The Omega.

As he swiveled his head toward the dreadful concentration, a cold blast of wind nailed him in the face, like Mother Nature was urging him in the opposite direction.

Tough shit. He had to get his roommate out of here.

V ran toward what he could sense of Butch, his shitkickers punching through the crusty snow. Up ahead, the full moon shone brightly at the margin of a cloudless sky, but the presence of evil was so vivid V could have followed the way blindfolded. And shit, Butch was close to that blackness.

Fifty yards later, V saw the coyotes. They were circling something on the ground, growling not as if they were hungry but as if the pack was being threatened.

And whatever had captured their interest was of such magnitude they didn't even notice V's approach. To break them up, he pointed his gun overhead and let off a couple of rounds. The coyotes scattered and—

V skidded to a halt. As he looked at what was on the ground, he couldn't swallow. Which was fine, because his mouth went dry.

Butch was lying in the snow on his side, naked, beaten, blood all over him, face swollen and bruised. His thigh was bandaged, but whatever wound was under the gauze had bled through. None of that was the horror, however. Evil was all around the cop . . . all around . . . shit, *he* was the black, foul footprint V had sensed.

Oh, sweet Virgin in the Fade.

Vishous did a quick scan of the environs, then dropped to his knees and gently laid his gloved hand on his friend. As a painful zinger shot up his arm, V's instincts told him to bolt because what he'd laid his palm on was to be avoided at all costs. *Evil.*

"Butch, it's me. Butch?"

With a groan, the cop stirred, a kind of hope flaring

in his battered face, as if he'd lifted his head to the sun. But then the expression faded.

Dear Lord, the man's eyes were frozen shut because he'd been crying and the tears hadn't gotten far in the cold.

"Don't worry, cop. I'm going to . . ." *Do what?* The male was about to die out here, but what the hell had been done to him? He was saturated by darkness.

Butch's mouth opened. The hoarse sounds that came out might have been words, but they didn't carry.

"Cop, don't say anything. I'm going to take care of you—"

Butch shook his head and began to move. With pathetic weakness, he stretched out his arms and grabbed at the ground, trying to pull his broken body through the snow. Away from V.

"Butch, it's me—"

"No . . ." The cop went all frantic, clawing, dragging himself. "Infected . . . don't know how . . . infected . . . you can't . . . take me. Don't know why . . ."

V used his voice like a slap, making it sharp and loud. "Butch! Stop it!"

The cop settled down, although whether it was because he was following orders or had run out of steam wasn't clear.

"What the hell did they do to you, my man?" V whipped out a Mylar blanket from his jacket and put it around his roommate.

"Infected." Butch awkwardly rolled onto his back and shoved the silver sheath down, his busted-up hand falling onto his belly. "In . . . fected."

"What the fuck . . ."

There was a fist-sized black circle on the cop's stomach, something like a bruise with highly defined edges. In the center of it, there seemed to be . . . a surgical scar.

"Shit." They'd put something in him.

"Kill me." Butch's voice was a chilling rasp. "Kill me now. Infected. Something . . . inside. Growing . . ."

V sat back on his heels and grabbed at his hair. Forcing his emotions to the back burner, he put his mind to work and prayed that his overdose of gray matter would come to the rescue. Moments later, the conclusion he reached was radical but logical, and it focused him to the point of calmness. He unsheathed one of his black daggers with a perfectly steady hand and leaned in to his roommate.

What shouldn't be in there needed to come out. And given the evil that it was, the extraction had to be done here, in neutral territory, rather than at home or in Havers's clinic. Plus, death was breathing down the cop's neck, and the sooner he was decontam'd the better.

"Butch, buddy, I want you to take a deep breath, then hold still. I'm going to—"

"Be of care, warrior."

V whirled around in a crouch. Right behind him, hovering above the ground, was the Scribe Virgin. As always she was pure power, her black robes unruffled by the wind, her face hidden, her voice clear as the night air.

Vishous opened his mouth, but she cut him off. "Before you o'erstep your bounds and render inquiry, I will tell you, no, I cannot help directly. This is a matter of the sort I must stay out of. However, I will say this. You would be wise to unveil the curse you detest. Handling what is within him will bring you closer to death than ever you have been. And no one could remove it save you." She smiled a little, as if she read his thoughts. "Yes, this moment now is part of the reason you dreamed of him in the beginning. But there is another *why* of which you may see in time."

"Will he live?"

"Get to work, warrior," she said in a hard tone. "You shall make more progress toward his salvation if you act rather than offend me."

V leaned down to Butch and moved fast, drawing the knife over the cop's belly. As a moan left the man's cracked lips, a gaping hole opened up.

"Oh, Jesus." There was something black cocooned in the flesh.

The Scribe Virgin's voice was closer now, as if she were right over his shoulder. "Unsheathe your hand, warrior, and be of speed about it. How quickly that spreads."

V shoved his dagger back into his chest holster and ripped his glove off. He reached down, then stopped. "Wait, I can't touch anyone with this."

"The infection will offer the human protection. Do it now, warrior, and as you make contact, visualize the white glow of your palm all around you, as if you are skinned by light."

Vishous brought his hand forward while imagining himself surrounded by a pure, radiant incandescence. The moment he made contact with the black piece, his body shuddered and bucked. The thing, whatever it was, disintegrated with a hiss and pop, but, oh, shit, he felt ill.

"Breathe," the Scribe Virgin said. "Just breathe through it."

Vishous swayed and caught himself on the ground, his head hanging off his shoulders, his throat starting to pump. "I think I'm going to be—"

Yeah, he got sick. And as the retching tackled him again and again, he felt himself get eased off his arms. The Scribe Virgin supported him through the vomiting, and when it was over, he sagged into her. For a moment he even thought she was stroking his hair.

Then from out of nowhere, his cell phone appeared in

his good hand, and her voice was strong in his ear. "Go now, take this human, and trust that the seat of evil is in the soul, not the body. And you must bring back the jar of one of your enemies. Bring it to this place and use your hand upon it. Do this without delay."

V nodded. Unsolicited advice from the Scribe Virgin was not the kind you left at the roadside.

"And, warrior, keep your shield of light in place around this human. Further, use your hand to heal him. He may yet die unless enough light enters his body and heart."

V felt the power of her fade as another shot of nausea hit his gut. While he dealt with the lingering effects of touching that thing, he figured, Jesus, if he felt this bad, he couldn't imagine how Butch was doing.

When the phone rang in his hand, he realized he'd been lying on his back in the snow for some time. "Hello?" he said, all groggy.

"Where are you? What's happening?" Rhage's bass holler was a relief.

"I have him. I have"—V eyed the bloody mess that was his roommate—"Jesus, I need a pickup. Oh, shit, Rhage—" V put his hand to his eyes and started to shake. "Rhage—what they did to him . . ."

The tone of his brother's voice instantly gentled, as if the guy knew V had gone bye-bye. "Okay, just relax. Tell me, where are you?"

"Woods . . . I don't know . . ." God, his brain had totally shorted out. "Can you pinpoint me on the GPS?"

A voice in the background, probably Phury, yelled, "Got him!"

"All right, V, we got you and we're coming—"

"No, place is contaminated." As Rhage started in with the *whats*, V cut the brother off. "Car. We need a car. I'm going to have to carry him out. I don't want anyone else to come here."

There was a long pause. "All right. Head straight north, my brother. About a half mile you'll run into Route 22. We'll be there waiting for you."

"Call—" He had to clear his voice and wipe his eyes. "Call Havers. Tell him we're bringing in a trauma case. And tell him that we need a quarantine."

"Jesus . . . what the hell did they do to him?"

"Hurry, Rhage—wait! Bring a *lesser* jar with you."

"Why?"

"No time to explain. Just make sure you have one."

V shoved his phone into his pocket, stuffed his glowing hand back into its glove, and went to Butch. After making sure the Mylar blanket was in place, he gathered the cop in his arms and eased all that deadweight off the ground. Butch hissed with pain.

"This is going to be a rough ride," V said, "but we gotta get you moving."

Except then V frowned and looked at the ground. Butch wasn't bleeding much anymore, but holy hell, what about the footprints tracking out through the snow? If a *lesser* happened to come back, he might catch them on the way out.

From out of nowhere, storm clouds rolled in and snow started to fall hard.

Damn, the Scribe Virgin was good.

As V headed off through what was now nearly a blizzard, he imagined a white light of protection around both him and the man in his arms.

"You came!"

Marissa smiled as she shut the door to the cheery, windowless patient room. On the hospital bed, looking small and fragile, was a seven-year-old female. By her side, looking only somewhat larger but much more breakable, was the young's mother.

"I promised last night I would visit you again, didn't I?"

When the young grinned, there was a black hole where her front tooth was missing. "But still, you came. And you look so pretty."

"So do you." Marissa sat on the bed and took the young's hand. "How are you?"

"*Mahmen* and I have been watching *Dora the Explorer*."

The mother smiled a little, but the expression didn't touch much of her plain face or her eyes. Since the young had been brought in three days ago, the mother had seemed to be on some kind of numbed-out autopilot. Well, except when she jumped every time someone came into the room.

"*Mahmen* says that we can only stay here a little while longer. Is that true?"

The mother opened her mouth, but Marissa answered, "You don't have to worry about leaving. We need to take care of your leg first."

These were not wealthy civilians, probably couldn't pay for any of this, but Havers never turned anyone away. And he wasn't going to rush them out.

"*Mahmen* says that my leg is bad. Is that true?"

"Not for long." Marissa glanced down at the blankets. Havers was going to operate on the compound fracture momentarily. Hopefully it would heal right.

"*Mahmen* says I'll be in the green room for an hour. Can it be shorter than that?"

"My brother will keep you there only as long as he has to."

Havers was going to replace her shinbone with a titanium rod, which was better than losing the limb but still a hard path. The young would need more operations as she grew, and going by the mother's exhausted eyes, the female knew this was just the beginning.

"I'm not scared." The young tucked her tattered stuffed tiger in closer to her neck. "Mastimon is coming with me. The nurse said he could."

"Mastimon will protect you. He is fierce, as a tiger should be."

"I told him not to eat anybody."

"Wise of you." Marissa reached into the skirting pocket of her pale pink gown and took out a leather box. "I have something for you."

"A present?"

"Yes." Marissa turned the box to face the young and opened it. Inside, there was a gold plate about the size of a tea saucer, and the precious object was buffed to a high shine, all mirror bright, gleaming like sunshine.

"That's so pretty," the child breathed.

"This is my wishing plate." Marissa took it out and turned the thing over. "Do you see my initial on the back?"

The young squinted. "Yes. And look! There's a letter like as in my name."

"I had yours added. I'd like you to have this."

There was a little gasp from the mother in the corner. Clearly she knew what all that gold was worth.

"Really?" the young said.

"Hold your hands out." Marissa put the gold disk in the girl's palms.

"Oh, it's so heavy."

"Do you know how these wishing plates work?" When the young shook her head, Marissa took out a little piece of parchment and a fountain pen. "Think of a wish and I'll write it down. While you sleep, the Scribe Virgin will come and read it."

"If she doesn't give you your wish, does that mean you're bad?"

"Oh, no. It just means she has something better planned for you. So what would you like? It can be anything. Ice cream when you wake up. More Dora?"

The little female frowned in concentration. "I want my *mahmen* to stop crying. She tries to pretend she doesn't, but ever since I . . . fell down the stairs she's been sad."

Marissa swallowed, knowing full well the child hadn't broken her leg like that. "I think that's fine. I'll write that down."

Using the intricate characters of the Old Language, she penned in red ink: *If it would not offend, I would be grateful for my* mahmen's *happiness.*

"There. How is it?"

"Perfect!"

"Now we fold it and leave it. Perhaps the Scribe Virgin will reply to you while you are in the operating—the green room."

The child hugged her tiger closer. "I would like that."

As a nurse came in, Marissa stood up. In a rush of heat, she felt a near-violent urge to protect the young, to shield her from what had happened at her home and what was about to happen in the OR.

Instead, Marissa looked at the mother. "This is going to be fine."

When she went over and put her hand on a thin shoulder, the mother shuddered, then gripped Marissa's palm hard.

"Tell me he can't get in here," the female said in a low voice. "If he finds us, he'll kill us."

Marissa whispered, "No one can get into the elevator without identifying themselves in front of a camera. The two of you are safe. I swear to it."

When the female nodded, Marissa left so that the young could be sedated.

Outside the patient room, she leaned against the hallway wall and felt more heaving rage. The fact that those two were bearing the pain of a male's violent temper was enough to make her want to learn how to shoot a gun.

And God, she couldn't imagine setting that female and her young loose in the world because surely that *hellren* would find them when they left the clinic. Although most males put their mates higher than themselves, there had always been among the race a minority of abusers and the realities of domestic violence were ugly and far-reaching.

A door shutting to the left brought her head up, and she saw Havers come walking down the hall, his head buried in a patient chart. Odd . . . his shoes were covered with little yellow plastic booties, the kind he always put on when he donned a hazmat suit.

"Have you been in the lab again, brother mine?" she asked.

His eyes shot up from the chart and he pushed his horn-rimmed glasses higher on his nose. His jaunty red bow tie was cocked at a bad angle. "Come again?"

She nodded at his feet with a smile. "The lab."

"Ah . . . yes. I have." He reached down and took the covers off his loafers, crushing the yellow plastic in his hand. "Marissa, would you do me the favor of returning to the house? I've asked the *Princeps* Council *leahdyre* and seven other members to dinner on Monday next. The menu must be perfect and I would talk to Karolyn myself, but I'm due in the OR."

"Of course." Except then Marissa frowned, aware that her brother was still as a statue. "Is everything all right?"

"Yes, thank you. Go . . . go now. Do . . . yes, please go now."

She was tempted to pry, but she didn't want to keep him from the young's operation, so she kissed him on the cheek, straightened his bow tie, and walked away. When she reached the double doors that led into the reception area, though, something made her glance back.

Havers was stuffing what he'd been wearing on his feet into a biohazard bin, and his face was drawn into tight lines. With a deep breath, he braced himself, then pushed open the door to the surgical suite's anteroom.

Ah, she thought, so that's what it was. He was upset about operating on the young. And who could blame him?

Marissa turned back to the doors . . . then heard the boots.

She froze. Only one kind of male made that thunder when he approached.

Pivoting around, she saw Vishous striding down the hall, his dark head lowered, and behind him, Phury and Rhage were similar silent menaces. All three were dripping with weapons and weariness, and Vishous had dried blood on his leathers and his jacket. But why had they been in Havers's lab? That facility was the only thing back there, really.

The Brothers didn't notice her until they practically mowed her down. Coming to a stop as a group, their eyes quickly went elsewhere, no doubt because of her having fallen from Wrath's grace.

Dear Virgin, up close they looked truly awful. Sick, yet not unwell, if that made any sense.

"Is there anything I can do for you?" she asked.

"Everything's cool," Vishous said in a hard voice. "'Scuse us."

The dream . . . Butch lying in the snow . . . "Is someone hurt? Is . . . Butch . . ."

Vishous just shrugged her off and stepped past her,

punching open the doors into Reception. The other two offered stiff smiles, then did the same.

Following at a distance, she watched them walk by the nursing station to the access elevator. As they waited for the doors to open, Rhage reached out and put his hand on Vishous's shoulder, and the other Brother seemed to shudder.

The exchange made warning bells go off, and the instant the elevator doors closed Marissa headed for the wing of the clinic the three had originally come from. Moving quickly, she passed the sprawling, brilliantly lit lab, then put her head into the six older patient rooms. All of which were empty.

Why had the Brothers been here? Maybe just to talk to Havers?

On instinct, she went out to the front desk, logged on to the computer and scanned the admissions. Nothing about any of the Brothers or Butch came up, but that didn't mean a thing. The warriors were never entered into the system, and she had to imagine it would be the same for Butch if he were in-house. What she was after was how many beds were occupied of the thirty-five they had.

She got the number and did a quick walk around, scouting each room. Everything was accounted for. There was nothing out of the ordinary. Butch had not been admitted—unless he was in one of the other rooms in the main house. Sometimes patients who were VIPs stayed there.

Marissa picked up her skirts and hightailed it for the back stairs.

Butch curled into himself even though he wasn't cold, operating on the theory that if he could just bring his knees up high enough, the pain in his stomach would ease a little.

Yeah, right. The hot poker in his gut was not impressed by that plan.

He peeled his puffy eyelids apart, and after a lot of blinking and deep breathing, he came to the following conclusions: He was not dead. He was in a hospital. And shit that was no doubt keeping him alive was being pumped into his arm.

As he rolled over gingerly, he came to one more realization. His body had been used for a punching bag. Oh . . . and something nasty was in his belly, like his last meal had been rancid roast beef.

What the fuck had happened to him?

Only a vague series of snapshots came to mind: Vishous finding him in the woods. Him with a screaming instinct that the brother should leave him to die. Then some knife action and . . . something about that hand of V's, that glowing thing used to take out a vile piece of—

Butch lurched over into his side and gagged just from the memory. There had been evil in his belly. Pure, undiluted malice, and the black horror had been spreading.

With shaking hands, he grabbed the hospital johnny he was wearing and yanked it up. "Oh . . . Jesus . . ."

There was a stain on the skin of his stomach, like the scorch mark of a fire that had been snuffed out. In desperation, he weeded through his sloppy brain, trying to remember how the scarring had gotten there and what it was, but he just came up with a big fat zero.

So like the detective he'd been before, he examined the scene—which in this case was his body. Lifting one of his hands, he saw that his fingernails were a mess, as if something like a file or some small nails had been hammered under a number of them. A deep breath told him his ribs were cracked. And going by his swollen eyes, he had to assume his face had partied with a lot of knuckles.

He had been tortured. Recently.

Reaching into his mind again, he panned for memories, trying to get back to the last place he'd been. ZeroSum. ZeroSum with . . . oh, God, that female. In the bathroom. Having hardcore, who-cares sex. Then he'd gone out and . . . *lessers*. Fighting with those *lessers*. Getting shot and then . . .

His recollections came to the end of their train track at that point. Just shot off the edge of reasoning into a pit of *huh, what?*

Had he squealed on the Brotherhood? Betrayed them? Had he given his nearest and dearest away?

And what the hell had been done to his belly? God, he felt like there was sludge in his veins thanks to whatever had festered there.

Letting himself go limp, he breathed through his mouth for a while. And found there was no peace to be had.

As if his brain didn't want to stop working, or maybe because it was showing off, the thing kicked up random visions from the distant past. Birthdays with his dad glaring at him and his mom tense and smoking like a chimney. Christmases where his brothers and sisters got presents and he didn't.

Hot July nights that no fan could cool off, the heat driving his father into the cold beer. The Pabst Blue Ribbon driving his father into fist-cracking wake-up calls just for Butch.

Memories he hadn't thought of for years came back, all unwanted visitors. He saw his sisters and brothers, happy, shouting, playing on bright green grass. And remembered how he'd wished he could be among them instead of hanging back, the oddball who'd never fit in.

And then— Oh, God, no . . . not this memory.

Too late. He pictured himself as the twelve-year-old he'd been, scrawny and shaggy, standing at the curb in front of the O'Neal family row house in South Boston. It had been a clear, beautiful fall afternoon when he'd watched his sister Janie get into a red Chevy Chevette that had rainbow stripes down the side. With perfect recollection he saw her waving at him through the window in the back as the car drove off.

Now that the door to the nightmare was open, he couldn't stop the horror show. He recalled the police coming to the door that night and his mother's knees going out when they finished talking to her. He remembered the cops questioning him because he was the last person to see Janie alive. He heard his younger self telling the badges that he hadn't recognized the boys and had wanted to tell his sister not to get in.

Mostly, he saw his mother's eyes burning with a pain so great she had no tears.

Then flash forward twenty-plus years. God . . . when was the last time he'd spoken to or seen either of his parents? Or his brothers and sisters? Five years? Probably. Man, the family had been so relieved when he'd moved away and started missing holidays.

Yeah, around the Christmas table, everyone else had been part of the O'Neal family fabric and he'd been the stain. Eventually he'd stopped going home altogether, leaving them only phone numbers to reach him, numbers they never dialed.

So they wouldn't know if he died now, would they? Vishous no doubt knew everything about the O'Neal clan, down to their social security numbers and bank statements, but Butch had never spoken about them. Would the Brotherhood call? What would they say?

Butch looked down at himself and knew there was a good chance he wasn't walking out of this room. His body looked a lot like those he'd seen in Homicide, the kind he investigated in the woods. Well, natch. That's where he'd been found. Discarded. Used. Left for dead.

Rather like Janie.

Exactly like Janie.

Closing his eyes, he floated away on the pain in his body. And from out of the swill of agony, he had a vision of Marissa from the first night he'd met her. The image was so vivid, he could almost smell the ocean scent of her and he saw exactly what had been: the filmy yellow gown she'd had on . . . the way her hair had looked, down over her shoulders . . . the lemon-colored sitting room they'd been in together.

To him, she was the unforgettable woman, the one he'd never had and never would but who nonetheless reached into the core of him.

Man, he was so fricking tired.

He opened his eyes and took action before he really knew what he was doing. Reaching up to his inner forearm, he peeled the clear plastic tape off the skin around the IV insertion site. Sliding the needle out of his vein was easier than he'd thought it would be, but then again, the rest of him hurt so bad, messing around with that little piece of hardware was a drop in the bucket.

If he'd had the strength, he'd have gone looking for something with a little more punch to off himself. But time—time was the weapon he was going to use because that's what he had at his disposal. And going by how shitty he felt, it wasn't going to take long. He could practically hear his organs coughing up their livelihoods.

Closing his eyes, he let go of everything, only dimly aware that alarms were going off in the machinery behind the bed. A fighter by nature, the ease with which he gave up was a surprise, but then a heavy tide of exhaustion crashed over him. He knew instinctually that this was not the exhaustion of sleep but rather of death, and he was glad that it came so fast.

Drifting free of everything, he imagined that he was at the start of a long, blinding hallway at the end of which was a door. Marissa was standing in front of the portal and as she smiled at him she opened the way into a white bedroom full of light.

His soul eased as he took a deep breath and began to walk forward. He'd like to think he was going to heaven, in spite of all the bad things he'd done, so this made sense.

It wouldn't be paradise without her.

SIX

Vishous stood in the clinic's parking lot and watched as Rhage and Phury pulled out in the black Mercedes. They were going to grab Butch's phone from the alley behind Screamer's, then pick up the Escalade from the ZeroSum lot and head home.

It went without saying that V wasn't going back into the field tonight. The remnants of the evil he'd handled lingered in his body, making him weak. But more than that, seeing Butch worked out and nearly dead had done some kind of inner damage. He had the sense that a part of him had become unhinged, that some inner escape hatch was hanging open and segments of him were fleeing the core.

Actually, he'd had this feeling for a while now, ever since his visions had left him. But this horror movie of a night made it so much worse.

Privacy. He needed to be alone. Except he couldn't stand the idea of going back to the Pit. The silence there, the empty couch where Butch always sat, the weighty knowledge that there was something missing, would be unbearable.

So he went to his undisclosed place. Taking form again thirty stories in the air, he materialized on the terrace of his penthouse at the Commodore. The wind was howling and it felt good, biting through his clothes, making him feel something other than the gaping hole in his chest.

He went to the terrace's edge. Bracing his arms against the ledge, he looked over the lip of the skyscraper, down to the streets below. There were cars. People going into the lobby. Someone reaching into a cab, paying the driver. So normal. So very normal . . .

Meanwhile, he was up here dying.

Butch was not going to make it. The Omega had been inside him; that was the only explanation for what had been done to him. And although the evil had been taken out, its infection was beyond deadly and the harm was done.

V rubbed his face. What the hell was he going to do without that smart-ass, tough-talking, Scotch-sucking SOB? The rough bastard somehow smoothed the edges of life, probably because he was like sandpaper, a scratchy, persistent wrong-way-rub that left everything more even.

V turned away from the three-hundred-foot drop to the pavement. Going over to a door, he took a gold key out of his pocket and pushed it into the lock. The penthouse beyond was his private space, for his private . . . endeavors. And the scent of the female he'd had the night before lingered in the darkness.

At his will, black candles flared. The walls and the ceilings and the floors were black and the chromatic void absorbed the light, sucking it in, eating it up. The only true piece of furniture was a king-sized bed that was likewise covered in black satin sheets. But he didn't spend a lot of time on the mattress.

The rack was what he relied on. The rack with its hard table-top and its restraints. And he also used the things hanging beside it: the leather straps, the lengths of cane, the ball gags, the collars and spikes, the whips—and always the masks. He had to have the females anonymous, had to cover their faces as he tied up their bodies. He didn't want to know them as anything more than the equipment for his deviant workouts.

Shit, he was depraved about sex and he knew it, but after trying out a lot of things, he'd finally found what worked for him. And fortunately there were females who liked what he did to them, craved it as he craved the release he got when he mastered them singly or in pairs.

Except . . . tonight as he looked at his equipment, his perversions made him feel dirty. Maybe because he never came here unless he was ready to use what he had, so he'd never given the place a look-see when his head was clear.

His cell phone's ring startled him. As he glanced at the number, he numbed out. Havers. "Is he dead?"

Havers's voice was all professional-doctor sensitive. Which was the tip-off that Butch was hanging by a spider's thread. "He coded, sire. He pulled the IV out and his vitals dipped. We brought him back, but I don't know how long he can keep going."

"Can you restrain him?"

"I did. But I want you to be prepared. He's just a human—"

"No, he is *not*."

"Oh . . . of course, sire, but I didn't mean it like—"

"Shit. Look, I'm coming back. I want to be with him."

"I would prefer you didn't. He gets agitated whenever anyone's in the room and that doesn't help things. Right now he's as stable as I can make him and as comfortable as possible."

"I don't want him dying alone."

There was a pause. "Sire, we all die alone. Even if you were in the room with him, he would still leave unto the Fade . . . alone. He needs to be kept calm so his body can decide whether it's going to revive. We're doing everything we can for him."

V put a hand over his eyes. In a small voice that he didn't recognize, he said, "I don't . . . I don't want to lose him. I, ah . . . yeah, don't know what I would do if he—" V coughed a little. "Fuck."

"I shall care for him as mine own. Give him a day to try and stabilize."

"Nightfall tomorrow, then. And you will call me if his condition gets worse."

V hung up the phone and found himself staring at one of the lit candlewicks. Over its black wax torso, the captured little head of light weaved in the currents of the room.

The flame got him thinking. The bright yellow of it was . . . well, it was kind of like the color of blond hair, wasn't it?

He whipped out his cell, deciding that Havers was wrong about the no-visitors thing. It just depended on who the visitor was.

As he dialed, he resented the only option he had. And knew that what he was doing probably wasn't fair. Probably would cause a helluva lot of trouble, too. But when your best friend was doing the tombstone two-step with the Reaper, you kind of didn't give a shit about a lot of things.

"Mistress?"

Marissa looked up from her brother's desk. The seating chart for the *Princeps* dinner was in front of her, but she couldn't concentrate. All that searching of the clinic and the house and she'd come up with nothing. Meanwhile, her senses were screaming that something was wrong.

She forced a smile for the *doggen* in the doorway. "Yes, Karolyn?"

The servant bowed. "A call for you. On line one."

"Thank you." The *doggen* inclined her head and left as Marissa picked up the receiver. "Hello?"

74

"He's in the room down by your brother's lab."

"Vishous?" She jumped to her feet. "What——?"

"Go through the door marked HOUSEKEEPING. There's a panel to the right that you push open. Make sure you put on a hazmat suit before you go in to see him——"

Butch . . . dear God, *Butch*. "What——"

"Do you hear me? Put the suit on and keep it on."

"What ha——"

"Car accident. Go. Now. He's dying."

Marissa dropped the phone and ran from Havers's study, nearly mowing down Karolyn out in the hall.

"Mistress! What's wrong?"

Marissa shot through the dining room, punched open the butler's door, and stumbled into the kitchen. As she made the corner to the back stairs, she lost one of her high heels, so she kicked off the other and kept going in her stocking feet. At the bottom of the steps, she entered the security code to the rear entrance of the clinic and burst into the ER's waiting room.

Nurses called out her name, but she ignored them as she raced for the lab's corridor. Tearing past Havers's laboratory, she found the door marked HOUSEKEEPING and slammed it open.

As she panted, she looked around at . . . nothing. Just mops and empty buckets and smocks. But Vishous had said——

Wait. There were faint marks on the floor, a little pattern of wear that suggested a hidden door opening and closing. She shoved the smocks out of the way and found a flat panel. Clawing with her nails, she forced it open and frowned. It was some kind of dimly lit monitoring room with a high-tech setup of computers and vitals readouts. Leaning in to the blue glow of one of the screens, she saw a hospital bed. On top of it, a male was lying spread-eagled and restrained with tubes and wires coming out of him. *Butch*.

She barged past the yellow hazmat suits and facial masks hanging next to the door and pushed into the room, the air lock breaking with a hiss.

"Virgin in the Fade . . ." Her hand went to her throat.

He was definitely dying. She could sense it. But there was something else—something frightening, something that set off her survival instincts sure as if she were confronted by an attacker with a gun. Her body screamed for her to run, get out, save herself.

But her heart brought her to his bedside. "Oh . . . God."

The hospital johnny left his arms and his legs bare, and it seemed as if he was bruised everywhere. And his face . . . good Lord, he was desperately battered.

As he made a groaning noise in the back of his throat, she reached out to take his hand—oh, no, not there, too. His blunt fingers were swollen at the tips, the skin purple, some of the nails missing.

She wanted to touch him, but there was no place that she could. "Butch?"

His body jerked at the sound of her voice and his eyes opened. Well, one of them did.

As he focused on her, a ghost of a smile pulled at his lips. "You're back. I just . . . saw you at the door." His voice was weak, a tinny echo of the bass it normally was. "I saw you then . . . lost . . . you. But here you are."

She sat gingerly on the edge of the bed and wondered which nurse he thought she was. "Butch—"

"Where did . . . the yellow dress go?" His words were garbled, his mouth not moving much, as if his jaw were broken. "You were so beautiful . . . in that yellow dress . . ."

Definitely a nurse. Those suits hanging next to the door were yello—*shoot*. She hadn't put one on, had she? Holy hell, if his immune system was compromised, she needed to protect him.

"Butch, I'm going to go out and get a—"

"No—don't leave me . . . don't go . . ." His hands started twisting in the binds, the leather restraints creaking. "Please . . . dear God . . . don't leave me . . ."

"It's okay, I'll be right back."

"No . . . woman I love . . . yellow dress . . . don't leave me . . ."

Not knowing what else to do, she leaned down and softly laid her palm on his face. "I won't leave you."

He dragged his bruised cheek into her touch, his cracked lips brushing her skin as he whispered, "Promise me."

"I—"

The air lock broke with a hiss and Marissa looked over her shoulder.

Havers burst into the room as if he'd been torpedoed inside. And through the yellow mask he wore, the horror in his stare was as obvious as a scream.

"Marissa!" He swayed in the protective suit he had on, his voice muffled and frantic. "Sweet Virgin in the Fade, what are you—*you should have a hazmat on!*"

Butch started to struggle on the bed, and she lightly stroked his forearm. "Shh . . . I'm right here." When he'd calmed a little, she said, "I'll put one on right now—"

"You have no idea—oh, God!" Havers's whole body shook. "You're compromised now. You could be contaminated."

"Contaminated?" She looked down at Butch.

"Surely you felt it when you came in!" Havers launched into all kinds of words, none of which she heard.

As her brother kept at it, her priorities realigned themselves, steel locking into steel. It didn't matter that Butch

77

had no idea who she was. If the mistaken identity kept him alive and fighting, that was all that mattered.

"Marissa, are you hearing me? You're contam—"

She glanced over her shoulder. "Well, if I'm contaminated, then it looks like I'm staying with him, doesn't it."

SEVEN

John Matthew squared off at his target and tightened his grip on his blade. On the far side of the gym, across a sea of blue mats, there were three punching bags hanging from the bottom lip of the bleacher section. As he concentrated, the middle one became a *lesser* in his mind. He pictured the white hair and the pale eyes and the pasty skin that haunted his dreams, and he started to run, his bare feet slapping over thick plastic skin.

His little body had neither speed nor strength, but his will was enormous. And sometime in the next year or so, the rest of him would catch up to the power of his hatred.

He. Couldn't. Fucking. *Wait*. For his transition to hit.

Lifting his blade over his head, he opened his mouth to scream a war cry. Nothing came out, because he was a mute, but he imagined he was making a whole lot of noise.

As far as he was concerned, the *lessers* had killed his parents. Tohr and Wellsie had taken him in, told him what he really was, showed him the only love he'd known. When those bastard slayers had murdered her and Tohr had disappeared, John had been left with nothing but his revenge—revenge for them and the other innocent life that had been lost back in January.

John approached the bag running flat out, with his arm above his shoulder. At the last instant, he ducked into a ball, rolled on the mats, then shot up off the ground with the blade, hitting the bag from underneath. If it had been a real combat scenario, the knife would have gone into the *lesser*'s gut. Deep.

He twisted the hilt.

Then he sprang to his feet and spun around, imagining the undead falling to its knees, holding on to the hole in its abdomen. He stabbed the bag from up top, seeing himself bury the blade in the back of the neck—

"John?"

He whirled around, panting.

The female who approached made him tremble—and not just because she'd surprised the shit out of him. It was Beth Randall, the half-breed queen, the female who was also his sister, or so blood tests proved. Strangely, whenever she was around, his head went on a little vacation, his brain seizing up, but at least he didn't pass out anymore. Which had been his first reaction to meeting her.

Beth came across the mats, a long, lean female dressed in jeans and a white turtleneck, her dark hair the exact color of his. As she came closer, he could smell Wrath's bonding scent on her, a dark perfume specific to her *hellren*. John suspected the marking happened through sex, as the spice was always strongest at First Meal when they came down from their bedroom.

"John, will you join us up at the house for the last meal of the night?"

I have to stay and practice, he signed in American Sign Language. Everyone in the household had learned ASL, and the concession to his weakness, to his lack of voice, irked him. He wished they didn't have to make any allowances for him. He wished he were normal.

"We'd like to see you. And you spend so much time here."

Practice is important.

She eyed the blade in his hand. "So are other things."

As he continued to stare at her, her dark blue eyes

looked around the gym as if she were trying to find an appealing argument.

"Please, John, we're . . . I'm worried about you."

At one time, three months ago, he would have loved to have heard those words from her. From anybody. But no more. He didn't want her concern. He wanted her to get out of his way.

When he shook his head, she took a deep breath. "All right. I'm going to leave more food in the office, okay? Please . . . eat."

He inclined his head once, and when she lifted her hand as if to reach out, he stepped away. Without another word, she turned around and walked back across the blue mats.

When the door shut behind her, John jogged back to the far side of the gym and crouched to start running. As he took off once again, he lifted his blade high, rank hatred powering his arms and legs.

Mr. X flipped into action at high noon, walking into the garage of the house he recharged in, getting into the don't-notice-me minivan that disguised him among Caldwell's human traffic.

He had no interest in his assignment, but you acted when the master called in a command and you were the *Fore-lesser*. It was either that or you got canned, something Mr. X had been through once before and not enjoyed: Having the Omega slap a pink slip on you was about as much fun as eating a barbed-wire salad.

The fact that Mr. X was back on the flipping planet and in this role once again was still a shocker to him. But it seemed as if the master had grown tired of his revolving door of *Fore-lessers* and wanted to make one stick. As Mr. X had evidently been the best of the lot in the last fifty or sixty years, he'd been called into service for another round.

Reissued out of hell.

And so he was going to work today. As he pushed the key into the ignition and the Town & Country's anemic engine coughed over, he was utterly uninspired, no longer the leader he'd first been. But it was hard to get motivated in this kind of lose/lose situation. The Omega was going to get pissed off again and take it out on his number one. It was inevitable.

In bright noonday sun, Mr. X headed out of the fresh and perky subdivision, passing by Monopoly houses that had been built in the late 1990s. The things all shared a common architect, the gene pool of features locking the homes into cheap variations on duck-and-bunny adorable. Lot of front porches with insubstantial molding. Lot of plastic shutters. Lot of seasonal decorations, this time themed out on Easter.

Perfect hiding place for a *lesser*: a bramble of frazzled soccer moms and hassled midmanagement daddies.

Mr. X took Lily Lane out to Route 22, pausing at the STOP sign to the big road. Using a GPS tracker, he got a ballpark location on the place in the woods that the Omega had asked him to pay a visit to. Travel time to destination was twelve minutes and that was good. The master was all impatient, eager to see if his plan with that Trojan human had worked, all jonesing to know if the Brotherhood had taken their little pal back.

Mr. X thought about the guy, sure that the two of them had met before. But even as he wondered about the where and when of it, none of that mattered today. And it hadn't mattered when Mr. X had been working the tough bastard over, either.

Jesus, that had been a hard SOB. Not one word about

the Brotherhood had passed the man's lips, no matter what was done to him. Mr. X had been impressed. Guy like that would have been quite an asset if they could have turned him.

Or maybe that had already happened. Maybe that human was one of them now.

A little later, Mr. X parked the Town & Country on Route 22's shoulder and hoofed it into the woods. Snow had fallen last night in some freak March storm, and it padded the pine boughs, like the trees had geared up to play football with each other. Kind of pretty, actually. If you were into the nature shit.

The farther he went through the forest, the less he needed the tracker because he could feel the master's essence, sure as if the Omega was up ahead. Maybe the human hadn't gotten picked up by the Brothers—

Well, what do you know.

As Mr. X emerged into a clearing, he saw a scorched circle on the ground. The heat that had flared there had been great enough to melt the snow and mud-up the ground for a time and the now refrozen earth showed the contours of the burst. All around, remnants of the Omega's presence lingered, like the stink of summer garbage long after the trash had been picked up.

He breathed in through his nose. Yup, there was something human in the mix, too.

Holy shit, they'd killed the guy. The Brotherhood had exterminated that human. Interesting. Except . . . why hadn't the Omega known the man was dead? Maybe there hadn't been enough in him to have him get called home to the master?

The Omega wasn't going to like this report. He was allergic to failure: it made him itchy. And itchy led to bad things for *Fore-lessers*.

Mr. X knelt down to the withered earth and envied the human. Lucky bastard. When a *lesser* bit it, what waited for him on the other side was an endless liquid misery, a horror bath that was every Christian's vision of hell times a thousand: After slayers were killed, they returned to the veins of the Omega's body, circling and recircling in an evil swill of other dead *lessers*, becoming the very blood the master put in you when you were inducted into the Society. And for these reconstituting slayers, there was no end to the burning cold or the driving starvation or the crushing pressure because you remained conscious. For eternity.

Mr. X shuddered. An atheist in life, he hadn't thought of death as anything other than a dirt nap. Now, as a *lesser*, he knew exactly what was waiting for him when the master lost patience and "fired" him again.

And yet there was hope. Mr. X had found a little loophole, assuming the pieces fell together right.

By a stroke of luck, he might have found a way out of the Omega's world.

EIGHT

Butch took three long, trippy days to wake up and he resurfaced from his coma in the manner of a buoy, popping out of the depths of nothingness and wobbling on top of reality's lake of sights and sounds. Eventually, he put things together enough to understand that he was looking at a white wall in front of him and hearing a soft beeping in the background.

Hospital room. Right. And the ties on his arms and legs were now gone.

Just for kicks and giggles, he rolled over onto his back and pushed his head and shoulders off the bed. He kept himself upright because he liked the sensation of the room going around. It distracted him from his Whitman's Sampler of aches and pains.

Man, he'd had bizarre, wonderful dreams. Marissa at his bedside caring for him. Stroking his arm, his hair, his face. Whispering to him to stay with her. That voice of hers had been what kept him in his body, what kept him back from the white light that any idiot who'd seen *Poltergeist* knew was the afterlife. For her, he'd somehow hung on, and going by the steady, strong beat of his heart, he knew he was going to make it.

Except, of course, the dreams had all been a gyp. She wasn't here and now he was stuck in this bag of skin of his until the next badass thing took him down.

Goddamn it, just his rotten luck to have kept breathing.

He looked up at the IV pole. Eyeballed the catheter bag. Then glanced over at what appeared to be a bathroom. Shower. Oh, God, he'd give his left nut for a shower.

As he shifted his legs around, he was aware that what he was about to do was probably a very bad call. But he told himself, as he hung up the catheter bag next to his IV meds, that at least the room spins had mostly stopped.

A couple of deep breaths and he grabbed the IV pole to use as a cane.

Feet hit the cold floor. Weight eased onto his legs.

Knees buckled without hesitation.

As he fell back on the bed, he knew he wasn't going to make it to the bathroom. With no hope of hot water, he turned his head and eyed the shower with naked lust—

Butch inhaled like he'd been cracked on the back of the head.

Marissa lay sleeping on the floor in the corner of the room, curled up on her side. Her head rested on a pillow and a beautiful gown of pale blue chiffon spilled over her legs. Her hair, that incredible waterfall of pale blond, that medieval romance novel rush of waves, was all around her.

Holy shit. She had been with him. She had truly saved him.

His body had newfound strength as he stood and lurched across the linoleum. He wanted to kneel down but knew he'd probably get stuck on the floor, so he settled for standing over her.

Why was she here? Last thing he knew, she didn't want to have anything to do with him. Hell, she'd refused to see him back in September when he'd come to her hoping for . . . everything.

"Marissa?" His voice was shot to shit and he cleared his throat. "Marissa, wake up."

Her lashes flicked open and she snapped upright. Her eyes, those pale blue, sea-glass-colored eyes, shot to his. "You're going to fall!"

Just as his body swayed backward and he toppled off

his heels, she leaped to her feet and caught him. In spite of her willowy body, she took all of his weight easily, reminding him that she was no human woman and was likely stronger than he was. As she helped him back onto the bed and pulled the sheets over him, the fact that he was weak as a child and she was treating him like one out of necessity bit into his pride.

"Why are you here?" he asked, his tone as sharp as his embarrassment.

When her eyes didn't meet his, he knew she also was uncomfortable with their situation. "Vishous told me you were hurt."

Ah, so V had guilted her into this Florence Nightingale routine. That bastard knew Butch was a simpering idiot for her and that the sound of her voice would do exactly what it did and bring him around. But it was a helluva position for her to be in, a reluctant rope to the proverbial lifeboat.

Butch grunted as he rearranged himself. And also from the knock his pride was taking.

"How do you feel?" she said.

"Better." Comparatively. Then again, he could have been dragged under a bus and still been miles ahead of what the *lesser* had done to him. "So you don't have to stay."

Her hand drifted off the sheet and she took a slow breath, her breasts rising under the expensive bodice of her gown. As she wrapped her arms around herself, her body became an elegant s-curve.

He looked away, ashamed because part of him wanted to take advantage of her pity and keep her with him. "Marissa, you can go now, you know."

"Actually, I can't."

He frowned and glanced back at her. "Why not."

She paled, but then lifted her chin. "You're under—"

There was a hiss and an alien walked into the room, the figure dressed in a yellow suit and a breathing mask. The face behind the molded plastic was female, but the features indistinct.

Butch looked back at Marissa with horror. "Why the *fuck* aren't you wearing one of those getups?" He had no idea what kind of infection he had, but if it was bad enough that the medical staff was pulling a Silkwood, he had to imagine he was deadly.

Marissa cringed, making him feel like a total thug. "I . . . I'm just not."

"Sire?" the nurse interrupted gently. "I'd like to take a blood sample if you don't mind?"

He kicked out a forearm while still glaring at Marissa. "You were supposed to be wearing one of those when you came in, weren't you? *Weren't you?*"

"Yes."

"Goddamn it," he snapped. "Why didn't you—"

As the nurse nailed him a good one in the crook of his elbow, Butch's strength ran out of him like she'd popped the balloon of his energy with that needle of hers.

Dizziness slammed into him and his head fell back against the pillow. But he was still pissed off. "You should have one of those on."

Marissa didn't respond, just paced around.

In the silence, he glanced over at the little vial that was plugged into his vein. As the nurse swapped it for an empty one, he couldn't help noticing that his blood seemed darker than usual. Much darker.

"Good God . . . what the hell's coming out of me?"

"It's better than it was. Much so." The nurse smiled through the mask.

"Then what color was it before," he muttered, thinking the shit looked like brown sludge.

When the nurse was done, she shoved a thermometer under his tongue and checked the machines behind the bed. "I'll bring you some food."

"Has she eaten," he mumbled.

"Keep your mouth closed." There was a beeping noise and the nurse took the plastic-covered stick from his lips. "Much better. Now, is there anything you'd like?"

He thought of Marissa risking her life because of guilt. "Yeah, I want her to get out of here."

Marissa heard the words and stopped walking around. Easing back against the wall, she glanced down at herself and was surprised to find that her gown still fit her the same. She felt half her usual size. Small. Insubstantial.

As the nurse left, Butch's hazel eyes burned. "How long do you have to stay?"

"Until Havers tells me I can go."

"Are you sick?"

She shook her head.

"What are they treating me for?"

"Your injuries from the car accident. Which were extensive."

"Car accident?" He looked confused, then nodded at the IV as if he wanted to change the subject. "What's in there?"

She linked her arms over her chest and recited the antibiotics, the nutrients, the pain meds, and the anticoagulants he was on. "And Vishous comes in to help as well."

She thought of the Brother and his disarming diamond eyes and the tattoos at his temple . . . and his obvious dislike of her. He was the only one who came into the room without protective clothing on and he dropped by twice a day, at the beginning and the end of night.

"V's been here to visit?"

"He lays his hand above your belly. It eases you." The first time that warrior had stripped the sheets from Butch's body and pulled up the hospital johnny, she'd been speechless both at the intimate sight and the Brother's authority. But then she'd grown mute for another reason. Butch's belly wound had been frightening—and then Vishous had scared her, too. He'd taken off the glove she'd always seen him wear, revealing a glowing hand that was tattooed front to back.

She'd been terrified about what would happen next, but Vishous just hovered that palm of his about three inches over Butch's belly. Even in the coma, Butch had sighed raggedly in relief.

Afterward, Vishous had rearranged the hospital johnny and the bedsheets and turned to her. He'd told her to close her eyes, and though she was scared of him, she did. Almost immediately a profound peace had come over her, as if she were bathed in white, calming light. He did that to her each time before he left, and she knew he was protecting her. Although she couldn't think of why, given that he clearly despised her.

She refocused on Butch and thought about his wounds. "You weren't in a car accident, were you?"

He closed his eyes. "I'm very tired."

As he shut her out, she sat on the bare floor and clasped her arms around her knees. Havers had wanted to bring things in like a cot or a comfortable chair, but she'd been concerned that if Butch's vitals crashed again, the medical staff wouldn't be able to get the necessary equipment to the bedside fast enough. Her brother hadn't disagreed.

After God only knew how many days of this, her back was stiff and her eyelids were like sandpaper, but she hadn't felt tired when she'd been fighting to keep Butch alive. Hell, she hadn't even noticed the passage of time, had always been surprised when food was brought in or the nurses or Havers came. Or Vishous arrived.

So far, she wasn't sick. Well, she had felt ill before Vishous stopped by for the first time. But ever since he'd started doing whatever he did with that hand of his, she'd been fine.

Marissa glanced up to the hospital bed. She was still curious why Vishous had called her to this room. Surely that warrior's hand was doing more good than she was.

As the machines beeped softly and the air blower came on up in the ceiling, her eyes drifted down the length of Butch's still body. A flush hit her face as she thought of what was underneath the covers.

She knew what every inch of him looked like now.

His skin was smooth over all his muscle and he was tattooed on the small of his back with black ink—a series of lines grouped in fours with each bundle carrying a slash that ran at an angle. Twenty-five of them, if she added correctly, some having faded, as if made years ago. She wondered what they commemorated.

As for the front of him, the dusting of dark hair across his pectorals had been a surprise, as she hadn't known humans weren't bare-skinned as her kind were. He didn't have a lot of hair on his chest, though, and it narrowed quickly, becoming a thin line under his belly button.

And then . . . She was ashamed of herself, but she'd looked at his male sex. The hair at the juncture of his legs was dark and very dense, and from the midst, he had a thick stalk of flesh almost as wide as her wrist. What was below was a heavy, potent sack.

He was the first male she'd ever seen naked and the nudes from Art History just weren't the same as the real thing. He was beautifully made. Fascinating.

She let her head fall back and stared at the ceiling. How

unattractive was it that she'd invaded his privacy? And how unattractive that her body stirred just remembering?

God, how much longer now before she could get out of here?

She absently fingered the fine fabric of her gown and tilted her head so she could look at the fall of pale blue chiffon. The lovely creation by Narciso Rodriguez should have been utterly comfortable, but her corset, which she wore always as was proper, was really starting to bug the hell out of her. The thing was, though, she wanted to look nice for Butch, even though he wouldn't care and not because he was ill. He just wasn't attracted to her anymore. Didn't want her around, either.

Still, she would continue to dress well when fresh clothes were brought in.

Pity that what she wore here had to go into the incinerator. What a shame to burn all those dresses.

NINE

That pale-haired fucker was back, Van Dean thought as he glanced through heavy chicken-wire fencing.

Third week in a row the guy'd come to Caldwell's fight underground. Against the cheering crowd around the fight cage he stood out like a neon sign, although Van wasn't clear exactly why.

As a knee made contact with his side, he refocused on what he was doing. Drawing back his bare fist, he snapped his arm out and connected with his opponent's face. Blood exploded from the guy's nose, a starburst of red that landed on the mat right before the man's body did.

Van planted his feet and stared down at his opponent, drops of his sweat landing on the guy's abs. There was no referee to stop Van from throwing more head punches. No rules to keep him from kicking this side of beef in the kidneys until the bastard needed dialysis for the rest of his life. And if there was even one twitch from that human throw rug, Van was going to let loose.

Bringing death with his bare hands was what the special part of him wanted to do, what the special part of him craved to do. Van had always been different, not just from his opponents but from everyone else he'd ever met: the seat of his soul was that of not merely a fighter but a warrior of the Roman kind. He wished he lived back in the times when you eviscerated your opponent when he fell before you . . . then you found his home and raped his wife and slaughtered his children. And after you looted his shit, you burned whatever was left down to the ground.

But he lived in the here and now. And there was another complication of late. The body holding in this special part was starting to age on him. His shoulder was killing him and so were his knees, though he made sure no one knew it, in or out of the fight cage.

Extending his arm to the side, he heard a pop and hid a wince. Meanwhile; the crowd of fifty roared and rattled the ten-foot-high chain-link fence. God, the fans loved him. Called him by his name. Wanted to see more of him.

They were largely irrelevant to his special part, though.

In the midst of the peanut gallery, he met the stare of the pale-haired man. Damn, those were some freaky eyes. Flat. No glow of life in them. And the guy wasn't cheering either.

Whatever.

Van nudged his opponent with his bare foot. The guy groaned but didn't open his eyes. Game over.

The fifty or so men around the cage went apeshit with approval.

Van sprang up to the lip of the fence and swung his two-hundred-pound body over the top. As he landed, the crowd roared louder but backed out of his path. When one of them had gotten in his way last week, flyboy had ended up spitting out a tooth.

The fighting "arena," such as it was, was in an abandoned underground parking garage, and the owner of the concrete wasteland brokered the matches. The whole thing was shady by def, with Van and his opponents nothing more than the human equivalent of fighting cocks. The pay was good, however, and so far there hadn't been any busts—although that was always an issue. Between the blood and the betting, the CPD badges wouldn't have been into the scene at all, so it was a private-membership-club kind of thing, and if you squealed you got tossed. Literally.

The owner had a six-pack of thugs who kept shit in line.

Van went over to the money man, got his five hundred bucks and his jacket, then headed for his truck. His Hanes undershirt was bloodstained, but he didn't care. What he was worried about was his aching joints. And that left shoulder.

Fuck. Every week it seemed like it was taking more and more out of him to serve his special part and put the guys on the ground. Then again, he was getting up there. Thirty-nine was denture time in the fight world.

"Why did you stop?"

As he came up to his truck, Van looked into his driver's side windshield. He was not surprised that the pale-haired man had come after him. "I don't answer to fans, buddy."

"I'm not a fan."

Their eyes stayed locked together on the flat surface of the glass. "Then why you been coming to my fights so much?"

"Because I have a proposition for you."

"I don't want a manager."

"I'm not one of those either."

Van looked over his shoulder. The guy was big and carried himself like a fighter, all jacked shoulders and loose arms. Ironpan hands on this one, the kind that could crank into a fist as big as a bowling ball.

So that was the deal, huh. "You want to get into the ring with me, you arrange it over there." He pointed to the money man.

"Not after that either."

Van turned around, thinking the twenty-questions thing was for shit. "So what do you want?"

"First I have to know why you stopped."

"He was down."

Annoyance flashed over the guy's face. "So."

"You know what? You're beginning to piss me off."

"Fine. I'm looking for a man who fits your description."

Oh, that narrowed the field. Busted nose in a regular joe face with a military haircut. Snooze. "Lotta men look like me."

Well, except for his right hand.

"Tell me something," the guy asked, "did you have your appendix removed?"

Van narrowed his eyes and put his truck's keys back in his pocket. "One of two things are about to happen and you get to pick. You walk away and I get into my ride. Or you keep talking and shit goes down. Your choice."

The pale man got in close. Jesus, he smelled funny. Like . . . baby powder?

"Don't threaten me, *boy*." The voice was low and the body that backed up the words was coiled for action.

Well, well, well . . . what do you know. A real contender.

Van pushed his face even closer. "Then get to your fucking point."

"Appendix?"

"Not anymore."

The man smiled. Eased back. "How would you like a job?"

"I have one. And this."

"Construction. Knocking strangers around for cash."

"Honest work, both of them. And just how long have you been nosing around my biz?"

"Long enough." The guy stuck out his hand. "Joseph Xavier."

Van let that palm hang out there. "Not interested in meeting you, Joe."

"That's Mr. Xavier to you, son. And surely you wouldn't mind listening to a proposition."

Van cocked his head to the side. "You know something, I'm a lot like a whore. I like to get paid by jerkoffs. So how about you palm me a benji, Joe, then we'll see about your proposition."

As the man just stared, Van felt an unexpected shot of fear. Man, something about this guy was not right.

The bastard's voice was even lower as he spoke. "Say my name properly first, son."

Whatever. For a hundred bucks, he'd flap his gums even for a freak like this. "Xavier."

"That's *Mr.* Xavier." The guy smiled like a predator, all teeth, no jolly. "Say it, son."

Some unknown impulse had Van opening his mouth.

Right before he let the words fly, he had a vivid memory of when he'd been sixteen years old and had taken a dive into the Hudson River. In midair, he'd seen the massive underwater stone he was going to hit and knew there would be no change in course. Sure enough, his head had made contact as if the collision had been preordained, as if there had been an invisible string around his neck and the rock had pulled him home. But it hadn't been a bad thing, at least not right away. Immediately after the crack of impact, there had been a floating, a sweet, satisfied calm, as if destiny had been fulfilled. And he'd known instinctively that the sensation was a forerunner of death.

Funny, he had that same spacy disorientation now. And the same sense that this man with the paper-white skin was like death: inevitable and fated—and coming specifically for him.

"Mr. Xavier," Van whispered.

When the hundred-dollar bill appeared in front of him, he reached forward with his four-fingered hand and took it.

But he knew he would have listened without the cash.

* * *

Hours later, Butch rolled over and the first thing he did was look for Marissa.

He found her sitting in the corner of the room, a book open next to her. Her eyes weren't on the pages, though. She was staring at the pale linoleum tiles, tracing the pattern of flecks with one long, perfect finger.

She looked achingly sad and so beautiful that his eyes stung. God, the idea he could infect her or endanger her in any way made him want to slit his own throat.

"I wish you hadn't come in here," he croaked. As she winced, he thought about his choice of words. "What I mean is—"

"I know what you mean." Her voice hardened. "Are you hungry?"

"Yeah." He struggled to push himself up. "But I'd really like a shower."

She got to her feet, rising like mist she was so graceful, and his breath caught as she walked to him. Man, that pale blue dress was the exact color of her eyes.

"Let me help you to the bath."

"No, I can do it."

She crossed her arms over her chest. "If you try to get to the bathroom on your own, you will fall and you will hurt yourself."

"Call a nurse, then. I don't want you to touch me."

She stared at him for a moment. Then blinked her eyes once. Twice.

"Will you excuse me for a moment?" she said in a level tone. "I need to use the lavatory. You can call the nurse by pushing that red button on the remote there."

She went into the bathroom and shut the door. Water started to run.

Butch reached for the little button pad, but stopped as the rush of the sink continued to bleed through the door.

The sound was uninterrupted, not as if someone was washing their hands or their face or filling a glass.

And it continued, on and on.

With a grunt, he shuffled off the bed and stood up, hanging himself on the IV pole until the thing shook from the effort of keeping him upright. He put one foot in front of the other until he got to the bathroom door. He pressed his ear against the wood. All he could hear was water.

For some reason, he knocked softly. Then knocked again. He gave it one more shot, then turned the knob, even though he would embarrass the hell out of them both if she was using the facilities—

Marissa was on the toilet, as it turned out. But the seat was down.

And she was weeping. Shaking and weeping.

"Oh . . . Jesus, Marissa."

She let out a shriek, as if he were the last thing on the planet she wanted to see. "Get out!"

He lurched in and sank to his knees in front of her. "Marissa . . ."

Burying her face in her hands, she snapped, "I would like some privacy, if you don't mind."

He reached over and shut the water off. As the basin emptied with a little gurgle, her muffled breathing took over where the sound of the faucet had left off.

"It's all right," he said. "You'll leave soon. You'll get out—"

"Shut up!" She dropped her hands long enough to glare at him. "Just go back to bed and call the nurse if you haven't already."

He sat back on his heels, woozy but determined. "I'm sorry you got trapped with me."

"I *bet* you are."

He frowned. "Marissa—"

The sound of the air lock being broken cut him off.

"Cop?" V's voice was unmuffled by protective gear.

"Hold up," Butch called out. Marissa didn't need more of an audience.

"Where are you, cop? Something wrong?"

Butch meant to stand up. He really did. But when he grabbed onto the IV pole and pulled, his body gave out, just went right to rubber on him. Marissa tried to grab him, but he slid from her grasp, ending up sprawled on the bathroom tile, his cheek next to the seal around the toilet base. Dimly, he heard Marissa talking in urgent bursts. Then V's goatee came into his line of sight.

Butch looked at his roommate . . . and shit, his vision got blurry, he was so happy to see the bastard. Vishous's face was just the same, the dark bearding around his mouth right where it should be, the tattoos on the temple unchanged, those diamond-bright irises still glowing. Familiar, so familiar. Home and family wrapped up in a vampire package.

Butch didn't let any tears fall, though. He was already hopelessly incapacitated next to a toilet, for chrissakes. Sapping out would be the cap to this gown of shame he'd pulled on.

Blinking fiercely, he said, "Where's your fucking gear, man? You know, the yellow suit."

V smiled, his eyes a little shiny as if he too were choked up. "Don't worry, I'm covered. So, I guess you're back, true?"

"And ready to rock and roll."

"Really."

"For sure. I'm thinking about a future in contracting. Wanted to see how this bathroom was put together. Excellent tile work. You should check it."

"How about I carry you back to bed?"

"I want to look at the sink pipes next."

Respect and affection clearly drove V's cool smirk. "At least let me help you up."

"Nah, I can do it." With a groan, Butch gave the vertical move a shot, but then eased back down onto the tile. Turned out lifting his head was a little overwhelming. But if they left him here long enough—a week, maybe ten days?

"Come on, cop. Cry uncle here and let me help."

Butch was suddenly too tired to front. As he went totally limp, he was aware of Marissa staring at him and thought, man, could he look any weaker? Shit, the only saving grace was that there wasn't a cold breeze on his butt.

Which suggested the hospital gown had stayed closed. Thank you, God.

V's thick arms tunneled under him and then he was lifted easily. As they went forward, he refused to let his head rest on his friend's shoulder, even though it gave him the sweats to keep the thing upright. When he was back on the bed, shivers racked his whole body and the room spun.

Before V straightened, Butch grabbed the male's arm and whispered, "I need to talk to you. Alone."

"What's doing?" V said with equal quiet.

Butch looked over at Marissa, who was hovering in the corner.

With a flush, she glanced at the bathroom, then picked up two large paper bags. "I think I'll take a shower. Will you excuse me?" She didn't wait for a response, just disappeared into the loo.

As the door shut, V sat on the edge of the bed. "Talk to me."

"What kind of danger is she in?"

"I've taken care of her and three days in, she seems fine. She can probably leave soon. We're all pretty convinced by now there's no cross-infection thing going on."

"What's she been exposed to? What was I exposed to?"

"You know you were with the *lessers*, true?"

Butch lifted one of his busted-up hands. "And here I thought I'd been to Elizabeth Arden."

"Smart-ass. You were there about a day—"

Abruptly, he grabbed V's arm. "I didn't crack. No matter what they did to me, I didn't say a thing about the Brotherhood. I *swear*."

V put his hand over Butch's and squeezed. "I know you didn't, my man. I know you wouldn't."

"Good."

As they both let go, V's eyes went to Butch's finger-tips, as if he were imagining what had been done to them. "What do you remember?"

"Only the feelings. The pain and the . . . dread. Fear. Pride . . . the pride is how I know I didn't squeal, how I know they didn't break me."

V nodded and drew a hand-rolled out of his pocket. Just before he lit up, he looked at the oxygen feed, cursed, and put the cig back. "Listen, buddy, I gotta ask . . . you okay in the head? I mean, going through something like that—"

"I'm cool. Always was too dumb to have PTSD or some shit, and besides, I've got not real memory of what went down. As long as Marissa can walk out of here okay, then, yeah, I'm fine." He scrubbed his face, feeling the itch of his beard growth, then dropped his arm. As his hand landed on his abdomen, he thought of the black wound. "You have any idea what they did to me?"

When V shook his head, Butch cursed. The guy was like a Walking Google link, so him not knowing was a bad thing.

"But I'm on it, cop. I will find an answer for you, I promise." The brother nodded at Butch's stomach. "So how's it look?"

"Don't know. Been too busy being in a coma to worry about my six-pack."

"Mind if I?"

Butch shrugged and pushed the covers down. As V lifted up the hospital johnny, they both looked down at his belly. The skin was not right around the wound, all gray and puckered.

"Does it hurt?" V asked.

"Like a mother. Feels . . . cold. Like there's dry ice in my gut."

"Will you let me do something?"

"What?"

"Just a little healing thing I've been throwing at you."

"Sure." Except when V brought up his business hand and started talking off that glove, Butch recoiled. "What are you going to do with that thing?"

"Trust me, true?"

Butch barked a laugh. "Last time you said that I ended up with a vampire cocktail, remember?"

"Saved your ass. That's how I found you."

So that had been the *why* of it. "Well, then, fly me some of that hand."

Still, as V put the glowing thing close, Butch winced.

"Relax, cop. This isn't going to hurt."

"I've seen you toast a house with that bastard."

"Point taken. But the Firestarter routine isn't going down here."

V hovered his tattooed, glowing hand over the wound, and Butch let out a ragged groan of relief. It was as if warm, fresh water was pouring into the wound, then flowing over him, through him. Cleaning him out.

Butch's eyes rolled back in his head. "Oh . . . God . . . that feels good."

He went limp, and then he was floating, free of the pain, sliding into some kind of dream state. He let his body go, let himself go.

He could actually feel the healing, as if his body's regenerative processes had kicked into high gear. As seconds passed, as minutes went by, as time drifted into the infinite, he felt like whole days of rest and eating well and being at peace were coming and going, leapfrogging him from the battered state he was in to the miraculous gift of health.

Marissa tilted her head back and stood right under the showerhead, letting the water fall down her body. She felt shaken loose and thin-skinned, especially after watching Vishous carry Butch to the bed. The two of them were so close, the mutual bond clear in the way their eyes met and held.

After a long while, she got out, toweled herself off roughly, then blew her hair dry. As she reached for a fresh set of undergarments, she looked at the corset and thought, the hell she was putting that on. She shoved it back into a bag, unable to bear having that iron grip around her rib cage right now.

As she put her peach gown on over her naked breasts, it felt strange, but she'd had it with being uncomfortable. At least for a little while. Besides, who would know?

She folded up the pale blue Rodriguez and put it into a bio-hazard bag along with her old underwear. Then she braced herself and opened the door out into the patient room.

Butch was sprawled on the bed, the hospital gown pushed up onto his chest, the sheets down around his hips.

Vishous's glowing hand was resting about three inches above the blackened wound.

In the silence between the two males, she was an intruder. With nowhere to go.

"He's asleep," V grunted.

She cleared her throat, but couldn't think of anything to say. After a long silence, she finally murmured, "Tell me . . . does his family know what's happened?"

"Yeah. The Brotherhood all know."

"No, I mean . . . his human family."

"They are irrelevant."

"But shouldn't they be—"

V looked up with impatience, his diamond eyes hard and a little mean. For some reason, it occurred to her now just how fully armed he was with his black daggers crossing his thick chest.

Then again, his sharp expression went with the weapons.

"Butch's 'family' doesn't want him." V's voice was strident, as if the explanation were none of her business and he was elaborating just to shut her up. "So they are irrelevant. Now come over here. He needs you to be close to him."

The contradiction between the Brother's face and his command to come closer tangled her up. So did the reality that that hand was the biggest help.

"He most certainly does not need me or want me here," she murmured. And wondered once again why the hell V had called her three nights ago.

"He's worried about you. That's why he wants you to go."

She flushed. "Wrong, warrior."

"I'm never wrong." With a quick flash, those navy-rimmed white irises flipped up to her face. They were so frigid that she stepped back, but Vishous shook his head.

"Come on, touch him. Let him feel you. He needs to know you're here."

She frowned, thinking the Brother was crazy. But she walked to the far side of the bed and reached out to stroke Butch's hair. The instant she made contact, he turned his face toward her.

"See?" Vishous went back to staring at the wound. "He craves you."

I wish he did, she thought.

"Do you really?"

She stiffened. "Please don't read my mind. It's rude."

"I didn't. You spoke out loud."

Her hand faltered on Butch's hair. "Oh. Sorry."

They grew quiet, both focused on Butch. Then Vishous said in a hard tone, "Why'd you shut him down, Marissa? When he came to see you back in the fall, why'd you turn him away?"

She frowned. "He never came to see me."

"Yeah, he did."

"I beg your pardon?"

"You heard what I said."

As they locked eyes, it occurred to her that although Vishous was scary as all get out, he was not a liar. "When? When did he come to me?"

"He waited for a couple weeks after Wrath was shot. Then he went to your house. When he got back, he said you wouldn't even come down in person. Man, that was a cold move, female. You knew he was feeling you, but you turned him away through a servant. *Nice.*"

"No . . . I never did that . . . He didn't come, he . . . No one told me he—"

"Oh, *please.*"

"Do *not* take that tone with me, warrior." As Vishous's eyes shot to her face, she was too pissed off to care who or what he was. "At the end of last summer I was flat on my back with the flu, thanks to feeding Wrath too much and then working in the clinic. When I didn't hear from Butch, I assumed he'd had second thoughts about us. As I . . . haven't had a lot of luck with males, it took me a while to work up the nerve to approach him. When I did, three months ago here in the clinic, he made it clear he didn't want to see me. So do me the favor of *not* blaming me for something I did *not* do."

There was a long silence and then Vishous surprised the hell out of her.

He actually smiled at her a little. "Well, what do you know."

Flustered, she looked down at Butch and resumed stroking his hair. "I swear to you, if I had known it was him, I would have dragged myself out of bed to answer that door myself."

In a low voice Vishous murmured, "Good deal, female. Good . . . deal."

In the silence that followed, she thought about the events of the previous summer. The convalescence she'd taken hadn't been just about the flu. She'd been overwhelmed by her brother's attempt on Wrath's life—by the fact that Havers, ever the calm, even-tempered healer, had gone so far as to betray the king's location to a *lesser*. Sure, Havers had done it to *ahvenge* her because of the way she had been cast aside for the queen, but that in no way excused the actions.

Dear Virgin in the Fade, Butch had tried to see her, but why hadn't she been told?

"I never knew you came," she murmured, smoothing his hair back.

Vishous removed his hand, and yanked up the sheet. "Close your eyes, Marissa. It's your turn."

She looked up. "I didn't know."

"I believe you. Now close."

After he had healed her, V walked over to the door, his big shoulders rolling with his gait.

At the air lock, he looked back over his shoulder. "Don't think I was the only reason he healed. You're his light, Marissa. Don't ever forget that." The Brother's eyes narrowed. "But here's something to keep in mind. You ever hurt him on purpose and I will consider you my enemy."

John Matthew sat in a classroom that was right out of Caldwell High School. There were seven long tables facing the blackboard, and all but one had a pair of trainees plugged into them.

John was alone in the back. Which was also just as it had been at CHS.

The difference between this class and the stuff he'd taken in school, though, was that now he took careful notes and stared up front like the chalkboard was running a *Die Hard* marathon.

Then again, geometry wasn't ever the subject on deck around here.

This afternoon, Zsadist was at the head of the class, pacing back and forth, talking about the chemical composition of C4 plastic explosives. The Brother was wearing one of his trademark black turtlenecks and a pair of loose nylon track pants. With that scar down his face, he looked exactly like he'd done what people said he had: killed females, desecrated *lessers*, attacked even his Brothers without provocation.

But the strange thing was, he was a helluva teacher.

"Now for detonators," he said. "Personally, I prefer the remote variety."

As John turned over a fresh page in his notebook, Z sketched a 3-D mechanism on the board, some kind of box with wiring circuits. Whenever the Brother drew, what he put up was so detailed and realistic you could almost reach out and touch the thing.

When there was a lull, John checked his watch. Another fifteen minutes, then it was time to have a light meal and hit the gym. He couldn't wait.

When he'd started school here, he'd hated the mixed martial arts training. Now he loved it. He was still last in the class in terms of technical skills, but lately he'd more than made up for that in rage. And his aggression had caused a realignment in social dynamics.

Back in the beginning, three months ago, his classmates had ridiculed him. Accused him of sucking up to the Brothers. Derided him for his birthmark because it looked like the pectoral star scar of the Brotherhood. Now the other guys watched it around him. Well, everyone except for Lash. Lash still rode him, singling him out, cutting him down.

Not that John cared. He might be in this class with the rest of the trainees, he might technically be living in the compound with the Brothers, he might supposedly be linked to the Brotherhood by the blood of his father, but ever since he'd lost Tohr and Wellsie, he was a free agent so far as he was concerned. Bound to no one.

So the other folks in this room were nothing to him.

He shifted his stare to the back of Lash's head. The guy's long blond hair was in a ponytail that rested smoothly down a jacket made by some fancy designer. And how did John know about the designer thing? Because Lash always told everyone what he was wearing when he walked in for class.

Had also mentioned tonight that his new watch was iced out by Jacob the Jeweler.

John narrowed his eyes, getting juiced up just thinking about the sparring the two of them would do in the gym. As if the guy felt the heat, Lash turned, his diamond earring sparkling. His lips lifted into a nasty little smile, then pursed as he blew John a kiss.

"John?" Zsadist's voice was hard as a hammer. "Mind showing me some respect here?"

As John flushed and looked up front, Zsadist continued, tapping the board with a long forefinger. "Once a mech like this is activated it's triggered by a variety of things, sound frequency being the most common. You can call in from a cell phone, a computer, or use a radio signal."

Zsadist started drawing again, the scratch of chalk loud in the room.

"Here's another kind of detonator." Zsadist stepped back. "This one is typical of car bombs. You wire the action box into the car's electrical system. Once the bomb's armed, whenever the car's started, *tick, tick, boom.*"

John's hand suddenly gripped his pen and he started to blink fast, feeling dizzy.

The redheaded trainee named Blaylock asked, "Does it go off right away after ignition?"

"There's a delay of a couple of seconds. I'd note also that because the car's wiring has been redirected, the engine won't catch. The driver will turn the key and hear nothing but a series of clicks."

John's brain began firing in a rapid, flickering sequence.

Rain . . . black rain on a car's windshield.

A hand with a key in it, reaching forward toward a steering wheel column.

An engine turning over but failing to catch. A feeling of dread, that someone was lost. Then a bright light—

110

John flipped out of his chair and hit the ground, but he was unaware he'd gone into a seizure: Too busy screaming in his head, he didn't feel a thing physically.

Someone was lost! Someone . . . was left behind. He'd left someone behind . . .

TEN

As dawn arrived and the steel shutters came down all around the mansion's billiards room, Vishous bit into an Arby's roast beef sandwich. Thing tasted like a phone book, through no fault of the ingredients.

At the soft smack of pool balls, he looked up. Beth, the queen, was just straightening from the felt.

"Nice shot," Rhage said as he lounged against a silk wall.

"Careful training." She walked around the table, sizing up her next stroke. When she leaned down again and braced the cue on her left hand, the queen's Saturnine Ruby flashed on her middle finger.

V wiped his mouth with a paper napkin. "She's going to beat you again, Hollywood."

"Probably."

Except she didn't get the chance. Wrath plowed through the doorway, clearly in a mood. His long black hair, which was down almost to his leather-covered ass now, flared behind him, then came to rest on his thick back.

Beth put her cue down. "How is John?"

"Who the hell knows." Wrath went over and kissed her on the mouth, then on both sides of her neck over her veins. "He won't go to see Havers. Refuses to get anywhere near the clinic. Kid's asleep in Tohr's office now, just exhausted."

"What was the trigger for the seizure this time?"

"Z was doing a class on explosives. Kid just whacked out, ended up on the floor. Same as before, when he first saw you."

Beth wrapped her arms around Wrath's waist and leaned into her *hellren*'s body. Their black hair mixed together, his straight, hers wavy. God, Wrath's was so damn long now. But word had it that Beth liked the stuff so he'd grown it out for her.

V wiped his mouth again. *Weird, how males do shit like that.*

Beth shook her head. "I wish John would come stay in the house with us. Sleeping in that chair, staying in the office . . . He spends so much time alone and he doesn't eat enough anymore. Plus Mary says he won't talk about what happened with Tohr and Wellsie at all. He just refuses to open up."

"I don't care what he talks about as long as he goes to the damn doctor." Wrath's wraparound sunglasses shifted over to V. "And how's our other patient? Christ, I feel like we need an in-house physician around here."

V reached for the Arby's bag and took out sandwich number two. "Cop's healing up. I think he'll be out in a day or so."

"I want to know what the fuck was done to him. The Scribe Virgin's giving me nothing on this one. She's silent as stone."

"I started the research yesterday. Began with the Chronicles." Which were eighteen volumes in the Old Language of vampire history. God, talk about your wall-bangers. The damn things were about as much fun as reading and inventory list for a hardware store. "If I don't find anything, there are some other places to check. Compendiums of oral tradition that were reduced to writing, that kind of shit. It is highly improbable that in our twenty thousand years of taking up space on the planet something like this hasn't happened before. I'm going to spend today working on it."

Because as usual there'd be no sleep for him. It had been over a week since he'd REM'd out, and there was no reason to think things were going to be any different this afternoon.

Holy hell . . . being up for eight days straight was not good for his brain wave activity. Without going into a dream state regularly, psychosis could easily take root and rewire your circuits. It was a wonder he hadn't lost it already.

"V?" Wrath said.

"Sorry? What?"

"You okay?"

Vishous bit into his roast beef and chewed. "Yeah, fine. Just fine."

When night fell some twelve hours later, Van Dean stopped his truck underneath a maple tree on a nice, tidy little street.

He did not like this situation.

The house on the other side of the shallow lawn wasn't trouble on the surface, just another whatever Colonial in this whatever neighborhood. The problem was the number of cars parked in the driveway. Four of them.

He'd been told he was meeting Xavier one-on-one.

Van cased the place from inside his truck. Shades were all down. Only two lights on inside. Porch light was off.

But there was a lot on the line. Saying yes to this gig meant he could kick the construction shit to the curb, reducing the wear and tear on his body. And he could make more than he did now by double so he could save something to survive on when he couldn't fight anymore.

He got out and walked up to the front stoop. The ivy-themed welcome mat that he planted his boots on was just too frickin' creepy.

The door swung open before he hit the bell. Xavier was on the other side, all big and bleached-out looking. "You're late."

"And you said we'd be meeting alone."

"Worried you can't handle company?"

"Depends on what kind it is."

Xavier stepped to the right. "Why don't you get in here and find out?"

Van stayed on the mat. "Just so you know, I told my brother I was coming here. Address and everything."

"Which brother, the older or the younger?" Xavier smiled as Van narrowed his eyes. "Yes, we know about them. As you say, their addresses and everything."

Van put his hand into the pocket of his parka. The nine-millimeter he was packing slid into his palm like the thing was finding home.

Money, think about the money.

After a moment, he said, "We going to get down to it or keep yakking it up in this draft?"

"I'm not the one on the wrong side of the door, son."

Van came in, keeping an eye on Xavier. Inside, the place was cold, like the heat was down low or maybe the house was abandoned. The lack of furniture suggested the latter.

When Xavier reached into his back pocket, Van tensed up. And what came forward was a weapon of sorts: ten perfectly crisp hundred-dollar bills.

"So do we have a deal?" Xavier asked.

Van looked around. Then took the money and stashed it. "Yeah."

"Good. You start tonight." Xavier turned and walked to the back of the house.

Van followed, staying on high alert. Especially as they went down into **the** basement and he saw six more of Xavier standing around at the bottom of the stairs.

The men were all tall, pale-haired, and smelling like old lady.

"Looks like you've got a few brothers of your own," Van said casually.

"They're not brothers. And don't use that word around here." Xavier glanced over at the hardasses. "These will be your trainees."

Moving under his own steam, but watched by a nurse in full hazmat dress, Butch got back into bed after having had his first shower and shave. The catheter and the IV were out and he'd managed to suck back a good meal. He'd also slept soundly for eleven out of the past twelve hours.

Man . . . he was beginning to feel human again, and the speed with which he was rebounding was a gift from God as far as he could tell.

"You did well, sire," the nurse said.

"Next stop, the Olympics." He pulled the sheets up himself.

After the nurse left, he glanced at Marissa. She was sitting on the cot that he'd insisted be brought in for her and her head was bent over the needlepoint she was doing. Ever since he'd woken up about an hour ago she'd been acting a little strange, as if she was on the verge of saying something that she couldn't quite manage to let out.

His eyes went from the bright crown of her head, to her delicate hands, to the peach gown that overflowed her makeshift bed . . . and then he eased his stare back up to the bodice of the dress. There were dainty buttons going all the way down the front. Like a hundred of them.

Butch shifted his legs around, feeling restless. And found himself wondering how long it would take him to slip each of those pearls loose.

His body stirred, the blood pooling between his legs, making him swell up hard.

Well, what do you know. He *really* was better.

And man, he was a sonofabitch.

He rolled away from her and closed his eyes.

Trouble was, with his lids down, all he saw was him kissing her on Darius's second-story porch last summer. Oh, shit, he remembered it clear as a photograph. He'd been sitting down and she'd been between his legs and his tongue had been in her mouth. They'd ended up on the floor when he broke the chair—

"Butch?"

He opened his eyes and jerked back. Marissa was right in front of him, her face on his level. In a panic, he glanced down to make sure the sheets hid what was doing between his thighs.

"Yeah?" he said with so much gravel he had to repeat himself. Christ, his voice box always had rough edges, his words perpetually a little hoarse, but if there was one sure thing that made that worse it was thinking about getting naked. Especially with her.

As her eyes scanned his face, he feared that she saw everything, right down to the core of him. Where his obsession with her was the strongest.

"Marissa, I think I should go to sleep now. You know, rest and all that."

"Vishous said you came to see me. After Wrath was shot."

Butch squeezed his lids shut again. His first thought was that he was going to drag his sorry ass out of bed, find his roommate, and beat the guy. Goddamn, V—

"I wasn't told," she said. As he looked at her and frowned, she shook her head. "I didn't know you'd been by until Vishous told me last night. Who did you see when you came? What happened?"

117

She hadn't known? "I, ah, a *doggen* answered the door. After she went upstairs, she said you weren't receiving and you'd call. When you never did . . . I wasn't going to stalk you or something."

Well, okay . . . he'd stalked her a little. She'd just never known about it, thank God. Unless of course, V, that loose-lipped fool, had filled her in on that, too. *Bastard.*

"Butch, I got sick and I needed some time to regroup. But I wanted to see you. That's why I asked you to come calling when I ran into you back in December. When you said no, I thought . . . well, you'd lost interest."

She'd wanted to see him? Had she said that?

"Butch, I wanted to see you."

Yeah, she had. Twice.

Well, now . . . didn't that perk a guy up.

"Shit," he breathed, meeting her eyes. "Do you have any idea how many times I drove past your house?"

"You did?"

"Practically every night. I was pathetic." Hell, he still was.

"But you wanted me to leave this room. You were angry to see me here."

"I was pissed—er, angry because you weren't wearing a suit. And I assumed you'd gotten roped into being here." With a shaky hand, he reached out for a lock of her hair. God, it was so soft. "Vishous can be very persuasive. And I didn't want your compassion or your pity to put you someplace you didn't want to be."

"I wanted to be here. I *want* to be here." She grabbed his hand and squeezed.

In the *oh-my-God-this-has-to-be-Christmas* silence that followed, he struggled to recorder the last six months, to catch up with this reality they'd somehow missed. He wanted her. She wanted him. Was it true?

Felt true. Felt good. Felt . . .

He let incautious, desperate words fly. "I am pathetic over you, Marissa. Yeah, totally fuc—er . . . really pathetic. Over you."

Her pale blue eyes teared up. "Me . . . too. For you."

Butch wasn't even aware of making the big move. But one moment they were separated by air. The next, he was putting his mouth on hers. When she gasped, he pulled back.

"Sorry—"

"No—I—I was just surprised," she said, eyes on his lips. "I want you to . . ."

"Okay." He tilted his head to the side and brushed her mouth. "Come closer to me."

With a tug on her arm, he eased her onto the bed, then pulled her over so she was lying on top of him. The weight of her was little more than warm air and he loved it, especially as he was surrounded by her blond hair. Putting both hands to her face, he stared up at her.

As her lips parted in a gentle smile just for him, he saw the tips of her fangs. Oh, God, he had to get into her, had to penetrate her in some way, so he leaned up and led with his tongue. She moaned while he licked into her mouth and then they were kissing deep, his hands threading into her hair and cradling the back of her head. He spread his legs and her body eased between them, increasing the pressure where he was hard and thick and hot.

From out of nowhere, a question shot into his mind, one he had no right to ask, one that tripped him up and had him losing his rhythm. He pulled back from her.

"Butch, what is it?"

He stroked her mouth with his thumb, wondering if she'd had a man. In the nine months since he'd kissed her before, had she taken a lover? Maybe had more than one?

"Butch?"

"Nothing," he said, even as a fierce possessive streak clawed into his chest.

He took her mouth again, and now he kissed her with an ownership he had no right to, one hand shooting down to the small of her back, pressing her into his arousal. He felt this urgent need to stake a claim on her so that anything male would know whose woman she was. Which was nuts.

Abruptly she jerked back. As she sniffed the air, she seemed confused. "Do human males bond?"

"Ah . . . we get emotional, sure."

"No . . . bond." She buried her face in his neck, inhaled, then started to rub her nose against his skin.

He gripped her hips, wondering just how far things were going to go. He wasn't sure he had the strength for sex, even though he was totally erect. And he didn't want to presume anything. But Jesus God in heaven he wanted it from her.

"I love the way you smell, Butch."

"It's probably the soap I just used." As her fangs dragged up his neck, he groaned, "Oh, shit . . . don't . . . stop . . ."

ELEVEN

Vishous came into the clinic and headed straight back to the quarantine room. No one at the nursing station questioned his right to barge on through, and as he went down the hall, the medical staff tripped over their own feet to get out of his way.

Smart. He was heavily armed and edgy as hell.

The day had been a wasteland. He hadn't found anything in the Chronicles that approached what had been done to Butch. Nothing in the Oral Histories either. And worse, he was sensing things in the future, parts of people's destinies realigning, but he could see nothing of what his instincts told him was happening. It was like watching theater with the curtain down: Every once in a while he would see the velvet drape move as a body brushed the far side or he would hear indistinct voices or the lighting would shift under the tasseled hem. But he knew no particulars, his gray cells shooting blanks.

He strode past Havers's lab and went into the house-keeping closet. As he stepped through the concealed door, he found the anteroom empty, the computers and the monitors carrying on their sentry duties alone.

V stopped dead.

On the glowing screen closest to him, he saw Marissa lying on the bed on top of Butch. The cop's arms were around her, his bare knees split wide to accommodate her body as the two of them moved against each other in waves. V couldn't see their faces, but it was obvious their mouths were fused and their tongues wrapped.

V rubbed his jaw, dimly aware that under his weapons and his leathers, his skin had grown hot. God . . . damn . . . Butch's palm was slowly sliding up Marissa's spine now, going under her profusion of blond hair, finding, caressing the back of her neck.

The guy was totally sexed up, but he was so gentle with her. So tender.

V thought of the sex he'd had the night Butch had been taken. Nothing gentle about that. Which had been the point for both parties involved.

Butch shifted and rolled Marissa over, making a move to mount her. As he did, the hospital johnny broke open, the ties ripping free and revealing his strong back and powerful lower body. The tattoo at the base of his spine flexed as he pushed his hips through her skirts, trying to find home. And as he worked what was no doubt a rock-hard erection against her, her long, elegant hands snaked around and bit into his bare ass.

As she scored him with her nails, Butch's head lifted, no doubt to let out a moan.

Jesus, V could just hear the sound . . . Yeah . . . he could hear it. And from out of nowhere an odd yearning feeling flickered through him. *Shit.* What exactly in this scenario did he want?

Butch's head dropped back down into Marissa's neck, and his hips started to surge and retract, then surge again. His spine undulated and his heavy shoulders shrugged and released as he found a rhythm that made V blink really quick. And then not at all.

Marissa arched up, her chin lifting, her mouth opening. Christ, what a picture she was under her male, her hair strewn all over the pillows, some of it tangled around Butch's thick bicep. In her passion, in her vibrant peach gown, she was a sunrise, a dawn, a promise of warmth, and Butch was basking in what he was lucky enough to touch.

The anteroom's door opened and V wheeled around, blocking the monitor with his body.

Havers put Butch's medical chart down on a shelf and reached for a hazmat suit. "Good evening, sire. You've come to heal him again, have you?"

"Yeah . . ." V's voice cracked and he cleared his throat. "But now's not a good time."

Havers paused, suit in hand. "Is he resting?"

Not in the slightest. "Yeah. So you and I are going to leave him alone right now."

The doctor's brows shot up behind his horn-rimmed glasses. "I beg your pardon?"

V picked up the chart, shoved it at the doctor, then grabbed the suit and hung it back up. "Later, doc."

"I—I need to do an examination. I think he may be ready to go home—"

"Great. But we're leaving."

Havers opened his mouth to argue and V got bored with the conversation. Clamping a hand on the doctor's shoulders, he looked into the male's eyes and willed him into agreement.

"Yes . . ." Havers murmured. "Later. T-tomorrow?"

"Yeah, tomorrow works."

As V frog-marched Marissa's brother back out into the hall, all he could think about were the images on that screen. So wrong of him to watch.

So wrong of him to . . . want.

Marissa was on fire.

Butch . . . good Lord, Butch. He was heavy on top of her

123

and big, so big her legs were stretched wide beneath her gown to accommodate him. And the way he moved . . . the rhythm of his hips was making her crazy.

When he finally broke the kiss, he was breathing hard and his hazel eyes were full of sexual hunger, a rank male starvation. Maybe she should have been overwhelmed because she had no idea what she was doing. Instead, she felt powerful.

As silence stretched, she said, "Butch?" Though she wasn't exactly sure what she was asking for.

"Oh . . . God, baby." With a light brush, his hand went down her neck to her collarbone. He paused as he got to the top of her dress, clearly asking for permission to take off her gown.

Which cooled her down fast. Her breasts seemed average enough, but it wasn't as if she'd seen any other female's to compare. And she couldn't bear to catch the sort of disgust males of her kind had looked at her with. Not on Butch's face, and especially not if she were naked. That distaste had been hard enough to bear fully clothed and coming from males she didn't care about.

"It's okay," Butch said, removing his hand. "I don't want to push you."

He kissed her lightly and rolled off her, dragging a sheet over his hips as he eased onto his back. He covered his eyes with his forearm, his chest going up and down like he'd been running.

Marissa looked down at her bodice and realized she was clutching the fabric so hard her knuckles were white. "Butch?"

His arm dropped and his head turned on the pillow. His face was still swollen in places, one of his eyes still black and blue. And she noticed that his nose had been broken, but not recently. Yet to her he was beautiful.

"What, baby?"

"Have you . . . have you had many lovers?"

He frowned. Inhaled. Looked like he didn't want to reply. "Yeah. Yeah, I have."

Marissa's lungs turned to concrete as she imagined him kissing other females, unclothing them, mating. She was willing to bet the vast majority of his lovers hadn't been clueless virgins.

God, she was going to throw up.

"Which is another reason it's good that we stop," he said.

"How so?"

"I'm not saying it would have gone this far, but I would need a condom."

Well, at least she knew what one of those was. "But why? I'm not fertile."

The long pause didn't inspire confidence. And neither did the way he cursed under his breath. "I haven't always been careful."

"With what?"

"Sex. I've had . . . a lot of sex with people who might not have been clean. And I did it without protection." He flushed as if ashamed of himself, the color riding up his neck and slamming into his face. "So yeah, I'd need a condom with you. I don't have any idea what I'm carrying."

"Why weren't you more careful with yourself?"

"Just didn't give a sh—er, yeah . . ." He reached out and took a piece of her hair. As he carried it to his lips and kissed it, he said under his breath, "Now I wish I were a goddamned virgin."

"I can't catch human viruses."

"I wasn't just with humans, Marissa."

Now she went completely cold. For some reason, if it was with females of his own species, with women, that struck her as different. But another vampire?

"Who?" she asked tightly.

"Somehow I don't think you'd know her." He dropped the strand of hair and put his arm back over his eyes. "God, I wish I could undo that. Undo a lot of things."

Oh . . . Jesus. "It happened recently, didn't it."

"Yeah."

"Do you . . . love her?"

He frowned and looked over at her. "God, no. I didn't even known her—oh, shit, that sounds worse, doesn't it."

"Did you take her into your bed? Did you sleep beside her afterward?" *Why in the hell was she asking these questions?* It was like poking at a cut with a steak knife.

"No, it was in a club." Shock must have shown on her face, because he cursed again. "Marissa, my life isn't pretty. The way you've known me, being with the Brotherhood, dressed in fancy clothes . . . that's not the way I lived before. And that's really not who I am now."

"Who are you, then?"

"No one you'd ever know. Even if I were a vampire, our paths would never cross. I'm a blue-collar kind of guy." At her look of confusion, he said, "Lower-class."

His tone was factual, as if he were reciting his height or weight.

"I don't think of you as lower-class, Butch."

"Like I said, you don't really know me."

"When I lie this close to you, when I smell your scent, when I hear your voice, I know everything that matters." She looked down the length of him. "You are the male I want to mate with. That's who you are."

A dark, spicy scent came out of his skin in a rush, the kind of thing that were he a vampire she would have said was his bonding mark. As she drew it in through her nose, she took strength in the response.

With fingers that shook, she went to the first of the little buttons on her bodice.

He captured both her hands in one of his. "Don't force yourself, Marissa. There are things I want from you, but I'm in no hurry."

"But I want to. I want to be with you." She pushed him away and started working at the buttons, except she didn't get far because she was trembling so badly. "I think you're going to have to do it."

His breath went in on an erotic hiss. "You sure?"

"Yes." When he hesitated, she nodded at the bodice. "Please. Get this off me."

In slow succession, he freed each of the pearl buttons, his battered fingers sure, the dress opening little by little as he went. Without her corset on, her naked skin was revealed in the shallow V that formed.

As he got to the last one, her whole body started to quake.

"Marissa, you're not okay with this."

"It's just . . . No male has ever seen me before."

Butch went motionless. "You are still . . ."

"Untouched," she said, hating the word.

Now his body trembled and that dark scent flowed from him even more strongly. "It wouldn't have mattered if you weren't. I need you to know that."

She smiled a little. "I do. Now will you . . ." As his hands came up, she whispered, "Just be kind, all right?"

Butch frowned. "I'm going to love what I see because it's you." When she didn't meet his eyes, he leaned forward. "Marissa, you're beautiful to me."

Impatient with herself, she gripped the bodice and bared her breasts. Closing her eyes, she found she couldn't breathe.

"Marissa. You're beautiful."

She lifted her lids, bracing herself. Except he wasn't staring at what she'd revealed.

"But you haven't looked at me yet, have you?"

"I don't need to."

Tears speared into the corners of her eyes. "Please . . . just look."

His eyes drifted downward and he inhaled sharply through his teeth, the hiss cutting through the room. Ah, hell, she knew there was something wrong—

"Jesus, you're perfect." With a quick pass, his tongue licked over his lower lip. "May I touch you?"

Overwhelmed, she nodded with a jerk of the chin and his hand slipped under the bodice, smoothed up her rib cage and caressed the side of her breast, soft as a breath. She surged at the contact and then settled down. At least until he brushed her nipple with his thumb.

Then she arched involuntarily.

"You're . . . very perfect," he said in his hoarse voice. "You blind me."

Butch's head went down, his lips finding the skin at her sternum, then kissing the way up her breast. Her nipple gathered up on itself, straining for . . . yes, his mouth. *Oh . . . God, yes . . . his mouth.*

His eyes stared into hers as he latched on to the tip of her breast, pulling her between his lips. He sucked on her for a heartbeat before releasing and blowing across the glistening tip. Between her legs, she felt a warm rush.

"You okay?" he said. "This okay?"

"I didn't know . . . they could feel like that."

"No?" He brushed his lips over her nipple again. "Surely you've touched this beautiful place? No? Not ever?"

She couldn't think straight. "Females in my class . . . we're taught that we shouldn't . . . do such things. Unless we are with a mate and even then . . ." God, what were they talking about?

"Ah . . . well, I'm here now, aren't I?" His tongue came out and licked over her nipple. "Yeah, I'm here now.

So give me your hand, Marissa." When she did, he kissed her palm. "Let me show you what perfection feels like."

He took her forefinger into his mouth and sucked on it, then popped it free and brought it to her distended nipple. He ran circles around the tip, touching her through her own hand.

She let her head fall back, but kept her eyes on his. "It's so . . ."

"Soft and tight at the same time, isn't it." He lowered his mouth, covering her nipple and her fingertip, a smooth, licking warmth. "Feels good?"

"Yes . . . dear Virgin in the Fade, *yes*."

His hand went to her other breast and rolled her nipple, then he massaged the swell beneath. He was so big looming over her, the hospital gown slipping from his bunched-up shoulders, his heavy arms clenched from holding himself above her body. As he switched sides and went to work on her other nipple, his dark hair brushed against her pale skin, soft and silky.

Lost in the heat and a growing restlessness, she didn't notice as her skirts started moving . . . until they were up around her thighs.

As she stiffened, he asked against her breast, "Will you let me keep going a little farther? If I swear I'll stop anytime you want?"

"Um . . . yes."

His palm slid onto her bare knee, and she jerked, but when he went back to work on her breast, she forgot the fear. With slow, lazy circles, his hand went higher and higher until it slipped between her thighs—

Abruptly, she felt something spill out of her. In a panic, she clamped her legs together and pushed at him.

"What, baby?"

Blushing fiercely, she muttered, "I feel something . . . different . . ."

"Where? Down here?" He stroked her inner thigh.

As she nodded, his smile was slow, sexy. "Oh, really?" He kissed her, lingering with their mouths together. "Want to tell me what it is?" As she flushed even more, his hand kept up the caressing. "What kind of different?"

"I'm . . ." She couldn't say it.

His mouth shifted so it was next to her ear. "Are you wet?" When she nodded, he growled deep in his throat. "Wet is good . . . wet's right where I want you to be."

"It is? Why—"

With a smooth, quick move, he touched her panties between her legs, and they both jumped at the contact.

"Oh . . . God," he groaned, his head dropping on her shoulder. "You're so with me right now. You're *so* right here with me."

Butch's erection pounded as he kept his hand on the warm, damp satin over Marissa's core. He knew if he pushed the panties aside, he was going to dive into a whole lot of honey, but he didn't want to shock her out of the moment.

Curling his fingers around her, he rubbed the heel of his palm against the top of her slit, right where it would feel best. As she gasped, her hips pushed forward, then followed his slow rhythm. Which naturally put him through the roof. To maintain control, he rolled his hips so his stomach was sitting on that arousal of his, trapping it against the mattress.

"Butch, I need . . . something . . . I . . ."

"Baby, have you ever—" Ah, hell, no way she'd ever pleasured herself. She'd been surprised at what her nipple felt like.

"What?"

"Never mind." He eased off her core and stroked her panties, just running his fingertips over her. "I'm going to take care of you. Trust me, Marissa."

He kissed her mouth, sucking at her lips, getting her lost. Then he slipped his hand under the lip of satin at her core—

"Oh . . . *fuck*," he breathed, hoping she was too dazed to hear the curse.

She tried to pull back. "What's wrong with me?"

"Easy, easy." He held her in place by putting his thigh over her legs. And then worried that he might have orgasmed . . . given the rocket launch sensation that had just ridden up his shaft. "Baby, there's nothing wrong. It's just you're . . . oh, God, you're bare here." He moved his hand, his fingers sliding into her folds . . . holy heaven, she was so smooth. So honeyed. So hot.

He was getting lost in all that slick flesh when her confusion registered through the haze. "You have no hair," he said.

"Is that bad?"

He laughed. "It's beautiful. It's exciting to me."

Exciting? Try explosive. All he wanted to do was crawl up under her skirt and lick at her and swallow and suck her off, but all that was definitely too far.

And shit, he was such a Neanderthal, but the idea he was the only one who'd put his hand where it was was erotic as hell.

"How's this feel?" he asked, tuning things up a little.

"God . . . *Butch*." She arched wildly on the bed, her head kicking back so that her neck bent in a lovely upward curve.

His eyes latched on to her throat, and the strangest instinct went through him: He wanted to bite her. And his mouth opened like he was prepared to do just that.

Cursing, he shrugged off the bizarre impulse.

"Butch . . . I *ache*."

"I know, baby. I'm going to take care of that." He latched on to her breast with his mouth and started to touch her seriously, finding a rhythm with the stroking, being careful to stay on the outside so she didn't get thrown.

Turned out he was the one who got tossed. The friction and the feel of her and the scent of it all snowballed on him until he realized he was shadow-pumping her, pushing his hips into the mattress in tempo with his hand. As his head fell between her breasts because he couldn't hold it up anymore, he knew he had to stop the cock massage he was giving himself. He needed to pay attention to her.

He looked up. Her eyes were wide and a little frightened. She was just on the verge and she was getting rattled.

"All right, baby, it's okay." He didn't stop working between her legs.

"What's happening to me?"

He put his mouth to her ear. "You're about to come. Just let yourself feel it. I'm right here, I've got you. Hold on to me."

Her hands bit into his arms and as her nails drew blood, he smiled, thinking that was so perfect.

Her hips tilted up sharply. "*Butch . . .*"

"That's it. Come for me."

"I can't . . . I can't . . ." She shook her head back and forth, getting trapped between what her body wanted and what her mind was having trouble assimilating. She was going to lose the momentum unless he did something fast.

Without even thinking or knowing why it would help, he buried his face in her throat and bit her, right over her jugular. That was what did it. She cried out his name and started convulsing, her hips jerking, her body flexing all along her spine. With profound joy, he helped her ride

132

the orgasm's pulses and he talked to her the whole time—although God only knew what he was saying.

When she'd come down, he lifted his head from her neck. Between her lips, he saw the tips of her fangs and was struck by a compulsion he couldn't fight. He pushed his tongue into her mouth and licked at the sharp points, feeling them rasp over his flesh. He wanted them in his skin . . . he wanted her to suck at him, fill her belly, live off of him.

He forced himself to stop and the retreat was so damn hollow. He strained from unmet needs and they weren't all sexual. He needed . . . things from her, things he didn't understand.

Her eyes opened. "I didn't know . . . it would be like that."

"Did you like it?"

Her smile was enough to make him forget his own name. "Oh, yes."

He kissed her gently, then rearranged her skirts and did up the buttons of her bodice, rewrapping the gift of her body. Easing her into the crook of his arm, he got good and comfortable. She was fading into sleep already and he was so damned content to watch her slide. It just seemed like the perfect thing to do, to stay awake while she rested, to watch over her.

Although for some reason, he wished he had a weapon.

"I can't keep my eyes open," she said.

"Don't even try."

He stroked some of her hair and thought, in spite of the fact that in about ten minutes he was going to have the worst case of blue balls known to mankind, that everything was right in his world.

Butch O'Neal, he thought, *you have found your woman.*

TWELVE

"He does so look like his grandfather."

Joyce O'Neal Rafferty leaned over the crib and tucked the blanket around her three-month-old son. This debate had been on going since his birth, and she was tired of it. Her son clearly took after her father.

"No, he looks like you."

As Joyce felt her husband's arms wrap around her middle, she fought the need to pull away. He didn't seem to mind the baby weight, but it made her anxious as hell.

Hoping to get him focused elsewhere, she said, "So next Sunday you have a choice. You can either handle Sean by yourself or you can pick up Mother. What do you want to do?"

He dropped his hold on her. "Why can't your father get her from the nursing home?"

"You know Dad. He doesn't deal with her all that well, especially in the car. She'll get agitated, he'll get frustrated with her, and we'll have a mess at the baptism when they get there."

Mike's chest rose and fell. "I think you better deal with your mother. Sean and I will be fine. Maybe one of your sisters can come with us?"

"Yeah. Colleen, maybe."

They were silent a while, just watching Sean breathe. Then Mike said, "Are you going to invite him?"

She wanted to curse. In the O'Neal family, there was only one "him." Brian. Butch. The "him." Of the six children Eddie and Odell O'Neal had had, two of them had been lost. Janie had been murdered, and Butch had basically disappeared after high school. The latter had been a blessing, the first a curse.

"He won't come."

"You should invite him anyway."

"If he shows up, Mother will become unglued."

Odell's rapidly escalating dementia meant she sometimes thought Butch was dead and that was why he wasn't around. Her other option for dealing with the loss was making up crazy stories about him. Like how he was running for mayor down in New York. Or how he was going to medical school. Or how he wasn't his father's son and that was why Eddie couldn't stand him. All of which were nuts. The first two for obvious reasons and the third because while it was true Eddie had never liked Butch, it wasn't because he was a bastard child. Eddie had never particularly liked any of his children.

"You should invite him anyway, Joyce. This is his family."

"Not really."

Last time she'd talked to her brother had been . . . God, at her wedding five years ago? And no one else had seen or heard much from him since then, either. Word in the family had it that her father had gotten a message from Butch back in . . . August? Yeah, end of summer. He'd given a number he could be reached at, but that was about it.

Sean let out a little whiffle through his nose.

"Joyce?"

"Oh, come on, he won't show if I ask him."

"So you get the credit for putting the offer out and won't have to deal with him. Or maybe he'll surprise you."

"Mike, I'm not calling him. Who needs more drama in this family?" Like her mother being crazy *and* having Alzheimer's wasn't enough of a problem?

She made a show of checking her watch. "Hey, is *CSI* on?"

With determination, she pulled her husband out of the nursery, distracting him from things that were none of his business.

Marissa wasn't sure what time it was when she woke up, but she knew she'd been asleep for a long while. As her eyes opened, she smiled. Butch was out cold and crowding her at her back, his thick thigh between her legs, his hand cupping her breast, his head in her neck.

As she rolled over slowly and faced him, her eyes drifted down his body. The sheet he'd pulled up earlier had slid off him, and underneath the thin hospital gown, something thick rested at his hips. Good Lord . . . an erection. He was aroused.

"What you looking at, baby?" Butch's low voice was mostly gravel.

She jumped and glanced up. "I didn't know you were awake."

"I never went to sleep. Been watching you for hours." He pulled the sheet back into place and smiled. "How you doing?"

"Good."

"You want we call for some break—"

"Butch." Exactly how was she going to put this? "Males do what you made me do, right? I mean, last night when you were touching me."

He flushed and tugged at the sheet. "Yeah, we do. But you don't need to worry about that."

"Why?"

"Just don't have to."

"Would you let me look at you?" She nodded at his hips. "Down there?"

He coughed a little. "You want that?"

"Yes. God, yes . . . I want to touch you there."

With a soft curse, he muttered, "What happens might shock you."

"I was shocked when your hand was between my legs. Is it shocking like that? In that good kind of way?"

"Yeah." His hips shifted, as if they'd rotated on the base of his spine. "Jesus . . . Marissa."

"I want you naked." She sat up on her knees and reached for his johnny. "And I want to strip you."

He took her hands in a hard grip. "I, ah . . . Marissa, do you have any idea what happens when a man comes? Because sure as shit, that's going to happen if you start handling me. And it's not going to take long."

"I want to find out. With you."

He closed his eyes. Took a deep breath. "Dear Lord in heaven."

Lifting his upper body off the bed, he leaned forward so she could slip the two halves of the gown down his arms. Then he let himself fall back on the mattress and his body was revealed: the thick neck plugged into those broad shoulders . . . the heavy pads of his pectorals that were dusted with hair . . . the ribbed expanse of his belly . . . and . . .

She pulled back the sheet. Good God, his sex was . . . "It's gotten so . . . huge."

Butch barked out a laugh. "You say the nicest things."

"I saw it when it was . . . I didn't know it got . . . "

She just couldn't take her eyes off his erection as it lay against his belly. His hard sex was the color of his lips and shockingly beautiful, the head blunt with a graceful ridge, the shaft perfectly round and very thick at the base. And the twin weights below were heavy, shameless, virile.

Maybe humans were larger than her kind?

"How do you like to be touched?"

"If it's you, any way."

"No, show me."

He squeezed his eyes shut for a moment, and his chest expanded. When he lifted his lids, his mouth parted and he slowly eased his hand down his pecs and his belly. Moving one of his legs out to the side, he captured himself in his palm, fisting that dark pink flesh of his, his man hand broad enough to hold the thing. With a slow, smooth movement, he stroked his arousal, base to tip, riding the shaft.

"Or something like this," he said hoarsely, keeping it up. "Good God, look at you . . . I could come right now."

"No." She pushed his arm out of the way and the erection bounced stiffly on his stomach. "I want to make you do that."

As she took hold of him, he groaned, his whole body undulating.

He was hot. He was hard. He was soft. He was so thick she couldn't close her palm all the way around him.

Hesitant at first, she followed his example, running her grip up and down, marveling at how his satin skin slid over the stone core of him.

When he gritted his teeth, she stopped. "Is this all right?"

"Yeah . . . damn . . ." His chin tilted back, the veins in his neck popping. "More."

She put her other hand on him, stacking her palms, moving them together. His mouth fell wide open, his eyes rolling back in his head, a sheen of sweat breaking out over his body.

"How does this feel, Butch?"

"I'm so close already." He clamped his jaws together and breathed through teeth that were locked light.

But then he grabbed her hands, stilling them. "Wait! Not yet . . ."

His erection pulsed, kicking in their grips. A crystal drop appeared at the tip.

He took in a ragged breath. "Hold me out. Make me work for it, Marissa. The longer you burn me, the better the end will be."

Using his gasps and the spasms of his muscles as a guide, she learned the peaks and valleys of his erotic response, figured out when he was getting close and just how to suspend him at the tip of the sexual blade.

God, there was power in sex, and right now she had it all. He was defenseless, exposed . . . just as she'd been the night before. *She loved this.*

"Please . . . baby . . ." She loved that hoarse breathlessness. Loved the straining cords in his neck. Loved the command she had as she held him in her hand.

Which made her think. She let go and attended to his sack, sliding her hand under the weight of it, cupping him. With a curse, he knotted the sheets up in fists until his knuckles went white.

She kept going at him until he was twitchy and covered with sweat and shaking. Then she bent down and pressed her mouth to his. He gobbled her up, grabbing her neck and holding her against his lips, mumbling, kissing, thrusting with his tongue.

"Now?" she said in the midst of the kiss.

"Now."

Taking him in hand, she moved her palm faster and faster, until his face contorted into a beautiful mask of agony and his body grew tight as a cable.

"Marissa . . ." With no coordination, he grabbed the hospital gown and pulled it over his hips, shielding him from her eyes. Then she felt him jerk and shudder and

something warm and thick came out of him in pulses, covering her hand. She knew instinctively not to lose her rhythm until it was over.

When his eyes finally opened, they were fuzzy. Satiated. Full of a worshiping warmth.

"I don't want to let go of you," she said.

"Then don't. Ever."

He was softening in her palm, a retreat from the hard staff he'd been. Kissing him, she took her hand out from under the hospital johnny and looked down, curious as to what had come out of him.

"I didn't know it would be black," she murmured with a little smile.

Horror flooded his face. *"Oh, Christ!"*

Havers walked down the hallway to the quarantine room.

On the way, he checked on the little female he'd operated on days before. She was healing well, but he worried about sending her and her mother back out into the world. That *hellren* was violent and there was a good chance they would be back in the clinic again. But what could he do? He couldn't let them stay here indefinitely. He needed the bed.

He kept going, passing his laboratory, waving at a nurse who was processing various samples. When he got to the HOUSEKEEPING door, he hesitated.

He hated that Marissa was locked up with that human.

But the important thing was she hadn't been contaminated. According to the physical they'd done on her early yesterday, she was just fine, so her lapse in judgment evidently wasn't going to cost her her life.

And as for the human, he was going home. His last blood sample had been very close to normal and he was getting stronger at an astonishing rate, so it was time to

140

get him the hell away from Marissa. Havers had already called the Brotherhood and told them to come get the man.

Butch O'Neal was dangerous, and not just because of the contamination issue. That human wanted Marissa—it was in his eyes. And that was unacceptable.

Havers shook his head, thinking that he'd tried to keep them apart back in the fall. At first, he'd assumed Marissa was going to drain the human and that would have been fine. But when it became obvious that she was pining for him in her illness, Havers had had to step in.

God, he'd hoped she'd find a true mate at some point, but certainly not an inferior, roughneck human. She needed someone worthy, though it was unlikely that would happen anytime soon, given the *glymera*'s opinion of her.

But maybe . . . well, he was aware of how Rehvenge watched her. Maybe that would work. Rehv was from very good bloodlines on both sides. He was a little . . . hard, perhaps, but he was appropriate in the eyes of society.

Perhaps that pairing should be encouraged? After all, she was untouched, as clean as the day she was birthed. And Rehvenge had money, lots of it, though no one knew how or why. Even more important, he was unswayed by the *glymera*'s opinions.

Yes, Havers thought. That would be a good pairing. The best she could hope for.

He pushed open the closet door, feeling a little better. That human was on the way out of the clinic, and no one had to know the two of them had been locked in together for days. His staff was blessedly discreet.

God, he could only imagine what the *glymera* would do to her if they knew she'd been in close contact with a human male. Marissa's tattered reputation just couldn't withstand any more controversy, and frankly, Havers couldn't take it either. He was utterly exhausted by her social failures.

He loved her, but he was at the end of his rope.

Marissa had no idea why Butch was dragging her into the bathroom at a dead run.

"Butch! What are you doing?"

He cranked on the sink, forced her hands under the water, and grabbed for a bar of soap. As he washed her off, the panic in his face stretched his eyes and flattened his mouth.

"What the hell is going on here!"

Marissa and Butch both wheeled around to the doorway. Havers was standing in it without benefit of a hazmat suit—more furious than she'd ever seen him.

"Havers—"

Her brother cut her off by lunging forward and yanking her out of the bathroom.

"Stop it—ouch! Havers, that hurts!"

What happened next was too fast for her to track.

Havers was suddenly just . . . gone. One minute he was pulling at her and she was fighting against him, and the next Butch had him flattened facefirst against the wall.

Butch's voice was a nasty drawl. "I don't care if you're her brother. You don't handle her like that. *Ever.*" He pushed his forearm into the back of Havers's neck to emphasize the point.

"Butch, let him—"

"We clear?" Butch growled over her words. When her brother gasped and nodded, Butch released him, walked over to the bed, and calmly wrapped a sheet around his hips. As if he hadn't just manhandled a vampire.

Meanwhile, Havers stumbled and caught himself on

the edge of the bed, his eyes crazed as he rearranged his glasses and glared at her. "I want you to leave this room. *Now*."

"No."

Havers's jaw went slack. "I beg your pardon?"

"I'm staying with Butch."

"You most certainly are not!"

In the Old Language, she said, "*If he would have me, I would stand at his side as his* shellan."

Havers looked as if she'd slapped him: shocked and disgusted. "*And I would forbid you. Have you no nobility?*"

Butch cut off her reply. "You really should go, Marissa."

She and Havers looked over at him. "Butch?" she said.

That harsh face she adored softened for a moment, but then grew grim. "If he'll let you out, you should go."

And not come back, his expression said.

She glanced at her brother, heart starting to pound. "Leave us." When Havers shook his head, she shouted, "*Get out of here!*"

There were times when female hysteria got everyone's attention, and this was one of them. Butch went quiet and Havers seemed nonplussed.

Then her brother's eyes shifted to Butch and narrowed into slits. "The Brotherhood are coming to pick you up, human. I called them and told them you are free to go." Havers tossed Butch's medical chart on the bed as if he were giving up on the whole situation. "Don't come back here again. Ever."

As her brother left, Marissa stared at Butch, but before she could get any words past her tight throat, he spoke.

"Baby, please understand. I'm not well. There's something still in me."

"I'm not afraid of you."

"I am."

She linked her arms around her stomach. "What's going to happen if I leave here now? Between you and me?"

Bad question to ask, she thought in the silence between them.

"Butch—"

"I need to find out what was done to me." He looked down and fingered the puckered black wound next to his belly button. "I need to know what's inside me. I want to be with you, but not like this. Not the way I am now."

"I've been with you for four days and I'm fine. Why stop—"

"Go, Marissa." His voice was haunted and sad. So were his eyes. "As soon as I can, I'll come find you."

The hell you will, she thought.

Dear Virgin in the Fade, this was Wrath all over again, wasn't it. Her waiting, always waiting, while some male with better things to do was out into the world.

She'd already put in three hundred years of baseless anticipation.

"I'm not going to do that," she murmured. With more force, she said, "I'm not waiting anymore. Not even for you. Almost half my life is over now and I've wasted it sitting at home hoping that a male would come for me. I can't do that anymore . . . no matter how much I . . . care about you."

"I care about you, too. That's why I'm telling you to leave. I'm protecting you."

"You're . . . 'protecting' me." She eyed him up and down, knowing damn well he'd been able to peel Havers off her only because Butch had had the element of surprise working for him and the male in question had been a civilian. If her brother were a fighter, Butch would have been leveled. "You're *protecting* me? Christ, I could lift you over my head with one arm, Butch. There's nothing you can do physically that I can't do better. So don't do me any favors."

It was, of course, the perfectly wrong thing to say.

Butch's eyes shifted away and he crossed his arms over his chest, his lips narrowing flat.

Oh, God. "Butch, I don't mean that you're weak—"

"I'm very glad you reminded me of something."

Oh, God. "Of what."

His tight smile was ghastly. "I'm on the lower end of things on two counts. Socially and evolutionarily." He nodded to the door. "So . . . yeah, you go on, now. And you're absolutely right. Don't wait for me."

She started to reach out to him, but his cold, empty eyes held her back. Damn it, she'd blown it.

No, she told herself. There hadn't been anything to blow. Not if he was going to shut her out of the ugly parts of his life. Not if he was going to take off and leave her and maybe come back at some indefinable, probably-never point in time.

Marissa went to the door and had to look back at him once more. The image of him with that sheet wrapped around his hips, his chest bare, bruises still healing all over him . . . was one she was going to wish she could forget.

She walked out, the air lock sealing him in with a hiss.

Holy shit, Butch thought as he sagged down onto the floor. So this was what getting skinned alive felt like.

Scrubbing his jaw, he sat there staring into space, lost though he knew exactly what room he was in, alone with the remnants of the evil in him.

"Butch, my man."

He jerked his head up. Vishous was standing just inside the room and the brother was dressed for fighting, a big-ass, leather-wearing, stabbing machine. The Valentino garment bag dangling from his gloved hand seemed totally out of place, just as whacked as a butler toting an AK-47.

"Fuuuuck, Havers has got to be nuts to release you. You look like crap."

"Bad day, s'all." And there were going to be a lot more of those, so he should get used to it.

"Where's Marissa?"

"She left."

"Left?"

"Don't make me say it again."

"Oh. Hell." Vishous took a deep breath and swung the bag onto the bed. "Well, got you some threads and a new cell phone—"

"It's still in me, V. I can feel it. I can . . . taste it."

V's diamond eyes did a quick up and down. Then he came over and held out his hand. "Rest of you is healing up good. Healing up quick."

Butch took his roommate's palm and got pulled to his feet. "Maybe if I'm free of here we can figure this out together. Unless you've found—"

"Nothing yet. But I haven't lost hope."

"That makes one of us."

Butch unzipped the bag, dropped the sheet, and dragged on some boxers. Then he punched his legs into a pair of black slacks and stuffed his arms into a silk shirt.

Putting on street clothes made him feel like a fraud because the truth was he was a patient, a freak, a nightmare. Jesus Christ . . . what had come out of him as he'd orgasmed? And Marissa . . . at least he'd washed her as soon as he could.

"Your levels look good," V said as he read the chart Havers had tossed. "Everything seems back to normal."

"I ejaculated about ten minutes ago and the stuff was black. So everything is *not* normal."

Silence greeted that happy little announcement. Man, if he had hauled off and sucker-punched V, he would have gotten less of a shocked-out reaction.

"Oh, Christ," Butch muttered, slipping his feet into his Gucci loafers and grabbing the black cashmere dress coat. "Let's just go."

As they went to the door, Butch glanced back at the bed. The sheets were still tangled from him and Marissa getting all over each other.

He cursed and walked out into a monitoring room, then V led the way through a little closet stocked with cleaning supplies. Outside, they went down a hall, past a lab, and came into the clinic proper, going by patient rooms. As he went, he looked inside each one until he stopped short.

Through the doorway he saw Marissa, sitting on the edge of a hospital bed, that peach gown all around her. She was holding the hand of a little girl and talking softly while an older female, probably the young's mother, looked on from the corner.

The mother was the one who glanced up. As she saw Butch and V, she retracted in on herself, bringing her pilled sweater closer to her body and dropping her eyes to the floor.

Butch swallowed hard and kept going.

They were at the bank of elevators, waiting for one, when he said, "V?"

"Yeah?"

"Even though it's nothing concrete, you have an idea of what was done to me, don't you?" He didn't look at his roommate. V didn't look at him.

"Maybe. But we're not alone here."

An electronic *ding* sounded and the doors opened. They rode up in silence.

When they'd walked out of the mansion and into the night, Butch said, "I bled black for a while, you know."

"They noted in your chart that the color came back."

Butch snagged V's arm and wheeled the male around. "Am I part *lesser* now?"

There. It was out on the table. His biggest fear, his reason for running from Marissa, the hell he was going to have to learn to live with.

V stared into his eyes. "No."

"How do we know?"

"Because I reject that conclusion."

Butch dropped his hold. "Dangerous to put your head in the sand, vampire. I could be your enemy now."

"Bull. Shit."

"Vishous, I could—"

V grabbed him by the lapels and yanked him up against his body. The brother was trembling from head to foot, his eyes glowing like crystals in the night. *"You are not my enemy."*

Instantly pissed off, Butch gripped V's powerful shoulders, bunching up the leather jacket in his fists. *"How do we know for sure."*

V bared his fangs and hissed, his black eyebrows cranking down hard. Butch gave the aggression right back, hoping, praying, ready for them to start clocking each other. He was jonesing to hit and get hit back; he wanted blood all over the both of them.

For long moments, they stayed locked together, muscles straining, sweat blooming, right on the edge.

Then Vishous's voice came out into the space between their faces, the cracked tone riding a panting, desperate breath and getting bucked off. "You are my only friend. Never my enemy."

No telling who embraced who first, but the urge to beat the living shit out of the other guy bled from their bodies, leaving only the bond between them. They wound up tight together and stood for a time in the cold wind. When they stepped back, it was awkwardly and with embarrassment.

After some throat clearing on both sides, V took out a hand-rolled and lit it. As he exhaled, he said. "You're not a *lesser*, cop. The heart is removed when that happens. Yours is still beating."

"Maybe it was a partial job? Something that was interrupted?"

"That I can't answer. I went through the race's records, looking for something, anything. Didn't find shit the first trip through, so I'm reading the Chronicles all over again. Hell, I'm even checking in the human world, looking for obscure shit on the Internet." V blew out another cloud of Turkish smoke. "I'll find out. Somehow, some way, I'll find out."

"Have you tried to see what's coming?"

"You mean the future?"

"Yeah."

"Of course I have." V dropped the hand-rolled, crushed it with his shitkicker, then bent down and picked up the butt. As he slipped the deadie into his back pocket, he said, "But I'm still getting nothing. Shit . . . I need a drink."

"Me, too. ZeroSum?"

"You sure you're up for that?"

"Not in the slightest."

"All right then, ZeroSum it is."

They walked over to the Escalade and got in, Butch riding shotgun. After putting on his seat belt, his hand went to his stomach. His abdomen was hurting like a bitch now because he'd been mobile, but the pain didn't matter. Matter of fact, nothing really seemed to.

They were just pulling out of Havers's drive when V said, "By the way, you got a telephone call on the general line. Late last night. Guy named Mikey Rafferty."

Butch frowned. Why would one of his brothers-in-law be calling, especially that one? Of all his sisters and brothers, Joyce disliked him the most—which was really saying something, considering how the others felt. Had his father finally had the heart attack that had been waiting in the wings all these years?

"What did he say?"

"Baptizing a kid. Wanted you to know so you could show if you were into it. It's this Sunday."

Butch looked out the window. Another baby. Well, Joyce's first, but it was grandchild number . . . how many? Seven? No . . . eight.

As they drove along in silence, heading toward the city's urban hub, the lights from oncoming cars flared and faded. Houses were passed. Then stores. Then turn-of-the-century office buildings. Butch thought of all the people living and breathing in Caldwell.

"You ever want kids, V?"

"Nope. Not interested."

"I used to."

"No more?"

"Not gonna happen for me, but it doesn't matter. Plenty of O'Neals in this world now. Plenty."

Fifteen minutes later, they were downtown and parked behind ZeroSum, but he found it hard to get out of the Escalade. The familiarity of it all—the car, his roommate, his watering hole—unsettled him. Because even though it was just the same, he had changed.

Frustrated, cagey, he reached forward and got a Red

Sox hat out of the glove compartment. As he put it on, he opened the door, telling himself he was being melodramatic and this was all business as usual.

The moment he stepped foot out of the SUV, he froze.

"Butch? What is it, my man?"

Well, wasn't that the million-dollar question. His body seemed to have turned into some kind of tuning fork. Energy was vibrating through him . . . drawing him . . .

He turned and started walking down Tenth Street, moving fast. He just had to find out what it was, this magnet, this homing signal.

"Butch? Where you going, cop?"

When V grabbed his arm, Butch snapped free and broke into a jog, feeling like he was on the end of a rope and something was pulling him.

He was dimly aware of V jogging next to him and talking as if he'd gotten on his cell phone. "Rhage? I got me a situation here. Tenth Street. No, it's Butch."

Butch began to run flat out, the cashmere coat flapping behind him. When Rhage's towering body materialized in his path from out of nowhere, he made a shift to get around the male.

Rhage jumped right in his way. "Butch, where you going?"

When the brother grabbed at him, Butch shoved Rhage back so hard the guy slammed against a brick building. "Don't touch me!"

Two hundred yards of hauling it later, he found what was calling him: Three *lessers* coming out of an alley.

Butch stopped. The slayers stopped. And there was a hideous moment of communion, one that brought tears to Butch's eyes as he recognized in them what was inside of him.

"Are you a new recruit?" one of them asked.

"'Course he is," another said. "And you missed check-in tonight, idiot."

No . . . no . . . oh, God, no . . .

In a synchronized movement, the three slayers looked over his shoulder at what had to be V and Rhage coming around the corner. The *lessers* prepared to strike, falling into combat stance, bringing up their hands.

Butch took a step toward the trio. Then another.

"Butch . . ." The aching voice behind him was Vishous. "God . . . *no.*"

THIRTEEN

John shuffled his little body around and closed his eyes again. Wedged into the seat of a beat-up, ugly-ass, avocado green armchair, he smelled Tohr with every inhale he took: The decorator's nightmare had been the Brother's favorite possession and Wellsie's *"seatus non grata."* Exiled here to his office at the training center, Tohr had spent hours doing admin work in it while John studied.

John had used the thing as a bed since the killings.

Aggravated, he twisted himself around so his legs were draped over one arm and his head and shoulders were shoved back into the top half of the chair. He squeezed his eyes closed even harder and prayed for some rest. Trouble was, his blood was buzzing through his veins and his head was spinning with a whole lot of nothing specific, everything urgent bullshit.

God, class had ended two hours ago and he'd worked out even after the other trainees had left. Plus he hadn't slept well for a week. You'd think he'd be out like a light.

Then again, maybe he was still worked up over Lash. That SOB had been all over him about passing out in front of the whole class yesterday. Man, John hated that kid. He really did. That arrogant, rich, snarky—

"Open your eyes, boy, I know you're awake."

John went into a full-body jerk and nearly landed on the floor. As he hauled himself back up, he saw Zsadist in the doorway to the office, dressed in that uniform of skintight turtle-neck and loose sweats.

The expression on the warrior's face was as hard as his body. "Listen up, because I'm not going to say this again."

John gripped the arms of the chair. He had a feeling what this was about.

"You don't want to go to Havers's, fine. But cut the shit. You're skipping meals, you look like you haven't slept for days, and your attitude is beginning to irritate the fuck out of me."

Yeah, this wasn't like any parent/teacher conference John had ever had. And he wasn't taking the criticism well: Frustration swirled in his chest.

Z jabbed his forefinger across the room. "You stop marking Lash, we clear? Leave the fucker alone. And from now on, you come up to the house for meals."

John frowned, then reached for his pad so he'd be sure Z would understand what he wanted to say.

"Forget about a response, boy. I'm not interested." As John started to get downright pissed, Z smiled, revealing monstrous fangs. "And you know better than to get up in my grill, don't you."

John looked away, certain the Brother could break him in half without any effort at all. And resentful as hell about that fact.

"You will quit it with Lash, you feel me? Do *not* make me get involved with the two of you. Neither of you will like it. Nod so I know you understand."

John nodded, feeling ashamed. Angry. Exhausted.

Choking on all the aggression inside of him, he blew out a breath and rubbed his eyes. God, he'd been so calm all his life, maybe even timid. Why was everything setting him off lately?

"You're getting close to the change. That's the why of it."

John slowly lifted his head. He'd heard that right, hadn't he?

Am I? he signed.

"Yeah. That's why it is imperative that you learn how to control yourself. If you make it through the transition, you're going to come out the other side with a body capable of things that will floor you. I'm talking about raw physical strength. The brute kind. The kind that can kill. You think you got problems now? Wait'll you have to deal with handling that load. You need to learn your control *now*."

Zsadist turned away, but then paused and looked over his shoulder. Light fell on the scar that ran down his face and distorted his upper lip. "One last thing. Do you need someone to talk to? About . . . shit?"

Yeah, right, John thought. Over his dead body he was going back to Havers to see that therapist.

Which was why he refused to go get checked out. Last time he'd tangled with the race's physician, the guy had blackmailed him into a therapy session he hadn't wanted, and he had no intention of repeating the Dr. Phil hour. With everything going on recently, he wasn't getting into his past again, so the only way he was going back to that clinic now was if he was bleeding out.

"John? You want to talk to someone?" When he shook his head, Z's eyes narrowed. "Fine. But you get the message about you and Lash, right?"

John looked down and nodded.

"Good. Now drag your ass up to the house. Fritz has made you dinner and I'm going to watch you eat it. And you *will* eat all of it. You need to be strong for the change."

Butch walked closer to the slayers and they weren't threatened by him at all. If anything, they were annoyed, like he wasn't doing his job.

"Behind you, dumb ass," the one in the middle said. "Your target's behind you. Two Brothers."

Butch circled around the *lessers*, reading their imprints instinctively. He sensed that the tallest one had been inducted within the last year or so: There was some trace of human still in him, although Butch wasn't sure how he knew this. The other two were far older in the Society and he was certain of this not just because their hair and skin had paled out.

He stopped when he was behind the three and stared through their big bodies at V and Rhage . . . who were looking like they'd watched a good friend die in their arms.

Butch knew exactly when the *lessers* were going to attack and he moved forward with them. Just as Rhage and V sank down into fighting stances, Butch grabbed the middle slayer around the neck and flipped him onto the ground.

The *lesser* hollered and Butch jumped on top of him, even though he knew he wasn't up to fighting. Sure enough, he was kicked off and the *lesser* took the driver's seat, sitting on him, choking him. The bastard was brutally strong and pissed off, nothing less than a sumo wrestler with rabies.

As Butch struggled to keep from getting his head ripped off his shoulders, he was dimly aware of a flash of light and a pop. And then another. Clearly, Rhage and V had cleaned house and Butch heard them pound it over. Thank God.

Except it was just as they arrived that the freak show started.

Butch looked deeply into the undead's eyes for the first time and something clicked into place, just locked the two of them up tight as if there were iron bars encircling their bodies. As the slayer went utterly still, Butch felt this overwhelming urge to . . . well, he didn't know what. But the instinct was strong enough to have him opening his lips to breathe.

And that was when the inhaling started. Before he knew what he was doing, his lungs began to fill in one long, steady draw.

"No . . ." the slayer whispered, trembling.

Something passed between their mouths, some cloud of blackness leaving the *lesser* and getting drawn into Butch—

The connection was broken with a brutal attack from above. Vishous grabbed the slayer and yanked the undead free, throwing the thing against a building headfirst. Before the bastard could recover, V fell upon it, black blade slicing down.

As the spark and sizzle faded, Butch's arms fell limp against the asphalt. Then he rolled over onto his side and curled in on himself, arms linking tight against his stomach. His gut was killing him, but more to the point, he felt nauseous as shit, a nasty echo of what he'd struggled with when he'd been at his sickest.

A pair of shitkickers came into his line of sight, but he couldn't bear to look up and see either one of the brothers. He didn't know what the hell he had done or what had happened. All he knew was that he and the *lessers* were kin.

V's voice was as thin as Butch's skin. "Are you okay?"

Butch squeezed his eyes shut and shook his head. "Think it's best . . . that you get me out of here. And don't you dare take me home."

Vishous unlocked his penthouse and muscled Butch inside while Rhage held the door open. The three of them had taken the cargo elevator up the back of the building, which made sense. The cop was a dead load, weighing more than he looked like he did, as if the pull of gravity had singled him out for special attention.

They laid the cop flat on the bed and he eased over onto his side, bringing his knees up until they hit his chest.

There was a long stretch of silence, during which Butch seemed to pass out.

Like he was walking off anxiety, Rhage started pacing around, and shit, after that showdown, V was all up in his head, too. He lit up and inhaled hard.

Hollywood cleared his throat. "So, V . . . this is where you go with the females, huh." The brother went over and fingered a pair of chains bolted into the black wall. "We heard stories, of course. Guess they're all true."

"Whatever." V headed to his bar and poured a long/tall of Grey Goose. "We've got to hit those *lessers'* houses tonight."

Rhage nodded toward the bed. "What about him?"

Miracle of miracles, the cop lifted his head. "I'm not going anywhere right now. Trust me."

V narrowed his eyes on his roommate. Butch's face, which normally got all Irish ruddy if he exerted himself, was utterly blushless. And he smelled . . . faintly sweet. Like baby powder.

Jesus Christ. It was like being around those slayers had brought out something else in him—something Omega in him.

"V?" Rhage's voice was soft. Real close. "You want to stay here? Or maybe take him back to Havers?"

"I'm fine," Butch croaked.

A lie on so many levels, V thought.

He polished off his vodka and looked at Rhage. "I'm coming with you. Cop, we'll be back and I'll bring food, true?"

"No. No food. And don't come back tonight. Just lock me in so I can't get out and leave me."

Fuck. "Cop, if you hang yourself in the bathroom, I swear I will kill you all over again, ya herd me?"

Dull hazels opened up. "I want to know what was done to me more than I want to off my ass. So don't worry."

Butch squeezed his lids shut again and after a moment, Vishous and Rhage walked out to the balcony. As V locked the doors, he realized he was more worried about keeping Butch inside than protecting the guy.

"Where we going?" he asked Rhage. Even though he was usually the one with the plans.

"First wallet has an address of Four five nine Wichita Street, Apartment C-four."

"Let's hit it."

FOURTEEN

When Marissa opened the door to her bedroom, she felt like an intruder in her own space: A wiped-out, heart-broken, lost . . . stranger.

Looking around aimlessly, she thought, God, it was such a pretty white room, wasn't it? With its big canopied bed and its chaise lounge and antique dressers and side tables. Everything was so feminine, except for the art on the walls. Her collection of Albrecht Durer woodcuts didn't match the rest of the décor, those stark lines and hard edges more fitting to a male's eyes and a male's things.

Except that the images spoke to her.

As she went over to look at one, she had a passing thought that Havers had always disapproved of them. He'd thought that Maxfield Parrish paintings of romantic, dreamy scenes were more appropriate for a female *Princeps*.

They never had agreed on art, had they? But he'd bought the woodcuts for her anyway because she'd loved them.

Forcing herself into action, she closed her door and went for the shower. She had little time before the regularly scheduled *Princeps* Council meeting tonight, and Havers always liked to arrive early.

As she stepped under the water, she thought how strange life was. When she'd been with Butch in that quarantine room, she'd forgotten all about the council and the *glymera* and . . . everything. But now, he was gone and it was all back to normal.

The return struck her as tragic.

After blowing her hair dry, she dressed in a teal Yves St. Laurent gown from the 1960s, then went to her jewelry cabinet and chose an important suite of diamonds. The stones were heavy and cold around her neck, the earrings weighty on her lobes, the bracelet a lock on her wrist. As she stared at the flashing gems, she thought that females in the aristocracy were really just display mannequins for their families' wealth, weren't they.

Especially at *Princeps* Council meetings.

Going downstairs, she dreaded seeing Havers, but figured it would be good to get it over with. He wasn't in his study, so she headed for the kitchen, thinking he might be having a bite to eat before they left. Just as she was pushing her way into the butler's pantry she saw Karolyn coming out of the door to the basement. The *doggen* was carrying a heavy load of collapsed cardboard boxes.

"Here, let me help you," Marissa said, rushing forward.

"No, thank you . . . mistress." The servant flushed and looked away, but that was the way of the *doggen*. They hated accepting aid from those they served.

Marissa smiled gently. "You must be packing up the library for its new paint job. Oh! Which reminds me. I'm late right now, but we do need to talk about tomorrow evening's dinner menu."

Karolyn bowed very low. "Forgive me, but master indicated the party with the *princeps leahdyre* was canceled."

"When did he say this?"

"Just now, before he left for the Council."

"He's gone already?" Maybe he assumed she would want to rest. "I'd better hurry off then—Karolyn, are you all right? You don't look well."

The *doggen* bowed so deeply the boxes brushed the floor. "I am well, indeed, mistress. Thank you."

Marissa raced out of the house and dematerialized to the Tudor home of the current council *leahdyre*. As she knocked, she hoped Havers had cooled down. She could understand his anger considering what he'd walked in on, but he didn't have a thing to worry about. It wasn't like Butch was in her life or anything.

God, she felt like throwing up every time she thought about that.

She was let in by a *doggen* and shown to the library. As she walked into the meeting, none of the nineteen at the polished table acknowledged her presence. This was not unusual. What was different was that her brother did not lift his eyes. Nor was there even a seat saved for her on his right. Nor did he even come around and settle her in her chair.

Havers had not cooled down. Not in the slightest.

Well, no matter, she would talk to him after the meeting. Calm him. Reassure him, though it killed her, because she could have used some support from him right now.

She sat at the far end of the table, in the middle of three empty chairs. As the last male walked into the meeting, he froze as he saw that all the seats were taken save for those on either side of her. After an awkward pause, a *doggen* rushed in with another and the *princeps* squeezed in elsewhere.

The *leahdyre*, a distinguished pale-haired male of great bloodline, shuffled some papers around, rapped on the table with the tip of a gold pen, and cleared his throat. "I hereby call this meeting to order and I am tabling the agenda you have all received. One of the members of the council has drafted an eloquent appeal to the king, which I believe we should consider with alacrity." He lifted a creamy piece of stationery and read from the thing. "'In light of the brutal killing of the *Princeps* Wellesandra, mated of the Black Dagger warrior Tohrment son of Hharm and blooded daughter of the *Princeps* Relix, and in light of the abduction of the *Princeps* Bella, mated of the Black Dagger warrior Zsadist son of Ahgony and blooded daughter of the *Princeps* Rempoon and blooded sister of the *Princeps* Rehvenge, and in light of the numerous deaths of males from the *glymera* who have been taken in their youth by the Lessening Society, it is evident that the clear and present danger facing the species has grown more dire of late. Therefore, this council member respectfully seeks to resurrect the practice of mandatory *sehclusion* for all unmated females of the aristocracy such that the bloodlines of the race may be preserved. Further, as it is this council's duty to safeguard all members of the species, this council member respectfully seeks to have this *sehclusion* practice extended to all class levels.'" The *leahdyre* looked up. "As per *Princeps* Council practice, we shall now entertain the motion with discussion."

Warning bells went off in Marissa's head as she looked around the room. Of the twenty-one council members present, six were females, but she was the only one to whom the writ would apply. Though she'd been Wrath's *shellan*, he'd never taken her, so she qualified as unmated.

As a consensus of approval and support swelled in the library, Marissa stared at her brother. Havers would now have complete control of her. Well played of him, wasn't it.

If he was her *ghardian*, she couldn't leave the house without his permission. Couldn't remain on the Council unless he agreed. Couldn't go anywhere or do anything because he would own her as his property, for all intents and purposes.

And there was no hope of Wrath turning down the

recommendation if the *Princeps* Council voted *yes* on the motion. Given the way things were with the *lessers,* there was no rational standing for a veto, and although no one could unseat Wrath by law, a lack of confidence in his leadership could lead to civil unrest. Which was the last thing the race needed.

At least Rehvenge wasn't in the room, so they couldn't do anything tonight. The venerable laws of procedure for the *Princeps* Council provided that only representatives from the six original families could vote, but all of the Council had to be present for a motion to be passed. So even though the bloodlines were at the table, with Rehv not in attendance, there would be no resolution now.

While the Council enthusiastically discussed the proposal, Marissa shook her head. How could Havers have opened up this can of worms? And it was all for nothing because she and Butch O'Neal were . . . nothing. Damn it, she had to talk to her brother and get him to derail this ridiculous proposal. Yes, Wellesandra had been killed and that was beyond tragic, but forcing all females underground was a step backward.

A retreat into the dark ages when females were totally unseen and all but possessions.

With icy clarity, she pictured that mother and her young with the broken leg back at the clinic. Yes, this was not just repressive, it was dangerous if the wrong *hellren* was in charge of a household. Legally, no one had any recourse against a *sehcluded* female's *ghardian.* At his discretion, he could do whatever he wished to her.

Van Dean stood in another basement of another house in another part of Caldwell, a whistle between his lips as his eyes tracked the movements of the pale-haired men in front of him. The six "students" were in a line, knees bent, fists up. They were striking the empty air in front of them with blurring speed, alternating left and right, shifting their shoulders accordingly. The air was heavy with their sweet smell, but Van didn't notice that shit anymore.

He blew the whistle twice. As a unit, the six brought both hands up as if grabbing a man's head like a basketball, and then they slammed their right knees forward repeatedly. Van blew the whistle again and they switched legs.

He hated to admit it, because it meant he was over the hill, but training men to fight was so much easier than going hand to hand in the ring. And he appreciated the break.

Plus he was good at the teaching, evidently. Although these gang members learned fast and hit hard, so he had something to work with.

And these were definitely gang members. Dressed the same. Colored their hair the same. Packed the same weapons. What was not so obvious was what they were about. These boys had the focus of military men; none of that sloppy bullshit most street thugs covered up with bravado and bullets. Hell, if he didn't know better he'd have assumed they were government: There were squads of them. They had top-notch gear. They were intense as shit. And there were a lot of them. He'd only been on board a week and he'd taught five classes a day, each filled with different guys. Hell, this was only his second trip through the park with this particular bunch of men.

Except why would the feds use someone like him to teach?

He blew the whistle for a long beat, stopping them all. "That's it for tonight."

The men broke ranks and went for their bags of gear. They said nothing. Didn't interact with each other. Didn't pull any of that macho, nut-busting routine that guys usually did when they were in a group.

As they filed out, Van went to his own bag and got his water bottle. Sucking back some, he thought about how he had to head across town now. He had a fight scheduled in an hour. No time to food up, but he wasn't that hungry anyway.

He put his windbreaker on, jogged up the basement steps, and did a quick tour of the house. Empty. No furniture. No eats. Nothing. And every single one of the other places had been exactly the same. Shells of houses that from the outside looked all cheery normal.

Fucking weird.

He went out the front, made sure he locked the door, and headed to his truck. The locations they met at had been different each day and he had a feeling they always would be. Every morning at seven a.m., he got a call with an address, and he stayed put when he got there, the men cycling through, the classes on mixed martial-arts fighting lasting two hours apiece. The schedule ran like clockwork.

Maybe they were paramilitary whack jobs.

"Evening, son."

Van froze then looked over the hood of his truck. A minivan was parked across the street, and Xavier was leaning up against the thing as casual as the mommy-mommy who should have been driving the POS.

"What up?" Van said.

"You're doing well with the men." Xavier's flat smile matched his flat, pale eyes.

"Thanks. I'm just leaving now."

"Not yet." Van's skin prickled as the guy eased off the

car and crossed the street. "So, son, I've been thinking you might want to become more closely involved with us."

More closely involved, huh? "I'm not interested in crime. Sorry."

"What makes you think what we do is criminal?"

"Come on, Xavier." The guy hated it when he dropped the *Mr.* So he did it often. "I've done time once. It was boring."

"Yes, that carjacking ring you fell into. I bet your brother had a lot to say about that, didn't he? Oh—I don't mean the one you did the stealing with. I'm talking about the law abider in the family. The clean one. Richard, isn't it?"

Van frowned. "Tell you what. You don't bring my family into this, I won't drop a dime and turn in these houses you use to the CPD. I mean, cops would love to come for Sunday dinner, I'm damn sure. Wouldn't need to ask 'em over twice."

As Xavier's face became remote, Van thought, *Gotcha.*

But then the man just smiled. "And I'll tell *you* what. I can give you something no one else can."

"Oh, yeah?"

"Undoubtedly."

Van shook his head, unimpressed. "Isn't this a little early to invite me in? What if I'm not trustworthy?"

"You will be."

"Your faith in me is so fucking sweet. But the answer's no. Sorry."

He expected argument. All he got was a nod.

"As you wish." Xavier turned and walked back to the minivan.

Weird, Van thought as he got into his truck. These boys were definitely weird.

But at least they paid on time. And well.

* * *

Across town, Vishous took form on the side lawn of a nicely kept apartment building. Rhage was right behind him, materializing into flesh and blood in the shadows.

Shit, V thought. He wished he'd taken a moment for another smoke before he'd come here. He needed a cigarette. He needed . . . something.

"V, my brother, you okay?"

"Yeah. Perfect. Let's do this."

After pulling a little mind bend with the lock system, they walked in the front door. The inside of the place smelled like air freshener, a fake orange stench that coated the nostrils like paint.

They skipped the elevator because it was in use and hit the stairwell. When they got to the second floor, they headed past apartments C1 and C2 and C3. V kept his hand under his jacket and on his Glock, although he had a feeling the worst thing that could come at them would be a hall monitor. The place was neat as a pin and QVC cutesy-pie: Fake flower bouquets hung on doors. Welcome mats with hearts or ivy on them were on the floor outside each apartment. Framed inspirational pictures of pink and peach sunsets alternated with ones of fuzzy puppies and clueless kitties.

"Man," Rhage muttered, "someone hit this place with the Hallmark stick."

"Until it broke."

V stopped in front of the door marked C4 and willed the locks to shift.

"What are you doing?"

He and Rhage wheeled around.

Holy shit, it was one of the frickin' Golden Girls: Three feet high with a crown of kinky white on her head, the old lady was decked out in a bunchy quilted robe, like she was wearing her bed.

Trouble was, she had the eyes of a pit bull. "I asked you young men a question."

Rhage took over, which was good. He was better with the charm. "Ma'am, we're just here visiting a friend."

"You know Dottie's grandson?"

"Ah, yes, ma'am. We do."

"Well, you look like you would." Which was evidently not a compliment. "I think he should move out, by the way. Dottie died four months ago and he doesn't fit in here."

And neither do you, those eyes tacked on.

"Oh, he's moving out." Rhage smiled pleasantly while keeping his lips together. "Moved out, really. Yeah, tonight."

V cut in, "'Scuse me, I'll be right back."

As Rhage shot him a *don't-you-dare-leave-me-with-this-hot-potato* glare, V stepped inside and shut the door on his brother's face. If Rhage couldn't handle the biddy, he could just swipe her memories, although that would be a last resort. Older humans sometimes didn't deal well with the erasing, their brains no longer resilient enough to withstand the invasion.

So yeah, Hollywood and Dottie's neighbor were going to get tight while V cased the place.

With a sneer, he glanced around. Man, everything smelled of *lesser*. Sickly sweet. Like Butch.

Shit. Do not think about that.

He forced himself to focus on the apartment. Unlike most *lesser* pads, this one was furnished, though obviously by its former occupant. And Dottie's taste had run toward flower prints, doilies, and cat figurines. She fit *right* in with this building.

Chances were good the *lessers* had read about her passing in the paper and had copped her identity. Hell, maybe it even was her grandson camping out here after he'd been inducted into the Society.

V walked through the kitchen and out again, not surprised there was no food in the cabinets or the refrigerator. As he headed for the other half of the apartment, he thought it was so curious that the slayers didn't hide where they crashed. Hell, most died with ID on them that was accurate. Then again, they wanted to encourage conflicts—

Hello.

V went over to a pink and white desk where a Dell Inspiron 8600 was cracked open and running. He swiped his finger across the mouse and did a quick poke around. Encrypted files. Everything password protected up the wazoo. Blah, blah, blah . . .

Although *lessers* were all welcome mat about their cribs, they were very tight about their hardware. Most slayers had a compy at home, and the Lessening Society pulled a lot of the same protections and coding maneuvers that V did at the compound. So basically their shit was impenetrable.

Good thing he didn't know the meaning of *impenetrable.*

He clapped the Dell shut and unplugged the power line from the unit and the wall. He stuffed the electrical cord in his pocket, zipped up his jacket, and tucked the laptop in close to his chest. Then he went deeper into the apartment. Bedroom looked like a chintz bomb had gone off with flower and frill shrapnel covering the mattress and the windows and the walls.

And then there it was. On a little table beside the bed, sitting next to a phone, a four-month-old issue of *Reader's Digest* and a colony of orange pill bottles: a ceramic jar about the size of a quart of milk.

He flipped open his phone and dialed Rhage. When the

brother picked up, V said, "I'm outtie. I've got a laptop and the jar."

He hung up, palmed the ceramic container and held it tightly against the hard body of the laptop. Then he dematerialized to the Pit, thinking how handy it was that humans didn't line their walls with steel.

FIFTEEN

As Mr. X watched Van drive off, he knew the ask had come too soon. He should have waited until the guy was a little more hooked on the power trip he went on when he trained the slayers.

Except time was passing.

It wasn't that he was worried about the loophole closing. The prophecy hadn't said anything about that kind of thing. But the Omega had been righteous pissed when Mr. X had left him last. Hadn't taken at all well the news that the contaminated human had been offed by the Brothers in that clearing in the woods. So the stakes were mounting, and not in X's favor.

From out of nowhere, the center of his chest began to warm, and then he felt a beating where his heart once had been. The rhythmic pulse made him curse. Speak of the devil, the master was calling him.

Mr. X got into the minivan, started the thing up, and drove seven minutes across town to a shitty ranch house on a ratty lot in a bad neighborhood. Place still reeked like the meth lab it had been up until its former owner had been shot by a professional associate. Thanks to the lingering toxicity, the Society had gotten the digs at a discount.

Mr. X parked in the garage and waited until the door squeaked shut before getting out. After killing the security alarm he'd installed, he headed for the back bedroom.

As he went along, his skin was irritated and itchy, like he had a case of prickly heat all over his body. The longer he put off responding to the master, the worse it would get. Until he was crazed from the need to scratch at himself.

Settling on his knees and lowering his head, he didn't want to get anywhere near the Omega. The master had radar instincts and Mr. X's goals were now his own, not the Society's. Problem was, when the *Fore-lesser* was called, he came as summoned. That was the deal.

As soon as Vishous walked into the Pit, he heard the quiet and hated it. Fortunately, within fifteen minutes of his cracking open that *lesser*'s laptop on his desk, there was a pounding on the door. He glanced at a monitor, then sprang the locks with his mind.

Rhage walked in munching on something, his hand shoved in a Ziploc bag. "Having any luck with Mr. Dell's fine product?"

"What are you eating?"

"The last of Mrs. Woolly's banana nut bread. It's awesome. Want some?"

V rolled his eyes and went back to the laptop. "No, but you could bring me a bottle of Goose and a glass from the kitchen."

"No problem." Rhage made the delivery, then leaned against the wall. "So you find anything in there?"

"Not yet."

When silence expanded until it crowded out the air in the Pit, V knew there was more to the visit than a check-in on the Dell.

Sure enough, Rhage said, "Listen, my brother—"

"I'm not much for company right now."

"I know. That's why they asked me to come."

V glanced over the top of the computer. "And who's 'they'?" Even though he knew.

"The Brotherhood's worried about you. You're getting

damn tight, V. Twitchy as shit and don't deny it. Everyone's noticed."

"Oh, so Wrath asked you to come play Rorschach on me?"

"Direct order. But I was on my way over here anyway."

V rubbed his eyes. "I'm fine."

"It's okay if you aren't."

No, it really was not. "If you don't mind, I'd like to go through this PC."

"We going to see you at Last Meal?"

"Yeah. Sure." Right.

V fiddled with the mouse and kept scanning through the computer's file systems. As he stared at the screen, he noticed absently that his right eye, the one with the tats on its side, had started to flicker like the lid was shorting out.

Two massive fists knuckled down on the desk and Rhage leaned in tight. "You come or I come for you."

As Vishous glared up at his brother, Rhage's teal gaze just stared back from his towering height and his mind-bending beauty.

Oh, so they were going to play chicken with the eyeballs, huh? *Well, fuck you,* V thought.

Except Vishous was the one who lost. Moments later, he looked down at the laptop, trying to make like he was just checking on something. "You need to back off, okay. Butch is my roommate, so of course I'm going to be bleeding for him. But it's no big thing—"

"Phury told us. About your visions drying up."

"Christ." V burst out of his chair, pushed Rhage out of the way, and walked around. "That gum-flapping motherfu—"

"If it's any consolation, Wrath didn't really give him a choice."

"So the king brass-knuckled it out of him?"

"Come on, V. When I've whacked out, you've been there for me. This is no different."

"Yeah, it is."

"Because it's you."

"Bingo." Man, V simply couldn't talk about this shit. He, who spoke sixteen languages, just had no words for the mind-bending fear he had over the future: Butch's. His own. The whole race's. His visions of what was coming had always pissed him off, but they were a strange comfort, too. Even if he didn't like what was around the bend, at least he'd never been surprised.

Rhage's hand landed on his shoulder and he jumped. "Last Meal, Vishous. You show or I'm picking you up like mail, dig?"

"Yeah. Fine. Now get the fuck out of here."

As soon as Rhage left, V went back to the laptop and sat down. Except instead of returning to IT land, he called Butch's new phone.

The cop's voice was all gravel. "Hey, V."

"Hey." V held his phone between his ear and his shoulder and poured himself some vodka. As the juice hit the glass, there was the sound of shuffling over the line, like Butch was rolling over in bed or maybe taking his jacket off.

They were silent for a long time, nothing but an open cellular connection.

And then V had to ask, "Did you want to be with them? You feel like you should be with the *lessers*?"

"I don't know." Deep inhale. Long, slow exhale. "I won't front. I recognized those bastards. Felt them. But when I was looking into the eyes of that slayer, I did want to destroy him."

V lifted his glass. As he swallowed, the vodka burned down his throat in the nicest possible way. "How you feeling?"

"Not so hot. Queased out. Like I lost some ground."
More silence. "Is this what you dreamed of? Back in the
beginning, when you said I was supposed to come with
the Brotherhood . . . did you dream of me and the Omega?"

"No, I saw something else."

Although with everything that was going down, he
couldn't see a path to what had been shown to him, couldn't
see it on a lot of levels: The vision had been of him naked
and Butch wrapped around him, the two of them high up
in the sky, entwined in the midst of a cold wind.

Jesus Christ, he was *deranged. Deranged and perverted.*
"Look, I'll come at sundown and hit you with a little hand
action."

"Good. That always helps." Butch cleared his throat.
"But V, I can't sit here and just wait this out. I want to
go on the offensive. What say we pick up a few *lessers* and
work them over, get them to do some talking for a change."

"Hard-core, cop."

"You get a look at what they did to me? You think I'm
worried about the frickin' Geneva Convention?"

"Lemme talk to Wrath first."

"Do it soon."

"Today."

"Good deal." There was another long silence. "So . . .
you got some tube in this place?"

"Flat screen's up on the wall to the left of the bed.
Remote's . . . I don't know where it is. I don't usually . . .
yeah, TV's not on my mind when I'm there."

"V, man, what is this setup?"

"Pretty self-explanatory, don't you think?"

There was a little chuckle. "I guess this was what Phury
was talking about, huh?"

"When he said what?"

"That you were into some kinky shit."

V had a sudden vision of Butch on top of Marissa, the male's body surging while she gripped his ass with her beautiful hands.

Then he saw Butch's head lift up and heard in his mind the hoarse, erotic moan that broke free of his roommate's lips.

Despising himself, Vishous hammered a shot of vodka and quickly poured another. "My sex life is private, Butch. So are my . . . unconventional interests."

"I hear ya. No one's biz but yours. One question, though."

"What."

"When the females tie you down, do they paint your toe-nails and shit? Or just do your makeup?" As V laughed in a loud crack, the cop said, "Wait . . . they tickle your pits with a feather, right?"

"Smart-ass."

"Hey, I'm just curious." Butch's own laughter faded. "Do you hurt them, though? I mean . . ."

More with the vodka. "It's all about consent. And I don't cross the line."

"Good. Little freaky for my Catholic ass, granted . . . 'cept, hey, it's whatever gets you off."

V swirled the Goose around in his glass. "So, cop, mind if I ask you something?"

"Fair's fair."

"Do you love her?"

After a while, Butch muttered, "Yeah. Fuck me, but yeah."

As the laptop's screen saver came on, V put his fingertip on the mouse square and interrupted the metastasizing pipes. "What's that feel like?"

There was a grunt as if Butch were rearranging himself and was stiff as a board. "Hell, right at this moment."

V played with the arrow on the screen, making it whip around the desktop. "You know . . . I like her with you. The two of you make sense to me."

"Except for the fact that I'm a blue-collar human who could be part *lesser,* I'd say I agree with you."

"You're not turning into a—"

"I took some of that slayer in me tonight. When I inhaled. I think that's why I smelled like one afterward. Not because we'd been fighting, but because some of the evil was—is—in me again."

V cursed, hoping like hell that wasn't the case. "We're going to figure this out, cop. I'm not going to leave you in the dark."

They hung up a little later and V stared at the laptop while swirling the arrow around. He kept up the forefinger workout until he became thoroughly unimpressed with the time he was wasting.

As he stretched his arms over his head, he realized that the cursor had landed on RECYCLE BIN. Recycle . . . Recycle . . . *to reprocess in order to use again.*

What was it with Butch and the inhale thing? Now that V thought about it, when he'd pulled that *lesser* off the cop, he'd been aware he was breaking some kind of connection between them.

Restless, he took his Goose and glass and went over to the couches. As he sat down and swallowed some more, he looked at the pint of Lag that was on the coffee table.

V leaned forward and grabbed the Scotch. Unscrewing it, he lifted it to his lips and took a slug. Then he brought the Lag to the lip of his glass of vodka and poured. With low-lidded eyes, he watched the swirling combination, seeing the two blend, the vodka and the Scotch both diluted of their pure essence and yet stronger together.

V brought the combo to his lips, tilted his head back,

and swallowed the whole damn thing. Then he eased back into the couch.

He was tired . . . way fucking tired . . . ti—

Sleep came to him so fast it was like getting slammed in the head. But the shut-eye didn't last long. The Dream, as he was coming to think of it, woke him up minutes later with its characteristic violence: He came to on a scream with a splitting feeling in his chest, as if someone were using a rib-spreader on him. As his heart skipped, then pounded, sweat broke out all over him.

Ripping his shirt open, he looked down at his body.

Everything was where it should be, no gaping wound to be seen. Except the feelings remained, the horrible pressure of being shot, the crushing doom that death had come upon him.

He breathed raggedly. And figured that was it for shut-eye.

He left the vodka behind and lurched over to his desk, determined to get good and intimate with that laptop.

When the *Princeps* Council broke up, Marissa was totally drained. Which made sense, as dawn was close. There had been a lot of discussion about the *sehclusion* motion, none of the talk negative, all of it centered around the *lesser* threat. Clearly, when the vote was taken, not only would it pass, but if Wrath didn't issue a proclamation, the Council was going to look at it as evidence that the king lacked commitment to the race.

Which was something Wrath's detractors were dying to have come to the forefront. Three hundred years of him passing on the throne had left a bitter taste in the mouths of some of the aristocracy, and they were after him.

Desperate to leave, Marissa waited and waited by the library's door, but Havers kept talking to the others.

Eventually, she went outside and dematerialized back home, figuring she'd camp out in his bedroom if she had to in order to talk with him.

As she came in the front door of their mansion, she didn't call for Karolyn as she usually did, but went straight upstairs to her bedroom. Pushing the door open, she—

"*Oh . . . my God.*" Her room was . . . a ghost town.

Her walk-in closet was open and empty, not even a single hanger remaining. Her bed was stripped, her pillows gone, along with her sheets and blankets. All of the pictures were down. And cardboard boxes were stacked up against the far wall next to every piece of Louis Vuitton luggage she owned.

"What . . ." Her voice dried out as she went into the bathroom. The cabinets of which were all barren.

As she stumbled from the bath, Havers was standing by the bed.

"What is this?" She swept her arm around.

"You need to leave this house."

At first all she could do was blink at him. "But I live here!"

He took out his wallet, removed a thick wad of bills, and spread them on the bureau. "Take this. And go."

"All because of Butch?" she demanded. "And how's this going to work with that *sehclusion* proposal you put to the council? *Ghardians* have to be around their—"

"I didn't propose the motion. And as for that human . . ." He shook his head. "Your life is your own. And seeing you with a naked human male who had just engaged in a sexual act—" Havers's voice cracked and he cleared his throat. "Go now. Live as you wish. But I will not sit back and watch you destroy yourself."

"Havers, this is ridiculous—"

"I can't protect you from yourself."

"Havers, Butch is not—"

"I threatened the king's life to *ahvenge* your honor!" The sound of his voice ricocheted around the walls. "And then to find you with a human male! I—I can't have you near me anymore. I don't trust this anger you bring out in me. It triggers acts of such violence. It—" He shuddered and turned away. "I have told the *doggen* they are to deposit you wherever you wish to go, but after that, they will return to this household. You will have to find your own."

Her body went completely numb. "I am still a member of the *Princeps* Council. You will have to see me there."

"No, because I am not required to render you mine eyes. And you assume you will stay on the council, which is doubtful. Wrath will have no cause to deny the *sehclusion* motion. You will be without a mate and I will not function as your *ghardian*, so you will have no one to grant permission for your presence to be out in the open. Not even your bloodline can override the law."

Marissa's jaw unhinged. Holy heaven . . . she would be a total social outcast. A veritable . . . no one. "How can you do this to me?"

He glanced over his shoulder. "I am tired of myself. Tired of fighting the urge to defend you from choices you make—"

"Choices! Living as a female in the aristocracy I have no choices!"

"Untrue. You could have been a proper mate to Wrath."

"He didn't want me! You knew that, you saw it with your own two eyes! That's why you wanted to have him killed!"

"But now when I think on it, I wonder . . . why did he feel nothing for you? Perhaps you didn't work hard enough to engage his interest."

Marissa felt a raw fury. And the emotion grew hotter

as her brother said, "And as for choices, you could have stayed out of that human's hospital room. You chose to go in there. And you chose to . . . you could have . . . not layed with him."

"Is that what this is about? For God's sake, I'm still a virgin."

"Now you lie."

The three words snapped her out of her emotions. As the heat drained away, clarity came, and for the first time, she truly saw her brother: brilliant of mind, devoted to his patients, loving of his dead *shellan* . . . and utterly rigid. A male of science and order who liked rules and predictability and enjoyed a precise vision of life.

And he was clearly willing to protect that worldview at the cost of her future . . . her happiness . . . her very self.

"You are absolutely correct," she said with a strange calm. "I do have to go."

She glanced at the boxes that were filled with the clothes she'd worn and the things she'd bought. Then her eyes found him again. He was doing the same, staring at them as if measuring the life she'd led.

"I shall let you keep the Dürers, of course," he said.

"Of course," she whispered. "Good-bye, brother."

"I am Havers to you now. Not brother. And never again." He dropped his head and walked out of the room.

In the silence that followed there was the temptation to fall on the bare mattress and cry. But there was no time. She had maybe an hour before light.

Dear Virgin, where would she go?

SIXTEEN

When Mr. X came back from meeting the Omega on the other side, he felt like he had heartburn. Which seemed logical, as he'd been fed his own ass.

The master had been teed up about a variety of things. He wanted more *lessers*, more vampires bleeding out, more progress, more . . . more . . . But the thing was, no matter what he was given, he would always be unsatisfied. Maybe that was his curse.

Whatever. The calculus of Mr. X's failure was up on the blackboard, the mathematical equation of his destruction outlined in chalk. The unknown in the algebra was time. How long before the Omega snapped and Mr. X got recalled for eternity?

Things needed to move faster with Van. That man had to get on board and in place ASAP.

Mr. X went over to his laptop and fired the Dell up. Sitting down next to the dried brown stain of a blood pool, he called up the Scrolls and found the relevant passage. The lines of the prophecy calmed him:

There shall be one to bring the end before the master,
a fighter of modern time found in the seventh of the
    twenty-first,
and he shall be known in the numbers he bears:
One more than the compass he apperceives,
Though mere four points to make at his right,
Three lives has he,
Two scores on his fore,

*and with a single black eye, in one well will he be birthed
and die.*

Mr. X eased back against the wall, cracked his neck, and looked around. The stinky remnants of the meth lab, the filth in the place, the air of bad deeds done without remorse were like a party he didn't want to be at but couldn't leave. Just like the Lessening Society.

Except it was going to be okay. At least he'd spotted the *lesser* exit.

God, it had been so weird how he'd found Van Dean. X had gone to the ultimate fighting brawls to troll for new recruits and Van had immediately stood out from the others. There was just something special about him, something that elevated him above his opponents. And watching the guy move that first night, Mr. X had thought he'd spotted an important addition to the Society . . . until he'd noticed the missing finger.

He didn't like to bring in anyone with a physical defect.

But the more he saw Van fight, the more clear it was that an absent pinkie was no liability at all. Then a couple nights later he saw the tattoo. Van always fought with a T-shirt on, but at one point the thing got shoved up around his pecs. On his back, in black ink, an eye stared out from between his shoulder blades.

That had been what sent Mr. X into the Scrolls. The prophecy was buried deep in the text of the Lessening Society's handbook, an all-but-forgotten paragraph in the midst of the rules of induction. Fortunately, when Mr. X had become *Fore-lesser* the first time, he'd read the passages thoroughly enough to remember the damn thing was there.

As with the rest of the Scrolls, which had been translated into English in the 1930s, the wording of the prophecy was abstract. But if you were missing a finger on your right hand, then you had only four points to make. "Three lives" was childhood, adulthood, and then life in the Society. And according to the fight crowd, Van was homegrown, born in the city of Caldwell, which was also known as the Well.

But there was more. The man's instincts were twitchy as hell. All you had to do was watch him in that chicken-wire ring to know that north, south, east, and west were only part of what he was sensing: He had a rare talent for anticipating the way his opponent was going to move. It was the gift that set him apart.

The clincher, however, was the appendix removal. The word *score* could be construed in a variety of ways, but it very conceivably referred to scarring. And everyone had a belly button, so if you'd had your appendix removed as well, you'd have two scars on your "fore," wouldn't you?

Plus it was the right year to find him.

Mr. X reached for his cell phone and called one of his subordinates.

As the line rang, he was aware that he needed Van Dean, that modern fighter, that four-fingered bastard, more than anyone he'd met in his life. Or after his death.

When Marissa materialized in front of the dour gray mansion, she put her hand up to her throat and tilted her head back. God, so much stone rising from the earth, whole quarries stripped to gather the load. And so many leaded-glass windows, the diamond panes looking like bars. And then there was the twenty-foot-high retaining wall that wrapped around the courtyard and the grounds. And the security cameras. And the gates.

So secure. So cold.

The place was precisely as she'd expected it to be, a fortress not a home. And it was surrounded by a buffer of what in the Old Country was called *mhis* so that unless you were supposed to be here, your brain couldn't process the location well enough for you to find your way around. Hell, the only reason she'd made it to the Brotherhood's compound was because Wrath was inside. After three hundred years of living off his pure blood, she had so much of him in her that she could find him anywhere. Even through the *mhis*.

As she faced the mountain before her, her nape tingled like she was being stalked, and she looked over her shoulder. In the east, the light of day was gathering momentum, and the radiance made her eyes burn. She was almost out of time.

Hand still on her throat, she walked up to a pair of massive brass doors. There was no doorbell or knocker, so she tried one side. It opened, which was a shock—at least until she stood in the vestibule. Ah, here was where you were screened.

She put her face in front of a camera and waited. No doubt an alarm had gone off when she'd breached the first door, so someone would either come and let her in . . . or refuse her. In which case she was on to her second choice. At a dead run.

Rehvenge was the only other person she could have turned to, but he was complicated. His *mahmen* was a spiritual counselor of sorts to the *glymera* and would no doubt be highly offended by Marissa's presence.

With a prayer to the Scribe Virgin, she smoothed her hair with her palm. Maybe she'd gambled wrong, but she'd assumed that Wrath wouldn't turn her away this close to dawn. For all she'd endured with him, she figured he could spare her one day under the cover of his roof. And he was a male of honor.

At least Butch didn't live with the Brotherhood as far

as she knew. He'd stayed at another place somewhere else over the summer and she guessed he still had it. Hoped he did.

The heavy wooden doors ahead of her opened, and Fritz, the butler, seemed very surprised to see her. "Madam?" The elderly *doggen* bowed low. "Are you . . . expected?"

"No, I'm not." She was about as far away from *expected* as it got. "I, ah—"

"Fritz, who is it?" came a female voice.

As footsteps got closer, Marissa clasped her hands together and lowered her head.

Oh, Lord. Beth, the queen. It would have been so much better to see Wrath first. And now she could only assume this wasn't going to work out.

Surely her majesty would let her use the phone to call Rehvenge? God, did she even have time to dial?

The doors creaked open even wider. "Who is . . . *Marissa*?"

Marissa kept her eyes on the floor and curtsied, as was custom. "My queen."

"Fritz, will you excuse us?" A moment later Beth said, "Would you like to come in?"

Marissa hesitated, then stepped through the door. She had a peripheral sense of incredible color and warmth, but she couldn't lift her head to take it all in.

"How did you find us?" Beth asked.

"Your . . . *hellren*'s blood lingers within me. I . . . I have come to him for a favor. I would speak to Wrath, if it would not offend?"

Marissa was shocked when her hand was grasped. "What's happened?"

When she lifted her eyes to the queen, she nearly gasped. Beth was so genuinely concerned, so worried. To be greeted with any kind of warmth was disarming, especially from this female who by all rights might be tempted to kick her out.

"Marissa, talk to me."

Where to start. "I am . . . ah, I am in need of a place to stay. I have nowhere to go. I have been cast out. I am—"

"Wait, slow down. Just slow down. What happened?"

Marissa took a deep breath and gave a condensed version of the story, one that avoided any mention of Butch. The words ran out of her like dirty water, spilling onto the brilliant mosaic floor, staining the beauty beneath her feet. The shame of the recounting stung her throat.

"So you will stay with us," Beth pronounced when it was over.

"Just the one night."

"For however long you want." Beth squeezed Marissa's hand. "However. Long."

As Marissa shut her eyes and tried not to break down, she became dimly aware of a pounding sound, of heavy boots descending carpeted stairs.

Then Wrath's deep voice filled the cavernous three-story foyer. "What the hell's going on?"

"Marissa is moving in with us."

While Marissa dropped into another curtsy, she was totally stripped of her pride, as vulnerable as if she were naked. To have nothing and throw yourself on the mercy of others was a strange kind of terror.

"Marissa, look at me."

Wrath's hard tone was utterly familiar, the one he'd always used with her, the one that had made her cringe for three centuries. In desperation, she eyed the open door to the vestibule even though she was by now officially out of time.

The wooden panels slammed shut as if the king had willed it so. "Marissa, talk."

"Back off, Wrath," the queen snapped. "She's been through too much tonight already. Havers threw her out."

"*What*? Why?"

Beth made quick work of the story, and hearing it from a third party only increased Marissa's humiliation. As her vision blurred, she struggled not to lose it.

And the battle was lost when Wrath said, "Jesus Christ, that idiot. Of course she stays here."

With a shaking hand, she brushed under both eyes, capturing her tears and quickly rubbing them away between her fingertips.

"Marissa? Look at me."

She lifted her head. God, Wrath was just the same, his face too cruel to be truly handsome, those wraparound sunglasses making him look even more intimidating. Absently, she noted that his hair was much longer than when she'd known him, down nearly to the small of his back.

"I'm glad you came to us."

She cleared her throat. "I would be grateful for a short tenure here."

"Where are your things?"

"They're all packed up at my house—er, my brother's— I mean, Havers's house. I came back from the *Princeps* Council and everything I own was in boxes. But it can remain there until I figure out—"

"Fritz!" When the *doggen* came running in, Wrath said, "Go to Havers's and pick up her stuff. You better take the van and an extra set of arms."

Fritz bowed and took off, moving faster than you would think an old *doggen* could.

Marissa tried to find words. "I—I—"

"I'm going to show you to your room," Beth said. "You look like you're about to collapse."

The queen took Marissa over to the grand staircase, and as they went, Marissa glanced over her shoulder. Wrath had an utterly ruthless expression on his face, his jaw set like concrete.

She had to stop. "Are you sure?" she asked him.

His glower got worse. "That brother of yours has a real knack for pissing me off."

"I don't mean to inconvenience you—"

Wrath rolled right over her words. "This was about Butch, wasn't it. V told me that you went to the cop and pulled him through. Let me guess—Havers didn't appreciate you getting too tight with our human, right?"

Marissa could only nod.

"Like I said, your brother really pisses me off. Butch is our boy even if he isn't in the Brotherhood and anyone who cares for him cares for us. So you take up residence here for the rest of your natural goddamned life as far as I'm concerned." Wrath headed around the base of the stairs. "Fucking Havers. Fucking *idiot*. I'll go find V and let him know you're here. Butch isn't around, but V'll know where to find him."

"Oh—no, you don't have to—"

Wrath didn't stop, didn't even hesitate, reminding her that you didn't tell the king to do anything. Even if it was not to worry about something.

"Well," Beth murmured, "at least he's not armed right now."

"I'm surprised he cares this much."

"Are you kidding? It's appalling. To turn you out right before dawn? Anyway, let's get you settled."

Marissa resisted the female's gentle pull. "You welcome me so graciously. How can you be so—"

"Marissa." Beth's navy blue eyes were level. "You saved the man I love. When he was shot and my blood wasn't strong enough, you kept him alive by giving him your wrist. So let's be perfectly clear. There is absolutely *nothing* I wouldn't do for you."

As dawn arrived and light poured into the penthouse, Butch woke up fully aroused and in the process of grinding his hips into a twist of satin sheets. He was covered with sweat, his skin hypersensitized, his erection pulsing.

Groggy, confused as to what was reality and what he just hoped was real, he reached downward. Undid his belt. Burrowed through his slacks and his boxers.

Images of Marissa swirled in his head, half the fantasy he'd been so gloriously lost in, half memories of the feel of her. He fell into a rhythm with his hand, unsure whether he was the one who was doing the stroking . . . Maybe it was her . . . God, he wanted it to be her.

He closed his eyes and arched his back. *Oh, yeah. So good.*

Except then he woke up.

As he realized what he was doing, he became vicious. Angry with himself and so much of what was going on, he handled his sex roughly until he barked a curse and ejaculated. He couldn't even call it an orgasm. More like his cock swore out loud.

With sickening dread, he braced himself and looked down at his hand.

Then just sagged from relief. At least something was back to normal.

After kicking out of his trousers and wiping up with the boxers, he went into the bathroom and turned on the shower. Under the spray, all he could think about was Marissa. He missed her with a stinging hunger, a kind of craving pain that reminded him of when he'd quit smoking the year before.

And shit, no Nicoderm for this.

191

When he came out of the bath with a towel around his hips, his new cell phone was ringing. He fumbled around the pillows and finally found the thing.

"Yeah, V?" he rasped. Man, his voice was always shot to shit in the morning and today was no different. He sounded like a car engine that wouldn't turn over.

Okay, so that was two normals in his favor.

"Marissa's moved in."

"*What?*" He sank down onto the mattress. "What the hell are you talking about?"

"Havers kicked her out."

"Because of me?"

"Yup."

"*That bastard—*"

"She's here in the compound, so you don't worry about her safety. But she's rattled as hell." There was a long silence. "Cop? You there, my man?"

"Yeah." Butch fell back on the bed. Realized his thigh muscles were twitching with the need to get to her.

"So like I said, she's okay. You want me to bring her to you tonight?"

Butch put his hand up to his eyes. The idea that someone had hurt her in any way made him positively mental. To the point of violence.

"Butch? Hello?"

As Marissa settled into a canopied bed, she pulled the covers up to her neck and wished she weren't naked. Trouble was, she had no clothes.

God, even though no one would bother her here, being bare just . . . felt wrong. Scandalous, though no one would ever know.

She glanced around. The room she'd been given was lovely, done in a delphinium blue toile, with the pastoral scene of a lady and a kneeling suitor repeated on the walls, the drapes, the bedcovers, the chair.

Not exactly what she wanted to look at. The two French lovers crowded her, striking her as not visual but audible, a chaotic staccato of what she didn't have with Butch. Wouldn't ever have with Butch.

To solve the problem, she turned off the light and closed her eyes. And the ocular version of earplugs worked like a charm.

Dear Virgin, what a mess. And she had to wonder in what manner things were going to get worse. Fritz and two other *doggen* had gone over to her brother's—to *Havers's*—and she half expected them to come back with nothing. Maybe Havers would decide to just get rid of her things in the meantime. Like he'd done with her.

While she lay there in the dark, she sifted through the rubble of her life, trying to see what was still usable and what she had to abandon as unsalvageable. All she found was depressing litter, a hodgepodge of unhappy memories that gave her no direction. She had absolutely no idea what she wanted to do or where she should go.

And didn't that make sense. She'd spent three centuries waiting and hoping for a male to notice her. Three centuries trying to fit in with the *glymera*. Three centuries working desperately to be someone's sister, someone's daughter, someone's mate. All those external expectations had been the laws of physics that had governed her life, more pervasive and grounding than gravity.

Except where had trying to meet them gotten her? Orphaned, unmated, and shunned.

All right, then, her first rule for the rest of her days: no more looking outside for definitions. She might not have any clue who she was, but better to be lost and searching than shoved into a social box by someone else.

The phone next to the bed rang and she jumped. After five rounds of chiming, she answered the thing only because it refused to stop going off. "Hello?"

"Madam?" A *doggen*. "You have a call from our master Butch. Are you receiving?"

Oh, great. So he'd heard.

"Madam?"

"Ah . . . yes, I am."

"Very well. And I've given him your direct dial. Please hold."

There was a click and then that telltale gravel voice. "Marissa? Are you okay?"

Not really, she thought, but it was none of his business. "Yes, thank you. Beth and Wrath have been very charitable to me."

"Listen, I want to see you."

"You do? Then may I assume that all your problems have magically disappeared? You must be thrilled to be back to normal. Congratulations."

He cursed. "I'm worried about you."

"Kind of you, but—"

"Marissa—"

"—we wouldn't want to endanger me, would we?"

"Listen, I just—"

"So you better stay away so I don't get hurt—"

"*Damn you*, Marissa. Goddamn this whole thing!"

She closed her eyes, mad at the world and at him and at her brother and herself. And with Butch getting angry, too, this conversation was a hand grenade about to go off.

In a low voice she said, "I appreciate you checking in on me, but I'm fine."

"Shit . . ."

"Yes, I believe that covers the situation well. Good-bye, Butch."

As she hung up the phone, she realized she was shaking all over.

The ringer went off again immediately and she glared at the bedside table. With a quick lean-and-grab, she reached over and yanked the cord out of the wall.

Shoving her body down through the sheets, she curled over on her side. There was no way she was going to go to sleep, but she shut her eyes anyway.

As she fumed in the dark, she came to a conclusion. Even though everything was . . . well, *shit*, to use Butch's eloquent summation . . . she could say this at least: Being pissed off was better than having a panic attack.

Twenty minutes later, with his Sox cap pulled down low and a pair of sunglasses in place, Butch walked up to a dark green '03 Honda Accord. He looked left and right. No one was in the alley. There were no windows on the buildings. No cars passing by on Ninth Street.

Bending down, he picked up a hunk of rock from the ground and punched a hole in the driver's side window. As the alarm went apeshit, he stepped away from the sedan and melted into the shadows. No one came running. The noise died off.

He hadn't stolen a car since he was sixteen and a juvenile delinquent in South Boston, but he was back in the groove now. He walked over calmly, popped the door, and got in. The sequence that came next was quick and efficient, proving that crime, like his Southie accent, was something he'd never quite lost: He ripped off the panel underneath the dash. Found the wires. Put the right two together and . . . *vroom*.

Butch knocked out the rest of the shattered glass with his elbow and took off at a leisurely roll. As his knees were nearly up to his chest, he reached down, hit the release and shoved the seat back as far as it could go. Propping his arm on the window, like he was just taking in the early spring air, he leaned back, all casual.

When he got to the stop sign at the end of the alley, he hit the directional signal and came to a full-tire halt: Following traffic laws when you were in a stolen vehicle and had no ID on you was mission critical.

As he hung a louie and headed down Ninth, he felt bad for whatever Joe he'd just royally fucked over. Losing your wheels was not fun, and at the first stoplight he came to, he flipped open the glove compartment. Car was registered to one Sally Forrester. 1247 Barnstable Street.

He vowed to return the Honda to her ASAP and leave her a couple of grand to cover the inconvenience and the busted window.

Speaking of busted things . . . he tilted the rearview mirror toward himself. Oh, Christ, he was a train wreck. He needed a shave and his face was still a mess from the beatings. With a curse, he repositioned the glass so he didn't have to look at his road map of ugly.

Unfortunately, he still had a pretty clear picture of what was doing.

Heading out of town in Sally Forrester's Accord, sporting a puss like a punching bag, he got nailed with a good shot of self-awareness that he didn't appreciate. He'd always straddled that line between good and bad, had always been willing to bend the rules to suit his purposes. Hell, he'd cracked suspects around until they broke. Turned a blind eye on occasion if it would get him information on a case. Done drugs even after he'd joined the force—at least until he'd kicked his coke habit.

Only no-no's had been accepting bribes or sexual favors in the line of duty.

So, yeah, guess those two made him a hero.

And what was he doing now? Going after a female whose life was already a mess. Just so he could join the shit parade that was marching all over her.

Except he couldn't stop himself. After he'd called Marissa back on the phone over and over again, he'd been unable to keep himself from this road trip. Obsessed before, now he was possessed by her. He just had to see if she was all right and . . . well, hell, he was thinking maybe he could explain himself a little better.

There was one good thing, though. He truly seemed to be normal on the inside. Back at V's lair, he'd given himself a fresh slice in the arm with a knife because, hand-job results notwithstanding, he'd had to check his blood. The stuff had been red, thank God.

He took a deep breath—and then frowned. Putting his nose down to his bicep, he inhaled again. What the hell was this? Even with the wind rushing around in the car, and even through his clothes, he could smell something and no, not the cloying baby powder bullshit, which had fortunately faded. Now there was something else coming out of him.

Christ. Lately, it was like his body was a Glade PlugIn that couldn't make its mind up. But at least this spicy scent he liked—

Whoa. It couldn't be . . . No, it wasn't. Just wasn't. Right?

Absolutely not. He took out his cell phone and hit speed dial. As soon as he heard V's "hello," he said, "Heads up, I'm coming in."

There was a rasp and an inhale like Vishous had lit up. "I'm not surprised. But how are you getting here?"

"Sally Forrester's Honda."

"Whose?"

"No idea, I stole it. Look, I'm not pulling anything

197

strange." Yeah, right. "Well, the *lesser* kind of strange. I just need to see Marissa."

There was a long silence. "I'll let you in through the gates. Hell, the *mhis* has kept those slayers off this property for seventy years, so it's not like they could track you here. And I don't believe you're coming after us. Unless I've got my head wedged?"

"Damn straight I'm not."

Butch repositioned the Sox cap, and as his wrist passed by his nose, he got another whiff of himself. "Ah, V . . . listen, there is something a little weird going down with me."

"What?"

"I smell like men's cologne."

"Good for you. Females dig that kind of thing."

"Vishous, I smell like Obsession for Men, only I'm not *wearing* any, you feel me?"

There was silence on the line. Then, "Humans don't bond."

"Oh, really. You want to tell that to my central nervous system and my sweat glands? They'd appreciate the news flash, I'm sure."

"You noticed it after you two were in that patient room together?"

"It's been worse since then, but I thought I smelled something like it one other time."

"When?"

"I watched her get into a car with a male."

"How long ago?"

"Like three months. Palmed a Glock when I saw it happen."

Silence. "Butch, humans do not bond like we do."

"I know."

More silence. Then, "Any chance you were adopted?"

198

"No. And there are no fangs in the family, if that's what you're thinking. V, man, I drank some of you. Are you sure that I haven't become—"

"Genetics is the only way. That bite/turning thing's just bullshit folklore. Look, I'll let you through the gates and we'll talk after you see her. Oh, and check it. Wrath has no problem working over *lessers* to find out what happened to you. But he doesn't want you involved."

Butch's hand cranked hard on the steering wheel. "Fuck. That. I spent hours earning the right for payback, V. I *bled* for the right to knock those assholes around and get my own answers."

"Wrath—"

"Is a nice guy, but he ain't my king. So he can lay down on this."

"He just wants to protect you."

"Tell him I don't need the favor."

V let off a foul-sounding line or two in the Old Language, then muttered, "Fine."

"Thank you."

"One last deet, cop. Marissa's a guest of the Brotherhood's. If she doesn't want to see you, we're going to haul your ass out, true?"

"If she doesn't want to see me, I'll leave on my own. I swear."

SEVENTEEN

When Marissa heard a knock on the door, she cracked her eyes open and checked the clock. Ten in the morning and she hadn't slept at all. God, she was exhausted.

But maybe it was Fritz with a report on her things. "Yes?"

The door opened to reveal a big dark shadow with a baseball hat.

She sat up, keeping the covers to her bare breasts. "Butch?"

"Hi." He removed the cap from his head, crushing it in one hand, scrubbing his hair around with the other.

She willed a candle to light. "What are you doing here?"

"Ah . . . I wanted to make sure you were okay in person. Plus your phone . . ." His eyebrows lifted as if he'd caught sight of the cord she'd ripped out of the wall. "Um, yeah . . . your phone isn't working. Mind if I come in for a minute?"

As she took a deep breath, all she smelled was him, the scent going in her nose and blooming all over her body.

Bastard, she thought. *Irresistible bastard.*

"Marissa, I won't crowd you, I promise. And I know you're pissed off. But can we just talk?"

"Fine," she said, shaking her head. "But don't think we're going to solve anything."

As he stepped forward, it dawned on her that this was a bad idea. If he wanted to talk, she should meet him downstairs. After all, he was very male. And she was very naked. And they were now . . . yup, shut in a bedroom together.

Good planning. Excellent work. Maybe she should jump out a window next.

Butch leaned back against the door he'd closed. "First, are you all right here?"

"Yes, I am." God, this was awkward. "Butch—"

"I'm sorry I got all Humphrey Bogart, big man on you." His bruised face assumed a wince. "It's not that I don't think you can take care of yourself. I'm absolutely scared shitless of myself and I can't handle the idea of you getting hurt."

Marissa stared at him. See, this was simply awful. This humble apology stuff was liable to get through to her if he kept it up. "Butch—"

"Wait, please—just hear me out. Hear me out and then I'll leave." He inhaled slowly, his big chest expanding under his fine black coat. "Keeping you away from me seems like the only way to make sure you're safe. But that's about me being dangerous, not you being weak. I know you don't need to be sheltered or have some kind of caretaker."

In the long silence that followed, she measured him. "So prove it, Butch. Tell me what really happened to you. There was no car accident, was there?"

He rubbed his eyes. "I got jacked by some *lessers*." As she gasped, he said quickly, "It was no big deal. Honestly—"

She put her hand up. "Stop. Give me all of it or none of it. I don't want half-truths. It demeans us both."

He cursed. Did some more eye scrubbing.

"Butch, talk or get out."

"Okay . . . okay." His hazel stare lifted to her face. "As far as we can figure, I was interrogated for twelve hours."

She gripped the sheets hard enough to numb out her fingers. "Interrogated . . . how?"

"I don't remember much, but based on the damage, I'd say pretty standard stuff."

"Standard . . . stuff?"

"Electroshock, bare-knuckle punches, under-the-fingernail shit." As he stopped, she was very certain the list continued.

A wash of bile bubbled up her throat. "Oh . . . God . . ."

"Don't think about it. It's over. Done with."

Sweet Virgin in the Fade, how could he say that?

"Why—" She cleared her throat. And thought that she'd wanted the whole story so she damn well better show him she could handle it. "Why were you quarantined, then?"

"They put something in me." He untucked his silk button-down and flashed his black abdominal scar. "V found me left for dead in the woods and took out whatever it was, but now I'm like . . . connected to the *lessers*." As she stiffened, he dropped the shirt. "Yeah, the slayers, Marissa. The ones who are trying to exterminate your kind. So believe me when I tell you, my need to know what was done to me isn't some kind of kumbaya, find-my-inner-self bullshit. Your enemies tampered with my body. They put something *inside* of me."

"Are you . . . one of them?"

"I don't want to be. And I don't want to hurt you or anyone else. But see, this is the problem. There's too much shit I don't know."

"Butch, let me help you."

He cursed. "What if—"

"*What ifs* don't cut it." She took a deep breath. "I won't lie. I'm scared. But I don't want to turn my back on you and you're a fool to try and make me."

He shook his head, respect in his eyes. "You always been this courageous?"

"No. But it appears that for you, I guess I am. Are you going to let me in?"

"I want to. I feel like I need to." But it was quite a

while before he crossed the room. "Is it okay for me to sit next to you?"

When she nodded and moved over, he lowered himself onto the bed, the mattress dipping down from his weight, her body sliding into his. He stared at her for the longest time before reaching for her hand. God, his palm was so warm and big.

He bent down and brushed his lips over her knuckles, then rubbed his mouth back and forth. "I want to lie down next to you. Not for sex. Not for anything like that. Just—"

"Yes."

As he stood up, she lifted the sheets, but he shook his head. "I stay on top."

He took off his coat and stretched out beside her. Pulled her up close. Kissed the top of her head.

"You seem really tired," he said in the candlelight.

"I feel really tired."

"So sleep and let me watch over you."

She wedged herself even more tightly against his big body and exhaled. It was so good just to rest her head on his chest and feel his warmth and smell him up close. He stroked her back slowly, and she fell asleep so fast she didn't realize she'd gone under until she felt the bed moving and woke up.

"Butch?"

"I've got to go talk with Vishous." He kissed the back of her hand. "You keep resting. I don't like how pale you are."

She smiled a little. "No caretaking."

"That was just a suggestion." His lips lifted on one side. "How about we meet before First Meal? I'll wait for you downstairs in the library."

When she nodded, he leaned down and ran his fingertip

across her cheek. Then he glanced at her lips and the scent he was throwing off abruptly got stronger.

Their eyes locked.

It took less than a second before a craving lit off in her veins, a kind of burning, clenching need. Of their own accord, her eyes shifted from his face to his throat and her fangs began to throb as her reality shrunk to nothing but instinct: She wanted to pierce his thick vein. She wanted to feed from him. And she wanted him to have sex with her body while she did.

Bloodlust.

Oh, God. That's why she was so tired. She hadn't been able to feed from Rehvenge the other night, and then there had been all the stress of Butch being so ill, followed by his taking off. Plus the thing with Havers.

Not that the whys mattered at the moment. All she knew was the hunger.

Her lips parted and she started to reach forward—

Except what would happen if she drank from him?

Well, that was easy. She'd drain him dry trying to satisfy herself because his human blood was so weak. She would kill him.

But God, he would taste good.

She cut off the voice of the bloodlust, and in an act of iron will, put her arms under the sheets. "I'll see you tonight."

As Butch straightened, his eyes dulled and he put his hands over the front of his hips, like he was hiding an erection. Which naturally made the urge to grab him get even stronger.

"You take care of yourself, Marissa," he said in a low, sad tone.

He was at the door when she said, "Butch?"

"Yeah?"

"I don't think of you as weak."

He frowned as if wondering where that came from. "Neither do I. Sleep well, beautiful. I'll see you soon."

When she was alone, she waited for the hunger to pass and it did. Which gave her some hope. With everything that was going on right now, she would love to put feeding off for a little while. Getting so close to Rehvenge just seemed wrong.

EIGHTEEN

Van drove downtown as night came rolling over Caldwell. After getting off the highway, he took a half-assed access road to the river, easing his truck along a pothole-riddled strip that ran beneath the city's big bridge. Stopping under a pylon marked F-8 in orange spray paint, he got out and looked around.

Traffic overhead rushed by, semis bumping along with echoing thunder, cars letting off the occasional horn blast. Down here, at river level, the Hudson was almost as loud as the din from above. The day had been the first to carry a shot of spring warmth, and the water was flowing fast from the runoff of melting snow.

The dark gray rush looked like liquid asphalt. Smelled like dirt.

He scanned the area, instincts hackling up. Man, alone under the bridge was never a good place to be. Especially as daylight faded.

Fuck this, he shouldn't have come. He turned back to his truck.

Xavier stepped from the shadows. "Glad you made it, son."

Van sucked back his surprise. Shit, the guy was like some kind of ghost. "Why couldn't we do this over the phone?" Well, didn't that sound weak. "I got things I have to fucking do."

"I need you to help me with something."

"I told you I wasn't interested."

Xavier smiled a little. "Yes, you did, didn't you."

The sound of wheels on loose gravel percolated into Van's ears and he looked to the left. The Chrysler Town & Country, that gold-toned, utterly forgettable minivan, was pulling up right next to him.

Keeping his eyes on Xavier, Van put his hand in his pocket and slipped his finger into the trigger of his nine. If they were going to try and whack him, they were going to get a lead fight.

"There's something in the back for you, son. Go ahead. Open her up." There was a pause. "Afraid, Van?"

"Fuck that." He walked over, ready to pull out his heat. But when he slid back the door, all he could do was recoil. His brother, Richard, was tied up with nylon rope, and had strips of duct tape over his mouth and his eyes.

"*Jesus, Rich . . .*" When he reached forward, he heard a gun get cocked and he looked up at the minivan's driver. The pale-haired bastard behind the wheel was pointing what appeared to be a Smith & Wesson forty right in Van's face.

"I'd like you to rethink my invitation," Xavier said.

Behind the wheel of Sally Forrester's Honda, Butch cursed as he took a left at a stoplight and saw a Caldwell PD patrol car parked at the Stewart's on the corner of Framingham and Hollis. Holy hell. Driving around in a lifted car with two grand in cash did not make a guy feel relaxed.

Good thing he had backup. V was right on his ass in the Escalade as they headed to the Barnstable Road address.

Nine and a half minutes later, Butch found Sally's little Cape Cod. After he killed the headlights and let the Accord roll to a stop, he broke the wire connection to cut off the engine. The house was dark, so he walked right up to the front door, shoved the envelope with the cash through the mail slot, and then beat feet across the road for the Escalade. He wasn't worried about getting caught on this quiet street. If anyone asked questions, V would just do a mental Windex on them.

He was getting into the SUV when he froze, an odd feeling rushing through him.

For no apparent reason, his body started to ring—that was the only way he could describe it. Like there was a cell phone smack dead in the center of his chest.

Down the street . . . down the street. He had to go down the street.

Oh, God—*lessers* were there.

"What is it, cop?"

"I feel them. They're close."

"Game on, then." Vishous slipped out from behind the wheel and they both shut their doors. As V hit the alarm, the Escalade's lights flashed once. "Go with it, cop. Let's see where this takes us."

Butch started walking. Then fell into a jog.

Together they ran through the shadows of the peaceful sub-division, staying out of the pools of light thrown by porches and streetlamps. They cut through someone's backyard. Dodged around an aboveground pool. Sidled past a garage.

The neighborhood got shittier. Dogs barked in warning. A car passed by with no headlights on and rap thumping. And then an abandoned house. Followed by an empty lot. Until finally they came up to a decrepit two-story from the seventies that was surrounded by a nine-foot-high wooden fence.

"In here," Butch said, looking around for a gate.

"Give me your leg, cop."

As Butch grabbed the top of the fence and cocked his

knee, V tossed him over the thing like he was the morning newspaper. He landed in a crouch.

There they were. Three *lessers*. Two of whom were dragging a male out of the house by his arms.

Butch went into an instant overboil. He was radioactive angry about what had been done to him, frustrated by his fears for Marissa, trapped by his human nature—and those slayers became the focal point of his aggression.

Except V materialized next to him and grabbed his shoulder. As Butch wheeled around to tell the brother to fuck off, Vishous hissed, "You can have at them. Just keep it quiet. We've got eyes everywhere and without Rhage around, I need to fight on all cylinders, true? So I can't pull off no *mhis*. I'm not going to be able to mask this one."

Butch stared at his roommate, realizing this was the first time he'd ever been given free rein to go fight. "Why are you letting me in now?"

"We gotta be sure whose side you're on," V said, unsheathing a dagger. "And this is how we'll know. So I'll take the two with the civilian and you hit the other one."

Butch nodded once, then sprang forward, aware of a great roaring between his ears and within his body. As he gunned for the *lesser* that was about to move in on the house, the thing turned like he heard the approach.

The bastard merely looked annoyed as Butch ran up on him. "About time you backups showed." The slayer pivoted away. "There are two females in here. The blonde's really fast, so I want her—"

Butch tackled the *lesser* from behind and made like a vise, clamping on to the fucker's head and shoulders. It was like mounting a rodeo horse. The slayer went shit wild and spun around, grabbing at Butch's legs and arms.

When that didn't work, the thing slammed the two of them back against the house hard enough to dent the aluminum siding.

Butch stayed locked on, his forearm tight against the *lesser*'s esophagus, his other hand on his straining wrist, pulling back. To get an even better hold, he linked his legs around the slayer's hips, crossed his ankles, and squeezed with his thighs.

It took a while, but asphyxia and exertion eventually slowed the undead down.

Except, holy hell, by the time the *lesser*'s knees started to wobble, Butch knew what a pinball felt like. He'd been knocked against the house's exterior, then its front doorjamb, and now they were in the hall and he was getting banged back and forth in the narrow space. His brains were pinging around the inside of his skull and his internal organs were like scrambled eggs, but, goddamn it, he was not letting go. The longer he kept the *lesser* occupied, the more chance those females had to escape—

Oh, shit, it was Tilt-A-Whirl time. The world spun and Butch hit the floor first, the *lesser* turtling over on top of him.

Bad place to be. Now he was the one who couldn't breathe.

He threw out a leg, kicked against the wall, and slid out from under, wrenching the *lesser*'s torso. Unfortunately, the bastard pulled a twist move, too, and the two of them started rolling around and around on the nasty orange carpet. Finally, Butch's strength wore out.

With little effort, the slayer flipped him over so they were face-to-face, then cranked Butch into a submission hold, immobilizing him.

Okay . . . now would be a great time for V to show up.

Except then the *lesser* looked down and met Butch's eyes, and everything just slowed down. Ground to a halt. Stopped. Dead.

Another kind of viser action bolted them together, but this was a locking of stares and Butch was the one in control, even though he was on the bottom of the body pile. The *lesser* became transfixed and Butch followed his instincts.

Which meant he opened his mouth and began to inhale slowly.

But he wasn't taking in air. He was taking in the slayer. Absorbing him. Consuming him. It was as before in the alley, but now no one stopped the process. Butch just kept sucking in an endless draw, a streaming black shadow passing from the *lesser's* eyes and nose and mouth and going into Butch.

Who felt like a balloon filling up with smog. Who felt like he was assuming the mantle of the enemy.

When it was over, the slayer's body just disintegrated into ash, the fine mist of gray particles falling onto Butch's face, chest, and legs.

"Holy shit."

In utter despair, Butch shifted his eyes around. V was leaning in through the front door, holding on to the frame as if the house was the only thing keeping him standing.

"Oh, God." Butch rolled over onto his side, the ugly carpet scratchy on his cheek. He was wretchedly sick to his stomach, and his throat burned like he'd been hammering Scotch for hours. But worst, the evil was back in him, running through his veins.

As he breathed through his nose, he smelled baby powder. And he knew it was him, not remnants of the *lesser*.

"V . . ." he said with desperation, "what did I just do?"

"I don't know, cop. I have no idea."

Twenty minutes later, Vishous shut himself and his roommate in the Escalade and hit all the locks. As he dialed his cell phone and put it up to his ear, he eyed Butch. The cop was looking multifactorial ill in the passenger seat, like he was seasick and jet-lagged and coming down with the flu all at the same time. And he reeked of baby powder, as if he were sweating out the scent through every one of his pores.

While the phone rang, Vishous started the SUV, threw it into drive, and thought back to Butch working some kind of mojo shit on that *lesser*. To steal a phrase from the cop, *Holy Mary, Mother of God*.

Man . . . that suck job was a hell of a weapon. But the complications were legion.

V glanced over again. And realized it was to reassure himself that Butch wasn't eyeing him as a *lesser* would.

Fuck.

"Wrath?" V said as his call was answered. "Listen, I—shit . . . our boy here just consumed a *lesser*. No . . . not Rhage. Butch. Yes, *Butch*. What? No, I saw him . . . consume the thing. I don't know how, but the *lesser* disappeared into dust. No, no knife involved. He inhaled the damn thing. Look, just to be conservative, I'm going to take him to my place and let him sleep it off. Then I'm coming home, true? Right . . . No, I have no clue how he did it, but I'll give you the blow-by-blow when I get to the compound. Yup. Right. Uh-huh. Oh, for God's—*yes* I'm *fine* and quit asking me that. Later."

As he hung up and tossed the phone onto the dash, Butch's voice drifted over, all weak and hoarse. "I'm glad you're not taking me home."

"Wish I could, though." V took out a hand-rolled and lit it, drawing hard on the thing. As he blew smoke, he cracked one of the windows. "Jesus Christ, cop, how did you know you could do that?"

"I didn't." Butch coughed a little, like his throat was bothering him. "Lemme have one of your daggers."

V frowned and looked at his roommate. "Why?"

"Just give it to me." As V hesitated, Butch shook his head with sadness. "I'm not going to come after you with it. I swear on my mother."

They hit a red light and V shifted his seat belt out of the way so he could unsheathe one of his blades from his chest holster. He gave the weapon to Butch handle first, then checked the road ahead. When he glanced back over, Butch had shoved up his sleeve and was slicing himself on the inside of his forearm. They both stared at what came out.

"I'm bleeding black again."

"Well . . . not a surprise."

"I smell like one, too."

"Yeah." Man, V did not like the way the cop was fixated on that dagger. "How 'bout you give my blade back, buddy?"

Butch handed the thing over and V wiped the black steel on his leathers before resheathing the weapon.

Butch wrapped his arms around his middle. "I don't want to be anywhere around Marissa when I'm like this, okay?"

"No problem. I'll take care of everything."

"V?"

"What?"

"I will die rather than hurt you."

V's eyes shot across the space between them. The cop's face was grim and his hazels were dead serious, the words not a mere expression of thought but a vow: Butch O'Neal was prepared to take himself out of the game if shit got critical. And he was fully capable of doing the job.

V inhaled on his hand-rolled again and tried not to get even more attached to the human. "Hopefully it won't come to that."

Please, God, let it not come to that.

NINETEEN

Marissa paced another circle around the Brotherhood's library and ended up back at the windows that looked out over the terrace and the pool.

The day must have been a warm one, she thought. There were patches in the snow that had melted through, revealing black slate at the terrace or brown ground over the lawn—

Oh, who the hell cared about the goddamned landscape.

Butch had left after First Meal, saying he had a quick errand to run. Which was fine. Dandy. A-okay. But that had been two hours ago.

She wheeled around as someone came into the room. "*Butch*—oh . . . it's . . . you."

Vishous stood in the archway, a full-blooded warrior framed by the extravagant gold-leaf molding around him.

Dear Virgin in the Fade . . . his expression was utterly blank, the kind of thing you put on your face when you had bad news to deliver.

"Tell me he is alive," she said. "Save my life right here and now and tell me he is alive."

"He is."

Her knees buckled and she grabbed on to one of the wall-to-wall bookshelves. "But he isn't coming, is he?"

"No."

As they stared at each other, she noticed absently that he was wearing a fine white shirt with his black leathers: a Turnbull and Asser button-down. She recognized the cut. It was what Butch wore.

Marissa wrapped an arm around her waist, overwhelmed by Vishous even though he was all the way across the room. He seemed like such a dangerous male—and not because of the tattoos on his temple or the black goatee or that fearsome body. The Brother was cold to the core, and someone that removed was capable of anything.

"Where is he?" she asked.

"He's okay."

"Then why isn't he here?"

"It was just a quick fight."

A . . . *quick* . . . *fight*. Her knees loosened again as memories of being at Butch's bedside crashed over her. She saw him lying on hospital sheets in that johnny, beaten up, almost dying. Contaminated by something evil.

"I want to see him."

"He's not here."

"Is he at my brother's?"

"No."

"And you're not going to tell me where he is, are you?"

"He's going to call you in a little bit."

"Was it with the *lessers?*" When all Vishous did was continue to stare at her, her heart kicked into overdrive. She couldn't bear for Butch to be involved in this war. Look what had already been done to him. "Goddamn it, tell me if it was with the slayers, you smug bastard."

Only silence. Which of course answered the question. And also suggested that Vishous didn't care whether or not she was pissed off at him.

Marissa gathered up her skirts and marched over to the warrior. Up close, she had to crane her neck to look at his face. God, those eyes, those diamond white eyes with the midnight blue lines around the irises. Cold. So very cold.

She did her best to hide her shiver, but he caught it. Tracked it in her shoulders.

216

"Scared of me, Marissa?" he said. "Exactly what do you think I'd do to you?"

She ignored that. "I don't want Butch fighting."

One black eyebrow cocked. "Not your call."

"It's too dangerous for him."

"After tonight, I'm not so sure about that."

The Brother's hard smile made her take a step back, but anger saved her from a full-on retreat. "You remember that hospital bed? You saw what they did to him last time. I thought you cared about him."

"If it turns out he's an asset, and he's willing, he will be used."

"I don't like the Brotherhood right now," she blurted. "Or you."

She started to go past him, but his hand shot out, grabbing her arm and jerking her close, holding her, though not hurting her. His eyes went over her face, her neck, then swept down her body.

And that was when she saw the fire in him. The volcanic heat. The interior inferno that was caged by all that glacial self-control.

"Let go of me," she whispered, heart beating hard.

"I'm not surprised." His reply was quiet . . . quiet as a sharp knife laid on a table.

"About w-what?"

"You're a female of worth. So you shouldn't like me." Those glittering eyes narrowed on her face. "You know, you really are the great beauty of the species, aren't you."

"No . . . no, I am not—"

"Yeah, you are." Vishous's voice grew lower and lower, softer, until she wasn't sure whether she was hearing it or he was in her mind. "Butch is a wise choice for you, female. He'll take good care of you, if you let him. Will you, Marissa? Will you let him . . . take care of you?"

As those diamond eyes hypnotized her, she felt his thumb move over her wrist, shifting back and forth. Her heart rate gradually slowed to the lazy rhythm.

"Answer my question, Marissa."

She swayed. "What . . . what did you ask?"

"Will you let him take you?" Vishous leaned down and put his mouth at her ear. "Will you take him inside of you?"

"Yes . . ." she breathed, aware they were talking about sex, but too seduced in the moment not to reply. "I will have him within me."

That hard hand loosened, then stroked her arm, traveling over her skin warmly, strongly. He looked down at where he was touching her, an expression of deep concentration on his face. "Good. That's good. The two of you are beautiful together. A fucking inspiration."

The male turned on his heel and stalked out of the room.

Disoriented, shocked, she stumbled over to the library's doorway and saw Vishous going up the stairs, his heavy thighs eating the distance with no effort.

Without warning, he stopped and snapped his head her way. Her hand fluttered to her throat.

Vishous's smile was as dark as his eyes were pale. "Come on, Marissa. Did you really think I was going to kiss you?"

She gasped. That was exactly what had been going through her—

Vishous shook his head. "You're Butch's female and whether you end up with him or not, you always will be to me." He started up again. "Besides, you're not my type. Your skin's too soft."

V walked into Wrath's study and shut the double doors, thinking that little chat with Marissa had been disturbing as hell on a variety of levels. God, he hadn't gotten into anyone's thoughts for weeks now, but he'd read hers clear as day. Or maybe he'd just hazarded a guess. Hell, more likely the latter. Going by those saucer-wide eyes of hers, she'd clearly been convinced he was going to lay his mouth on her.

Wrong. The reason he'd stared at her was because she fascinated him, not attracted him. He wanted to know what it was about her that made Butch lay with her with such warmth and love. Was it something in her skin? Her bones? Her beauty? How did she do it?

How did she take Butch to a place were sex was communion?

V rubbed the center of his chest, aware of a piercing loneliness.

"Hello? My brother?" Wrath leaned onto his dainty desk, all heavy forearms and big hands. "You here to report or make like sculpture?"

"Yeah . . . sorry. Distracted."

Vishous lit up and replayed the fight, especially the final part when he'd watched a *lesser* disappear into the thin air, thanks to his roommate.

"God damn . . ." Wrath breathed.

V went to the fireplace and chucked the ass end of his hand-rolled into the flames. "Never seen anything like it."

"Is he okay?"

"Don't know. I'd take him to Havers to get checked out, but there's no going back to the clinic with the cop. Right now, he's at my place with his cell phone. He'll call me if things get ratty and I'll think of something."

Wrath's brows disappeared behind his mirrored wrap-arounds. "How confident are you that the *lessers* can't trace him?"

"Damn confident. In both cases, he's the one that went

after them. It's like he smelled them or something. When he gets up close, they seem to recognize him, but it's always him engaging first."

Wrath looked down at the stacks of paper on his desk. "Don't like him out there alone. Don't like it at all."

There was a long pause and then V said, "I could go get him. Bring him home."

Wrath took off his sunglasses. As he rubbed his eyes, the king's ring, that massive black diamond, sparkled on his middle finger. "We got females here. One of whom is pregnant."

"I could watch him. I could make sure he stays in the Pit. I could seal off the tunnel access."

"Hell." Those sunglasses got slid back on. "Go get him. Bring our boy home."

For Van, the scariest part of his induction into the Lessening Society was not the physical conversion or the Omega or the involuntary nature of it all. Not that that shit wasn't horrifying. It was. Jesus Christ . . . to know that evil actually existed and walked around and . . . did things to people? Yeah, huge wake-up call in a bad way.

But not the scariest part.

With a grunt, Van pushed himself up on the bare mattress he'd been on for God only knew how long. Staring down at his body, he extended his arm out from his shoulder socket, then curled it in tight.

No, the scariest part was the fact that when he'd finally stopped throwing up and managed to catch his breath, he couldn't quite remember why he hadn't wanted to join in the first place. Because the power was back in his body; the roar from his twenties was parked in his garage once again. Thanks to the Omega, he was returned to himself, no longer a faded, washed-up shadow of what he once had been. Sure, the means had been a mind bender of terror and disbelief. But the ends . . . were glorious.

He flexed his bicep again, just feeling the muscles and bones, loving them.

"You're smiling," Xavier said as he came into the room.

Van looked up. "I feel great. Really . . . fucking . . . great."

Xavier's eyes were distant. "Don't let it go to your head. And listen up good. I want you to stay close to me. You never go anywhere without me. We clear?"

"Yeah. Sure." Van shifted his legs off the bed. He couldn't wait to run and see what that felt like.

As he stood, Xavier's expression was odd. Frustration?

"What's wrong?" Van asked.

"Your induction was so . . . average."

Average? Getting your heart taken out and your blood exchanged for something that looked like tar didn't count as average to him. And for chrissakes, Van wasn't interested in this buzz-kill routine. The world was fresh and new again as far as he was concerned. He was reborn.

"Sorry to disappoint you," he muttered.

"I'm not disappointed in you. Yet." Xavier checked his watch. "Get dressed. We leave in five."

Van went into the bathroom and stood over the toilet, only to realize he didn't have to go. And he wasn't thirsty or hungry either.

Okay, this was weird. It seemed unnatural not to follow his morning routine.

Leaning forward, he glanced at his reflection in the mirror above the sink. His features were the same, but his eyes were different.

With unease snaking through him, he rubbed his face with his palm to reassure himself that he was flesh and blood still. As he felt the bones of his skull through his thin skin, he thought of Richard.

Who was at home with his wife and two kids. Safe now.

Van would have no more contact with his family. Ever. But his brother's life seemed like a fair trade. Fathers mattered.

Besides, look at all he'd gained for that sacrifice. His special part was back in business.

"You ready to go?" Xavier called from down the hall.

Van swallowed hard. Man, whatever he was caught up in was so much darker and deeper than just a criminal life. He was an agent of evil now, wasn't he?

And that should have bothered him more.

Instead, he reveled in his power, ready to wield it. "Yeah. I am."

Van smiled at his reflection, feeling as if his special destiny had been realized. And he was exactly who he needed to be.

TWENTY

That following evening, Marissa was getting out of the shower when she heard the shutters lift for the night.

God, she was tired, but then it had been a busy day. Very busy.

Although the good thing was at least everything she'd had to do had kept her from obsessing about Butch. Well, mostly kept her mind off him. Okay, sometimes stopped her from thinking about him.

The fact that he'd been hurt by a *lesser* again was only part of her preoccupation. She wondered where he was and who was caring for him. Not her brother, obviously. But did Butch have someone else?

Had he spent the day with another female, being nursed by her?

Sure, Marissa had talked to him last night and he'd said all the right things: He'd reassured her he was okay. Hadn't lied about fighting with a *lesser*. Been up-front about not wanting to come see her until he felt more stable. And he'd told her he'd meet her at First Meal tonight.

She'd assumed if he'd been stilted, it was because he'd been rattled, and she didn't blame him. But it was only after they hung up that she realized everything she'd neglected to ask.

Disgusted with her insecurities, she marched over to the laundry chute and shoved her towel down the mouth of it. As she straightened, she got so dizzy she weaved on her bare feet and had to sink down into a crouch. It was either that or pass out cold.

Please let this need to feed pass. *Please*.

She breathed deeply until her head cleared, then slowly stood up and headed for the sink. As she cupped her hands under cold water and splashed her face, she knew she was going to have to go to Rehvenge. Just not tonight. Tonight she needed to be with Butch. She needed to see him up close and reassure herself that he was okay. And she had to talk to him. He was the important thing, not her body.

When she felt steady enough, she got dressed in that teal YSL gown. God, she really hated wearing the thing now. It held such bad associations for her, as if the scene with her brother was a nasty smell that had permeated the dress's fabric.

The knock she'd been waiting for came at precisely six o'clock. Fritz was on the other side of the bedroom door, the old male smiling as he bowed.

"Good evening, mistress."

"Good evening. Do you have the papers?"

"As you asked."

She took the file he held out and went to a bureau, where she leafed through the documents and signed on several lines. As she closed the top of the folder, she laid her hand on it.

"This is over so fast."

"We have good lawyers, don't we?"

She took a deep breath and handed the power of attorney and the rental papers back to him. Then she went to the bedside table and picked up the bracelet from the suite of diamonds she'd still had on when she'd arrived at the Brotherhood's compound. As she held the glittering length out to the *doggen*, she had a fleeting thought that her father had given her the set over a hundred years ago.

He would never have guessed how it would be used. Thank the Scribe Virgin.

The butler frowned. "Master does not approve."

"I know, but Wrath has been too kind to me already." The diamonds sparkled as they hung from her fingertips. "Fritz? Take the bracelet."

"Master really does not approve."

"He's not my *ghardian*. So it's not his call."

"He is king. Everything is his call." But Fritz took the piece of jewelry.

As he turned away, the *doggen* looked so stricken, she said, "Thank you for bringing me some of my undergarments and for dry-cleaning this gown. You are very thoughtful."

He brightened a little at a job well done. "Perhaps you should like me to retrieve a few of your dresses from your trunks?"

She looked down at the St. Laurent and shook her head. "I won't be here for long. Best to leave them packed."

"As you wish, mistress."

"Thank you, Fritz."

He paused. "You should know that I have put fresh roses in the library for your rendezvous this evening with our master Butch. He asked me to get some for your pleasure. He asked me to ensure they were as lovely and pale a gold as your hair."

She closed her eyes. "Thank you, Fritz."

Butch rinsed out his razor, tapped it on the edge of his sink, and shut off the water. According to the mirror, the shave hadn't helped much; in fact, it just showcased his bruises, which were now yellowing out. Crap. He wanted to look nice for Marissa, especially since last night had turned out to be such a mess.

As he stared at his reflection, he poked his front tooth, the one with the little chip out of it. Shit . . . if he wanted to look like he deserved her, he'd need plastic surgery, detox, and a full set of caps.

Whatever. He had other things to worry about if he was going to see her in ten minutes. She'd sounded like hell over the phone last night, and it looked like they were back to having distance between them. But at least she was willing to see his ass.

Which led to his big concern. He reached down and picked up a paring knife off the edge of the white sink. Extending his forearm, he—

"Cop, you're going to be full of holes if you keep this up."

Butch looked into the mirror. Behind him, V was leaning against the doorjamb, a glass of Goose and a cigarette in his hand. Turkish tobacco scented the air, pungent, masculine.

"Come on, V. I need to be sure. I know your hand works wonders, but . . ." He drew the blade over his skin, then closed his eyes, afraid of what was going to come out.

"It's red, Butch. You're okay."

He glanced at the wet crimson streak. "How do I know for sure, though?"

"You don't smell like a *lesser* anymore and you did last night." V came into the bathroom. "And secondly . . ."

Before Butch knew what was doing, V grabbed his forearm, bent down, and licked the cut, sealing it up quick.

Butch yanked out of his roommate's hold. "Jesus, V! What if that blood's contaminated!"

"It's fine. Just f—" With a boneless lurch, Vishous gasped and collapsed against the wall, eyes rolling back in his head, body twitching.

"Oh, God . . . !" Butch reached out in horror—

Only to have V cut the seizure off and calmly take a drink from his glass. "You're fine, cop. Tastes perfectly okay. Well, fine for human guy, which really ain't my 'tail of choice, you feel me?"

Butch hauled back and nailed his roommate in the arm with his fist. And as the brother cursed, Butch popped him another one.

V glared and rubbed himself. "*Christ*, cop."

"Suck it up, you deserve it."

Butch pushed by the brother and headed for his closet. As he tried to figure out what to wear, he was rough with his clothes, shoving them around on their hangers.

He stopped. Closed his eyes. "What the fuck, V. Last night I was bleeding black. Now I'm not. Is my body some kind of *lesser*-processing plant?"

V eased onto the bed, leaning back against the headboard, resting his glass on his leather-clad thigh. "Maybe. I don't know."

Man, he was so tired of feeling lost. "I thought you knew everything."

"Not fair, Butch."

"Shit . . . you're right. I apologize."

"Can we screw the 'sorry' part and let me hit you back instead?"

As they both laughed, Butch forced himself to pick a suit and ended up tossing a blue/black Zegan on the bed next to V. Then he fingered his ties. "I saw the Omega, didn't I. That thing in me was part of him. He put part of himself in me."

"Yeah. That's what I think."

Butch felt a sudden need to go to church and pray for his salvation. "No going back to normal for me, is there."

"Probably not."

Butch stared at his tie collection, getting swamped by the colors and the choices. As he stood frozen with indecision, for some reason he thought about his family in South Boston.

Talk about normal . . . and they were unchanging, too, so relentlessly the same. For the O'Neal clan, there had been one pivotal event, and that tragedy had thrown the chessboard of the family up in the air. When the pieces had fallen, they'd landed in glue: After Jane had been raped and murdered when she was fifteen, everyone had stayed in their places. And he was the unforgiven outsider.

To cut off his train of thought, Butch pulled a bloodred Ferragamo from the rack. "So what's on deck for you tonight, vampire?"

"I'm supposed to be off."

"Good."

"No, bad. You know I hate not fighting, true?"

"You're strung too tight."

"Hah."

Butch glanced over his shoulder. "Do I need to remind you about this afternoon?"

V's eyes dropped to his glass. "Nothing doing."

"You woke up screaming so loud I thought you'd been shot. What the hell were you dreaming about?"

"Nothing."

"Don't try and fade me, it's annoying."

V swirled the vodka around. Swallowed it. "Just a dream."

"Bullshit. I've lived with you for nine months, buddy. You're stone quiet if you sleep at all."

"Whatever."

Butch dropped his towel, pulled on a pair of black boxers and took a starched white button-down out of the closet. "You should let Wrath know what's doing."

"How about we don't go there."

Butch put on the shirt, buttoned it up, then snapped the pin-striped pants off their hanger. "All I'm saying—"

"Can it, cop."

"God, you're a tight-lipped bastard. Look, I'm here if you want to talk, okay?"

"Don't hold your breath. But . . . 'preciate it." V cleared his throat. "By the way, I borrowed one of your shirts last night."

"That's cool. It's you whoring my socks that pisses me off."

"Didn't want to see your girl in fighting clothes. Which is all I got."

"She said you'd talked to her. I think you make her nervous."

V said something that sounded like "I should."

Butch looked over. "What did you say?"

"Nothing." V shot up off the bed and headed for the door. "Listen, I'm going to go hang at my other place tonight. Being here by myself when everyone's on the job makes me bat shit. You need me, come find me at the penthouse."

"V." As his roommate stopped and looked back, Butch said, "Thanks."

"For what?"

Butch lifted his forearm. "You know."

V shrugged. "Figured you'd feel better being around her that way."

John walked through the underground tunnel, his footsteps an echoing drumroll that made him feel how alone he was as nothing else could.

Well, alone except for his anger. That was with him always now, close as his own skin, coating him like his skin, too. Man, he couldn't wait for class to start tonight so he could let some of it out. He was twitching, over-activated, restless.

But maybe some of that was because, as he headed for the main house, he couldn't help remembering the first time he'd come this way with Tohr. He'd been so nervous then, and having the male next to him had been reassuring.

Happy fucking anniversary, John thought.

Three months ago tonight was when it had all gone down. Three months ago tonight, Wellsie's murder and Sarelle's murder and Tohr's disappearance had been dealt like bad-news Tarot cards. Bang. Bang. Bang.

And the aftermath had been a special kind of hell. For a couple of weeks following the tragedies, John had assumed Tohr would come back. He'd waited, hoped, prayed. But . . . nothing. No communication, no phone calls, no . . . nothing.

Tohr was dead. Had to be.

As John came up to the shallow set of stairs that led into the mansion, he could not bear to go through the hidden door into the foyer. He so wasn't interested in eating. Didn't want to see anyone. Didn't want to sit at the table. But sure as hell, Zsadist would come after him. The Brother had totally dragged him to the big house for meals the last couple of days. Which was embarrassing and pissed them both off.

John forced himself to go up the steps and into the mansion. To him, the foyer's blinding splash of color was an affront to the senses, no longer a feast for the eyes, and he headed for the dining room with his stare locked on the floor. When he walked under the grand arch, he saw that the table was set but not yet occupied. And he smelled roast lamb—Wrath's absolute favorite meal.

John's stomach rumbled with starvation, but he wasn't falling for it. Lately, however hungry he was, the instant he put food in his gut, even the kind specially made for a pre-trans, he got cramps. And he was supposed to eat more for the change? Yeah, right.

When he heard light, rushing footfalls, he turned his head. Someone was racing along the second-floor balcony.

Then laughter drifted down from above. Glorious feminine laughter.

He leaned out the archway and glanced at the grand staircase.

Bella appeared on the landing above, breathless, smiling, a black satin robe gathered in her hands. As she slowed at the head of the stairs, she looked over her shoulder, her thick dark hair swinging like a mane.

The pounding that came next was heavy and distant, growing louder until it was like boulders hitting the ground. Obviously, it was what she was waiting for. She let out a laugh, yanked her robe up even higher, and started down the stairs, bare feet skirting the steps as if she were floating. At the bottom, she hit the mosaic floor of the foyer and wheeled around just as Zsadist appeared in the second-story hallway.

The Brother spotted her and went straight for the balcony, pegging his hands into the rail, swinging his legs up and pushing himself straight off into thin air. He flew outward, body in a perfect swan dive—except he wasn't over water, he was two floors up over hard stone.

John's cry for help came out as a mute, sustained rush of air—

Which was cut off as Zsadist dematerialized at the height of the dive. He took form twenty feet in front of Bella, who watched the show with glowing happiness.

Meanwhile, John's heart pounded from shock . . . then pumped fast for a different reason.

Bella smiled up at her mate, her breath still hard, her hands still gripping the robe, her eyes heavy with invitation. And Zsadist came forward to answer her call, seeming to get even bigger as he stalked over to her. The Brother's bonding scent filled the foyer, just as his low, lionlike growl did. The male was all animal at the moment . . . a very sexual animal.

"You like to be chased, *nalla*," Z said in a voice so deep it distorted.

Bella's smile got even wider as she backed up into a corner. "Maybe."

"So run some more, why don't you." The words were dark and even John caught the erotic threat in them.

Bella took off, darting around her mate, going for the billiards room. Z tracked her like prey, pivoting around, his eyes leveled on the female's streaming hair and graceful body. As his lips peeled off his fangs, the white canines elongated, protruding from his mouth. And they weren't the only response he had to his *shellan*.

At his hips, pressing into the front of his leathers, was an erection the size of a tree trunk.

Z shot John a quick glance and then went back to his hunt, disappearing into the room, that pumping growl getting louder. From out of the open doors, there came a delighted squeal, a scramble, a female's gasp, and then . . . nothing.

He'd caught her.

John put his hand on the wall, steadying a lurch he hadn't realized he'd fallen into. As he thought about what they were doing, his body grew curiously loose and a little tingly. Like maybe something was waking up.

When Zsadist came out a moment later, he had Bella in his arms, her dark hair trailing down his shoulder as she lounged in the strength that held her. Her eyes were locked on Z's face while he looked where he was going, her hand stroking his chest, her lips curved in a private smile.

There was a bite mark on her neck, one that had very

definitely not been there before, and Bella's satisfaction as she stared at the hunger in her *hellren*'s face was utterly compelling. John knew instinctively that Zsadist was going to finish two things upstairs: the mating and the feeding. The Brother was going to be at her throat and in between her legs. Probably at the same time.

God, John wanted that kind of connection.

Except what about his past? Even if he made it through his transition, how was he ever going to be that comfortable and confident with a female? Real males hadn't been through what he had, hadn't been forced at knifepoint into a hideous submission.

Hell, look at Zsadist. So strong, so powerful. Females went for that kind of thing, not weaklings like John. And there was no mistaking it. No matter how big John's body got, that's what he would always be: a weakling, marked forever by what had been done to him.

He turned away and went to the dining room table, sitting down alone in the midst of all the china and silver and crystal and candles.

But alone was okay, he decided.

Alone was safe.

TWENTY-ONE

While Fritz went upstairs to get Marissa, Butch waited in the library and thought about what a good guy the *doggen* was. When Butch had asked for a favor, the old man had been thrilled to take care of the request. Even though it had been an odd thing to ask.

When the smell of an ocean breeze drifted into the room, Butch's body threw out an instantaneous and very noticeable response. As he turned around, he made sure his suit jacket was in place.

Oh, Christ, she was beautiful in that teal gown. "Hey, baby."

"Hello, Butch." Marissa's voice was quiet, her hand unsure as she smoothed her hair. "You look . . . well."

"Yeah, I'm fine." Thanks to V's healing palm.

There was a long silence. Then he said, "Is it okay if I greet you properly?"

When she nodded, he went over and took her hand. As he bent down and kissed her, her palm was cold as ice. Was she nervous? Or ill?

He frowned. "Marissa, you want to sit down for a minute before we go in to dinner?"

"Please."

He led her over to a silk-covered couch and noticed that she was unsteady as she gathered the skirting of her gown and sat down with him.

He tilted her head around. "Talk to me." When she didn't speak right away, he pushed. "Marissa . . . you've got something on your mind, right?"

There was an awkward pause. "I don't want you fighting with the Brotherhood."

So that's what it was. "Marissa, last night was unexpected. I don't fight. Truly."

"But V said if you were willing, they were going to use you."

Whoa. News to him. Far as he knew, that thing the night before had been about testing his loyalty, not bringing him into the field as a regular gig. "Listen, the brothers have spent the last nine months keeping me *out* of fights. I'm not getting involved with the *lessers*. That's not my deal."

Her tension eased. "I just can't bear the thought of you being hurt like before."

"You don't worry about that. The Brotherhood does their thing, it's got little to do with me." He tucked a lock of hair behind her ear. "You got anything else you want to talk about, baby?"

"I do have a question."

"Ask me anything."

"I don't know where you live."

"Here. I live here." At her confusion, he nodded toward the library's open doors. "Across the courtyard in the gatehouse. I live with V."

"Oh—so where were you last night?"

"Right over there. But I stayed put."

She frowned. Then blurted, "Do you have other females?"

As if anyone could measure up to her? "No! Why do you ask?"

"We haven't layed together and you are a male with obvious . . . needs. Even now, your body has changed, hardening, growing big."

Crap. He'd tried to hide the erection, he really had. "Marissa—"

"Surely you need to be eased regularly. Your body is *phearsom*."

That didn't sound good. "What?"

"Potent and powerful. Worthy of entering a female."

Butch closed his eyes, thinking Mr. Worthy was really rising to the occasion now. "Marissa, there's no one but you. No one. How could there be?"

"Males of my kind may take more than one mate. I don't know if humans—"

"I don't. Not with you. I can't imagine myself with another woman. I mean, could you see yourself with someone else?"

In the hesitation that followed, a blast of cold shot up his spine, racing from his ass right into the base of his skull. And while he freaked, she fiddled with her extravagant skirt. Shit, she was flushing, too.

"I don't want to be with anyone else," she said.

"What aren't you telling me, Marissa?"

"There is someone I've been . . . around."

Butch's brain started to misfire, like his neuropathways had just blown apart and there were no more roads left in his gray matter. "'Around,' as in how?"

"It's not romantic, Butch. I swear. He's a friend, but he is a male, and that's why I'm letting you know." She put her hand to his face. "You're the one I want."

Staring into her solemn eyes, he couldn't doubt the truth in what she said. But shit, he felt like he'd been two-by-foured. Which was ridiculous and petty and . . . oh, God . . . he totally couldn't handle her being with someone else—

Pull it together, O'Neal. Just yank your ass back to reality, buddy. Right now.

"Good," he said. "I want to be the one for you. The only one."

Shoving aside all his jealous-guy horseshit, he kissed her hand . . . and was alarmed by the tremors in it.

He smoothed her cold fingers out between his palms. "What's going on with this shaking thing? Are you upset or are you sick? Do you need a doctor?"

She waved off his concern with none of her usual grace. "I can take care of it. Don't worry."

The hell he wouldn't. Christ, she was totally weak here, her eyes dilated, her movements uncoordinated. Ill, definitely ill.

"Why don't I take you back upstairs, baby? It'll kill me not to see you, but you don't look as if you're up to dinner. And I can bring you something to eat."

Her shoulders sagged. "I was so hoping . . . Yes, I think that would be best."

She stood up and swayed. As he caught her arm, he cursed that brother of hers. If she needed medical help, who would they take her to?

"Come on, baby. Lean on me."

Taking it slow, he led her up to the second floor, then down past Rhage and Mary's room, past Phury's, and even farther, until they got to the corner suite she'd been given.

She put her hand on the brass knob. "I'm sorry, Butch. I wanted to spend time with you tonight. I thought I had more strength."

"Can I please call a doctor?"

Her eyes were dazed but curiously unconcerned as she looked up into his face. "It's nothing I can't handle on my own. And I'm going to be all right soon."

"Man . . . right now I want to caretake like you read about."

She smiled. "Not necessary, remember?"

"Does it count if I just do it to ease myself?"

"Yes."

As they stared at each other, he had a screaming thought flash through his pea brain: He loved this woman. He loved her to death.

And he wanted her to know it.

He stroked her cheek with his thumb and decided it was a crying shame he didn't have the gift of words. He wanted to say something smart and tender, to give the L-bomb a good intro. Except he just came up dry.

So he blurted out, with his typical lack of finesse, "I love you."

Marissa's eyes popped.

Oh, shit. Too much, too soon—

She threw her arms around his neck and held on hard, burying her head in his chest. As he wrapped his arms around her, and geared up to go full sap all over the place, voices drifted down the hall. Opening her door, he ushered her into the room, figuring they needed a little privacy.

As he took her to the bed and helped her lie down, he lined up all kinds of sissy words in his head, ready to romance it up. But before he could say anything, she grabbed his hand and squeezed so hard his bones bent.

"I love you, too, Butch."

The words made him forget how to breathe.

Totally knocked out, he sank down to his knees next to the bed and had to smile. "Now, why you want to go and do that, baby? I'd figured you as a smart female."

She laughed softly. "You know why."

"You pity me?"

"Because you are a male of worth."

He cleared his throat. "I'm really not."

"How can you say that?"

238

Well, let's see. He'd been canned from Homicide for busting the nose of a suspect. He'd fucked mostly whores and lowlifes. Shot and killed other men. Then, yeah, there was that former cokehead shit and the current and persistent Scotch sucking. Oh, and did he mention he'd been sort of suicidal since his sister's murder all those years ago?

Yup, he was worth something. But only a trip to a landfill.

Butch opened his mouth, about to spill the beans, but then stopped himself.

Shut your face, O'Neal. The woman tells you she loves you and she's more than you deserve. Don't ruin it with the ugly past routine. Start fresh, here and now, with her.

He rubbed his thumb over her flawless cheek. "I want to kiss you. You feel like letting me?"

As she hesitated, he couldn't say he blamed her. Last time they'd been together had been a mess with his body kicking out that nasty stuff and her brother walking in. Plus she was clearly tired now.

He pulled back. "I'm sorry—"

"It's not that I don't want to be with you. I do."

"You don't have to explain. And I'm happy to just be around you, even if I can't—" *Be inside of you.* "Even if we don't . . . you know, make love."

"I'm holding back because I'm afraid I'll hurt you."

Butch smiled fiercely, thinking if she ripped his back to shreds hanging on tight, that was perfectly fine with him. "Doesn't matter if I get hurt."

"It matters to me."

He started to get up. "That's sweet of you. Now, listen, I'll just bring you up some—"

"Wait." Her eyes glowed in the dimness. "Oh . . . God, Butch . . . Kiss me."

He stilled. Then sank back down to his knees. "I'll take it easy. I promise."

Leaning into her, he put his mouth on hers and brushed her lips. Good Lord, she was soft. Warm. Shit . . . he wanted in. But he wasn't going to push.

Except then she grabbed on to his shoulders and said, "More."

Praying for control, he stroked her mouth once again, then tried to ease back. She followed, keeping them linked . . . and before he could stop himself, he ran his tongue across her lower lip. With an erotic sigh, she opened herself and he had to slide inside, couldn't possibly turn down the opportunity to penetrate her.

As she tried to get even closer to him, he moved his torso up on the bed, pressing his chest into her. Which was not such a hot idea. The way her breasts absorbed his weight set off a five-alarm fire in his body, reminding him just how desperate a man could be when he had his woman horizontal.

"Baby, I should stop." Because in another minute he was going to have her under him with that dress yanked up around her hips.

"No." She slipped her hands under his jacket and slid it off of him. "Not yet."

"Marissa, I'm getting raw here. Fast. And you don't feel well—"

"Kiss me." She dug her nails into his shoulders, the sting cutting through his fine shirt in a series of delicious little flares.

He growled and took her mouth a hell of a lot less gently.

Again, bad idea. The harder he kissed her, the harder she kissed back until their tongues were dueling and every muscle in him was twitching to mount her.

"I have to touch you," he groaned, shifting his whole body up on the bed and swinging his leg over hers. He palmed her hip and squeezed, then moved his hand up onto her rib cage just below the swell of her breast.

Shit. He was so on the ledge right now.

"Do it," she said into his mouth. "Touch me."

As her back arched, he took what she offered, capturing her breast, stroking it through the silk bodice of the gown. With a gasp, she put her hand over his, holding him tighter to her.

"Butch . . ."

"Oh, shit, let me see you, baby. Can I see you?" Before she could respond, he captured her mouth, but the way she met his tongue gave him his answer. He sat her up and started in on the buttons down the back of her gown. His hands were clumsy, but by some miracle the satin parted.

Except there were so many other layers to get through. Goddamn it, her skin . . . he had to get to her skin.

Impatient, aroused, fixated, he stripped the front of the gown off her, then pushed the straps of her slip down so that the pale silk pooled at her waist. The white corset that was revealed was an erotic surprise and he ran his hands all over it, feeling the structure of its bones and the warmth of her body underneath. But then he couldn't stand it any longer and all but tore the thing from her.

As her breasts were freed, her head fell back, the long, elegant lines of her neck and shoulders stretching out for him. Eyes on her face, Butch bent down to her and took one of her nipples with his mouth, suckling. Sweet heaven, he was going to come, she was so good. He was panting like a dog, already deranged from the sex, and they were nowhere near naked.

But she was right there with him, straining, hot, needy, her legs scissoring under her skirts. Man, this whole situation was spiraling out of control, a combustion engine turning over faster and faster with every second. And he was powerless to stop.

"Can I take this off you?" Shit, his voice was totally gone. "This gown . . . the whole thing?"

"Yes . . ." The word was a groan, a frantic groan.

Unfortunately, the dress was a project and damn it, he didn't have the patience to keep working all those buttons in the back of it. He ended up bunching the floor-length skirt at her hips and drawing a pair of whisper-thin white panties down her long, smooth legs. Then he ran his hands up the insides of her thighs, parting them.

As she tensed up, he stopped. "If you want me to back off, I will. In a heartbeat. But I just want to touch you again. And maybe . . . look at you." When she frowned, he started to pull down the dress. "It's okay—"

"I'm not saying no. It's just . . . oh, God . . . what if I'm unattractive there?"

Jesus, he could not comprehend why she'd ever worry about that. "Not possible. I already know you how perfect you are. I've felt you, remember?"

She took a deep breath.

"Marissa, I loved the feel of you. I really did. And I have a beautiful picture of you in my mind. I just want to know the reality."

After a moment, she nodded. "All right . . . go ahead."

Keeping their gazes locked, he swept his hand between her thighs and then . . . oh, yeah, that soft, secret place of hers. So slick and hot he swayed and dropped his mouth to her ear.

"You're so beautiful here." Her hips surged as he stroked her, his fingers light and slippery from her honey. "Mmm,

yeah . . . I want to be inside of you. I want to put my"—
the word *cock* was definitely too coarse, but that's what he
was thinking—"myself in you, baby. Right here. I want
to be surrounded by all this, held in you tight. So you
believe me when I say you're beautiful? Marissa? Tell me
what I want to hear."

"Yes . . ." As he rubbed a little deeper, she shivered.
"God . . . yes."

"You want me to come inside of you someday?"

"Yes . . ."

"You want me to fill you up?"

"Yes . . ."

"Good, because that's what I want." He nipped at
her earlobe. "I want to lose it deep in you and have you
fist me as you come, too. Mmm . . . rub yourself against
my hand, let me feel you move for me. Oh, shit . . .
that's nice. That's . . . work your core for me . . . oh,
yeah . . ."

Shit, he had to stop talking. Because if she took direction any better he was going to explode.

Oh, screw it. "Marissa, spread your legs farther apart
for me. Spread them wide. And don't stop what you're
doing."

As she complied, he slowly, discreetly, shifted back and
looked down her body. On the other side of yards of
twisted, teal blue satin, her creamy thighs were split open,
his hand disappearing between them, her hips rolling in
a rhythm that made his cock pop in his pants.

Latching on to the closest breast, he gently smoothed
one of her legs even wider. Then he moved all that skirting
to the side, lifted his head and removed his hand. Down
the flat plane of her stomach, past the dimple of her belly
button, over the perfectly pale skin of her pelvic cradle,
he saw the graceful little slit of her sex.

His whole body trembled. "So perfect," he whispered. "So . . . exquisite."

Enthralled, he moved down the bed and filled himself with the sight of her. Pink, glistening, delicate. And he was catching a contact high from her scent, his brain shorting out in a flickering series of sparks. "Oh . . . Jesus . . ."

"What's wrong?" Her knees snapped together.

"Not a thing." He pressed his lips to the top of her thigh and stroked her legs, trying to part them gently. "Never seen anything so beautiful."

Hell, *beautiful* didn't even cut it and he licked his mouth, his tongue desperate for so much more of that action. In an absent voice, he said, "God, baby, I want to go down on you so badly right now."

"Go down?"

He flushed at her confusion. "I . . . ah, I want to kiss you."

She smiled and sat up, taking his face between her hands. But when she tried to draw him to her, he shook his head.

"Not on your mouth this time." As she frowned, he eased his hand back between her thighs. "Here."

Her eyes flared so wide he wanted to curse. *Way to make her feel relaxed, O'Neal.*

"Why . . ." She cleared her throat. "Why would you want to do that?"

Good Lord, hadn't she ever heard of . . . well, of course not. Aristocrats probably had very polite, very missionary sex, and if they even knew about the oral stuff, they certainly would *never* tell their daughters about it. No wonder she was shocked.

"Why, Butch?"

"Ah . . . because if I do it right, you'll really enjoy it. And . . . yeah, so will I."

He glanced down her body. Oh, God, would he enjoy it. Going down on a woman had never been something he'd *had* to do before. With her? He needed it. He craved it. When he thought about making love to her with his mouth, every square inch of him got hard.

"I just want to taste you so damned much."

Her thighs relaxed a little. "Go . . . slowly?"

Holy shit, she was going to let him? He started to tremble. "I will, baby. And I'm going to make you feel good. I promise."

He shifted farther down the mattress, staying to the side of her so she didn't feel crowded. As he got closer to her core, his body whacked out on him even more and the small of his back got tight, just like it did right before he had an orgasm.

Man, he was *so* going to have to go slow. For the both of them.

"I love your scent, Marissa." He kissed her belly button, then her hip, going downward inch by creamy inch. Lower . . . lower . . . until he finally pressed his closed mouth to the top of her cleft.

Which was great for him. The problem was she went totally rigid. And jumped as he laid his hand on her outer thigh.

He moved back up a little and rubbed his lips back and forth on her stomach. "I'm so lucky."

"W-why?"

"How would you feel if someone trusted you like this? Trusted you with such a private thing?" He blew into her belly button, and she laughed a little as if the warm air tickled. "You honor me, you know that? You really do."

He soothed her out with words and leisurely kisses that lingered a little longer and went a little lower each time. When she was ready, he swept his hand down the inside of her leg, clasped the back of her knee and gently separated her just a couple of inches for himself. He kissed her slit softly, again and again. Until the tension eased out of her.

Then he lowered his chin, opened his mouth, and licked her. She gasped and sat up.

"Butch . . . ?" As if she were checking to make sure he knew what he'd done.

"Didn't I tell you?" He bent down and lightly traced up her pink flesh with his tongue. "This is all about French kissing, baby."

As he repeated the slow sweeps, her head fell back, and the tips of her breasts rose as her spine curled. Perfect. Just where he wanted her to be. Not worried about modesty or anything like that, just enjoying the feel of someone loving her like she deserved.

With a smile, he kept going, gradually dragging deeper and deeper until he got a real honest-to-God taste of her.

His eyes rolled back in his head as he swallowed. She was like nothing he'd ever pulled down his throat. The ocean and ripe melon and honey all together, a cocktail that made him want to weep from the perfection of it. More . . . he needed more. But goddamn, he had to put a choke hold on himself before he could keep going. He wanted to feast on her, and she wasn't ready for that kind of gluttony.

As he took a little breather, she tilted her head up. "Is it over?"

"Not by a long shot." Man, he loved that glassy, sexed-up look in her eyes. "Why don't you lie back and let me do my thing. We're just getting started here."

As she relaxed a little, he looked down at her secrets, seeing the high gloss on the tender flesh, thinking there was going to be a whole lot more of that shine when he was through. He kissed her again, then lollipopped her, flattening his tongue out and trolling up nice and lazy-like. Then he swept his mouth from side to side, nuzzling in farther, hearing her moan. With gentle pressure, he opened her thighs more and latched on to her, drawing on her core in a rhythmic sucking.

When she started to thrash, a buzzing lit off in his head, the shrill warning a Danger, Will Robinson from the civilized part of him that things were about to go meteoric. But he couldn't quit, especially as she grabbed onto the sheets and arched up like she was going to come at any second.

"Feel good?" He tickled the top of her cleft, flicking over the most sensitive part. "You like this? You like me tonguing you? Or maybe you like this . . ." He sucked her into his mouth and she cried out. "Oh, yeah . . . God, my lips are covered with you . . . feel them, feel me . . ."

He took her hand and brought it to his mouth, moving her fingers back and forth, then licking them clean. She watched him with wide eyes, panting, nipples tight. He was pushing her hard and he knew it, but she was right there with him.

He bit her palm. "Tell me you want this. Tell me you want me."

"I . . ." Her body undulated on the bed.

"Tell me you want me." He nailed her harder with his teeth. Shit, he wasn't sure why he needed to hear it from her so badly, but he did. *"Say it."*

"I want you," she gasped.

From out of nowhere, a dangerous, greedy lust slapped hold of him and his control shattered. With a dark sound that came from his gut, he clamped his hands on the insides of her thighs, split her wide and literally dove between her legs. As he fell upon her flesh, penetrating her with his tongue, finding a rhythm with his jaw, he was dimly aware of some kind of noise in the room, a growling.

Him? Couldn't be. That was the sound of . . . an animal.

Marissa had been shocked by the act at first. The carnality of it. The sinful closeness, the scary vulnerability. But soon none of that mattered. Butch's warm tongue was so erotic she could hardly bear the slick, slippery sensation of it—and couldn't stand the idea that he'd ever stop what he was doing, either. Then he started sucking on her, sucking and swallowing and saying things that made her sex swell until the pleasure stung like pain.

But all that was nothing compared to when he let loose. With a surge of male need, his heavy hands held her down, his mouth, his tongue, his face going all over her . . . God, that sound coming out of him, that throaty, pumping purr . . .

She orgasmed wildly, the most shattering, beautiful thing she'd ever felt, her body arching into the liquid flashes of pleasure—

Except at the crest, the seething energy shifted, transformed, detonated.

Bloodlust roared along the sexual current between them, then pulled her down into a spiral of starvation. Hunger ripped through her civilized nature, shredding everything but the need to go for his neck, and she bared her fangs, ready to flip him over onto his back and strike at his jugular and drink hard—

She was going to kill him.

She cried out and struggled against his hold. "Oh, God . . . *no!*"

"What?"

Shoving at Butch's shoulders, she hauled her body away

from him, shooting off the side of the bed and falling to the floor. As he reached for her in confusion, she scrambled across the rug to the far corner, her dress dragging behind, the top hanging from her waist. When there was no farther to go, she curled into a ball and held herself in place. As her body shook uncontrollably, the pain in her belly hit in waves, redoubling each time it returned.

Butch came after her, panicked. *"Marissa . . . ?"*

"No!"

He hauled up short. His face was stricken, all the color run out of his skin. "I'm so sorry—dear God—"

"You've got to go." As tears came up her throat, her voice went guttural.

"Sweet Jesus, I'm sorry . . . I'm so sorry . . . I didn't mean to scare you . . ."

She tried to control her breathing so she could reassure him, but lost the fight: She was panting, crying. Her fangs throbbed. Her throat was dry. And all she could think of was launching herself onto his chest. Pushing him down on the floor. Closing her teeth on his neck.

God, the drinking. He would taste good. So good, she couldn't imagine ever getting enough of him.

He tried to come close to her again. "I didn't mean for things to go so far—"

She leaped up, opened her mouth, and hissed at him. "Get out! For God's sake, leave! Or I'm going to hurt you!"

She raced for the bathroom and locked herself in. As the sound of the door slamming shut faded, she skidded to a halt on the marble and caught the horrible sight of herself in the mirror. Her hair was tangled, her dress undone, her fangs showing white and long in her gaping mouth.

Out of control. Undignified. *Defective.*

She grabbed the first thing she saw, a heavy glass candle-holder, and hauled it against the mirror. As her reflection shattered, she watched through bitter tears as the pieces of herself fell apart.

TWENTY-TWO

Butch threw himself at the bathroom door and jerked the handle until his palm nearly tore open. On the other side he heard Marissa crying. Then a shattering noise.

He drove his shoulder into the wooden panels. "Marissa!"

He hit the door with his body again, but then stopped and listened. Wild fear bit into him when there was only silence. "Marissa?"

"Just go." The quiet desperation in her voice made his eyes sting. "Just . . . go."

He splayed his hand on the wood that separated them. "I'm so sorry."

"Go . . . just go. Oh, God, you have to leave."

"Marissa—"

"I won't come out until you're gone. Go!"

Feeling as if he were in a nightmare, he grabbed his jacket and stumbled out of the bedroom, all sloppy, loose-bodied, weak in the knees. Out in the hall, he sagged back against the wall and banged his head into the plaster.

Squeezing his eyes shut, all he could see was her cowering in the corner, her trembling body drawn in a defensive crouch, her gown hanging loose from her bare breasts as if it had been ripped off her.

Fuck. Him. She was a lovely virgin and he'd treated her like a whore, pushing her too far and too hard because he hadn't been able to control himself. Christ, no matter how hot she burned, she wasn't used to what a man wanted to do during sex. Or what happened when a man's instincts took over. And even though he'd *known* all of that, he'd still held her down on that bed by the thighs, trapping her while he tongue-fucked her, for God's sake.

Butch slammed the back of his skull into the wall again. Dear God, she'd been so scared, she'd even bared her fangs as if she had to protect herself from him.

With a nasty curse, he tore off down the stairs, trying to out-run how much he despised himself, knowing he couldn't go that fast or that far.

When he hit the foyer, someone yelled, "Butch? Yo, Butch! You okay?"

He burst outside, jumped into the Escalade, and cranked the engine. All he wanted to do was apologize to her until he was hoarse, but he was the last person on the planet she wanted to see at the moment. And he didn't blame her.

He gunned the SUV for downtown, heading straight for V's place.

By the time he'd curbed the Escalade and was riding up the high-rise's elevator, he was about to take the bridge he was such a mess. He threw open V's door—

Shit!

In the glow of black candles, Vishous was bent over with his head down, his leather-clad hips driving back and forth, his bare shoulders and massive arms flexed up hard. Beneath him, a female was tied down on the table at the wrists and ankles, her body wrapped in leather except for the tips of her breasts and where V was slamming into her core. Even though there was a mask over her face and a ball gag in her mouth, Butch was pretty damn sure she was on the verge of an orgasm. She was making little mewling noises, begging for more even as tears streaked down her leather-covered cheeks.

When V's head lifted from the female's neck, his eyes were glowing and his fangs were long as . . . well, she might need stitches, put it that way.

"My bad," Butch blurted and ducked out of the penthouse.

He went back down for the Escalade in a daze and couldn't seem to think of anywhere to go once he got to the SUV. He just sat in the driver's seat, key in the ignition, hand on the gearshift . . . picturing Vishous feeding.

The glowing eyes. The long fangs. The sex.

Butch thought about how unconcerned Marissa had been that she was ill. And her voice popped into his head. *I can take care of it.* Then, *I don't want to hurt you.*

What if Marissa needed to feed? What if that was why she'd sent him away? She was a goddamned vampire, for chrissakes. Or did he think those beautiful fangs of hers were just for decoration?

He put his head down on the steering wheel. Oh, man, this was so unattractive. He had no business looking for other explanations. Besides, why hadn't she just asked if she could take some of him? He would have let her in a heartbeat. Maybe even faster.

Hell, the mere thought of it gave him a massive hard-on. The idea that she would settle in at his neck and suck was a turn-on the likes of which he'd never come across before. He pictured her naked, sprawled on his chest, her face at his throat—

Careful, O'Neal. Be careful you're not just looking for an out here.

Except she had been aroused, hadn't she. He'd tasted it. In fact, when he'd gone hard-core on her, it had seemed as if that sweetness had flowed even more. But then why hadn't she just told him what was wrong?

Maybe she didn't want to drink from him. Maybe she figured because he was a human he couldn't take it.

Maybe because he was a human, he actually couldn't.

Yeah, fuck that. He'd rather die feeding her than know

some other man was taking care of his woman. The idea of Marissa's mouth on someone else's neck, her breasts against someone else's chest, her smell in someone else's nose . . . her swallowing someone else's blood . . .

Mine.

The word shot through his head. And he became aware his hand had moved into his coat and found the trigger of his Glock.

Hitting the gas, he took off for ZeroSum, knowing his next move had to be calming down and ironing his head out. Homicidal jealousy directed at some male vampire was so not on his to-do list.

When his cell phone started ringing in his pocket, he palmed the Razr. "Yeah?"

V's voice was low. "Sorry you had to walk in on that. I didn't expect you to come—"

"V, what happens when a vampire doesn't feed?"

There was a pause. "Nothing good. You get tired, real damn tired. And the hunger hurts. Think food poisoning. Waves of pain rolling through your gut. If you let it get too out of hand, you turn into an animal. It gets dangerous."

"I've heard those stories about Zsadist, back before he got with Bella. He lived off humans, right? And I know for a fact those women didn't die. I'd see them back in the club after he was finished with them."

"You thinking of your girl?"

"Yeah."

"Look, you headed for a drink?"

"More than one."

"I'll meet you."

When Butch pulled into ZeroSum's parking lot, V was waiting by the side of the club, smoking a hand-rolled. Butch got out and triggered the Escalade's alarm.

"Cop."

"V." Butch cleared his throat and tried not to think about what his roommate looked like feeding and having sex. He failed. All he saw was Vishous over that female, dominating her, pumping into her, his body moving like a piston.

Man, he was going to have to readjust his definition of hard-core, thanks to that eyeful.

V drew hard on his cigarette, then put it out on the heel of his shitkicker and slipped the butt into his back pocket. "You ready to go in?"

"Christ, yes."

The bouncers let them bypass the wait line and then they walked through the club's writhing, sweating, over-sexed crowd to the VIP section. Within moments, and without an order, a waitress brought over a Lagavulin double and some Grey Goose.

As V's phone went off and he started talking, Butch glanced around—only to stiffen with a curse. In the corner, in the dim shelter of some shadow, he saw that tall, muscled female. And Rehvenge's head of security was watching him, her eyes burning like she wanted a repeat of the bathroom action they'd had.

Not going to happen.

Butch looked down into his glass as V clipped his phone shut. "That was Fritz. Message from Marissa to you."

Butch's head jacked up. "What she say?"

"She wants you to know that she's okay. Said she needs to lay low for tonight, but she'll be fine tomorrow. Said she doesn't want you to worry and she . . . ah, she loves you and you didn't do anything wrong when you did whatever you did." He cleared his throat. "So what did you do? Or is that TMI?"

"Wicked TMI." Butch tossed his drink back and held his empty glass up. The waitress came immediately.

As she took off to get him a freshie, he looked down at his hands. And felt V's eyes boring into him.

"Butch, she's going to need more than you can give her."

"Zsadist survived on—"

"Z drank from a lot of different humans. You're just the one. Thing is, because your blood is so weak, she'll drain you in no time because she'll have to do it so often." V took a deep breath. "Look, she can use me if you want. You can even be there so you know what happens. Sex doesn't have to be involved."

Butch tilted his head and focused on his roommate's jugular. Then he imagined Marissa at that thick neck, the two of them together. Intertwined.

"V, you know I love you like a brother, right?"

"Yeah."

"You feed her and I'll tear your fucking throat out."

V smirked, then broke into a full smile. The grin was so wide he had to cover his fangs with the back of his gloved hand. "'Nuff said, my man. And just as well. I've never let someone take my vein before."

Butch frowned. "Never?"

"Nope. I'm a vascular virgin. Personally, I hate the idea of some female feeding off me."

"Why?"

"Not my bag." Butch opened his mouth and V held up his hand. "Enough. Just know I'm here if you change your mind and want to use me."

Not going to happen, Butch thought. *Ever.*

Taking a deep breath, he thanked God for Marissa's message. And he'd been right: She'd kicked him out because she needed to feed. That had to be it. Man, he was sorely tempted to head back home, except he wanted to respect her wishes and not behave like a stalker. Besides, tomorrow night, assuming this was about blood . . . well, then he had something for her, didn't he.

She was going to drink from him.

When the waitress came back with more Scotch, Rehvenge showed up at the table with her. The male's massive body blocked out the view of the crowd which meant Butch couldn't see the guy's security officer. Which meant he could take a deep breath.

"My people keeping you wet enough?" Rehv asked.

Butch nodded. "Very wet."

"That's what I like to hear." The Reverend slid into the booth, his amethyst eyes scanning the VIP section. He looked good, his suit black, his silk shirt black, his mohawk a dark cropped stripe that ran front to back on his skull. "So I want to share a little news."

"You getting married?" Butch tossed back half the new Lag. "Where you registered? Crate and Bury 'Em?"

"Try Heckler and Koch." The Reverend opened his jacket and flashed the butt of a forty.

"Nice little poodle shooter you got there, vampire."

"Put a hell of a—"

V cut in. "You two are like watching tennis, and racquet sports bore me. What's the news?"

Rehv looked at Butch. "He has such phenomenal people skills, doesn't he."

"Try living with him."

The Reverend smirked, then grew serious. As he spoke, his mouth barely moved and his words didn't carry far. "The *Princeps* Council met night before last. Issue was mandatory *sehclusion* for all unmated females. The *leahdyre* wants a recommendation passed and submitted to Wrath ASAP."

V whistled under his breath. "A lockdown."

"Precisely. They're using my sister's abduction and

Wellesandra's death as the rationales. Which is some powerful shit, as it should be." The Reverend locked eyes with V. "Word to your boss. The *glymera* is pissed off at these civilian losses all around town. This motion is their warning shot across Wrath's bow and they are dead serious about passing it. The *leahdyre*'s all up in my grill because they can't hold a vote unless every member of the council is in the room, and I'm a consistent no-show. I can put off the meeting for a little while, but not forever." At that moment, a cell phone went off in the Reverend's jacket and he took the thing out. "And what do you know, here's Bella now. Hey, sister mine—" The male's eyes flashed and his body shifted. *"Tahlly?"*

Butch frowned, getting the distinct impression that whoever was on that line was a female and not of the sister kind: Rehvenge's body was suddenly throwing off heat like a banked fire.

Man, you had to wonder what kind of woman would tangle with a piece of work like the Reverend. Then again, V was obviously getting laid, so those kind of females were out there.

"Hold on, *tahlly*." Rehv frowned and got to his feet. "Later, gentlemen. And drinks are on me tonight."

"Thanks for the heads-up," V said.

"I'm such a model fucking citizen, aren't I?" Rehv sauntered down to his office and shut himself away.

Butch shook his head. "So the Reverend's got a chippie, huh?"

V grunted. "Pity that female."

"For real." As Butch's stare drifted, he tensed up. That hard-ass female with the men's haircut still had her eyes on him in the shadows.

"Did you do her, cop?" V asked softly.

"Who." He kicked the tail end of the shot.

"You know exactly who I'm asking about."

"None of your biz, roommate."

As Marissa waited for Rehvenge's voice to come back on the line, she wondered where he was. There was a din coming over the connection—music, voices. A party?

The noise cut off sharply, as if he'd closed a door. *"Tahlly*, where are you? Or did Havers get his phones really encrypted?"

"I'm not at home."

Silence. Then, "Are you where I think you are? Are you with the Brotherhood?"

"How did you know?"

He muttered something, then said, "Only one number on the planet this phone can't trace, and it's where my sister calls me from. Now you're pulling the same no-show thing for an I.D. What the hell's going on?"

She glossed over the situation, telling him only that she and Havers had argued and she'd needed somewhere to stay.

Rehv cursed. "You should have called me first. I want to take care of you."

"It's complicated. Your mother—"

"You don't worry about her." Rehv's voice smoothed out into a purr. "Come stay with me, *tahlly*. All you have to do is materialize to the penthouse and I'll have you picked up."

"Thank you, but no. I'm only going to be here long enough to get settled somewhere else."

"Settled somewhere—what the hell? This stuff with your brother is *permanent*?"

"It'll be fine. Listen, Rehvenge, I . . . need you. I need to try again to . . ." She put her head in her hand. She hated using him, but who else could she go to? And Butch . . .

God, Butch . . . she felt like she was betraying him. Except what was her alternative?

Rehvenge growled, "When, *tahlly?* When do you want me?"

"Now."

"Just go to—ah, hell, I've got to meet the *Princeps leahdyre*. And then I've got some work-related issues I have to take care of."

She gripped the phone. Waiting was bad. "Tomorrow, then?"

"At nightfall. Unless you want to come and stay at my home. Then we could have . . . all day long."

"I'll see you first thing tomorrow evening."

"I can't wait, *tahlly*."

After she hung up, she stretched out on the bed and sank into utter exhaustion, her body becoming indistinguishable from the sheets and blankets and pillows, just another inanimate object on top of the mattress.

Oh, hell . . . maybe waiting until tomorrow was better. She could rest up then talk to Butch and let him know what was going on. As long as she wasn't sexually charged, she should be able to control herself around him and this was one conversation that was better to have in person: If humans who were in love were anything like bonded male vampires, Butch wasn't going to handle the fact that she needed to be with someone else well.

With a sigh, she thought about Rehv. Then the *Princeps* Council. Then her sex in general.

God, even if that *sehclusion* motion was defeated by some miracle, there really was no safe place for females to go if they were threatened at home, was there? With the disintegration of vampire society and all the fighting with the *lessers*, there were no social services for the race. No safety net. No one to help females and their young if the *hellren* in their house was violent. Or if the family turned the female away.

Good Lord, what would have happened to her if Beth and Wrath hadn't taken her in? Or if she didn't have Rehvenge?

She might well have died.

Down in the compound's training center, John was the first in the locker room after the in-class session was done. He changed quickly into his jockstrap and his *ji*, impatient for the fighting practice to begin.

"What's the hurry, John? Oh, wait, you like to get your ass kicked."

John looked over his shoulder. Lash was standing in front of an open locker, taking off a fancy silk shirt. His chest was no bigger than John's and his arms just as thin, but as the guy stared back, his eyes burned like he was the size of a bull.

John met that glare head-on, his body heating up. Man, he was jonesing for Lash to open his mouth and say something else. Just one more thing.

"You gonna pass out on us again, John? Like the pansy you are?"

Bingo.

John launched himself at the kid but didn't get far. Blaylock, the redhead, caught him and held him back, trying to derail the fight. But Lash didn't have any such deadweight. The bastard drew his fist back and threw a right hook so hard that John spun out of Blaylock's hold and hit the bank of lockers with a metal bang.

Stunned, breath knocked out of him, John reached out blindly.

Blaylock caught him again. "*Jesus Christ*, Lash—"

"What? He was coming at me."

"Because you were *begging* for it."

Lash's eyes narrowed. "What did you say?"

"You don't have to be such an asshole."

As Lash pointed at Blaylock, his Jacob & Co. watch sparkled under the lights like it was a battery-powered twinkler.

"Careful, Blay. Playing on his team ain't such a hot idea." The guy shook out his hand and dropped his pants. "Man, that felt good. How was it on your end, John-boy?"

John let that one go and pushed himself free. As his face throbbed to the beat of his heart, he thought of a car blinker for some absurd reason.

Oh, Lord . . . how bad was the damage? He stumbled over to the row of sinks, and in the long mirror that ran down the length of the wall, he got a look at his puss. Great. Just great. His chin and lip were already swelling.

Blaylock appeared behind him with a cold bottle of water. "Put this on it."

John took the icy Aquafina and eased it onto his face. Then he closed his eyes to avoid seeing either himself or the redhead.

"You want me to tell Zsadist you're not training tonight?"

John shook his head.

"You sure?"

Ignoring the question, John gave the water back and walked out to the gym. The other guys followed in a tense group, stomping over the blue mats and lining up next to him.

Zsadist came out of the Equipment Room, took one look at John's face and got good and pissed off. "Everyone put their hands out, palms down." He walked past each trainee until he stopped in front of Lash. "Nice knuckles. Over against the wall."

Lash sauntered across the gym, looking self-satisfied that he wasn't going to have to work out.

Zsadist stopped in front of John's hands. "Turn 'em over."

John did. There was a heartbeat of silence. Then Zsadist gripped John's chin and forced his head up. "Seeing double?"

John shook his head.

"Nauseous?"

John shook his head.

"This hurt?" Zsadist prodded the jaw a little.

John winced. Shook his head.

"Liar. But that's what I want to hear." Z stepped away and addressed the trainees. "Laps. Twenty. And each time you get to your classmate over there, you drop in front of him and do twenty push-ups. Marine style. Move it."

The groans were loud.

"Do I look like I care?" Zsadist whistled through his teeth. *"Move it."*

John started off with the rest of them, thinking this was going to be a really long night. But at least Lash wasn't looking quite so pleased with himself . . .

Four hours later, it turned out John was right.

By the end of the session, they were all exhausted. Z not only ground them into the mats, he kept them longer than usual. Like, centuries longer than usual. The damn training was so grueling. that not even John had the energy to keep practicing after they broke for the night. Instead, he went directly to Tohr's office and collapsed in the chair without even showering.

Curling his legs up tight, he figured he would just rest a minute, then go rinse off—

The door swung open. "You okay?" Zsadist demanded.

John didn't look over, just nodded.

"I'm recommending that Lash get kicked out of the program."

John jerked upright and started shaking his head.

"Whatever, John. That's the second time he's gone after you. Or do I have to remind you of the nunchakus thing a few months back?"

No, John remembered. Shit, though.

With too much to say to be able to sign and have Z catch everything, he reached for his pad and wrote with extra neatness: *If he gets kicked out, I look weak to the others. I want to fight with these guys someday. How can they trust me if they think I'm a lightweight?*

He handed the pad to Zsadist, who held the pages with care in his big hands. The Brother's head dropped low and his brows crunched together, his distorted mouth moving a little as if he were sounding out each word.

When Z was finished, he tossed the pad on the desk. "I won't have that little shit beating on you, John. Just won't have it. But you got a point. I'll slap Lash with some serious probation. But one more of these happy little episodes, and he's out."

Zsadist walked over to the closet where the tunnel access was hidden, then looked over his shoulder. "Listen up, John. I don't want a free-for-all during training. So no going after the bastard even though he deserves it. You just keep your head down and your hands to yourself. Phury and I'll watch him for you, okay?"

John looked away, thinking of how badly he'd wanted to clock Lash. How badly he still wanted to do that.

"John? We clear? No brawling."

After a long moment, John nodded slowly.

And hoped he'd be able to keep his word.

TWENTY-THREE

Hours and hours and hours later, Butch's ass was so numb he couldn't tell where the floor ended and his butt began. All day long, he'd been sitting in this hallway outside of Marissa's bedroom door. Like the dog he was.

He couldn't say it had been wasted time. He'd done a lot of thinking.

And had made a phone call that had been the right thing to do, though a cringer to get through: He'd bitten the bullet and called his sister Joyce.

Nothing had changed at home. Evidently his family back in South Boston still had no interest in having anything to do with him. And that didn't really bother him because it was the status quo. But it did make him feel bad for Marissa. She and her brother had been tight, so getting turned out by him must have been a truly nasty surprise.

"Master?"

Butch looked up. "Hey, Fritz."

"I have what you asked for." The *doggen* bowed low and held out a black velvet bag. "I believe it matches your specifications, but if it does not, I can find another."

"I'm sure it's perfect." Butch took the heavy satchel, split it open at the mouth, and poured the contents into his hand. The solid gold cross was three inches long and two inches wide, thick as a finger. Suspended at the end of a long, gold chain, it was exactly what he'd wanted and he put it around his neck with satisfaction.

The substantial weight was just as he'd hoped it would be, a tangible protection.

"Master, how is it?"

Butch smiled up at the *doggen*'s wrinkled face while unbuttoning his shirt and dropping the necklace inside. He felt the cross slide down his skin until it lay right over his heart. "Like I said, perfect."

Fritz beamed, bowed, and took off, just as the grand-father clock started chiming down at the other end of the corridor. Once, twice . . . six times.

The bedroom door in front of him swung open.

Marissa appeared before him as an apparition. After so many hours of thinking about her, his eyes were momentarily snowed, seeing her not as real but as a figment of his desperation, her dress ether not cloth, her hair a glorious golden aura, her face a haunting well of beauty. As he stared up at her, his heart transformed her into an icon from his Catholic childhood, the Madonna of salvation and love . . . and him her unworthy servant.

He dragged himself off the floor, his spine cracking as it supported his weight. "Marissa."

Ah, shit, his emotions were all right there in his rusted-out voice, the pain, the sadness, the regret.

She held her hand up. "I meant what I said in that message last night. I loved being with you. Every moment. That wasn't why you had to leave and I wish I could have explained myself better at the time. Butch, we need to talk."

"Yeah, I know. But do you mind if we go down the hall for this?" Because he had no intention of having an audience, and no matter what she said, he figured she'd prefer not to be in a bedroom alone with him. She was tense as hell.

When she nodded, they headed to the sitting room at the end of the corridor, and on the way, he was stunned by how weak she was. She moved slowly, as if she couldn't feel her legs, and she was terribly pale, nearly transparent from a lack of energy.

Once inside the peach and yellow room, she went over to the windows, away from him.

Her words were thin as breath as she spoke. "Butch, I don't know how to say this . . ."

"I know what's doing."

"You do?"

"Yes." He started toward her, arms out. "Don't you know I would do anything—"

"Don't come any closer." She stepped back. "You've got to stay away from me."

He dropped his hands. "You need to feed, don't you?"

Her eyes widened. "How did you—"

"It's all right, baby." He smiled a little. "It's *very* all right. I talked with V."

"So you know what I've got to do? And you don't . . . mind?"

He shook his head. "I'm fine with it. More than fine."

"Oh, thank the Scribe Virgin." She lurched over to a sofa and sat down as if her knees had buckled. "I was so afraid you'd be offended. It'll be hard on me as well, but it's the only safe way. And I can't wait any longer. It has to be tonight."

When she patted the couch seat, he went over with relief and sat beside her, taking her hands in his. God, she was so cold.

"I'm really ready for this," he said, with thick antici-pation. Man, he was suddenly dying to head back to her bedroom. "Let's go."

A curious expression crossed her face. "You want to watch?"

He stopped breathing. "Watch?"

"I, ah . . . I'm not sure that's a good idea."

As her words hit him, Butch became aware of a sinking feeling in his gut. Like someone had popped the stoppers on a number of his internal organs. "What are you talking about, *watch*?"

"When I'm with the male who lets me take his vein."

Abruptly, Marissa recoiled, giving him a good idea of what the expression on his face must be like.

Yeah, or maybe she was reacting to the fact that he'd started to growl.

"The other male," he said slowly, as he put it all together. "The one you told me you've been seeing. You've fed from him."

She nodded slowly. "Yes."

Butch jacked up to his feet. "Often?"

"Ah . . . four or five times."

"And he's an aristocrat, of course."

"Well, yes."

"And he'd make a socially acceptable mate for you, wouldn't he." Unlike a POS human. "Wouldn't he?"

"Butch, it isn't romantic. I swear."

Yeah, maybe on her side it wasn't. But it was damn hard to imagine any male not sexing her. The bastard would have to be impotent or some shit. "He's into you, isn't he. Answer the question, Marissa. Flyboy with the superhero plasma . . . he wants you, doesn't he? *Doesn't he?*"

God, where the hell was this wild jealousy coming from?

"But he knows I don't feel that way about him."

"Has he kissed you?"

When she didn't reply, Butch was very glad he didn't know the Joe's name and address. "You're not using him anymore. You have me."

"Butch, I can't feed from you. I'll take too—where are you going?"

He stalked across the room, shut the double doors, and

locked them in together. As he came back at her, he tossed his black suit jacket on the floor and ripped open his shirt, the buttons popping off and flying everywhere. Falling to his knees in front of her, he tilted back his head and offered his throat, himself, to her.

"You will use me."

There was a long silence. Then her scent, that gorgeous clean fragrance, intensified until it flooded the room. Her body began to shake, her mouth opening.

As her fangs unsheathed, he got an instant erection.

"Oh . . . yeah," he said in a dark voice. "Take me. I need to feed you."

"No," she moaned, tears glowing in her cornflower blue eyes.

She made a move to get up, but he jumped at her, taking her by the shoulders, holding her down on the couch. He moved himself between her legs, bringing their bodies together, getting all up in her. While she trembled against him and pushed at him, he kept her close, nuzzling her, nipping her ear, sucking on her jaw. Before long, she stopped fighting to get away. And started gripping the two halves of his shirt to pull him in tighter.

"That's right, baby," he growled. "You grab on to me. Let me feel those fangs get into me deep. *I want it*."

He palmed the back of her head and brought her mouth to his throat. As an arc of pure sexual power exploded between them, they both began to pant, her breath and tears hot on his skin.

But then she seemed to come to her senses. She struggled hard and he did his best to keep her in place, even though they were both going to end up with bruises. And even though he was ultimately going to lose the fight against her. As he was just a human, she was stronger, even though he outweighed her by well over a hundred pounds.

But hopefully she would give in and use him before his energy flagged.

"Marissa, please, *take me*," he groaned, his voice hoarse from the struggle and now the begging.

"*No . . .*"

His heart broke as she sobbed, but he didn't let her go. He couldn't. "Take what's inside of me. I know I'm not good enough, but take me anyway—"

"Don't make me do this—"

"I have to." God, he felt like crying with her.

"Butch . . ." Her body bucked and strained against his, their clothes flapping as they struggled. "I can't hold back . . . for much longer . . . let me go . . . before I hurt you."

"*Never.*"

It happened so fast. His name shot out of her on a yell and then he felt a searing blaze of pain at the side of his throat. Her fangs sinking into his jugular.

"Oh . . . *fuck* . . . *yes* . . . !" He loosened his grip and cradled her as she latched on to his neck. He barked her name at the first erotic draw, the first hard suck on his vein, the first swallow for her. As she repositioned for a better angle, pleasure swamped him, sparks flowing all through his body as if he were orgasming. This was *so* the way it had to be. He needed her to take from him in order to live—

Marissa broke the contact and dematerialized, right out of his arms.

Butch fell headfirst into the empty air where she'd been, face-planting into the sofa cushions. In a messy scramble, he shoved himself to his feet and spun around. "Marissa! *Marissa!*"

He threw himself at the doors and clawed at the lock, but couldn't get free.

Then he heard her broken, desperate voice on the other side. "I'll kill you . . . God help me, but I'll kill you . . . I want you too much."

He pounded on the door. "Let me out!"

"I'm sorry—" Her voice cracked, then grew strong. And he feared her resolve more than anything else. "I'm so sorry. I'll come to you afterward. After it is done."

"Marissa, don't do this—"

"*I love you.*"

He beat the wood with his fists. "I don't care if I die! Don't go to him!"

When the lock finally gave way, he burst into the hall and ran flat out for the staircase.

But by the time he threw open the mansion's front door she was gone.

Across town, in the underground parking garage where the brokered fights took place, Van hopped into the chicken-wire cage and bounced on the balls of his feet. The drumbeat of him warming up echoed through the concrete levels, cutting off the silence.

Tonight there was no crowd, just three people. But he was juiced like it was standing room only.

Van was the one who'd suggested the locale to Mr. X, and he'd shown them how to break into the place. As he knew the schedule of fights, he'd been sure there wouldn't be anyone around this evening and a big part of him wanted to have his glory, his resurrection here in this ring, not in some anonymous basement somewhere.

He tried out some kicks, so very satisfied with his strength, then eyed his opponent. The other *lesser* was just as lit for the hand-to-hand as he was.

From the other side of the cage, Xavier barked, "You don't stop until it's over. And Mr. D, on the ground unmoving is not 'over,' we clear?"

Van nodded, already used to being called by his last initial.

"Good." Xavier's palms clapped together and the fight was on.

Van and the other *lesser* circled each other, but Van had no intention of letting the slow-dance crap go on for long. He moved in first, throwing punches, forcing his opponent back against the cage. The guy took the bare-knuckled pounders like they were nothing more than spring rain on his cheeks and then tossed out a mean-ass right hook. The damn thing caught Van at an angle, splitting his lip open like an envelope.

It hurt, but the pain was good, a strengthener, something that focused him further. Van spun around and sent his foot out flying, a body bomb on the end of a steel chain. Sure as shit it took the *lesser* down, sprawling the guy flat. Van jumped on his opponent and cranked him into a submission hold, wrenching one arm back and around so the joints strained at the shoulder and elbow. Just a little tighter and he was going to pop this sucker right off—

The *lesser* pulled a smoothie, somehow nailing Van in the balls with his knee. Quick switch of positions and Van was on the bottom. Then another roll and they were up on their feet.

The fight went on and on, no time-outs, no breathers, the two of them battering the holy hell out of each other. It was flipping miraculous. Van felt like he could go for hours, no matter how beat up his body got. It was like he had an engine in him, a driving force, one that was not as dulled by exhaustion or pain as his old self had been.

When the break in the action finally came, the tipping factor was Van's special . . . whatever it was. Though the two of them were identically matched for strength, Van was the master at this, and he saw the opening for the win. He popped the other slayer in the gut, nailing a liver shot that would have left a human opponent shitting in his shorts. Then he picked his opponent up and slammed him down onto the ring floor. As he mounted the body and looked down, Van's blood welled from the cuts around his eyes and dropped onto the guy's face like tears . . . black tears.

The color momentarily freaked Van out, and the other *lesser* took advantage of the lapse in focus by spinning him over onto his back.

Yeah, not happening, not this time. Van balled his fist and rammed it into the guy's temple at exactly the right force and the right place, knocking the *lesser* stupid. With a quick surge, Van kicked his opponent over, straddled the slayer's chest and repeated the punch over and over again, battering the skull until the bone helmet went soft. And he just kept going, sticking to the task until the very structure of the man's face let go, the head becoming a loose bag, his opponent dead and then some.

"Finish him!" Xavier called from the sidelines.

Van looked up, panting hard. "I just did."

"No . . . *finish him*!"

"How?"

"You should know what to do!" Xavier's pale eyes shined with an eerie desperation. "You must!"

Van wasn't clear on exactly how much deader he could make the guy, but he grabbed the *lesser* by the ears and twisted until the neck snapped. Then he eased off the body. Though he had no heart that beat anymore, his lungs burned and his body was deliciously logy from exertion . . . except the logy didn't last.

He started to laugh. Already the strength was returning to him, just pouring in from somewhere else as if he'd eaten and slept and recovered for days.

Xavier's boots landed hard in the ring and the *Forelesser* strode over, furious. "I told you to finish him, goddamn it."

"Uh-huh. Right." *Christ*. Xavier just had to suck the triumph out of the moment. "You think he's walking away from this?"

Xavier shook with rage as he took out a knife. *"I told you to finish him."*

Van tensed up and leaped to his feet. But Xavier just bent over that messy punching bag of a *lesser* and stabbed the thing in the chest. There was a flash of light and then . . . gone. Nothing but black smudges on the ring's tarmac.

Van backed up until he hit the fencing. "What the hell . . ."

From across the way, Xavier pointed the knife right at Van's chest. "I have expectations for you."

"Like . . . what?"

"You should be able to do that"—he jabbed toward the disintegration mark with the blade—"on your own."

"So give me a knife next round."

Xavier shook his head, a bizarre kind of panic flaring in his face. "Fuck!" He paced around, then muttered, "It's just going to take time. Let's go."

"What about the blood?" Man, that oily black stuff suddenly made him dizzy.

"Like I give a shit?" Xavier picked up the dead *lesser*'s duffel bag and left.

As Van followed him out of the parking garage, he

found it really fucking annoying that Mr. X was playing it like this. The fight had been a good one and Van had won. He wanted to enjoy the feeling.

In strained silence, the two of them headed for the minivan, which was parked blocks away. As they went along, Van scrubbed his face with a towel and tried not to curse. When they got to the car, Xavier slid behind the wheel.

"Where are we going?" Van asked as he got in.

Xavier didn't answer, just started to drive, so Van stared out the windshield, wondering how he could get away from the guy. Not easily, he suspected.

As they passed by a new skyscraper that was going up, he eyed the men pulling the nightshift. Under electric lights, the union crews were all over the building like ants, and he envied them even though he'd hated doing what they did.

Man, if he were still one of them, he wouldn't be dealing with Mr. X's crap attitude.

On a whim, Van lifted his right hand and looked at his missing pinkie, remembering how he'd done it. So fucking stupid. He'd been at a construction site, cutting boards on a table saw, and decided to take the guards off the machine to make the process go faster. One lapse of focus later and his finger had ended up flying through the air with the greatest of ease. The blood loss had seemed tremendous, the stuff leaking all over him, covering the saw's flat back, soaking into the ground. Red, not black.

Van put his hand to his chest and felt nothing beating behind his breastbone.

Anxiety trembled down the back of his neck, like spiders slipping under his collar. He glanced at Xavier, the only resource he had. "Are we alive?"

"No."

"But that guy was killed, right? So we must be alive."

Xavier's eyes shot across the seat. "We're not alive. Trust me."

"What happened to him, then?"

Exhaustion flared in Xavier's pale, dead stare, the drooping of his lids making him look like he was a million years old.

"What happened to him, Mr. X?"

The *Fore-lesser* didn't answer, just kept on driving.

TWENTY-FOUR

Marissa materialized on the terrace of Rehvenge's penthouse and nearly collapsed. As she lurched for the sliding door, he opened it wide.

"Marissa, *good God*." He shot his arm around her and pulled her inside.

Overcome with bloodlust, she gripped his biceps, the thirst in her so strong she was liable to bite him where he stood. To keep from ripping his throat open, she yanked out of his hold, but he caught her and spun her around.

"Come over here right now!" He all but threw her on the couch. "You're about to shock out on me."

As she hit the cushions in a heap, she knew he was right. Her body was wildly off balance, her head spinning, her hands and feet numb. Her stomach was an empty, grinding pit, her fangs throbbing, her throat dry as winter, hot as August.

But when he yanked his tie off and popped the buttons on his shirt, she mumbled, "Not at your throat. I can't bear that . . . not your—"

"You're too far gone for the wrist. You won't get enough and we're out of time."

As if on cue, her vision started to dim and she began to pass out. She heard him swear and then he pulled her on top of him, shoved her face in his neck and . . .

Biology took over. She bit him so hard she felt his big body jerk and she sucked at him with mindless instinct. With a great roar, his strength poured into her gut and spread out to her limbs and made her body come back to life.

As she swallowed with desperation, her tears flowed as thick as his blood.

Rehvenge held Marissa loosely, hating the starvation that rode her so hard. She was such a fragile, delicate thing. She should never be in this desperate state, and he ran his hands up and down her willowy back, trying to calm her. While she cried silently, he got pissed. Christ, what was wrong with that male she was so into? How could he force her to come to another?

Ten minutes later, she lifted her head. There was a little streak of blood on her lower lip and Rehv had to grab onto the sofa arm so he didn't lean up and lick it off.

With satiated grace but a face marked by tears, Marissa eased back against the leather cushions at the other end of the couch and cradled herself with her thin arms. She closed her eyes and he watched the color float back into her wet cheeks.

God, look at that hair of hers. So fine. So lush. So perfect. He wanted to be naked and unmedicated and hard as a stone, with those blond waves all over his body. And if he couldn't have all that, he wanted to kiss her. Right now.

Instead, he reached for his suit coat, grabbed his handkerchief, and leaned over to her. She jumped as he blotted her tears, and she took the linen square from him quickly.

He went back to his corner of the sofa. "Marissa, come stay with me. I want to take care of you."

In the silence that followed, he thought about where she was staying—and figured the male she wanted had to be at the Brotherhood's compound. "You're still in love with Wrath, aren't you."

Her eyes flipped open. "What?"

"You said you couldn't feed from the male you wanted. Wrath's mated now—"

"It's not him."

"Phury, then? As a celibate—"

"No, and I—I just can't talk about it, if you don't mind." She looked down at his handkerchief. "Rehvenge, I would really love some time alone. May I sit here for a little while? By myself?"

Even though he wasn't used to being dismissed, especially not from his own turf, he was so willing to cut her some slack. "Stay as long as you like, *tahlly*. Just close the slider when you leave. I'll remote the alarm after you go."

As he put his suit coat on, he left his tie loose and his shirt collar open because she'd chewed him raw and the bite marks were too tender to be covered. Not that he cared in the slightest.

"You are so kind to me," she said, staring at his loafers.

"Actually, I'm not."

"How can you say that? You never ask for anything in return—"

"Marissa, look at me. *Look at me.*" Dear Virgin in the Fade, she was beautiful. Especially with his blood in her. "Don't kid yourself. I still want you as my *shellan*. I want you naked in my bed. I want you swelling up with my young in your body. I want . . . yeah, the whole thing with you. I don't do this to be nice, I do it to get under your skin. I do it because I hope I can someday, somehow get you where I want you to be."

As her eyes peeled wide, he kept the rest to himself. No reason to air the fact that the *symphath* in him wanted to crawl around in her head and own every emotion she ever felt. Or share the reality that sex with him would be . . . complicated.

Ah, the joys of his nature. And his anomaly.

"But I want you to trust in something, Marissa. I won't ever cross the line if you don't want me to."

Besides, Xhex was probably right. Half-breeds like him did better going solo. Even if *symphaths* weren't discriminated against and could mate and live like Normals, they should never be with someone who was defenseless against their dark side.

He pulled on his floor-length sable coat. "This male of yours . . . he better get with the program. Damn fucking waste of a female of worth like you." Rehv grabbed his cane and headed for the door. "If you need me, call me."

Butch walked into ZeroSum, went back to the Brotherhood's table, and took off his Aquascutum raincoat. He was going to be here for a while. Which wasn't a news flash, was it? Hell, he should just pitch a damn pup tent and move in.

As the waitress came up with a Scotch, he said, "Any chance you can just bring me a bottle?"

"Sorry, I can't."

"Okay, come here." He crooked his finger at her. When she leaned down, he put a hundred-dollar bill on her tray. "This is just for you. I want you to keep me nice and poured."

"Absolutely."

Alone at the table, Butch reached up to his neck, his fingertips running over the puncture wounds. As he felt where he'd been bitten, he tried not to imagine what Marissa was doing right now to someone else. To an aristocrat. To a well-bred bastard who was better than him, platinum to his nickel. *Oh, God.*

Like a mantra, he repeated what V had said. That it didn't have to be sexual. That it was a biological imperative.

That there was no choice. That it . . . didn't have to be sexual. He was hoping if he heard the litany often enough in his head, his emotions would calm the hell down so he could accept the necessity of what she had to do. After all, Marissa wasn't being cruel. She'd been as distraught as he was—

In a vivid flash, he saw her naked body and couldn't help but picture another man's hands smoothing over her breasts. Another man's lips traveling across her skin. Another man taking her virginity as he nourished her, his hard body moving on top of her, inside of her.

And all the while she was drinking . . . drinking until she had her fill, until she was satiated, replete.

Taken care of. By someone else.

Butch hammered his double Lag.

Holy fuck. He was going to crack in half. He was going to fall apart, right here, right now, his raw insides spilling onto the floor, his vitals getting ground down under the feet of strangers along with fallen cocktail napkins and credit card receipts.

The waitress, bless her heart, came over with more Scotch.

As he picked up the second glass, he lectured himself: *O'Neal, get your sack together and grow some pride. Have some faith in her, too. She would never sleep with another man. She just wouldn't.*

But the sex was just part of it.

As he downed the Scotch, he realized there was another dimension to the nightmare. She was going to have to feed regularly, wasn't she. They were going to have to do this over and over again.

Fuck. He'd like to think he was a big enough man, a confident enough man, to handle all this, but he was possessive and selfish. And the next time she fed, they would be back where they were now, her in another man's arms, him drinking in a club alone on the verge of hanging himself. Only it would be worse. And the time after that, even more so. He loved her so much, so deeply, that he would destroy them both and it wouldn't take long.

Besides, what kind of future could they have? With the way he'd been pounding the Scotch lately, he probably only had another ten years left in his liver and her kind lived for centuries. He'd just be a footnote in her long life, a pothole on the road to her eventually finding a mate who was right for her, who could give her what she needed.

When the waitress brought him a third double, Butch held up his forefinger to keep her by his side. He downed the glass while she waited, gave it to her, and she went back to the bartender.

As she returned with number four, that scrawny blond Eurotrasher with his trio of thick-necked bodyguard types started waving for her attention from two tables over.

Christ, seemed like every damn night the kid was in this place. Or maybe it was just a little of the idiot went a long way.

"Hey!" the kid called out. "We need service over here. Get the lead out."

"I'll be right over," the waitress said.

"Now," the ass snapped. "Not later."

"I won't be gone long," she murmured to Butch.

As she went over to the punk, Butch watched as she got majorly harassed. Goddamned bigmouthed show-offs, all of them. And they weren't going to improve as the night went on.

Then again, neither was Butch.

"You look a little aggressive there, Butch O'Neal."

He squeezed his eyes shut. When he opened them again, the female with the man's hair and the man's body was still in front of him.

"We going to have trouble with you tonight, Butch O'Neal?"

He wished she'd stop saying his name. "Nah, I'm good."

Her eyes flashed with an erotic light. "Oh, I know that. But let's get real. You going to be a problem tonight?"

"No."

She stared at him long and hard. Then smiled a little. "Well . . . I'll be watching you. So keep that in mind."

TWENTY-FIVE

Joyce O'Neal Rafferty met her husband at the door with the baby on her hip and a glare on her face. As Mike stood on the cold side of the welcome mat, he was clearly tired after pulling double shifts on the T, but she couldn't have cared less. "I got a telephone call today from my brother. Butch. You told him about the baptism, didn't you."

Her husband kissed Sean, but didn't try it with her. "Come on, honey—"

"This is not your business!"

Mike shut the door. "Why do you all hate him so much?"

"I am *not* going there with you."

As she wheeled away, he said, "He didn't kill your sister, Jo. He was twelve. What could he have done?"

She shifted her son in her arms and didn't turn around. "This is not about Janie. Butch turned his back on the family years ago. His choice, got nothing to do with what happened."

"Maybe all of you turned your back on him."

She glared over her shoulder. "Why are you defending him?"

"He was my friend. Before I met and married you, he was my friend."

"Some friend. When was the last time you heard from him?"

"Doesn't matter. He was good to me when I knew him."

"You are such a bleeding heart." She headed for the

stairs. "I'm going to feed Sean. I left you some dinner in the fridge."

Joyce marched up to the second floor, and when she hit the top landing, she glared at the crucifix that hung on the wall. Turning away from the cross, she went into Sean's room and sat down in the rocker by his crib. Baring her breast, she brought her son up and he latched on, his hand squeezing the flesh that was next to his face. As he fed, his little body was warm and pudgy with health, his lashes down on his rosy cheeks.

Joyce took a number of deep breaths.

Crap. Now she felt bad for yelling. And for forsaking the Savior's cross. She said a Hail Mary and then tried to calm herself by counting Sean's perfect toes.

God . . . if anything happened to him, she would die, her heart would literally never beat the same way again. How had her mother done it? How had she lived through the loss of a child?

And Odell had lost two, hadn't she. First Janie. Then Butch. Thank God the woman's mind was going soft. The relief from bad memories must be a blessing.

Joyce stroked Sean's fine dark hair and realized that her mother had never even gotten to say good-bye to Janie. The body had been too ruined to fix up for an open casket, and Eddie O'Neal, as the father, had done the ID at the morgue.

God, on that horrible fall afternoon, if only Butch had followed through and run into the house and told a grown-up that Janie had just left . . . maybe they could have saved her. Janie hadn't been allowed to get in cars with boys and everyone knew the rules. Butch knew the rules. If only . . .

Ah, hell. Her husband was right. The whole family

hated Butch. No wonder he'd taken off and all but disappeared.

With a whiffle, Sean's mouth went slack and his little hand eased up. But then he jerked awake again and got back with the program.

Talk about disappearing . . . Good Lord, her mother wasn't going to get a good-bye with Butch, either, was she? Her lucid moments were so few and far between. Even if Butch showed up at the church this Sunday, she might well not even recognize him.

Joyce heard her husband coming up the stairs, his footfalls slow.

"Mike?" she called out.

The man she loved and had married appeared in the doorway. He was developing a middle-aged belly, and he was losing the hair at the crown of his head even though he was only thirty-seven. But as she stared at him now, she saw his younger self: The high school jock. The friend of her older brother Butch. The hotshot football player that she'd had a crush on for years.

"Yeah?" he said.

"I'm sorry. For getting so pissed off."

He smiled a little. "It's some tough stuff. I understand."

"And you're right. Butch probably should have been invited. I just—I want the day of the baptism to be pure, you know? Just—pure. It's Sean's beginning and I don't want any shadows. Butch . . . he carries that shadow around and everyone would get tense, and with Mother being so sick, I don't want to deal."

"Did he say he was coming?"

"No. He . . ." She thought about the conversation. Funny, he'd sounded the same. Her brother had always had the strangest voice, so husky and hoarse. Like either his throat was deformed or there was too much that he

286

wasn't saying. "He said he was happy for us. Thanked you for the call. Said he hoped Mom and Dad were okay."

Her husband glanced down at Sean, who had melted into sleep again. "Butch doesn't know your mother's ill, does he?"

"No." In the beginning, when Odell had just been forgetful, Joyce and her sister had decided to wait until they knew what was wrong to tell Butch. But that had been two years ago, hadn't it. And they knew what was wrong, didn't they. Alzheimer's.

God only knew how much longer Mother was going to be around. The disease was progressing relentlessly.

"I am a thief not to tell Butch," she said softly. "Aren't I."

"I love you," Mike murmured.

Her eyes watered as she looked from her son's face up to his father's. Michael Rafferty was a good man. A solid man. He was never going to be Hugh Jackman handsome or Bill Gates rich or King of England powerful. But he was hers and he was Sean's and that was more than enough. Especially on nights like tonight, during conversations like this.

"I love you, too," she said.

Vishous materialized behind ZeroSum and walked down the alley to the front of the club. When he saw the Escalade curbed on Tenth Street, he was relieved. Phury had said Butch had split from the mansion like Jeff Gordon and not because he was a happy guy.

V went into the club and headed straight for the VIP section. But he didn't make it.

That female head of security stepped in front of him, her jacked body blocking his way. As he gave her a quick once-over, he wondered what it would be like to tie her up.

She'd probably leave scars in the process, and wouldn't that be a fun way to kill an hour or two.

"Your boy needs to leave," she said.

"He at our table?"

"Yeah, and you better get him out of here. Now."

"What's the damage?"

"None yet." They both took off for the VIP area. "But I don't want things to get that far, and we're right on the edge."

As they weeded in and out of the crowd, V glanced at those muscled arms of hers and thought about the job she had in the club. Hard-core for anyone, but especially a female. He had to wonder why she did it.

"Do you get off cracking males?" he said.

"Sometimes, but with O'Neal I prefer the sex."

V stopped dead.

The female glanced over her shoulder. "There a problem?"

"When did you do him?" Though he somehow knew it had been recently.

"The question is when I'll be with him again." She nodded toward the VIP checkpoint. "But it won't be tonight. Now go get him and haul him out of here."

V narrowed his eyes. "'Scuse the old-school, but Butch is OPP."

"Oh, really? Is that why he's in here almost every night getting faced? His mate must be a real darling."

"Don't go near him again."

The female's expression hardened. "Brother or not, you do *not* tell me to do anything."

V leaned in close and bared his fangs. "Like I said, you stay away from him."

For a split second, he thought they were going to go at it, he really did. He'd never thrown hand to hand with a female before, but this one . . . well, she didn't really seem female. Especially as she eyed his jaw like she was measuring her uppercut reach.

"You two want a room or a boxing ring?"

Vishous turned to see Rehvenge standing not three feet away, the male's amethyst eyes glowing in the dimness. Under the floodlights, that mohawk was as dark as the floor-length sable coat he wore.

"Do we have a problem?" Rehvenge glanced back and forth as he took off his fur and handed it to a bouncer.

"Not at all," V said. He glanced at the female. "Nothing doing, right?"

"Yeah," she drawled, crossing her arms over her chest. "Nothing."

V pushed past the bouncers in front of the velvet rope and went straight for the Brotherhood's table—*oh . . . man.*

Butch looked totally wasted and not just because he was drunk. His face was drawn in grim lines, his eyes half-closed. His tie was out of whack, his shirt partially unbuttoned . . . and there was a bite mark on his neck that had bled a little onto his collar.

And yup, he was spoiling for a fight, glaring at the rowdy table of highfliers two banquettes down. Shit, the cop was a hairbreadth away from jumping them, all coiled and ready to spring.

"Hey, my man." V sat down real slowly, thinking no sudden movements was a good plan. "What up?"

Butch threw back his Scotch without looking away from the class-A asses next door. "How're ya, V?"

"Good, good. So how many of those Lags you have?"

"Not enough. I'm still vertical."

"You want to tell me what's going on?"

"Not particularly."

"You got bit, buddy."

As the waitress came over and picked up the cop's empty, Butch touched the bite wounds on his throat. "Only because I forced her. And she stopped. She won't take me, not really. So she's with someone else. Right now."

"Shit."

"That's about the gist of it. As we're sitting here, my woman is with another man. He's an aristocrat, by the way. Did I mention that? A fancy-ass male is touching . . . yeah, anyway . . . Whoever he is, he's stronger than I am. He's giving her what she needs. He's feeding her. He's—" Butch cut off the tailspin. "So how's your night going?"

"I told you, the drinking doesn't have to be sexual."

"Oh, I know that." The cop leaned back as his next drink arrived. "You want some Goose? No? Okay . . . I'll hold it down for the both of us." He hammered half the Scotch before the waitress even turned around. "It's not just the sex. I can't stand the idea of someone else's blood in her. *I* want to feed her. *I* want to keep her alive."

"That's not logical, my man."

"Fuck logic." He looked down at the Scotch. "Jesus . . . didn't we just do this?"

"I'm sorry?"

"I mean . . . We were just here last night. Same drink. Same table. Same . . . everything. It's like I'm locked into this pattern and I'm sick of it. I'm sick of me."

"How about I take you home?"

"Don't want to go back to th—" Butch's voice cut off and he stiffened in his seat, his shot glass lowering slowly to the table.

V went on red alert. Last time the cop had sported that fixated expression there had been *lessers* in the fucking bushes. Except as Vishous looked around, he saw no one special, just the Reverend walking into the VIP area and heading for his office.

"Butch? My man?"

Butch stood up from the table.

Then moved so fast, V had no time to catch him.

TWENTY-SIX

Butch's body was out of his control and acting independently as he shot across the VIP section at Rehvenge. All he knew was that he'd caught Marissa's scent and tracked it over to the mohawk-sporting male. Next move was gunning for the guy like he was a felon.

He took the Reverend down hard, surprise working in his favor. As they hit the floor, the male's "What the fuck!" carried, and bouncers started homing in from all directions. Just before Butch got pulled off, he yanked Rehvenge's shirt collar open.

There they were. Puncture marks right on the guy's throat.

"No . . . shit, *no* . . ." Butch fought against the hard hands that grabbed at him, fought and kicked until somebody got in front of him, raised a fist and popped him one right in the face. As a bomb burst of pain went off in his left eye, he realized it was the female security guard who'd hit him.

Rehvenge plugged his cane into the floor and got up, his eyes a violent purple. "In my office. *Now*."

There was some conversation at that point, not that Butch was following much. The only thing he could focus on was the male in front of him and the evidence of the feeding. He pictured the guy's massive body underneath Marissa's, her face dropping down into his neck, her fangs piercing skin.

No doubt Rehvenge had satisfied her. No. Doubt.

"Why did it have to be you?" Butch yelled into the fray. "*I fucking like you*. Why did it have to be *you*?"

"Time to go." V cranked Butch into a headlock. "I'm taking you home."

"Not right now you aren't," Rehvenge snarled. "He took me down in *my* house. I want to know what the *fuck* was going through his head. And then you're gonna want to give me a good goddamn reason why I shouldn't cap both his knees."

Butch spoke up nice and loud. *"You fed her."*

Rehvenge blinked. Lifted his hand to his neck. "Excuse me?"

Butch growled at the bite marks, his body trying to break free again. God, it was like there were two halves of him. One that made a little sense. And one that was completely off the curve. Guess which side was winning.

"Marissa," he spat. "You fed her."

Rehv's eyes peeled wide. "You're the one? You're the one she's in love with?"

"Yeah."

Rehv sucked in a shocked breath. Then he rubbed his face and dragged his collar together, hiding the wounds. "Oh . . . hell. Oh . . . for fucking hell." He turned away. "Vishous, get him gone and sober him up. Jesus Christ, the world is too goddamned small tonight, it really is."

By this time, Butch's knees were going rubber and the club was starting to spin like a top. Man, he was much more drunk than he'd thought, and that blow to the puss hadn't helped.

Right before he passed out, he groaned, *"It should have been me. She should have used me . . ."*

Mr. X parked the minivan on an alley off Trade Street and got out. The city was gearing up for the night, the bars cranking their music and filling with the soon-to-be drunk and drugged.

Time to hunt for Brothers.

As Mr. X shut the door and adjusted his weapons, he looked over the Town & Country's hood at Van.

Man, he was still disappointed as hell at the guy's performance in the ring. Spooked, too. But then again, it was going to take a while for the power to coalesce. No *lesser* came out fresh from his initiation at full strength, and there was no reason to think that Van was any different just because he was the prophesied one.

Shit, though.

"How will I tell who's a vampire?" Van asked.

Ah, yes. The job at hand. X cleared his throat. "The civilians will recognize you because they can smell you, and you'll notice them when they get scared. As for the Brothers, there's no mistaking them. They're bigger and more aggressive than anything you've ever seen and they are first strikers. They will come after you if they see you."

They walked out onto Trade. The night was sharp as a slap, that combination of cold and damp that had always energized X to fight before. Now, though, his focus was different. He had to be out in the field because he was the *Fore-lesser*, but all he cared about was keeping him and Van on this side of reality until the guy matured into what he was.

They were about to duck into an alley when Mr. X stopped. Swiveling his head, he looked behind them. Then across the street.

"What is it—"

"Shut up." Mr. X closed his eyes and let his instincts go to work. Calming down, zoning out, he stretched his mental feelers through the night.

The Omega was nearby.

He flipped his lids open, thinking that had to be

bullshit, though. The master couldn't come over to this side without the *Fore-lesser*.

And yet the Evil was close.

Mr. X pivoted around on his combat boot. As a car drove down Trade, he stared over its roof at ZeroSum, that techno club. The master was in there. Definitely.

Oh, shit, had there been a change in *Fore-lesser*?

No, Mr. X would have been called home in that case. So maybe the Omega had used someone else to cross over? Could that even happen?

Mr. X jogged across the street to the club and Van was tight behind him, clueless but ready for anything.

ZeroSum's wait line was full of humans in flashy clothes, shivering and smoking and talking on cell phones. He paused. In the back . . . the master was around back.

Vishous pushed open ZeroSum's fire door with his hip and muscled Butch over to the Escalade. As he stuffed the cop into the backseat like a heavy rug roll, he prayed the bastard didn't wake up punching.

V was getting behind the wheel when he sensed something coming, his instincts flaring up, the ring-a-ding-ding setting off his adrenal gland. Although the Brotherhood didn't run from conflict by nature or training, his sixth sense told him to get Butch the fuck away from the club. *Now*.

He started the engine and peeled out. Just as he came to the mouth of the alley, he saw a pair of men coming toward the SUV, one of which was pale-haired. *Lessers*. Except how had those two known to head back here?

V stomped on the gas. Got him and Butch good and ghost.

As soon as he was satisfied they weren't being followed, he glanced back at the cop. Out. Cold. Man, that female security chief packed one hell of a punch. Then again, so had all that Lagavulin.

Butch didn't move for the whole trip to the compound. In fact, it wasn't until V carried the guy into the Pit and laid him out on his bed that the cop opened his eyes.

"Room's spinning."

"I'll bet."

"Face hurts."

"Wait 'til you see it and you'll know why."

Butch closed his lids. "Thanks for bringing me home."

Vishous was about to help the guy out of his suit when the doorbell rang.

With a curse, he went to the front of the gatehouse and checked the security monitors at his desk. He wasn't surprised at who it was, but holy hell, Butch was not ready for prime-time viewing right now.

V stepped into the vestibule and shut the door behind him before opening the outer one. As Marissa looked up at him, he could smell the sadness and the worry coming off her, the scent like dried roses.

Her voice was low. "I saw the Escalade pull up, so I know he's home now. I need to see him."

"Not tonight you don't. Come back tomorrow."

Her face hardened until it was like a marble depiction of her beauty. "I'm not leaving until he tells me to go."

"Marissa—"

Her eyes flashed. "Not until he tells me himself, warrior."

V measured her resolve and found she was packing with nothing lacking—kind of like that muscled head of security back at the club, just without the knuckles.

Well, wasn't this the night for female hard-asses.

V shook his head. "At least let me get him cleaned up, okay?"

Her eyes flared with panic. "Why would you have to?"

"Christ, Marissa. What did you think was going to happen when you fed from Rehvenge?"

Her mouth dropped open. "How did you know—"

"Butch went after him at the club."

"*What?* He . . . oh, God." Abruptly, her eyes narrowed. "You better let me inside. Right this minute."

V threw his hands up and muttered, "Fuck," as he opened the door.

TWENTY-SEVEN

Marissa marched past Vishous, and the Brother got out of her way. Which proved he was as smart as his reputation held.

When she got to the doorway of Butch's room, she stopped. From the glow of the hall light, she saw him lying on the bed on his back. His suit was all out of joint and there was blood on his shirt. Blood on his face, too.

She walked over and had to cover her mouth with her hand. "Dear Virgin in the Fade . . ."

One of his eyes was swollen and going black and blue again, and there was a cut on the bridge of his nose, which explained the blood. And he smelled like fresh Scotch.

From the doorway, Vishous's voice was uncharacteristically gentle. "You should really come back tomorrow. He's going to be pissed as hell that you saw him like this."

"Exactly who did this to him? And so help me God, if you say it was just a quick fight, I'm going to scream."

"Like I said, he went after Rehvenge. And Rehv happens to have a lot of bodyguards."

"Those must be big males," she said numbly.

"Actually, the one who nailed him was a female."

"A female?" Oh, why the hell did the particulars matter. "Can you bring me a couple of towels and some hot soapy water?" She went to Butch's feet and pulled off his shoes. "I want to wash him."

After V walked down the hall, she stripped Butch down to his boxers then sat beside him. The heavy gold cross that lay on his chest was a surprise. In the earlier frenzy up in the sitting room, she hadn't paid much attention to the thing, but now she wondered where he'd gotten it.

She looked farther down, to the black scar on his belly. Which seemed no better, no worse.

When V showed up with a bowl of suds and a short stack of terry cloth, she said, "Put it all on this table where I can reach it, then leave us, please. And shut the door behind you."

There was a pause. Which made sense. You didn't order around a member of the Black Dagger Brotherhood anywhere, much less in his own house. But her nerves were shot and her heart was breaking and she really didn't care what anyone thought of her.

It was her rule number one in action.

After a silent stretch, the things were placed where she wanted them and then the door clicked shut. Taking a deep breath, she wet one of the washcloths. As she touched Butch's face with it, he winced and muttered something.

"I'm so sorry, Butch . . . but it's over now." She returned the washcloth to the bowl, submerging it, then squeezing the excess water out. The dripping seemed very loud. "And nothing happened other than the feeding, I swear."

She got the blood off his face then stroked his hair, the thick waves damp from the washing. In response, he stirred and turned his face into her hand, but it was obvious he was dead drunk and not coming around.

"Are you going to believe me?" she whispered.

At any rate, she had proof. When she came to him a *newling*, he would know no other male had—

"I can smell him on you."

She jerked back at the harsh sound of his voice.

Butch's eyes opened slowly and they seemed black, not hazel. "I can smell him all over you. Because it wasn't from the wrist."

She didn't know how to respond. Especially as he focused on her mouth and said, "I saw the marks on his throat. And your scent was all over him, too."

When Butch reached out, she flinched. But all he did was stroke her cheek with his forefinger, light as a sigh.

"How long did it take?" he asked.

She stayed silent, instinct telling her the less he knew the better.

As he took his hand back, his face was hard and weary. Emotionless. "I believe you. About the sex."

"You don't look as if you do."

"Sorry, I'm a little distracted. I'm trying to convince myself I'm okay with tonight."

She looked down at her hands. "It felt all wrong to me, too. I cried the whole time."

Butch inhaled sharply, then all the tension went out of the air between them. He sat up and put his hands on her shoulders. "Oh, God . . . baby, I'm sorry I'm such a pain in the ass—"

"No, I'm sorry that I have to—"

"Shh, it's not your fault. Marissa, this is not your fault—"

"It feels that way—"

"My deficiency, not yours." His arms, those wonderful, heavy arms, slid around her and gathered her close to his bare chest. In return, she hung on to him for dear life.

As he kissed her temple, he murmured, "Not your fault. Ever. And I wish I could handle it better, I truly do. I don't know why I'm having such a hard time with this."

She pulled back abruptly, seized by an urgency she didn't question. "Butch, lay with me. Mate with me. Now."

"Oh . . . Marissa . . . I would love to, I really would." He smoothed her hair gently. "But not like this. I'm drunk and your first time should be—"

She cut him off with her mouth, tasting the Scotch and the male in him while she pushed him down on the mattress. When she slid her hand between his legs, he groaned and hardened right in her palm.

"I need you in me," she said roughly. "If not your blood, then your sex. In me. *Now*."

She kissed him again and as his tongue shot into her mouth she knew she had him. And oh, he was so good. He rolled her over and swept his hand from her neck to her breasts, then followed the path with his lips. When he got to the bodice of her gown, he stopped and his face grew hard again. With a savage movement, he gripped the silk and ripped the front of the dress clean apart. And he didn't stop at the waist. He kept going, his big hands and veined forearms working as he tore the satin right down the middle, all the way to the hem of the skirt.

"Take it off," he demanded.

She stripped the remnants from her shoulders, and when she lifted her hips, he yanked the dress out from under her, wadded it up, and pitched it across the room.

Eyes fierce, he came back at her, shoved her slip up, and spread her thighs. Looking at her over her body, his voice raw, he said, "Never wear that thing again."

As she nodded, he pushed her panties to the side and put his mouth right on her core. The orgasm he gave her was a claim staked, a mate's marking, and he made her ride it out until she was limp and shaking.

Then he tenderly eased her legs back together. Though she was the one who'd had the release, he was so much more relaxed as he prowled up her body. In a daze from what he'd done to her, she was weak and unresisting as he stripped her naked and then got up and took off his boxers.

As she looked at the size of him and realized what was

coming next, fear tickled the edges of her consciousness. But she was too blissed out to care much.

He was all male animal as he got back on the bed, his sex hard and thick, ready to penetrate. She opened her legs for him, except he lay beside her, not on top of her.

Now he went slowly. He kissed her long and sweet, his broad palm traveling to her breasts, touching her with care. Breathless, she curled her hands on to his shoulders and felt the muscles under his warm and supple skin bunch up as he stroked her hips, her thighs.

When he touched her between her legs, he was tender and unhurried, and it was a while before one of his fingers went inside of her. He stopped just as a strange internal tugging made her frown and move her hips back.

"Do you know what to expect?" he asked against her breast, his voice soft, low.

"Um . . . yes. I suppose." But then she thought of the size of his erection. How in God's name was it going to fit?

"I'll be as gentle as I can, but this . . . is going to hurt you. I had hoped maybe—"

"I know that's a part of it." She'd heard that there was a slight twinge involved, but then a wondrous ecstasy. "I'm ready."

He took back his hand and rolled on top of her, his body easing in between her legs.

Abruptly, everything came into sharp focus: the feel of his hot skin and the compression of his weight and the power in his muscles . . . and the pillow under her head and the mattress she was on and exactly how far her thighs were spread. She looked up at the ceiling. A swing of lights moved around above them as if a car had just pulled up in the courtyard.

She went tense; she couldn't help it. Even though it

was Butch and she loved him, the threat of the experience, the overwhelming nature of it, swamped her. Three hundred years and it had suddenly come down to here and now.

For some stupid reason, tears welled.

"Baby, we really don't have to do this." His thumbs wiped her cheeks and his hips pulled back as if he was going to get off.

"I don't want to stop." She grabbed on to the small of his back. "No—Butch, wait. I want this. I truly do."

He closed his eyes. Then dropped his head into her neck and worked his arms so they were all the way around her. Twisting to the side, he hugged her into his hard body and they stayed like that for a long time, his weight positioned so she could breathe, his arousal a hot, branding length on her thigh. She began to wonder if he was going to do anything at all.

Just as she was about to ask, he shifted and his hips fell solidly between her legs again.

He kissed her, a deep, drugging full-mouth seduction that got her burning until she was undulating under him, rubbing against his hips, trying to get closer to him.

And then it happened. He moved over a little to the left, and she felt his erection at her core, all hard and smooth. There was a broad, satin stroke and then some pressure. She went still, thinking about exactly what was pushing at her and where it wanted to go.

Butch swallowed hard enough for her to hear it and sweat broke out across his shoulders until it ran down his spine. As the pressure between her legs intensified, his breathing deepened until he was groaning on every exhale. When she winced in earnest, he abruptly backed off.

"What's wrong?" she asked.

"You're very tight."

"Well, you're very big."

He laughed in a burst. "Nicest things . . . you say the nicest things."

"Are you stopping?"

"Not unless you want me to."

When there wasn't any "no" coming from her, his body tensed up and the head of him found her entrance once again. His hand came up next to her face and he tucked her hair behind her ear.

"If you can, try and relax, Marissa. It'll go easier for you." He started a rocking motion, his hips easing into hers and retreating, a gentle to and fro. Except each time he tried to nudge in a fraction, her body resisted.

"You okay?" he said through gritted teeth.

She nodded even though she trembled. It all felt so strange, especially as they weren't making any real progress—

With a sudden slide he was in, slipping past some outer muscle until he came up against the barrier his finger had found. As she stiffened, Butch groaned and dropped his face into the pillow next to her head.

She smiled uneasily, the fullness in her unexpected. "I—ah, I feel like I should be asking whether you're all right."

"Are you kidding? I think I'm about to explode." He swallowed again, a desperate gulping. "But I hate the idea of hurting you."

"So let's get that part behind us."

She felt rather than saw his nod. "I love you."

With a quick jerk, he drew back his hips and sliced forward.

The pain was raw and fresh and she gasped, shoving against his shoulders to keep him from moving any farther in. Instinct had her body struggling under his, trying to find a way out or at the very least to get some distance.

Butch lifted his torso off her, and their bellies brushed while they both breathed hard. With his heavy cross swinging between them, she let out a raw curse. The pressure before had been mere discomfort. This wasn't. This hurt.

And she felt so invaded by him, taken over. God, that female chatter she'd overheard about how it was all lock-and-key wonderful, how the first time was magic, how everything was so easy—none of that was true for her.

Panic swelled. What if she really was broken on the inside? Was this the defect the males of the *glymera* had sensed? What if—

"Marissa?"

—she couldn't get through it at all? What if every time it hurt like this? Oh, Jesus . . . Butch was very male and he was very sexual. What if he went looking for other—

"Marissa, look at me."

She dragged her eyes to his face, but all she could pay attention to was the voice in her head. Oh, Jesus, it wasn't supposed to hurt this badly, was it? Oh, Jesus . . . she was defective . . .

"How you doing?" he said roughly. "Talk to me. Don't keep it inside."

"What if I can't stand it?" she blurted.

His expression went utterly bland, becoming a deliberate mask of calm. "I don't imagine many women like their first time. That romantic version of losing your virginity is a lie."

Or maybe it wasn't. Maybe she was the problem.

The word *defect* raced around her head even faster, even louder.

"Marissa?"

"I wanted it to be beautiful," she said with despair.

There was a horrible silence . . . during which all she

knew was the strain of his erection in her body. Then Butch said, "I'm sorry you're disappointed. But not all that surprised."

He started to pull out, and that was when something changed. As he moved, the dragging sensation caused a tingle to go through her.

"Wait." She grabbed on to his hips. "That's not all there is to it, right?"

"Pretty much. Just gets more invasive, though."

"Oh . . . but you haven't finished—"

"I don't need to anymore."

When his erection slipped free of her, she felt curiously empty. Then he moved off her body and she grew instantly cold. As he flipped a comforter over her, she felt his arousal brush against her thigh for an instant. The shaft was wet and had softened.

He settled on his back next to her, resting both forearms over his face.

God . . . what a mess. And now that she'd caught her breath, she wanted to ask him to keep going, but she knew what he would say. The "no" was in the stiffness of his body.

While they lay side by side, she felt like she should say something. "Butch—"

"I'm really tired and not at all coherent. Let's just go to sleep, okay?" He rolled away, punched a pillow, and exhaled in a long, uneven breath.

TWENTY-EIGHT

Marissa woke up later, surprised she'd slept at all. But that was feeding for you. No matter what, she always had to take rest afterward.

In the dimness, she checked the red glow of an alarm clock. Four hours to dawn and she had things to do that she needed the night for.

She looked over her shoulder. Butch was on his back, his hand on his bare chest, his eyes flickering to and fro under his lids as he slept deeply. His beard had grown in, his hair was all over the place, and he looked a lot younger. Handsome, too, in his slumber.

Why couldn't it have worked out better for them, she wondered. If only she could have held on a little longer, given it more of a chance, And now she had to go.

She slipped out from under the comforter, and the air was chilly on her skin. Moving quietly, she gathered up her slip, her corset . . . panties, where were her panties—

Stopping short, she looked down with surprise. On the inside of one of her thighs, there was a trickling warmth—blood. From when he'd taken her.

"Come here," Butch said.

She nearly dropped her clothes. "I—ah, I didn't know you were awake."

He held his hand out and she went to him. When she got close to the bed, he snaked his arm behind her leg and pulled her onto the mattress so her weight was resting on one knee. Then he leaned into her and she gasped as she felt his tongue on her inner thigh. In a warm stroke, he went up to her core and kissed away the remnants of her virginity.

She wondered where he'd learned the tradition from. Couldn't imagine human males practiced it on the females they took for the first time.

Whereas for her kind, it was a sacred moment between mates.

Shoot, she wanted to cry again.

Butch released her and lay back down, watching her with eyes that gave nothing away. For some reason, she felt so very naked before him, even with her slip clutched to her breasts.

"Take my robe," he said. "Put it on."

"Where is it?"

"Closet. Hanging on the door."

She turned around. His robe was deep red and marked with the scent of him, and she drew it on awkwardly. The heavy silk hung down to the floor and covered her feet, the tie so long she could have wrapped her waist four times with it.

She eyed the ruined dress on the floor.

"Leave it," he said. "I'll throw it out."

She nodded. Went over to the door. Grabbed the handle.

What could she say to make this better? She felt as if she'd made a mess of everything: first her biological reality driving a wedge between them, then her sexual deficiency exposed.

"It's okay, Marissa. You can just go. You don't need to say anything."

She dropped her head. "I'll see you at First Meal?"

"Yeah . . . sure."

In a numbed-out daze, she walked from the gatehouse to the mansion. When a *doggen* opened the vestibule's innermost door, she picked up the bottom of Butch's robe so she didn't trip . . . and was reminded she had nothing to change into.

Time to talk to Fritz.

After she found the butler in the kitchen, she asked him for the way to the garage.

"Are you looking for your clothes, mistress? Why don't I bring some up for you?"

"I'd rather go and pick out a few things myself." As he anxiously glanced to a door on the right, she walked in that direction. "I promise to call if I need you."

The *doggen* nodded, totally unappeased.

When she stepped into the garage, she stopped dead and wondered what the hell she'd walked into. There were no cars inside the six-bay space. No room for them. Good God . . . crates and crates and crates. No . . . not crates. Coffins? What was this?

"Mistress, your things are over here." From behind her, Fritz's voice was respectful but very firm, as if all those pine boxes were none of her business. "Please to follow me?"

He led her over to her four wardrobe trunks and her luggage and her boxes. "Are you sure I may not bring dresses up for you?"

"Yes." She touched the brass lock on one of her Vuittons. "Would you . . . leave me?"

"Of course, mistress."

She waited until she heard the door shut and then she freed the latch on the wardrobe trunk in front of her. As she pulled the two halves apart, skirts burst free, multi-hued, lush, beautiful. She remembered wearing the gowns to balls and *Princeps* Council meetings and her brother's dinners and . . .

Her skin crawled.

She went to the next trunk. And the next. And the

309

last. Then she started again with the first and went through each one again. And then again.

This was ridiculous. What did it matter what she wore? *Just pick something.*

She reached and grabbed . . . No, she'd had this on feeding from Rehvenge that first time. What about this one? No . . . that was the dress she'd worn at her brother's birthday party. Then what about . . .

Marissa felt the anger come upon her like a fire. Fury blew into her, overheated her, blazed through her blood. She grabbed gowns randomly and yanked them from their padded hangers, searching for one that didn't trigger a memory of being subjugated, caged, made fragile in fine cloth. She moved to another trunk and more dresses went flying, her hands wrenching, material ripping.

Tears began to flow and she wiped them away with impatience—until she couldn't see anything and had to stop. She scrubbed her face with her hands, then dropped her arms, just standing in the midst of a rainbow mess.

It was then that she spied a door in the far corner.

And beyond it, through its glass panes, she saw . . . the back lawn.

Marissa stared out at the patchy snow. Then she looked to the left, at the riding mower parked next to the door—and the red can sitting on the floor next to it. Her eyes kept going, moving over weed whackers and bins of what looked like fertilizer until they landed on a gas grill, which had a little box resting on its lid.

She glanced at the hundreds and hundreds of thousands of dollars' worth of haute couture.

It took her a good twenty minutes to drag each one of her gowns out into the backyard. And she was careful to include the corsets and the shawls in the pile as well. When she was finished, her clothes were ghostly in the moonlight, muted shadows of a life she would never go back to, a life of privilege . . . restriction . . . and gilded degradations.

She pulled out a sash from the tangle and went back into the garage with the pale pink strip of satin. Picking up the gas can, she grabbed the box of matches and didn't hesitate. She walked out to the priceless swirl of satins and silks, doused them with that clear, sweet accelerant, and positioned herself upwind as she took out a match.

She lit the sash. Then threw it.

The explosion was more than she'd expected, knocking her back, scorching her face, flaring into a great fireball.

As orange flames and black smoke rose, she screamed at the inferno.

Butch was lying on his back, staring up at the ceiling, when the alarms started going off. Shooting himself out of bed, he pulled on some boxers and slammed into Vishous as the brother bolted out of his bedroom and into the hallway. Together they scrambled to the computers.

"Jesus Christ!" V barked. "There's a fire on the back lawn!"

Some sixth sense sent Butch out the door immediately. Running barefoot across the courtyard, not even feeling the cold air or the pebbles under his feet, he cut around the front of the main house and ran into the garage. *Oh, shit!* Through the windows on the far side, he could see a great orange fury in the backyard.

And then he heard the screams.

As he burst through the rear door, Butch was overcome by heat and the treacle smells of gasoline and burning cloth. And he wasn't half as close as the figure right in front of the inferno.

"Marissa!"

311

Her body was angled forward toward the fire, her mouth wide open, her shrill hollering cutting through the night as surely as the flames did. She was crazed, roaming around the periphery . . . now running.

No! The robe! She was going to trip—

With horror, he saw it happen. His long, bloodred robe twisted around one of her legs and tangled up her feet. Lurching forward, she started to fall facefirst into the fire.

As panic hit Marissa's expression and her arms went out into thin air, everything went slo-mo: Butch ran hard, yet seemed not to move at all.

"*No!*" he screamed.

Just before she was lost to the flames, Wrath materialized behind her and scooped her up into his arms. Saving her.

Butch skidded to a halt, a paralytic weakness making his legs go jelly on him. With no air left in his lungs, he fell to the ground . . . just collapsed.

So he was on his knees, staring up as Wrath held Marissa in his arms and she sagged all over him.

"Thank God my brother got there in time," V muttered from somewhere close by.

Butch pushed himself to his feet, wobbling like he was on rocky ground.

"You okay?" V asked, reaching out.

"Yeah. Fine." Butch stumbled back to the garage and kept going, tripping through random doors, banging into walls. Where was he? Oh, inside the kitchen. Blindly, he looked around . . . and saw the butler's pantry. Pushing his way into the little room, he leaned back against the shelves and shut himself in with all the canned goods and the flour and the sugar.

His whole body started to shake until his teeth rattled, and his arms flapped like bird wings. God, all he could think about was Marissa burning. On fire. Helpless. In agony.

If it had been just him going for her, if Wrath hadn't somehow seen what was happening and dematerialized right to her, she would be dead now.

Butch wouldn't have been able to save her.

The thought naturally shot him right back to the past. With horrible precision, flashes of his sister getting in that car two and a half decades ago pinged around his skull. Shit, he hadn't been able to save Janie, either. Hadn't been able to pull her out of that Chevy Chevette in time.

Hell, maybe if Wrath had been around back then, the king could have rescued his sister, too.

Butch rubbed at his eyes, telling himself that the blurriness was just the aftereffects of all the smoke.

A half hour later, Marissa sat on the bed in the blue toile room, enveloped by a fog of mortification. Damn it, she'd taken her rule number one *way* too far.

"I'm so embarrassed."

Wrath, who was standing in the doorway, shook his head. "You shouldn't be."

"Well, I am." She tried to smile at him and missed the mark by a million miles. God, her face felt stiff, the skin tight from having been so close to all that heat. And her hair—her hair smelled like gas and smoke. So did the robe.

She shifted her eyes over to Butch. He was out in the hall, leaning back against the wall. He hadn't said a thing since appearing there a few minutes ago and he didn't look like he was coming into the room, either. He probably thought she was crazy. Hell, *she* thought she was crazy.

"I don't know why I did that."

"You're under a lot of stress," Wrath said, even though he wasn't the one she was looking at.

"That's no excuse."

"Marissa, don't take this the wrong way, but no one

313

cares. We want you safe and well. We could give a shit about the lawn."

When she just stared past Wrath at Butch, the king glanced over his shoulder. "Yeah, I think I'll leave you two alone. Try and get some z's, okay?"

As Wrath turned around, Butch said something that didn't carry. In response, the king clapped a hand to the back of the man's neck. More quiet words were shared.

After Wrath left, Butch came forward, but only as far as the doorway. "You going to be all right?"

"Ah, yes. After I have a shower." And a lobotomy.

"Okay. I'm going back to the Pit."

"Butch . . . I'm sorry I did what I did. It was just . . . I couldn't find one gown that wasn't contaminated with memories."

"I can understand that." Except clearly he didn't. He looked completely numb, as if he'd unplugged himself from everything. Especially her. "So . . . take care of yourself, Marissa."

She leaped to her feet as he backed away. "Butch?"

"You don't worry about anything."

What the hell did that mean?

She started to go after him, but Beth appeared in the doorway with a bundle in her hands. "Um, hi, you guys . . . Marissa, you have a minute?"

"Butch, don't go."

He nodded a greeting to Beth, then looked down the hall. "I need to sober up."

"Butch," Marissa said sharply, "are you saying good-bye here?"

He flashed her a haunting smile. "You're always going to be with me, baby."

He walked away slowly, like the floor was slippery under his feet.

Oh . . . Jesus . . .

Beth cleared her throat. "So, yeah, Wrath suggested you might like some clothes? I brought a few things if you'd like to try them on."

Marissa was desperate to go after Butch, but she'd already made a spectacle of herself tonight and he looked like he was in serious need of a break from the drama. Boy . . . she knew exactly how he felt, except for her there was no escape. Everywhere she went, there she was.

She looked at Beth, feeling like this was quite possibly the single worst twenty-four hours of her life. "Did Wrath mention that I burned my entire wardrobe?"

"Um . . . that did come up."

"I also left a crater in the lawn. It looks like a UFO landed. I can't believe he isn't upset with me."

The queen's smile was gentle. "The only thing he's not thrilled about is your giving Fritz that bracelet to sell."

"I can't have you two renting me somewhere to live."

"As a matter of fact, we wish you would just stay here."

"Oh . . . no, you've already been too kind. Actually, tonight, I'd planned . . . Well, before I got sidetracked by that gasoline and matches thing, I was going to go to my new place and look around. See what kind of furniture I'll need to buy."

Which would be everything.

Beth frowned. "About that rental house. Wrath wants Vishous to check out the security system before you move in. And chances are good that V will want to upgrade whatever is there."

"I don't think that's necessary—"

"Nonnegotiable. Don't even try it. Wrath wants you to stay here at least until that's done, okay? Marissa?"

She thought about Bella getting abducted. As much as

independence was a good thing, there was no reason to be stupid. "Yes . . . I . . . all right. Thank you."

"So would you like to try on some clothes?" Beth nodded at what was in her arms. "I don't have many dresses, but Fritz can get you some."

"You know what?" Marissa eyed the blue jeans the queen had on. "I've never worn a pair of pants before."

"I've got two pairs here if you want to try them out."

Well, wasn't this a night for firsts. Sex. Arson. Pants. "I think I would like to . . ."

Except Marissa burst into tears. Just totally lost it. And the meltdown was so bad, all she could do was sit on the bed and weep.

When Beth shut the door and knelt in front of her, Marissa wiped up quickly. What a nightmare. "You are queen. You shouldn't be before me like this."

"I'm the queen, so I can do anything I want." Beth put the clothes aside. "What's wrong?"

Yeah, now there was a list.

"Marissa?"

"I think . . . I think I might need someone to talk to."

"Well, you have someone right here. You want to give me a shot?"

God, there was so much, but one thing mattered more than all the rest. "Fair warning, my queen, this is about an improper subject. Sex, actually. It's about . . . sex."

Beth eased back and arranged her long legs yoga style. "Hit me."

Marissa opened her mouth. Shut it. Opened it. "I was taught not to speak of this kind of thing."

Beth smiled. "Just you and me in this room. No one has to know."

Okay . . . deep breath time. "Ah . . . I was a virgin. Up until tonight."

"Oh." After a long pause, the queen said, "And?"

"I didn't . . ."

"Like it?" When she couldn't respond, Beth said, "I wasn't into it my first time, either."

Marissa looked up. "Really?"

"It was painful."

"You hurt, too?" When the female nodded, Marissa was stunned. Then a little relieved. "It wasn't all painful. I mean, what led up to it was . . . *is* amazing. Butch makes me . . . he's just so . . . the way he touches me, I get . . . Oh, God, I can't believe I'm talking like this. And I can't explain what it's like with him."

Beth chuckled. "That's all right. I know what you mean."

"Really?"

"Oh, yeah." The queen's dark blue eyes glowed. "I know *exactly* what you mean."

Marissa smiled, then went back to the talking. "When it was time to . . . you know, when it happened, Butch was really gentle and all. And I wanted to like it, I honestly did. I was just overwhelmed and it was very painful. I think there's something wrong with me. Inside."

"There's nothing wrong with you, Marissa."

"But I . . . it really hurt." She wrapped her arms around her stomach. "Butch said most females have a difficult time with it in the beginning, but I just didn't . . . That's certainly not what the *glymera* says."

"No offense, because you're a part of the aristocracy, but I wouldn't take the *glymera's* word on anything."

The queen probably had a point. "How did you get through it with Wrath when you . . . ah . . ."

"My first time wasn't with him."

"Oh." Marissa flushed red. "Pardon me, I didn't mean—"

"No problem. Actually I didn't like sex until Wrath.

I'd been with two guys before him and just . . . whatever. I mean, I didn't understand what all the fuss was about. Frankly, though, even if Wrath had been my first, it probably wouldn't have been any easier given the size of his—" Now the queen was flushing. "Anyway . . . you know, sex is an invasion for the woman. Erotic and wonderful, but an invasion just the same, and it takes a little getting used to. And for some, the first time is quite painful. Butch will be patient with you. He'll—"

"He didn't finish. I got the impression he . . . couldn't."

"If he hurt you, I can understand why he'd want to stop."

Marissa threw up her arms. "God, I feel so damned ashamed. When it happened, my head got all tangled . . . I had all this stuff shooting through my brain. And before I left, I wanted to talk to him, but I couldn't find the words. I mean, I love him."

"Good. That's good." Beth took Marissa's hand. "And it's going to be all right, I promise you. You two just need to try it again. Now that the pain is over for you, you shouldn't have a problem."

Marissa stared into the queen's midnight blue eyes. And realized that in her whole life, no one had ever talked to her candidly about a problem she had. In fact . . . she'd never had a friend before. And that's what the queen felt like. A . . . friend.

"You know something?" Marissa murmured.

"What?"

"You're very kind. I can see why Wrath has bonded with you so."

"Like I said before, I'd do anything to help you."

"You really have. Tonight . . . you totally have." Marissa cleared her throat. "May I—ah, may I try the pants on?"

"Absolutely."

Marissa picked up the clothes, got a change of underwear from the bureau, and went into the bathroom.

When she came out, she had on a pair of slim black pants and a turtleneck. And she couldn't stop staring down at herself. Her body seemed so much smaller without all the skirting.

"How do they feel?" Beth asked.

"Odd. Light. Easy." Marissa walked around in her bare feet. "A little like I'm naked."

"You're thinner than I am, so they're a little baggy. But they look great."

Marissa went back into the bathroom and stared at herself in the mirror. "I think I like them."

When Butch returned to the Pit, he lurched down to his suite and started the shower. He kept the lights off because he had no interest in seeing how drunk and freaked out he still was, and he got under the spray, even though it was cold, in the hopes that the Antarctic wash would help sober him up.

With rough hands, he worked himself over with a bar of soap, and when he got to his privates, he didn't look down. Couldn't bear it. He knew what he was washing off his body, and his chest burned at the thought of the blood that had been on the inside of Marissa's thighs.

Man . . . seeing that had been a killer. Then he'd shocked the shit out of himself by doing what he did. He had no idea why he'd put his mouth to her or where the idea had come from. It had just seemed like the thing to do.

Oh . . . hell. He couldn't think about all that.

Quick shampoo. Quick rinse. And then he was out. He didn't bother toweling off, just went dripping to his bed and sat down. The air was freezing cold on his wet skin, and the chill felt like a proper punishment as he rested his chin on his fist and stared across the room. In the dim glow coming under the door, he saw the pile of clothes Marissa had taken off him earlier. Then that dress of hers on the floor.

He went back to looking at what he'd been wearing. That suit wasn't really his, was it. Neither was the shirt— or the socks or the loafers. Nothing he wore was his.

He glanced at the watch on his wrist. Took the thing off. Let it fall onto the carpet.

He didn't live in his own place. He didn't spend his own money. He had no job, no future. He was a well-kept pet, not a man. And as much as he loved Marissa, after what just happened on that back lawn, it was clear things couldn't work out between them. The relationship was flat-out destructive, especially for her: she was distraught, blaming herself for shit that wasn't her fault, suffering, and it was because of him. Goddamn it, she deserved so much better. She deserved . . . oh, shit, she deserved Rehvenge, that thick-blooded aristocrat. Rehv would be able to take care of her, give her what she needed, take her out socially, be her mate for centuries.

Butch got up, walked to the closet, and took out a Gucci duffel . . . then realized he didn't want to take anything of this life with him when he bailed.

Tossing the bag aside, he pulled on a pair of jeans and a sweatshirt, shoved his feet into some running shoes, and found the old wallet and set of keys he'd brought with him when he moved in with Vishous. As he looked at the metal tangle on its simple silver ring, he remembered that back in September he hadn't bothered to do anything with his apartment. So after all this time, his landlord must have long ago busted in and cleared out his stuff. Which was fine. It wasn't like he wanted to go back there anyway.

Leaving the keys, he headed out of his room, only to

realize he had no wheels. He glanced down at his feet. Looked like he was walking it down to Route 22, then hitching a ride from there.

He had no coherent plan for what he was going to do or where he would go. He knew only that he was leaving the brothers and Marissa and that was it. Well, he also knew that to make it stick, he was going to have to get out of Caldwell. Maybe he could head west or something.

When he walked into the living room, he was relieved V wasn't around. Saying good-bye to his roommate was nearly as awful as leaving his woman. So no reason to have that bon voyage convo.

Shit. What was the Brotherhood going to do about him pulling out? He knew a lot about them— *Whatever*. He couldn't stay, and if that meant action had to be taken, it would sure as hell put him out of his misery.

And as for what the Omega did to him? Well, he didn't have much of an answer for the whole *lesser* thing. But at least he wouldn't have to worry about hurting the brothers or Marissa. Because he wasn't planning on ever seeing them again.

His hand was on the vestibule's doorknob when V said, "Where you going, cop?"

Butch swiveled his head around as V stepped out of the shadows of the kitchen.

"V . . . I'm leaving." Before there was a response, Butch shook his head. "If that means you have to kill me, just do it quick and bury me fast. And don't let Marissa know."

"Why you pulling out?"

"It's better this way, even if it means I'm dead. Hell, you'll be doing me a favor if you have to off me. I'm in love with a woman I can't really have. You and the Brotherhood are the only friends I've got and I'm giving you up, too. And what the fuck do I have out in the real world waiting for me? Nothing. I got no job. My family thinks I'm whacked. The only good thing is that I'll be on my own with my own kind."

V approached, a tall, menacing shadow.

Shit, maybe this would all be over with tonight. Right here. Right now.

"Butch, man, you can't get out. I told you from the beginning. No getting out."

"So like I just said . . . snuff me. Grab a dagger and do me. But hear me clear. I will not stay in this world as an outsider one more minute."

As their eyes met, Butch didn't even brace himself. He wasn't going to fight. He was going to go gently into the good night, carried there by his best friend's hand on a good, clean kill.

There were worse ways to go, he thought. Many, many worse ways.

Vishous's eyes narrowed. "There may be another way."

"Another . . . V, buddy, a set of plastic fangs ain't going to make this better."

"Do you trust me?" When there was only silence, V repeated, "Butch, do you trust me?"

"Yeah."

"Then give me an hour, cop. Let me see what I can do."

TWENTY-NINE

Time dragged and Butch prowled around the Pit while waiting for V to get back. Finally, unable to shake the Scotch haze and still dizzy as shit, he went in and lay down on his bed. As he closed his eyes, it was more to dim the light than with any hope of sleep.

Surrounded by a dense quiet, he thought about his sister Joyce and that new baby of hers. He knew where the baptism had been held today: Same place he'd been dipped. Same place all the O'Neals had been dipped.

Original sin washed away.

He put his hand on his stomach, on that black scar, and thought that evil had certainly come back for him, hadn't it. Ended up right inside of him.

Palming his cross, he fisted the gold until it cut into his skin, and decided he needed to go back to church. Regularly.

He was still gripping the crucifix when exhaustion took him by stealth, leaching his thoughts away, replacing them with a nothingness he would have been relieved by if he'd been conscious.

Sometime later, he woke up and glanced at the clock. He'd slept for two hours straight, and now he was in the hangover phase of things, his head one big, dull ache, his eyes supersensitive to the light coming in under the door. He rolled over and stretched, his spine cracking.

An eerie moan drifted down the hall.

"V?" he said.

Another moan.

"You okay there, V?"

From out of nowhere, there was a crashing noise, like something heavy had been dropped. Then choking sounds, the kind you made when you were too hurt to cry out and scared to death. Butch sprang off his bed and ran into the living room.

"Jesus Christ!"

Vishous had thrown himself off the couch and landed facefirst on the coffee table, scattering bottles and glasses. As he flailed around, his eyes were squeezed shut and his mouth gaped with screams unvoiced.

"Vishous! Wake up!" Butch grabbed on to those heavy arms, only to realize V had taken his glove off: That god-awful hand of his was glowing like the sun, burning holes in the wood of the table and the leather of the couch.

"*Fuck!*" Butch leaped out of the strike zone as he nearly got swiped.

All he could do was call out Vishous's name as the brother struggled in the grip of whatever monster held him. Finally, something got through. Maybe the sound of Butch's voice. Maybe V knocked himself around hard enough to wake himself up.

As Vishous opened his eyes, he was panting and shivering, covered with fear sweat.

"My man?" When Butch knelt down and touched his friend on the shoulder, V shrank back, cowering. Which was the scariest part. "Hey . . . easy, you're home. You're safe."

V's stare, usually so cool and calm, was glassy. "Butch . . . oh, my God. Butch . . . the death. The death . . . The blood down the front of my shirt. A shirt of mine . . ."

"Okay, just go easy. We're going to cool out here, big guy." Butch clamped a hand under V's right armpit and hoisted the brother back on the couch. Poor bastard flopped against the leather cushions like a rag doll. "Let's get you a drink."

Butch headed for the galley kitchen, picked up a fairly clean glass off the counter, and rinsed it out. He filled the thing with cold water, even though V would no doubt rather it be Goose.

When he came back, Vishous was lighting up a cigarette with hands that were like flags in the wind.

As V took the glass, Butch said, "You want something stronger?"

"Nah. This is good. Thanks, man."

Butch sat down on the other end of the sofa. "V, I think it's time we did something about this nightmare thing."

"Not going there." V inhaled deeply and let out a steady stream of smoke from his lips. "Besides, I've got good news. Kind of."

Butch would rather have stayed on the V dreamland shit, but that was clearly not happening. "So talk. And you should have woken me up as soon as you—"

"Tried. You were out cold. Anyway . . ." Another exhale. This one more normal. "You know I've looked into your past, right?"

"I figured."

"Had to know what was doing, if you were going to live with me—with us. I traced your blood back to Ireland. Lot of pasty-white bog people in your veins, cop."

Butch got real still. "Did you find . . . anything else?"

"Not when I searched nine months ago. And not when I retraced you an hour ago."

Oh. Buzz kill. Although, Christ, what was he thinking? He wasn't a vampire. "So why are we talking about this?"

"You sure you don't have any weird-ass stories in your family? Especially back in Europe? You know, some female in your line getting pinched at night? Maybe a pregnancy that came out of the blue? Like someone's daughter who disappeared and maybe came back with a child?"

Actually, there hadn't been a lot of O'Neal lore passed along. For his first twelve years, his mother had been busy raising six kids and working as a nurse. Then after Janie's murder, Odell had been too shattered to carry stories. And his father? Yeah, right. Pulling nine to five for the telephone company and then hitting the night shift as a security guard didn't make for a lot of quality chat time with the kidlets: When Eddie O'Neal had been home, he'd been drinking or asleep.

"I don't know of anything."

"Well, here's the deal, Butch." V inhaled, then talked through the smoke as he breathed out. "I want to see if you've got any of us in you."

Whoa. "But you know my family tree, right? And wouldn't my blood tests at the clinic, or even throughout my life, have shown something?"

"Not necessarily and I have a very precise way of finding out. It's called ancestor regression." V brought up his glowing hand and clenched it into a fist. "Goddamn, I hate this thing. But this is how we do it."

Butch eyed the scorched coffee table. "You're going to torch me like kindling."

"I'll be able to channel it to the purpose. Not saying it will be fun for you, but it shouldn't kill you. Bottom line? That shit with Marissa and the feeding and the way you reacted to it? The fact that you're telling me you throw off scent around her? Plus god knows, you're aggressive enough. Who knows what we'll find."

Something warm tingled in Butch's chest. Something like hope. "And what if I have a vampire relative?"

"Then we might . . ." V took a very deep drag on the hand-rolled. "We might be able to turn you."

326

Holy. *Shit*. "I thought you couldn't do that."

V nodded over at a thigh-high stack of leather volumes by the computers. "There is something in the Chronicles. If you've got some of our blood in you, we can give it a shot. It's very risky, but we could try."

Man, Butch was *so* on board with that plan. "Let's do the regression. Now."

"Can't. Even if you have the DNA, we need to get clearance from the Scribe Virgin before we even think about jump-starting any kind of change. That kind of shit is not to be done lightly, and there's the added complication of what the *lessers* did to you. If she won't allow us to proceed, it won't matter whether you've got relatives with fangs, and I don't want to put you through an ancestor regression if there's nothing we can do about it."

"How long until we know?"

"Wrath said he'd talk to her tonight."

"Jesus, V. I hope—"

"I want you to take some time and think about this. The regression is a bitch to go through. Your brain's going to stroke out on us and I understand the pain's no party. And you might want to talk to Marissa about it, also."

Butch thought of her. "Oh, I'll get through it. You don't worry about that."

"Don't get cocky—"

"I'm not. This has to work."

"Might well not, though." V stared at the lit tip of his hand-rolled. "Assuming you come out the other side of the regression okay, and we can find a living relative of yours to use to jump-start the change, you could die in the middle of the transition. There's only a small chance you'll survive."

"I'll do it."

V laughed in a short burst. "I can't decide whether you have serious balls or a death wish."

"Never underestimate the power of self-hatred, V. It's a hell of a motivator. Besides, we both know what the only other option is."

As their stares met, Butch knew V was thinking the same thing he was: No matter what the risks were, anything was better than Vishous having to kill him outright because he had to leave.

"I'm going to Marissa now."

Butch paused on his way out the door to the tunnel. "You sure there isn't something we can do about these dreams of yours?"

"You got enough on your plate."

"I'm an excellent multitasker, buddy."

"Go to your female, cop. Don't worry about me."

"You're such a pain in the ass."

"Said the SIG to the Glock."

Butch cursed and hit the tunnel, trying not to be totally pumped. When he got to the big house, he went up to the second floor and passed by Wrath's study. On impulse, he knocked on the jamb. After the king called out, Butch was in there maybe ten minutes tops before he went on to Marissa's room.

He was about to knock when someone said, "She's not there."

He pivoted around and saw Beth coming out of the sitting room at the end of the hall, a vase of flowers in her hands.

"Where is Marissa?" he asked.

"She went with Rhage to check out her new place."

"What new place?"

"She's rented a house for herself. About seven miles from here."

Shit. She was moving out. And she hadn't even told him. "Exactly where is it?"

After Beth gave him the address and assured him the rental was safe, his first instinct was to race over there, but he canned that idea. Wrath was going to the Scribe Virgin right now. Maybe they could get the regression over with and there'd be good news to share on the other side.

"She's coming back tonight, right?" Man, he wished she'd told him about the move out.

"Definitely. And Wrath is going to ask Vishous to work on the security system, so she'll stay here until that's done." Beth frowned. "Hey . . . you don't look so good. Why don't you come down and get some food with me?"

He nodded, even though he had no idea what she'd said to him. "You know I love her, right?" he blurted, not sure why he was going there.

"Yes, I do. And she loves you."

Then why didn't she talk to him?

Yeah, and just how easy had he made that for her lately? He'd freaked out about the feeding. Taken her virginity while he was drunk. Hurt her in the process. Christ.

"I'm not hungry," he said. "But I'll watch while you eat."

Back at the Pit, Vishous stepped out of the shower and yelped like a nancy, slamming back against the marble wall. Wrath was standing in the bathroom, a big leather-clad male the size of the goddamned Escalade.

"*Christ*, my lord. Scare a brother, why don't you."

"Little jumpy there, V, huh?" Wrath handed over a towel. "So I just came back from the Scribe Virgin."

V paused with the terry cloth under an arm. "What did she say?"

"She wouldn't see me."

"Goddamn it, why?" He wrapped up his hips.

"Some shit like 'wheels turning.' Who knows. One of

the Chosen met me." Wrath's jaw went so tight it was a wonder he could talk at all. "Anyway, I go back tomorrow night. Straight up, it doesn't look good."

As frustration spiked, V felt his eyelid start to flicker. "Shit."

"Yeah." There was a pause. "And while we're on the subject of crap, let's talk about you."

"Me?"

"You're strung tighter than cable and your eye's twitching."

"Yeah, because you just Friday-the-thirteenthed me." V pushed past the king and went into his bedroom.

As he put his glove on his hand, Wrath leaned against the jamb. "Look, Vishous . . ."

Oh, they were so not doing this. "I'm fine."

"Sure you are. So here's the deal. I'm giving you till the end of the week. If you haven't straightened up by then, I'm taking you out of rotation."

"What?"

"Vacation time. Can you say R&R, my brother?"

"Are you out of your mind? You realize we're down to four of us now with Tohr being gone, true? You can't afford to—"

"Lose you. Yeah, I know. And so you're not going to get killed because of whatever's going on in that head of yours. Or not going on, as is the case."

"Look, we're all on edge, what with—"

"Butch came by a little while ago. Told me about your repeating nightmare."

"That cocksucker." Man, he was going to pound his room-mate into the ground like a stake for blabbing.

"He was right to tell me. *You* should have told me."

V went over to his bureau, where his rolling papers and his tobacco were. He spun one up fast, needing something

330

in his mouth. It was either plug himself up or keep swearing.

"You need to get checked out, V."

"By who? Havers? No CAT scan or lab workup is going to tell me what's wrong, because it's not physical. Look, I'll get it together." He glanced over his shoulder and exhaled. "I'm the smart one, remember? I'll figure this out."

Wrath lowered his wraparounds, his pale green eyes burning like neon penlights. "You've got a week to fix this, or I'm going to the Scribe Virgin about you. Now get your ass dressed. I need to talk to you about something else involving the cop."

As the king took off for the living room. V drew hard on his cigarette and then looked around for his ashtray. Goddamn it, he'd left the thing out front.

He was about to head to the living room when he looked at his hand. Bringing the gloved nightmare up to his mouth, he peeled the leather off with his teeth and stared at his radiant curse.

Shit. The illumination was getting brighter and brighter every day.

Holding his breath, he pressed the lit cigarette into his palm. As the flaming end met his skin, the white glow beneath flared even stronger, backlighting the tattooed warnings until they appeared to be in 3-D.

The hand-rolled was consumed in a burst of light, the sting tingling his nerve endings. When only dust remained, he blew it off into the air, watching the little cloud rush forward and disintegrate into nothing.

Marissa took a tour through the vacant house and ended up back in the living room, where she'd started. The place was much bigger than she'd thought, especially given the six underground bedroom suites. God, she'd taken the lease because it had seemed so much smaller than her brother's—than Havers's—but size was so relative. This Colonial felt huge. And very empty.

As she pictured herself moving in, she realized that she'd never actually been in a house alone before. Back home, there had always been servants and Havers and patients and medical staff. And the Brotherhood's mansion was likewise full of people.

"Marissa?" Rhage's heavy boots came up behind her. "Time to go."

"I haven't measured the rooms yet."

"Have Fritz come back and do it."

She shook her head. "This is my house. I want to."

"Then there's always tomorrow night. But we have to get going now."

She took a last look around, then headed for the door. "Okay. Tomorrow."

They dematerialized back to the mansion, and as they came in through the vestibule, she could smell roast beef and hear talk drifting out of the dining room. Rhage smiled at her and started to disarm, stripping his dagger holster off his shoulders as he called out for Mary.

"Hey."

Marissa wheeled around. Butch was in the shadows of the billiards room, leaning on the pool table, a squat crystal glass in his hand. He was dressed in a fine suit and a pale blue tie . . . but as she stared at him, all she saw was him naked and propped up on his arms over her.

Just as heat swirled, his eyes shifted away. "You look different in pants."

"What—oh. They're Beth's."

He took a drink from his glass. "Heard you're renting a place."

"Yes, I've just come from—"

"Beth told me. So how much longer have you got here? A week? Less? Probably less, right."

"Probably. I was going to tell you, but I just rented it, and with all the other drama, I didn't have time to. I wasn't hiding it from you or anything." When he didn't reply, she said, "Butch? Are you—are we . . . okay?"

"Yeah." He looked down into his Scotch. "Or at least we're going to be."

"Butch . . . Look, about what happened—"

"You know I don't care about the fire."

"No, I mean . . . in your bedroom."

"The sex?"

She flushed and dropped her eyes. "I want to try it again."

When he said nothing, she glanced up.

His hazel stare was intense. "You know what I want? Just once, I want to be enough for you. Just . . . once."

"You are—"

He spread out his arms and glanced down at his body. "Not like this I'm not. But I'm going to make it so I can be. I'm going to take care of this problem of me."

"What are you talking about?"

"Will you let me escort you in to dinner?" As if to distract her, he came forward and offered her his arm. When she didn't take it, he said, "Trust me, Marissa."

After a long moment, she accepted his courtesy, thinking that at least he hadn't pulled away from her. Which was what she could have sworn he'd been doing just after the fire.

"Hey, Butch. Hold up, my man."

Both she and Butch looked over. Wrath was coming out of the hidden door underneath the stairs and Vishous was with him.

"Evening, Marissa," the king said. "Cop, I need you a sec."

Butch nodded. "What up?"

"Will you excuse us, Marissa?"

The expressions on the Brothers' faces were bland, their bodies relaxed. And she didn't buy the nothing special for an instant. But like she was going to hang around?

"I'll wait for you at the table," she told Butch.

She headed to the dining room, then paused and looked back. The three males were standing together, Vishous and Wrath towering over Butch as they did the talking. A surprised look hit Butch's face, his brows lifting up into his forehead. Then he nodded and crossed his arms over his chest—like he was braced and ready to go.

Dread washed over her. Brotherhood business. She just knew it.

When Butch came to the table ten minutes later, she said, "What did Wrath and V talk to you about?"

He snapped his napkin loose of its folds and put the damask in his lap. "They want me go through Tohr's house and pull a CSI. Try and see if the guy's been back or left any clues as to where he's gone."

Oh. "That's . . . good."

"It's what I did for a living for many years."

"Is that all you'll be doing?"

As a plate of food was set in front of him, he finished his Scotch. "Yup. Well . . . the brothers are going to start patrolling rural areas, so they've asked me to work up a route for them. I'm going to go with V and do that after sundown tonight."

She nodded, telling herself it was going to be fine. As long as he wasn't fighting. As long as he didn't—

"Marissa, what's wrong?"

"I, ah, I just don't want you to get hurt. I mean, you're human and all and—"

"So today I need to do some research."

Well . . . if that wasn't a door getting shut on her. And if she pressed the point, she'd only make it sound like she thought he was totally weak. "Research on what?"

He picked up his fork. "What happened to me. V's already been through the Chronicles, but he said I could give it a shot, too."

As she nodded, she realized they would not spend the day sleeping together, side by side, in his bed. Or hers.

She took a sip from her water glass and marveled at how you could sit so close to someone and still have him be totally far away from you.

THIRTY

The following afternoon, John took a seat in the classroom, all impatient for things to get rolling. The schedule of classes ran on a three-days-on, one-day-off rotation, and he was ready to get back to work.

While he went through his notes on plastic explosives, the other trainees yakked it up as they came in and got settled, the horsing around business as usual . . . until everyone fell silent.

John glanced up. There was a man in the doorway, a man who looked a little unsteady, or maybe drunk. What the hell—

John's mouth went slack as he stared at the face and the red hair. *Blaylock.* It was . . . Blaylock, only better.

The guy looked down and awkwardly walked to the back. Actually, he shuffled more than walked, as if he couldn't really control his arms and legs all that well. After he sat down, he moved his knees around under the table until they fit, then he hunched over as if trying to make himself look smaller.

Yeah, good luck on that. Jesus, he was . . . huge.

Holy crap. He had gone through the transition.

Zsadist walked into the classroom, shut the door, and glanced at Blaylock. Following a quick nod, Z went right into the teaching.

"Today we're going to do an intro to chemical warfare. We're talking tear gas, mustard gas—" The Brother paused. Then cursed as he obviously realized no one was paying any attention because they were all staring at Blay.

"Well, shit. Blaylock, you want to tell them what it was like? We're not going to get anything done here until you do."

Blaylock turned beet red and shook his head, tucking his arms around his chest.

"Okay, trainees, shoot your eyes up here." They all looked at Z. "You want to know what it's like, I'll tell you."

John got good and fixated. Z kept everything general, revealing nothing of himself, but it was all good information. And the more the Brother talked, the more John's body vibrated.

That's right, he told his blood and bones. *Take notes and let's do this soon.*

He was *so* ready to be a man.

Van got out of the Town & Country, shut the passenger-side door quietly, and stayed in the shadows. What he was looking at some hundred yards away reminded him of where he'd grown up: run-down house with a tar-paper roof and a rotting car in the side yard. The only difference was that this was in the middle of nowhere, and his neighborhood had been closer to town. But it was the same two steps up from poverty.

As he scanned the area, the first thing he noticed was an odd sound cutting through the night. It was a rhythmic hitting . . . like someone was chopping logs? No . . . it was closer to pounding. Someone was pounding on what was probably the back door of the house in front of him.

"This is your target for tonight," Mr. X said as two other *lessers* stepped out of the minivan. "The daylight details have been watching this place for the past week. No activity until after dark. Iron bars over the windows.

Drapes are always drawn. Goal is capture, but kill if you think they're going to get away from you—"

Mr. X stopped and frowned. Then looked around.

Van did the same and saw nothing out of whack.

Until a black Cadillac Escalade came down the drive. With its tinted windows and its spinning chrome, the thing looked like it was worth more than the house. What the hell was it doing out here in the sticks?

"Get armed," Mr. X hissed. *"Now."*

Van drew his fancy new Smith & Wesson forty, feeling the weight fill his palm. As his body primed for the fight ahead, he was so ready to engage an opponent.

Except Mr. X pegged him with hard eyes. "You stay back. I do not want you to engage. Just watch."

You fucker, Van thought, dragging a hand through his dark hair. *You miserable fucker.*

"We clear?" Mr. X's face was deadly cold. "You do *not* go in."

The best Van could manage was a dip of the chin and he had to look away to keep from cursing out loud. Training his eyes on the SUV, he watched as the thing got to the end of the ratty little cul-de-sac and stopped.

Clearly, it was some kind of patrol. Not cops, though. At least, not human ones.

The Escalade's engine was cut and two men got out. One was relatively normal-sized, assuming you were talking about linebackers. The other guy was *enormous*.

Jesus Christ . . . a Brother. Had to be. And Xavier was right. That vampire was bigger than anything Van had ever seen—and he'd gone into the ring with some monster-sized mofo's in his day.

Just like that, the Brother was gone. *Poof!* into thin air. Before Van could ask what the holy hell that was about, the vampire's partner turned his head and stared right at Mr. X. Even though they were all in the shadows.

"Oh, my God . . ." Xavier breathed. *"He's alive*. And the master . . . is with . . ."

The *Fore-lesser* lurched forward and kept walking. Right into the moonlight. Right into the middle of the road.

What the fuck was he thinking?

Butch's body trembled as he looked at the pale-haired *lesser* who emerged from the darkness. No question, this was the one who'd worked him over: Even though Butch had no conscious memories of the torture, his body seemed to know who had done the damage, its recollection embedded in the very flesh that had been torn and bruised by the bastard.

Butch was so ready to have at the *Fore-lesser*.

Except the shit hit the fan before he ever had the chance.

From somewhere behind the house, a chain saw started up with a roar, then settled into a high, whining scream. And at that exact moment, a second pale-haired *lesser* stepped out from the woods with his gun aimed at Butch.

As the semiautomatic went off and bullets whizzed by his head, Butch palmed his own Glock and jammed for cover behind the Escalade. Once he had some shield, he returned the *hi-how-are-ya*s, squeezing out rounds, his Glock kicking in his palm as he kept his vital organs out of the line of fire. When there was a breather in the exchange, he peered through bulletproof glass. The shooter was behind a rusted-out car carcass, no doubt reloading. Like Butch was.

And yet the first slayer, Butch's torturer, still hadn't armed himself. The guy was just standing in the middle of the road, staring at Butch.

Almost like eating lead would make his day.

So ready to fucking oblige, Butch leaned out around the SUV, pulled his trigger, and popped the guy right in the chest. With a grunt, the *Fore-lesser* staggered back, but he didn't go down. He seemed merely annoyed, throwing off the bullet's impact like it was nothing more than a bee sting.

Butch had no idea what to make of that, but now wasn't the time for wondering why his fancy bullets didn't slow that particular slayer down. Sticking his arm into the breeze, he started firing at the guy again, the shots kicking out of his muzzle in quick succession. Finally, the *lesser* yard-saled, falling backward in a sprawling heap—

Just as a slapping noise came from behind Butch, so loud he thought another gun was going off.

He swung around, two-fisting the Glock to keep it up in front and steady. *Oh, shit!*

A female with a child in her arms shot out of the house in a blind panic. And she had good reason to haul ass. Right on her heels was a hulking male with punishment on his face and a chain saw up over his shoulder. The lunatic was about to fall on the pair of them with that spinning blade, ready, willing, and able to kill.

Butch kicked up his gun muzzle two inches, aimed at the man's head, and pulled the trigger—

Right as Vishous appeared behind the guy, reaching for the saw.

"Fuck!" Butch tried to stop his forefinger from squeezing, but the gun bucked and the bullet flew—

And someone grabbed Butch around the throat: The second *lesser* with the gun had moved in fast.

Butch got flipped off his feet and slammed onto the hood of the Escalade like he was a baseball bat. On impact, he lost his Glock, the weapon bouncing away, metal on metal.

Fuck that, though. He shoved his hand into the pocket of his coat and felt for the switchblade he carried. Bless the damn thing's heart, it found his palm like it had come to a heel and he dragged his arm free. As the blade shot out, he jogged his torso to the left and stabbed the side of the slayer who held him down.

Howl of pain. Grip loosened.

Butch shoved hard against the chest above his, popping the *lesser* up off him. As the bastard hung in midair for a split second, Butch swung the knife in an arc. The switchblade streaked across the *lesser's* throat, opening up a fountainhead of black blood.

Butch kicked the slayer to the ground and turned to the house.

Vishous was holding his own against the guy with the chain saw, avoiding the roaring blade while throwing body shots. Meanwhile, the female with the child was running like hell across the side yard while another, pale-haired *lesser* closed in from the right.

"Called for Rhage," V had the presence of mind to holler.

"Going for vic," Butch yelled as he took off. He ran flat out, his feet gouging into the ground, knees kicking up to his chest. He prayed he would get there in time, prayed he'd be fast enough . . . *Please, just this once . . .*

He intercepted the *lesser* with a spectacular flying tackle. As they went down, he screamed for the female to keep going.

Gunshots went off somewhere, but he was too busy with a blurring struggle to care. He and the *lesser* rolled around in the patchy snow, punching and choking each other. He knew he was going to lose if they kept going like this, so out of desperation and some kind of driving instinct, he stopped fighting, let the slayer dominate him . . . and then locked stares with the undead.

That link, that horrible communion, that ironclad tie between them took root in an instant, rendering them both motionless. And with the bonding came an urge for Butch to consume.

He opened his mouth and began to inhale.

THIRTY-ONE

Lying in the middle of the road, bleeding like a sieve, Mr. X kept his eye on the contaminated human who was supposed to be dead. The guy handled himself, especially as he took down a *lesser* in the side yard, but he was going to get overpowered. And sure enough, he did. As the slayer flipped him on his back, he was going to get slaughtered in—

Except then the pair of them froze, and the dynamic shifted, the rules of strength and weakness getting scrambled. The slayer might have been on top, but the human was in charge.

Mr. X became breathless. Something was happening over there . . . something . . .

But then a blond-haired Brother materialized out of thin air right beside the two. The warrior swooped down and tore the *lesser* off the human, breaking whatever link had been forged—

From out of the shadows, Van came over and blocked Mr. X's view. "How'd you like to get out of here?"

Probably the safest course. He was about to pass out. "Yeah . . . and move fast."

As Mr. X got picked up and rushed to the minivan, his head bobbed like a half-stuffed doll's, and he watched through the wobbles as the blond Brother disintegrated the other *lesser* then knelt to check on the human.

Such fucking heroes.

Mr. X let his eyes go lax. And thanked a God he didn't believe in that Van Dean was too much of a new recruit to know that *lessers* didn't take their injured back home with them. Usually, a damaged slayer was left where he fell either for the Brothers to stab him back to the Omega or for him to gradually rot.

Mr. X felt himself get shoved into the minivan, and then the engine started and they were off. Easing over onto his back, he felt around his chest, assessing the damage. He was going to recover. It would take time, but his body wasn't so hurt that it couldn't regenerate.

As Van hung a sharp right, X was thrown against the door.

At his grunt of pain, Van looked back. "Sorry."

"Fuck it. Get us gone."

As the engine grew louder again, Mr. X closed his eyes. Man, that human showing up alive and breathing? Serious trouble. *Serious* trouble. What had happened? And why didn't the Omega know that the human still lived? Especially because the guy reeked of the master's presence?

Shit, who knew the whys. The more important thing was, now that X was aware that the man lived, did he tell the Omega? Or would that little news flash be what triggered another change in leadership and got X condemned forever? He'd sworn to the master that the Brothers had taken that guy out. He'd look like an idiot when it turned out not to be true.

The thing was, he was alive and on this side now, and he had to keep himself here until Van Dean came into his power. So, no . . . there would be no report on the Trojan human.

But the man was a dangerous liability. One that had to be eliminated ASAP.

Butch lay stiff on the snowy ground, trying to catch his breath, still caught in whatever the hell happened when he and one of those *lessers* got tight.

As his stomach rolled, he wondered where Rhage was. After Hollywood had cut off the link to the *lesser* and killed the bastard, he'd headed into the woods to make sure there were no others around.

So it was probably a good idea to get vertical and re-armed in case more came.

As Butch pushed himself up on his arms, he saw the mother and child across the lawn. They were cowering by a shed, wrapped up together as tight as vines. Shit . . . he recognized them; he'd seen them at Havers's. These were the two Marissa had been sitting with the day he'd finally left the quarantine room.

Yeah, this was definitely the pair. The young had a cast on her lower leg.

Poor things, he thought. Huddled as they were, they were like every human victim he'd ever seen on the job, the characteristics of trauma transcending species lines: The mother's wide eyes and pale skin and shattered illusions that life was okay were exactly what he'd dealt with before.

He got to his feet and went over to them slowly.

"I'm a—" He almost said *police detective*. "I'm a friend. I know what you are and I'm going to take care of you."

The mother's dilated eyes lifted from her daughter's messy hair.

Keeping his voice level and not taking one step closer, he pointed to the Escalade. "I'd like you both to go sit in that car. I'll give you the keys so you're in control and can lock yourself in. Then I'm going to do a quick check-in with my partner, okay? After that, you're going to Havers's."

He waited as the female surveyed him with a calculation he was very familiar with: Would he hurt her or her child? she was wondering. Did she dare trust someone of the opposite sex? What were her other options?

Keeping her daughter tight in her arms, she struggled to her feet, then held her hand way out. He came over and put his keys in her palm, knowing that V had another set so they could still get in the Escalade if they had to.

In a flash, the female turned and ran, her child a heavy, jangling load.

As Butch watched them go, he knew that little girl's face was going to keep him up at night. Unlike her mother, she was totally calm. Like this kind of violence was business as usual.

With a curse, he jogged over to the house and shouted, "V, I'm coming in."

Vishous's voice drifted down from the second floor. "There's no one else in here. And I didn't get a plate on that minivan that took off."

Butch checked out the body in the doorway. Male vampire, looked thirty-four years old or so. Then again, they all did until they started to age.

With his foot, Butch nudged the guy's head. It was loose as a bow on a present.

V's shitkickers came down the stairs. "He still dead?"

"Yup. You got him good—shit, your neck's bleeding. Did I shoot you?"

V put his hand up to his throat, then looked at the blood on his palm. "Don't know. He and I went at it in the back of the house and he nailed me with the saw, so this could be from anything. Where's Rhage?"

"Right here." Hollywood walked in. "I went through the woods. All clear. What happened to the mother and the kid?"

Butch nodded to the front door. "In the Escalade. They should go to the clinic. Mom has fresh bruises."

"Let's you and I take them," V said. "Rhage, why don't you get back to the twins?"

"Good deal. They're heading downtown now to hunt. Be safe, you two."

As Rhage dematerialized, Butch said, "What do you want to do with the body?"

"Let's put it around back. Sun'll be up in a couple of hours and that'll take care of it."

The two of them picked up the male, walked him through the grungy house, and laid him out next to the rotting shell of a Barcalounger.

Butch paused and looked at the hacked-out rear door. "So this guy shows up and goes all Jack Nicholson on his wife and kid. Meanwhile, the *lessers* have been scoping out the place and lucky, lucky they pick tonight to attack."

"Bingo."

"You get many domestic problems like this?"

"In the Old Country, sure, but here I haven't heard of many."

"Maybe they're just not being reported."

V rubbed his right eye, which was twitching. "Maybe. Yeah . . . maybe."

They went through what was left of the back door and locked it as best they could. On the way to the front exit, Butch saw a ratty stuffed animal in the corner of the living room, like it had been dropped there. He picked the tiger up, only to frown. The damn thing weighed a ton.

He tucked it under his arm, took out his cell phone, and made two quick calls as V worked on the front door to get it to shut. Then they walked over to the Escalade.

Butch cautiously approached the driver's side with his hands out, the tiger dangling from one palm. And Vishous went around the hood with the same nice-'n-easy routine, coming to a halt about three feet away from the passenger door. Neither of them moved.

The wind blew in from the north, a cold, wet rush that made Butch feel the aches from the fight.

After a moment, the locks in the car were released with a punching sound.

John couldn't stop staring at Blaylock. Especially in the shower. The guy's body was huge now, muscles sprouting from all different places, fanning out from his spine, filling his legs and shoulders, jacking up his arms. Plus he was easily six inches taller. Christ, he had to be six-foot-four now.

But the thing was, he didn't look happy. He moved awkwardly, facing the tiled wall for most of the time he washed. And going by his flinching, the soap he used seemed to irritate him, or maybe his skin itself was the problem. Plus he kept trying to get under the spray, only to step back and adjust the temperature.

"You going to fall in love with him now, too? Brothers might get jealous."

John glared over at Lash. The guy was smiling as he washed his little chest, a thick diamond chain catching the suds.

"Yo, Blay, you better not drop that soap. John-boy over here's eyeing your meat like you read about."

Blaylock ignored the comment.

"Yo, Blay. You heard me? Or you daydreaming about John-boy on his knees?"

John stepped in front of Lash, blocking his view of the other guy.

"Oh, please, like you're going to protect him?" Lash eyed Blaylock. "Blay doesn't need protecting by anyone, does he. He's a biiiiiiiiig man now, aren't you, Blay? Tell me, if John here wants to get you off, you going to let him? Bet you will. Bet you can't wait for it. The two of you are going to make such a—"

John lunged forward, took Lash down to the wet tile, and . . . beat him senseless.

It was like he was on autopilot. He just hit the guy in the face over and over again, his fists riding a wave of anger until the shower floor ran bright red all the way to the drain. And no matter how many hands grabbed at John's shoulders, he ignored them and kept pounding.

Until suddenly he was airlifted off of Lash.

He fought whoever it was that held him, fought and scratched even as he was dimly aware that the rest of the class had shrunk back in fear.

And John kept fighting and screaming without making a sound as he was hauled out of the shower. Out of the locker room. Down the hall. He clawed and punched until he was thrown onto the blue mats of the gym floor and the breath got knocked from him.

For a moment, all he could do was stare up at the caged ceiling lights, but when he realized he was being held down, the fight rushed back. Baring his teeth, he bit the thick wrist that was closest to his mouth.

Abruptly, he was flipped over onto his stomach and a huge weight gouged into his back.

"Wrath! No!"

The name registered only nominally. The queen's voice even less so. John was beyond angry, burning uncontrollably, flailing around.

"You're hurting him!"

"Stay out of this, Beth!" The king's hard voice shot into John's ear. "You finished yet, son? Or you want to go another round with those teeth of yours?"

John struggled even though he couldn't move and his strength was flagging.

"Wrath, please let him up——"

349

"This is between him and me, *leelan*. I want you to go to the locker room and deal with the other half of this mess. That kid on the tile is going to have to be taken to Havers."

There was a curse and then the sound of a door shutting.

Wrath's voice came back right next to the side of John's head. "You think popping one of those guys is going to make you a man?"

John heaved against the load on his back, not caring that it was the king. All that mattered, all that he felt, was the fury that ran through his veins.

"You think making that idiot with the fly mouth bleed is going to get you into the Brotherhood? Do you?"

John struggled harder. At least until a heavy hand landed on the back of his neck and his face had a communion with the floor mats.

"I don't need thugs. I need soldiers. You want to know the difference? Soldiers think." More pressure on his neck until John couldn't even blink for the bug eyes he was sporting. "Soldiers *think*."

All at once the weight was gone, and John took a heaving, sucking breath, the air dragging over his front teeth and hammering down his throat.

More breathing. More breathing.

"Get up."

Fuck you, John thought. But he pushed at the mat. Unfortunately, his stupid, weak-ass body felt like it was chained to the floor. He literally couldn't lift himself.

"Get up."

Fuck you.

"What did you say to me?" John got yanked off the ground by the armpits and came face-to-face with the king. Who was savagely pissed off.

Fear struck John hard, the reality of how badly he'd lost it dawning on him.

Wrath bared fangs that seemed as long as John's legs. "You think I can't hear you just because you can't talk?"

John's feet dangled for a moment and then he was dropped. When his knees failed him, he crumpled to the mats.

Wrath stared down with contempt. "It's a good goddamned thing Tohr isn't around right now."

Not fair, John wanted to yell. *Not fair*.

"You think Tohr would have been impressed by this?"

John thrust himself off the floor and wobbled to a stand, glaring up at Wrath.

Don't say that name, he mouthed. *Don't say his name*.

From out of nowhere, pain lanced through his temples. Then, in his mind, he heard Wrath's voice saying the word *Tohrment* again and again. Clamping his hands over his ears, he tripped over his feet, backing away.

Wrath followed, coming forward, the name getting louder until it was a screaming, relentless, pounding chant. Then John saw the face, Tohr's face, clear as if it were before him. The navy blue eyes. The short dark military hair. The hard features.

John opened his mouth and started to scream. No sound came out, but he kept at it until the crying took over. Swamped by heartache, missing the only father he'd known, he covered his eyes and hunched his shoulders, falling in on himself as he wept.

The instant he caved it all went away: His mind silenced. The vision disappeared.

Strong arms gathered him up.

John started screaming again, but now in agony, not anger. With nowhere to turn, he clutched at Wrath's huge shoulders. All he wanted was the hurting to stop . . . He wanted the pain in him, the stuff he tried to bury deep, to go away. He was raw with emotion from the losses in his life and the tragedies of circumstance, nothing but bruises on the inside.

"Shit . . ." Wrath rocked him gently. "It's all right, son. God . . . damn."

THIRTY-TWO

Marissa got out of the Mercedes then ducked back in. "Will you please wait, Fritz? I want to go to the rental house after this."

"Of course, mistress."

She turned and looked at the back entrance of Havers's clinic, wondering whether he would even let her in.

"Marissa."

She turned around. "Oh, God . . . Butch." She ran over to the Escalade. "I'm so glad you called me. Are you okay? Are they?"

"Yeah. They're getting checked out."

"And you?"

"Fine. Just fine. I figured I'd wait outside, though, because . . . you know."

Yes, Havers wouldn't be too happy to see him. Probably wasn't going to like running into her, either.

Marissa glanced toward the clinic's back entrance. "The mother and child . . . they can't go home after this, can they?"

"No way. The *lessers* know about the house, so it isn't safe. And frankly, there wasn't much there anyway."

"What about the mother's *hellren*?"

"He's been . . . taken care of."

God, she shouldn't feel relieved that there had been a death, but she was. At least until she thought of Butch in the field.

"I love you," she blurted. "That's why I don't want to have you fighting. If I lost you for any reason, my life would be over."

His eyes widened, and she realized they hadn't spoken of love for what seemed like forever. But she was rule number one-ing this. She'd hated spending the daylight hours away from him, hated the distance between them, and she wasn't letting it go on anymore on her side.

Butch stepped in close, his hands going to her face. "Christ, Marissa . . . you don't know what it means to hear you say that. I need to know that. Need to feel that."

He kissed her softly, whispering loving things against her mouth, and as she trembled, he held her with care. There were things still left awkwardly between them, but none of that mattered at the moment. She just needed to reconnect with him.

When he pulled back a little, she said, "I'm going to go inside, but will you wait? I'd like to show you my new house."

He ran his fingertip lightly down her cheek. Though his eyes grew sad, he said, "Yeah, I'll wait. And I would love to see where you're going to live."

"I won't be long."

She kissed him again and then headed off to the clinic entrance. As she felt like an intruder, it was a surprise to be admitted inside without a fuss, but she knew that didn't mean things were going to go smoothly. While she rode down in the elevator, she fiddled with her hair. She was nervous about seeing Havers. Would there be a scene?

When she walked into the waiting area, the nursing staff knew exactly what she'd come for and she was taken down to a patient room. She knocked on the door and stiffened.

Havers looked up from talking with the young in the cast and his face froze. As he seemed to lose track of the words he was speaking, he pushed up his glasses, then cleared his throat with a cough.

"You came!" the young called out to Marissa.

"Hi, there," she said, lifting her hand.

"If you'll excuse me," Havers murmured to the mother, "I'll get your discharge papers in order. But as I said, there's no hurry for you to leave."

Marissa stared at her brother as he came up to her, wondering whether he would even acknowledge her presence. And he did in a manner of speaking. His glance flicked over the pants she had on and he winced.

"Marissa."

"Havers."

"You look . . . well."

Nice enough words. But what he meant was she looked different. And he didn't approve. "I am well."

"If you'll excuse me."

As he left without waiting for a response, anger boiled up into her throat, but she didn't let the nasty words on her tongue fly. Instead, she went to the bedside and sat down. While she took the little female's hand, she tried to figure out what to say, but the young's singsong voice got there first.

"My father is dead," the child said factually. "My *mahmen* is scared. And we have nowhere to sleep if we leave here."

Marissa closed her eyes briefly, thanking the dear Scribe Virgin that at least she had an answer for one of those problems.

She looked over at the mother. "I know exactly where you should go. And I'm going to take you there soon."

The mother started to shake her head. "We have no money—"

"But I can pay rent," the young said, holding up her tattered tiger. She loosened the stitching on the back, dug her hand in and took out the wishing plate. "This is gold, right? So it's money . . . right?"

Marissa breathed in deeply and told herself not to cry. "No, that's a gift to you from me. And there is no rent to be paid. I have an empty home and it needs people to fill it." She glanced once again at the mother. "I would love it if you two would stay there with me as soon as my new house is ready."

When John finally went back to the locker room after his meltdown, he was all alone. Wrath had returned to the main house, Lash had been taken away to the clinic, and the other guys had gone home.

Which was good. In the resounding quiet, he took the longest shower of his life, just stood under the hot spray, letting the water run down him. His body felt achy. Sick.

Jesus Christ. Had he really bitten the king? Beaten a classmate?

John eased back against the tile. In spite of all the spray washing over him and the soap he'd used, nothing cleaned him off. He still seemed curiously . . . dirty. But then, disgrace and shame did make you feel like you were covered in pig shit.

Cursing, he looked down at the sparse muscles of his chest and the sunken pit of his stomach and the pointy knobs of his hips, looked past his utterly unimpressive sex to his little feet. Then followed the tile to the drain where Lash's blood had funneled out.

He could have killed the guy, he realized. He'd been that out of control.

"John?"

He jerked his head up. Zsadist was standing in the shower's entryway, his face utterly impassive.

"You finish, you come up to the main house. We'll be in Wrath's study."

John nodded and turned the water off. Chances were

very good that he was going to be kicked out of the training program. Maybe out of the house. And he couldn't blame them. But God, where would he go?

After Z left, John toweled dry, put his clothes on, and went across the hall to Tohr's office. He had to keep his eyes down as he passed through on his way to the tunnel. He couldn't bear any of his memories of Tohrment right now. Not a single one.

Couple minutes later he was in the mansion's foyer, staring up at the grand staircase. He climbed the red-carpeted steps slowly, feeling unbearably tired, and the exhaustion grew worse when he got to the top: The double doors to Wrath's study were open and voices spilled out, the king's and others'. How he would miss them all, he thought.

The first thing he noticed when he stepped into the room was Tohr's chair. The ugly green monster had been moved and was now behind and to the left of the throne. Odd.

John walked forward and waited to be acknowledged.

Wrath was bent over a fancy little desk piled with papers, a magnifying glass in his hand apparently helping him to read. Z and Phury were flanking the king, one on either side, both leaning over the map Wrath was looking at.

"This is where we found the first torture camp," Phury said, pointing to a big green stretch. "Here's where Butch was found. Here's where I was taken."

"Big spread between them all," Wrath muttered. "Lot of miles."

"What we need is an airplane," Z said. "Aerial review would be much more efficient."

"True that." Wrath shook his head. "But we'd have to watch it. Get too close to the ground and the FAA would crawl up our ass."

John inched a little closer to the desk. Craned his neck.

In a smooth move, Wrath pushed the big sheet of paper forward as if he'd finished reviewing it. Or maybe . . . was encouraging John to take a peek. Except instead of staring at the topographical spread, John looked at the king's forearm. The bite mark on that thick wrist mortified him and he stepped back.

Just as Beth walked in with a leather box of scrolls tied with red ribbons.

"Okay, Wrath, how about some briefing time. I've prioritized all these."

Wrath leaned back as Beth put the box down. Then the king captured her face, kissing her on the mouth as well as both sides of her throat. "Thanks, *leelan*. Right now's great, although V and Butch are coming by with Marissa. Oh shit, did I tell you the *Princeps* Council has a bright idea? Mandatory *sehclusion* for all unmated females."

"You're kidding me."

"Fools haven't passed it yet, but according to Rehvenge, the vote's coming soon." The king looked at Z and Phury. "You two check into the airplane situation. We got anyone who knows how to fly?"

Phury shrugged. "I used to. And we could bring V in on it—"

"Bring me in on what?" V said as he walked into the study.

Wrath looked around the twins. "Can you say Cessna, my brother?"

"Nice. We going airborne here?"

Butch and Marissa came in behind V. And they were holding hands.

John stepped to the side and just took it all in: Wrath falling deep into conversation with Beth while V and

Butch and Marissa started talking among themselves and Phury and Z headed out.

Chaos. Movement. Purpose. This was the monarchy, the Brotherhood at work. And John felt privileged to be in the room . . . for however short a time he had left before they kicked his sorry ass to the curb.

Hoping maybe they'd forget he was around, he looked for a place to sit and eyed Tohr's chair. Keeping on the sidelines, he walked over and lowered himself into the faded, torn leather. From here he could see everything: the top of Wrath's desk and whatever was on it, the door where people came and went, every corner of the room.

John curled his legs under him and tilted forward, listening in as Beth and Wrath talked about the *Princeps* Council. Wow. They worked really great together. She was giving him excellent advice and the king was taking it.

As Wrath nodded at something she'd said, his long black hair slipped over his shoulder and fell onto the desk. He pushed it back, then eased to the side and opened a drawer, pulling out a spiral-bound steno pad and a pen. Without looking, he held them out behind him, right in front of John.

John took the gift with shaking hands.

"Well, *leelan*, that's what you get when you deal with the *glymera*. A whole lot of crap." Wrath shook his head and then looked up at V and Butch and Marissa. "So what's up, you three?"

John dimly heard words exchanged, but he was too humbled to focus. God, maybe the Brothers weren't kicking him out . . . maybe.

He tuned in again to hear Marissa say, "They have nowhere to go, so they're staying in the house I just rented. But, Wrath, they need long-term assistance and I fear there are others out there just like them—females with no one to help them, either because their mates were taken by the *lessers* or died of natural causes or, God forbid, their males are abusers. I wish there was some kind of program—"

"Yeah, we definitely need one. Along with about eight thousand other things." Wrath rubbed his eyes under his wrap-arounds, then looked back at Marissa. "Okay, I'm putting you in charge of this. Find out what the humans do for their kind. Figure out what we need for the race. Tell me what you require for money and staffing and facilities. Then go out and do it."

Marissa's mouth fell open. "My lord?"

Beth nodded. "That's a fabulous idea. And you know, Mary used to work with social services when she was a volunteer at the Suicide Prevention Hotline. You could start with her. I think she's really familiar with DSS."

"I . . . yes . . . I'll do that." Marissa looked at Butch and in response, the guy smiled, a slow, very male expression of respect. "Yes, I . . . I'll do it. I . . ." The female crossed the room in a daze, only to stop at the door. "Wait, my lord? I've never done anything like this before. I mean, I've worked at the clinic, but—"

"You're going to handle it just fine, Marissa. And, as a friend of mine told me once, you're going to ask for help when you need some. Got it?"

"Uh . . . yes, thank you."

"Lot of work ahead of you."

"Yes . . ." She curtsied, even though she was wearing pants.

Wrath smiled a little, then looked at Butch, who was going after his female. "Yo, cop, you and V and I are getting together tonight. It's a go. Be back here in an hour."

Butch seemed to pale. But then he nodded and took off with Vishous in tow.

As Wrath refocused on his *shellan,* John quickly scribbled something on the pad and held it out to Beth. After she read it aloud for the king, Wrath inclined his head.

"You go right ahead, son. And yeah, I know you're sorry. Apology accepted. But you sleep up here from now on. Don't care if it's in that chair or in a bed down the hall, you sleep here now." As John nodded, the king said, "And one more thing. Every night at four a.m. you're taking a walk with Zsadist."

John blew a whistle in an ascending note.

"Why? Because I said so. Every night. Otherwise, you're out of the training program and you're out of here. Dig? Whistle twice if you understand me and agree to this."

John did as he asked.

Then he awkwardly signed *thank you.* And left.

THIRTY-THREE

Forty-five minutes later, Butch stood in the doorway to the kitchen, watching Marissa with Mary and John. The three were bent over a diagram explaining New York State's interlocking human services agencies. Mary was taking the case study approach to teaching Marissa how it all worked, and John had volunteered to be the case.

Jesus, the kid had had it rough. Born in the bathroom of a bus station. Picked up by a janitor and taken to the Catholic orphanage. Then housed with foster parents who didn't give a shit after Our Lady downscaled its program. And it got worse: Quitting school at sixteen. Running away from the system. Living in squalor while he supported himself as a busboy downtown. He was lucky to be alive.

And Marissa was clearly going to help kids like him.

As the discussion continued, Butch noticed that her voice changed. Deepened. Grew more direct. Her eyes sharpened and her questions got even sharper. She was, he realized, incredibly smart, and she was going to be good at this.

God, he loved her. And he wanted desperately to be what she needed. What she deserved.

As if on cue, he heard footsteps and smelled V's Turkish tobacco. "Wrath is waiting, cop."

Butch stared at his woman for a moment longer. "Let's do it."

Marissa looked up. "Butch? I would love to get your thoughts on a police force." She tapped the diagram. "I can see a lot of scenarios where we are going to need law enforcement intervention. Wrath is going to need to consider starting up some kind of civil guard."

"Anything you want, baby." His eyes memorized her face. "Just give me a few, okay?"

Marissa nodded, smiled in a distracted way, and went back to her work.

Unable to resist, he walked over and touched her shoulder. When she glanced up, he kissed her on the mouth and whispered, "I love you."

As her eyes flared, he kissed her again and turned away. Man, he hoped like hell this ancestor regression turned up something other than a shitload of Irish whitebread.

He and Vishous walked upstairs to the study and found the frilly French room empty except for Wrath . . . who was standing in front of the fire, one thick arm on the mantel. The king looked like he had brain strain as he stared into the flames.

"My lord?" V said. "This still a good time?"

"Yeah." Wrath motioned them in, his black diamond ring flashing on his middle finger. "Shut the doors."

"You mind if I get a little muscle?" V nodded down the hall. "I want Rhage in here holding the cop."

"Fine." As Vishous left, Wrath stared at Butch with such intensity, his eyes were like torches burning behind his wraparounds. "I didn't expect the Scribe Virgin to let us do this."

"I'm glad she is." Way glad.

"You understand what you're signing on for here? This is going to hurt like a bitch and you could end up a vegetable on the other side."

"V's done the full disclosure. I'm good."

"Check you out," Wrath murmured with approval. "You're so tight about this."

"What are my choices if I want to know? None. So getting all up in my head is not going to help."

The double doors clicked shut and Butch looked across the study. Rhage had damp hair and was wearing beat-to-shit blue jeans, a black fleece, and no shoes or socks. Absurdly, Butch noticed that even the guy's feet were gorgeous. Yeah, no hairy-knuckled, nasty-nail action for Hollywood. Bastard was head-to-toe perfection.

"Man, cop," the brother said. "You really going to do this?"

As Butch nodded, Vishous stepped in front of him and started to take off his glove. "Need you to lose the shirt, buddy."

Butch stripped to the waist, tossing his Turnbull & Asser on the sofa. "Can I keep the cross on?"

"Yup, shouldn't melt. Much." V shoved his glove into his back pocket, then whipped his black belt from his hips and held the leather strap out to Rhage. "I want you to put this thing in his mouth and hold it in place so he doesn't crack his teeth. But don't make any contact with him. You're going to get a sunburn anyway, being this close."

Rhage stepped in behind, but the sound of knocking on the doors interrupted everything.

Marissa's voice drifted through the wood panels. "Butch? Wrath?" More knocking. Getting louder. "My lord? Is there something going on?"

Wrath cocked an eyebrow at Butch.

Who replied, "Let me talk to her."

As Wrath willed the doors open, Marissa burst into the room. She took one look at V's ungloved hand and Butch's bare chest and went white as snow.

"What are you doing to him?"

Butch walked up to her. "We're going to find out if I have something of your kind in me."

Her mouth fell open. Then she wheeled on Wrath. "Tell them no. Tell them they can't do this. Tell them—"

"It's his choice, Marissa."

"It will kill him!"

"Marissa," Butch said, "it's worth the risk to find out about me."

She pivoted toward him, her stare furious, positively glowing with light. There was a pause. Then she slapped him across the face.

"That is for not caring about yourself." Without taking a breath, she slapped him again, another crack echoing into the ceiling. "And that is for not telling me what you were doing."

Pain blazed in his cheek, throbbed to the beat of his heart.

"Can you boys give us a minute?" he said softly, eyes not leaving her pale face.

When the brothers disappeared, Butch tried to take her hands, but she snapped them back, wrapping her arms around herself.

"Marissa . . . this is the only way out I can see."

"Way out of what?"

"There's a chance I can be who you need me to be—"

"Who I *need* you to be? I need you to be yourself! And I need you to be alive!"

"This is not going to kill me."

"Oh, and you've done it before, so you know that for sure? I'm *so* relieved."

"I have to do this."

"You do not—"

"*Marissa*," he snapped. "You want to put yourself in my shoes? You want to try on for size the idea that you love me but I have to be with someone else, live off someone else, while you can do nothing about it, month after month, year after year? You want to think about what it's like to know that you're going to die first and leave

365

me alone? You want to be a second-class citizen in the world I live in?"

"So you're saying you'd rather be dead than be with me?"

"I told you, this isn't going to—"

"But what comes next? You think I can't follow the logic? If you find out you've got a vampire descendant, you mean to tell me you aren't going to try something *truly* stupid?"

"I love you too much—"

"Goddamn it! If you loved me, you wouldn't do this to yourself. If you loved me—" Marissa's voice cracked. "If you loved me . . ."

Tears welled in her eyes, and with a jerky movement, she clamped her hands on her face and trembled. Just shook all over.

"Baby . . . it's going to be all right." Thank God, she let him put his arms around her. "Baby—"

"I am so angry at you right now," she said into his chest. "You're an arrogant, prideful fool who's breaking my heart."

"I'm a man who wants to take care of his woman."

"Like I said . . . a goddamned fool. And you promised, no more protecting me by leaving me out."

"I'm really sorry, I just wanted to tell you when it was over. And I trust V with my life, I truly do. I'm not going to kick it over this." He tilted her face up and thumbed away her tears. "I just keep thinking about the future. I'm thirty-seven and I've led a hard-drinking, hard-smoking life. I could be dead in ten years, who knows?"

"And if you die now, I will have missed out on that decade. I want those years with you."

"But I want centuries. Aeons. And I want you to stop feeding off of . . . Rehvenge."

She closed her eyes and shook her head. "I told you it's not romantic—"

"On your side. But can you honestly say that he doesn't want you?" When she didn't reply, he nodded. "That's what I thought. I don't blame him, but I don't like it. Even though . . . shit, you probably should be with someone like him, someone from your class."

"Butch, I don't care about the *glymera* anymore. I'm shut out of that life now, and you know what? It's for the better. In fact, I should thank Havers for forcing me to be independent. He did me a favor."

"Yeah, well, no offense, but I still want to beat his ass."

As he squeezed her harder, she sighed into his pecs. "What are they going to do if you have some of the race in you?"

"Let's talk about that afterward."

"No." She pushed him back. "You do *not* shut me out. You want to do this for us? Then I get a vote, damn it. We talk about it *now*."

He shoved a hand through his hair and braced himself. "They're going to try and jump-start the change if I do."

Her mouth opened slowly. "How?"

"V says he can do it."

"How?"

"I don't know. We haven't gotten that far."

Marissa stared at him for a long time, and he knew she was tallying his fuckups. After a moment, she said, "You broke your promise to me by keeping me out of all this."

"I . . . Yeah, I blew it." He put his palm over his heart. "But I swear, Marissa, I was going to come to you once I knew whether we had a shot at it. I never had any intention of going into the transition without talking to you first. I swear."

"I don't want to lose you."

"I don't want to be lost."

As she glanced at the door, silence expanded in the room until he could have sworn it became tangible, brushing against his skin like cold fog.

Finally, she said, "If you're going to do the regression, I want to be in the room."

Butch released his breath in a rush. "Come here, I need to hold you for a sec."

Pulling her to him, he wrapped his body around hers. Her shoulders were stiff, but her arms gripped him around the waist. Hard.

"Butch?"

"Yeah?"

"I'm not sorry I slapped you."

He dropped his head into her neck. "I deserved it."

As he pressed his lips to her skin, he breathed in deep, trying to hold her scent not just in his lungs but in his blood. When he pulled back, he looked at the vein running up her neck and thought, *Oh, God . . . please let me be something more than I am.*

"Let's get this over with," she said.

He kissed her and let Wrath, V, and Rhage back in.

"We going to do this?" Vishous asked.

"Yeah, we are."

Butch shut the doors, and then he and V went back over to the fireplace.

As Rhage moved in from behind and went to slide the belt in place, Butch looked at Marissa. "It's okay, baby. I love you." Then he glanced at Wrath. As if the king read minds, he went over and stood next to her. Ready to catch her. Or hold her back.

V got real close, so close their chests almost touched. With care, he repositioned the cross so it hung down Butch's back. "You good to go, cop?"

Butch nodded, finding as comfortable a bite as he could on the leather. He braced himself as V lifted an arm.

Except when his roommate's palm landed on his bare chest all he felt was a warm weight. Butch frowned. This was it? This was fucking it? Scaring the shit out of Marissa for no good—

He looked down, pissed off.

Oh, wrong hand.

"I want you to relax for me, my man," V said, slowly moving his palm in a circle, right over Butch's heart. "Just take some deep breaths. The calmer you are, the better it will be for you."

Funny choice of words. Exactly what Butch had said to Marissa when he'd—

Not wanting to get flustered, he dropped that thought and tried to loosen his shoulders. Got nowhere.

"Let's just breathe together for a minute, cop. That's it. In and out. Breathe with me. Yeah, good. We got all the time in the world."

Butch closed his eyes and concentrated on the soothing sensation rubbing over his chest. The warmth. The rotating movement.

"There you go, cop. That's nice. Feels good, true? Just chilling . . ."

The circling got slower and slower. And Butch's breathing got deeper and easier. His heart began to pause before beats, the intervals between pumps growing longer and longer. And all the time with V's voice . . . the lazy words seducing him, getting in his brain, trancing him out.

"Okay, Butch. Look at me. Show me those peepers of yours."

Butch lifted heavy lids and swayed as he stared up into V's face.

Then he tensed. The pupil of V's right eye was expanding until there was nothing but blackness. No white part. No iris. What the f—

"Nah, it's all good, Butch. You don't worry about what you're seeing. You just look inside of me. Come on, now. Look into me, Butch. Feel my hand on your chest. Good . . . now I want you to fall into me. Let yourself go. Fall . . . in . . . to . . . me . . ."

Butch fixated on the blackness and went back to focusing on the palm moving over his heart. From the corner of his eye, he saw the glowing hand come up, but he was too far gone to care. He was stumbling in the most marvelous, mild way, in the midst of a gentle trip through thin air, falling into Vishous . . .

Plunging into a void . . .

Of darkness . . .

Mr. X woke up and put his hand to his chest, feeling around for his wounds. He was satisfied with how fast they were healing, but he was far from his normal strength.

Lifting his head with care, he glanced at what had once been a cozy den for a nuclear family. Now that the Lessening Society was occupying the house, however, the room was just four walls, faded carpet, and wilted drapery.

Van walked in from the cheerful, empty kitchen and stopped dead. "You're awake. Jesus, I thought I was going to have to dig a hole in the backyard."

Mr. X coughed a little. "Bring me my laptop."

When Van brought the thing in, Mr. X heaved himself up so he was leaning against the wall. From the Windows XP start-up menu, he went into My Documents and opened a Word file titled "Operational Notes." He scrolled down to the header marked "July" and panned through entries made nine months ago. There was one for each day, back from when he'd been *Fore-lesser* the first time. Back when he'd given a shit.

As he searched, he was aware of Van hovering.

"We have a new purpose, you and I," Mr. X said absently.

"Oh, yeah?"

"That human we saw tonight. We're going to find him." X paused at the notes from the seventeenth of the month, but they didn't give him what he was after. "We're going to find that human, and we're going to take him out. Find him . . . take him out."

The guy had to die so that Mr. X's misread of the situation became fact and the Omega never knew his Trojan human hadn't been killed by the Brothers.

The actual assassination of the man would have to be carried out by another *lesser*, however. After this evening's show-down, Mr. X was taking himself out of the risk pool. He could not take a chance on another serious injury.

July . . . July . . . maybe he had the wrong month, but he could have sworn it was around then that a cop looking like that human had shown up at the Caldwell Martial Arts Academy, the Society's former HQ—ah . . . yes. Good record keeping was so helpful. And so was the fact that he'd demanded to see the guy's shield.

Mr. X spoke up. "His name is Brian O'Neal. CPD badge number eight five two. Address used to be over in the Cornwell Apartments, but I'm sure he's moved. Born Boston Hospital for Women, Boston, MA, to a Mr. Edward and a Mrs. Odell O'Neal." Mr. X glanced at Van and smiled a little. "What do you bet his parents are still in Boston?"

THIRTY-FOUR

Rain was falling onto Butch's face. Was he outside? Had to be.

Man . . . he must have passed out on some kind of bender or something. Because he was flat on his back and his head was nothing but 'slaw and the idea of opening his eyes was too much like work.

He should probably just lie here and wait a while. Yeah . . . he should just sleep for a little bit . . .

Except, holy hell, this rain was annoying. The shit tickled as it hit his cheeks and slid down into his neck. He lifted an arm to cover his face.

"He's coming around."

Whose deep voice was that? V's . . . yeah, and V was . . . his roommate? Or something. Yeah . . . roommate. He liked V a lot.

"Butch?" Now, a woman. A very scared woman. "Butch, can you hear me?"

Oh, he really knew her. She was . . . the love of his life . . . *Marissa*.

Butch's eyes lazed open, but he wasn't too sure what was reality and what was trippy nonsense. Until he saw his woman's face.

Marissa was bent over him and his head was in her lap. Her tears were what was falling on his face. And V . . . V was right next to her, down on his haunches, his mouth a thin, strained slash in the midst of his goatee.

Butch struggled to speak, but there was something in

his mouth. As he batted at it, trying to get it out, Marissa went to help him.

"No, not yet," V said. "I think he's got a couple more in him."

More what?

From out of nowhere, Butch heard a scramble of feet.

He lifted his head a little and was surprised to find that he was the one making the noise. His shoes were flopping up and down, and he watched as the spasms crawled up his legs. He tried to fight the progress, but the seizure took over, traveling into his hips and his torso, making his arms flap and his back slap against the floor.

He rode the wave as best he could, trying to hang on to consciousness until it was just impossible.

When he came back, he was dizzy.

"That one didn't last so long," Marissa said, smoothing his hair back. "Butch, can you hear me?"

He nodded and tried to lift his arm to her. But then his feet started up with the Fred Astaire routine again.

Three more trips through the seizure park and the belt was finally taken out of his mouth. As he tried to speak, he realized how truly drunk he was. His brain was barely kicking over, he was so wasted. Except . . . hold up—he couldn't remember hitting the Scotch.

"Marissa," he mumbled, taking her hand. "Don't want to see you drink so much." Wait, not really what he'd been going for. "Ah . . . don't you to see *me* drink so much . . . want."

Whatever. God . . . he was so confused.

V smiled a little, but it was the kind of falsey number doctors gave to patients who were about to throw up. "He's going to need something with sugar in it. Rhage, you got a lollipop on you?"

Butch looked over as a wicked handsome blond guy knelt down. "I know you," Butch said. "Hey . . . buddy."

"Hey, my man." Rhage reached into the pocket of his fleece and pulled out a Tootsie Pop. After ripping the wrapper off, he put the thing into Butch's mouth.

Butch groaned. Goddamn, that was the best thing he'd ever tasted in his whole life. Grape. Sweet. Ahhhh . . .

"Is he seizing again?" Marissa asked.

"I think he likes it," Rhage murmured. "That right, cop?"

Butch nodded and nearly lost the lollipop, so Rhage took control of the stick, holding it in place.

Man, they were so good to him. Marissa stroking his hair and holding his hand. V's palm a warm weight on his leg. Rhage making sure the Tootsie Pop stayed where it needed to be—

All of a sudden, higher reasoning and short-term memory came back in a rush, like his brain was being poured back into his skull. He wasn't drunk. The regression. The ancestor regression. V's hand on his chest. The blackness.

"What was the result?" he asked, panicked. "V . . . what did you find out? What was—"

Everyone around him took a deep breath and someone muttered, *Thank God he's really back.*

At that moment, two steel-toed shitkickers approached from the right. Butch's eyes latched on to them, then rose higher, taking in a pair of leather-clad legs, then a huge body.

Wrath towered over them all.

The king reached up and removed his wraparounds, revealing brilliant, gleaming, pale green eyes. As they didn't appear to have pupils, the stare was like getting hit with a pair of klieg lights.

Wrath smiled broadly, his fangs so very white. "What's doing . . . *cousin*."

Butch frowned. "What . . . ?"

"You've got some of me in you, cop." Wrath's smile stuck around as he slid his glasses back on. "'Course, I always knew you were a royal. Just didn't think it went past the pain-in-the-ass part, is all."

"Are you . . . serious?"

Wrath nodded. "You're of my line, Butch. One of mine."

As Butch's chest got tight, he braced himself for another seizure. And so did everyone else: Rhage took the lollipop out and reached for the belt. Marissa and V tensed up.

But what came out of him was a rush of laughter. A ridiculous, belly-rolling, tear-up, stupid-idiot wave of happy hysteria.

Butch laughed and laughed and kissed Marissa's hand. Then laughed some more.

Marissa felt the satisfaction and the excitement humming through Butch's body as he let loose. But when he beamed up at her, she couldn't share his joy.

He lost his smile. "Baby, it's going to be all right."

Vishous got to his feet. "Why don't we give you guys a minute alone?"

"Thank you," she said.

After the Brothers left, Butch sat up. "This is our chance—"

"If I asked, would you not do the transition?"

He froze. As if she'd slapped him again. "Marissa—"

"Would you?"

"Why don't you want me with you?"

"I do. And I would choose the future we have now over a hypothetical cast of centuries any day. Can't you understand that?"

He blew out a long breath, his jaw tightening. "Christ, I love you."

Okay, so clearly he didn't find her logic appealing. "Butch, if I asked you, would you not do it?"

When he didn't reply, she covered her eyes, though she had no tears left in her.

"I love you," he repeated. "So, yeah . . . if you asked me not to, I wouldn't."

She lowered her hand, her breath catching. "Swear to this. Here and now."

"On my mother."

"*Thank you* . . ." She pulled him into her arms. "Oh, God . . . thank you. And we can work through the . . . feeding issue. Mary and Rhage have. I just . . . Butch, we can have a good future."

They were silent for a time, just sitting on the floor. Then from out of the blue, he said gruffly, "I have three brothers and a sister."

"Excuse me?"

"I've never talked to you about my family. I have three brothers and one sister. Well, there had been two girls, but then we lost one."

"Oh." She sat back, thinking his tone was very odd.

And his hollow voice gave her the total creeps as he said, "My earliest memory is of my sister Joyce coming home from the hospital as an infant. I wanted to check her out, and I ran to her crib, but my father shoved me back so my older brother and sister could look at her. As I bounced off the wall, dad picked up my brother and lifted him so he could touch her. I'll never forget my father's voice . . ." Butch's accent changed, the vowels flattening out. "*This here's your sistah, Teddy. Yah gonna love'ah and take care'ahah*. I thought, what about me? I would like to love her and take care of her. I said, *Pa, I wanna help, too*. He didn't even look at me."

Marissa realized she was squeezing Butch's hand so hard she must be bruising his bones, but he didn't seem to notice. And she couldn't loosen the hold.

"After that," he went on, "I started watching my father and my mom, watching how they were different with the other kids. Main thing was on Friday and Saturday nights. My father liked to drink, and I was the one he went for when he needed to knock something around." When Marissa gasped, Butch shook his head with a total lack of regard. "No, it's fine. It was good. I can suck back punches like you read about, thanks to him, and trust me, that's come in handy. So anyway, one Fourth of July . . . Hell, I was almost twelve then . . ." He rubbed his jaw, his beard growth scratching. "Yeah, the Fourth of July came and we were doing the family thing out at my uncle's on the Cape. My brother skims some beers from the cooler and he and his buddies go 'round back of the garage and crack them open. I hid in the bushes because I wanted to be invited in. You know . . . I hoped my brother would . . ." He cleared his throat. "When my father came looking for them, the other boys took off and my brother about crapped in his pants. My father just laughed. Told Teddy to make sure my mother never found out. Then dad saw me crouched down in the shrubs. He came over, hauled me up by the collar, and backhanded me so hard I spit blood."

As Butch smiled in a hard way, she looked at the uneven edge of his front tooth.

"He told me it was for being a spy and a snitch. I swore to him I was just looking, I wasn't going to tell no one. He clipped me again and called me a pervert. My brother . . . yeah, my brother just watched the whole thing happen. Didn't say a word. And when I walked past my mother with my split lip and the chip out of my tooth, she just held my little sister Joyce closer and looked away."

He shook his head slowly. "Up at the house, I went to the bathroom and cleaned up, then headed for the room I was staying in. I didn't give a shit about God, but I went down on my knees, clapped my little hands together, and prayed like a good Catholic should. I begged God that this not be my family. *Please* let this not be my family. *Please* let there be someplace else I can go . . ."

She had a feeling he didn't know he'd switched into the present tense. Or that he'd reached up and was gripping the solid gold cross around his neck like his life depended on it.

His lips cracked into a half smile. "But God must have known I wasn't sure about Him because nothing came of it. Then that fall my sister Janie was murdered." As Marissa sucked in a breath, he pointed behind himself. "That's the tattoo on my back. I count the years since she's gone. I was the last one to see her alive, before she got in the car with those boys that just . . . desecrated her behind our high school."

She reached for him. "Butch, I'm so—"

"No, let me get this out, okay? This shit's like a train, now that it's moving, I can't stop it." He dropped the cross and shoved his hand through his hair. "After Janie disappeared and they found her body, my father never touched me again. Wouldn't come near me. Wouldn't look at me. Didn't talk to me, either. My mom went crazy after a little while and they had to put her in a psych ward. It was right around then that I started drinking. I ran the streets. Did drugs. Got in fights. The family just limped along. I never understood the change in my dad, though. I mean . . . for years he beat me, then . . . nothing."

"I'm so glad he stopped hitting you."

"No difference to me. The waiting to get clipped was as bad as getting my ass slammed. And to not know why . . . but I did find out. At my oldest brother's bachelor party. I was like twenty by then and had moved from Southie—er—South Boston to here because I was starting as a cop with the CPD. Anyway, I went back home for the party. We were in some guy's house with a lot of strippers. My father was pounding the beers hard. I was doing lines of cocaine and sucking back Scotch. Party comes to an end and I'm buzzing out of control. I'd done a lot of coke . . . man, I was so fucking polluted that night. So . . . Dad's leaving . . . getting a ride home from someone, and suddenly I had to talk to the sonofabitch.

"I end up chasing him out into the street, but he's all ignoring me and shit. So in front of all the guys, I just grabbed him. I was beyond pissed. I started going off on him, about how I thought he'd been a real shitty father to me, how I was surprised he stopped cracking me because he liked it so much. I went on and on, until my old man finally looked into my face. I just froze. There was . . . total terror in his eyes. He was completely scared of me. Then he said, *I left yah alone 'cause I couldn't have yah killin' any more of m' children, could I?* I was all . . . *What the fuck?* He starts to cry and says, *Yah knew she was my favorite . . . yah knew and that's why yah put hah in that cah w' those boys. Yah did it, yah knew what would happen.*" Butch shook his head. "Man, everyone heard it. All the guys. My oldest brother, too . . . My father actually thought I'd had my sister murdered to get back at him."

Marissa tried to embrace him, but again he shrugged her off and took a deep breath. "I don't go home anymore. Ever. Last I heard, Ma and Pa were spending some time in Florida every year, but otherwise were still in the house I grew up in. Like, my sister Joyce, her baby was just baptized? The only reason I knew about it was because her husband called me out of guilt.

"So here's my deal, Marissa. I've had a piece missing all my life. I've always been different from other people, not just in my family but when I was working here on the CPD force, too. I never fit in . . . until I met the Brotherhood. I met your kind . . . and, shit, now I know why. I was a stranger among humans." He cursed softly. "I wanted to go through the change not just for you, but for me. Because I felt like then . . . I could be who I'm supposed to be. I mean, hell, I've been living on the fringes all my life. I kind of wanted to know what being in the thick was like."

In a powerful move, he got off the floor. "So that's why I want . . . why I *wanted* to do this. It wasn't just about you."

He went over to a window and pushed aside the pale blue velvet drapery. As he stared out into the night, the glow from a lamp on the desk fell across the planes of his face, the heft of his shoulders, the thick pads of his chest. And the golden cross that lay over his heart.

God, how he yearned as he looked out of the window. Yearned so fiercely his eyes nearly glowed.

She thought of him the night she'd fed from Rehvenge. Saddened, hurt, paralyzed by biology.

Butch shrugged. "But . . . you know, sometimes you can't have what you want. So you deal and move on." He glanced back at her. "Like I said, you don't want me to, I won't."

THIRTY-FIVE

Butch looked away from Marissa and stared back out into the darkness. Against the dense black screen of the night, he saw images of his family, clip art that made his eyes sting. Holy fuck, he'd never put the whole story into words before. Never expected to.

Not a pretty picture, the whole lot of it.

Which was another reason he'd wanted to go through the transition. He could have used another shot at life, and the change would have been like birth, wouldn't it? A new beginning, where he was something else, something . . . improved. And purified, too. A kind of baptism by blood.

And man, he hungered to wipe the slate clean, all of it: the stuff with his family, the things he'd done as an adult, that shit with the Omega and the *lessers*.

He winced, thinking he'd gotten so close. "Yeah . . . ah, I'm just going to tell Wrath and them this is not—"

"Butch, I—"

He cut her off by going to the door and opening it. As he looked out at the king and V, his chest burned. "Sorry, fellas. Change in plan—"

"What will you do to him?" Marissa's voice was loud and all hard edges as it cut through the air.

Butch glanced over his shoulder. Across the study, she looked as grim as he felt.

"Well?" she demanded. "What will you do to him?"

Wrath nodded to his left. "Vishous, you better field that one."

V's answer was factual, straight to the point. Horrific.

Hell, any plan that ended with "and then we pray" was not a trip to Disneyland.

"Where would you do it?" she asked.

"Down in the training center," V replied. "The Equipment Room has a separate area for first aid and PT treatments."

There was a long silence, during which Butch stared at Marissa. Surely, she couldn't be—

"Okay," she said. "Okay . . . when do we do it?"

Butch's eyes popped. "Baby . . . ?"

Her gaze stuck to Vishous. "When?"

"Tomorrow night. His chances will be better if he has a little time to recover from the regression."

"Tomorrow night, then," Marissa said, wrapping her arms around herself.

V nodded, then looked at Butch. "I imagine you two are going to want some privacy today. I'm going to crash here at the main house, so you have the Pit to yourselves."

Butch was so stunned out, he couldn't make sense of anything. "Marissa, are you—"

"Yes, I'm sure. And I'm terrified." She walked past him, heading for the doorway. "Now, I'd like to go to the gatehouse if you don't mind."

He grabbed his shirt and went after her.

As they went along, he took her elbow . . . but had the sense that she was leading him.

When they got to the Pit, Butch could not read Marissa's mood. She was quiet, but she'd marched across the courtyard like a soldier, nothing but strength and focus.

"I'd like a drink," she said as he shut the door.

"Okay." This at least he could handle. Assuming they had anything but hard liquor in the house.

He went into the kitchen and cracked the fridge. Oh, man . . . decaying bags of Taco Hell and Arby's. Mustard packets. Two inches of milk that was now a solid. "I'm not sure what we've got. Um . . . water—"

"No, I want a *drink*."

He looked up over the icebox door. "All . . . right. We have Scotch and vodka."

"I'll try the vodka."

As he poured her some Grey Goose over ice, he watched her walk around. She checked out V's computers. The Foosball table. The plasma screen TV.

He went over to her. He wanted her in his arms; he gave her the glass.

She put it to her mouth, tilted her head back, took a long one . . . and coughed until her eyes watered. While she choked, he maneuvered her onto the couch and sat down next to her.

"Marissa—"

"Shut up."

Okaaay. He clasped his hands together as she struggled with the Goose. After she got down about half an inch, she put the stuff on the coffee table with a grimace.

She tackled him so fast, Butch never saw it coming. One second he was staring at his tightly laced fingers. The next, he was pressed into the sofa and she was straddling him and . . . oh, God, her tongue was in his mouth.

She felt so damned good, but the vibe was all wrong. The desperation and the anger and the fear just weren't appropriate background music. They were going to end up further apart if they kept going.

He held her back from him, even though his cock screamed in protest. "Marissa—"

"I want to have sex."

He closed his eyes. Christ, so did he. All night long. Except not like this.

He took a deep breath, trying to frame the words right . . . and when he opened his lids, she'd pulled off her turtleneck and was working the clasp of a black bra that totally knocked him out.

His hands tightened on her waist as those satin cups came off her and her nipples tightened in the chill. He leaned forward, ready to put his lips to the first piece of her he hit, when he stopped. He was not going to take her like this. The air was too hard between them.

He stopped her hands as they went to his pants. "Marissa . . . no."

"Don't say that."

He sat up, putting her back from his body. "I love you."

"Then don't stop me."

He shook his head. "I won't do this. Not as we are now."

She stared at him in disbelief. Then snatched her wrists out of his hold and turned her head from him.

"Marissa—"

She shrugged off his hands, batting them away. "I can't believe this. Our one night together and you say no."

"Let me . . . Christ . . . let me hold you. Come on, Marissa."

She rubbed her eyes. Laughed in a tragic little burst. "I am destined to go to my grave a virgin, aren't I? Sure, technically I'm not, but—"

"I didn't say I wouldn't be with you." She glanced over at him, tears glimmering on her lashes. "I just . . . Not with the anger. It'll pollute the whole thing. I want it to be . . . special."

So what if that line was right out of a high school play-book. It was the truth.

"Baby, why don't we just go into my bedroom and lie down in the dark." He handed her back the turtleneck and she put the thing to her breasts. "If we end up doing nothing but staring at the ceiling all night long, at least we'll be together. And if something happens? It won't be about pissed off and frustrated. Okay?"

She wiped off the two tears that had fallen. Pulled her shirt on over her head. Looked at the vodka she'd tried to drink.

He got to his feet and offered her his hand. "Come back with me."

After a long moment, her palm met his and he pulled her up and took her down to his bedroom. When he shut the door, everything went pitch-black, so he clicked on the little lamp on the dresser. The low-watt bulb glowed like embers in a fireplace.

"Come here." He drew her over to the bed, laid her down, and eased himself next to her so he was on his side and she on her back.

As he smoothed some of her hair out on the pillow, she closed her eyes and took a shuddering breath. Gradually, the tension loosened in her body.

"You're right. That wouldn't have gone well."

"It isn't because I don't want you." As he kissed her on the shoulder, she turned her face to his hand and pressed her lips to his palm.

"Are you scared?" she said. "About what'll happen to you tomorrow?"

"No." The only thing he worried about was her. He didn't want her to watch him die. Prayed it wouldn't come to that.

"Butch . . . about your human family. Do you want them to be told if you—"

"Nope, there's no need to tell them anything. And don't

talk like that. I'll be fine." *Please, God, let her not have to see me pass.*

"But won't they care?" When he shook his head, her expression grew sad. "You should be mourned by your blood."

"I will be. By the Brotherhood." As her eyes watered, he kissed her. "And no more about mourning. That's not part of the plan. Forget about it."

"I—"

"Shh. We're not going there. You and me are staying right here."

He lay his head down next to hers and continued running his hands through her beautiful blond hair. When her breathing grew deep and even, he shuffled a little closer, tucked her against his bare chest, and shut his eyes.

He must have fallen asleep as well, because a little later he woke up. In the best possible way.

He was kissing her throat and his hand was moving up her side, heading for her breast. He'd thrown a leg over both of hers, and his erection was pushed up against her hip. With a curse, he backed off, but she followed, staying with him until she was half on top of him.

Her eyes flipped open. "Oh . . ."

He swept his hands up to her face and pushed her hair back. Their eyes met.

Lifting his head off the pillow, he kissed her softly on the mouth. Once. Twice. And . . . again.

"Is . . . something happening?" she whispered.

"Yeah. I think something's happening."

He drew her back into a kiss, then entered her with his tongue, stroking against hers. As he kept at it, their bodies began to move together, mimicking the sex act, his hips advancing and retreating, hers absorbing him, rubbing against him.

There was no rush and he took it slowly, undressing her with care. When she was naked, he eased back and looked at her body.

Oh . . . God. All that soft female skin. Her perfect breasts with their nipples straining. Her secrets. And her face was the best of all: It showed no fear, just erotic anticipation.

Which meant he was going to finish this between them. If there had been a lick of doubt in her eyes, he would have just pleasured her and left it at that. But she wanted the same thing he did, and he was certain there would be no pain for her this time.

Butch stood up and slipped off his loafers, the Guccis making a thunking sound one by one. She watched with wide eyes as his hands went to the waistband of his slacks and he popped the button, then unzipped. Boxers hit the floor with the pants and his erection shot straight out from his body. He covered himself with his hand, folding his cock against his belly, not wanting her to get unnerved.

As he lay down, she rolled into him.

"Oh, God," he breathed as their skin met.

"You're so very naked," she whispered against his shoulder.

He smiled into her hair. "So are you."

She ran her hands up and down his sides, and he felt the heat in him go nuclear, especially as she slipped one arm between their bodies and her palm headed south. When she hit his lower belly, his erection pulsed with the desperate need to be touched, to be stroked, to be squeezed until it exploded.

But he captured her wrist and withdrew her hand. "Marissa, I want you to do something for me."

"What?"

"Let me see you through this, okay? Let's have this time be all about you."

Before she could protest, he covered her mouth with his own.

Butch treated her with such exquisite care, Marissa thought. And with total restraint. Every touch was soft and gentle, every kiss was easy, unhurried. Even when his tongue was in her mouth and his hand was between her legs and she was going wild from the way he went after her, he was in control of himself.

So when he rolled over onto her and his thigh parted hers, she didn't flinch or hesitate. Her body was ready to take him inside. She knew it by the slippery feel of his fingers when he'd touched her. Knew it from her hunger for his sex, too.

He settled his weight on her comfortably and that gloriously hard part of him burned her core as it brushed against her. With a shift, his shoulders bunched up and he put his hand down between their bodies. The head of him found the doorway to her.

Butch propped himself up on his thick arms and stared down into her eyes as he started with that light rocking motion she remembered from before. She deliberately relaxed herself, trying to get as loose as possible even as she became a little nervous.

"You're so beautiful," he groaned. "You okay?"

She ran her hands up his ribs, feeling all the heavy bones under his skin. "Yes."

Pressure and release, pressure and release, a little deeper each time. She closed her eyes, feeling his body moving on top of her, inside of her. This time the stretching, the way her interior yielded to him, the fullness, struck her as delicious, not scary. On instinct, she arched, and as her hips came back to level, she realized that his pelvis and hers had come together.

She lifted her head and looked down. He was all the way in.

"How does it feel? You all right?" Butch's voice was ragged as his muscles flickered under sweat-soaked skin. And then his erection jerked.

A stinging pleasure lit off deep inside of her and she moaned. "Dear Virgin in the Fade . . . do that again. I can feel you when you do that."

"I have a better idea."

As he drew his hips back, she grabbed onto his shoulders to stop the gliding retreat. "No, don't stop—"

He moved forward, pushing back into her flesh, filling her once more. Marissa's eyes popped and she shuddered, especially as he went again with the retreat and the advance.

"Yes . . ." she said. "Better. This is even better."

She watched him as he rode her so carefully, his pecs and his arms flexed up hard, his belly muscles curling and uncurling as his hips rolled into her and relented.

"Oh . . . Butch." The vision of him, the feel of him. She closed her eyes so she could concentrate on every subtle thing.

God, she hadn't expected sex to sound so erotic. With her lids closed, she heard the catch of his breath, the soft creaking of the bed, the rustle of the sheets as he repositioned one of his arms.

With every push and pull, she was getting hotter. And so was he. In no time, his slick skin went fever-baked and he began to breathe in short sucks of air.

"Marissa?"

"Yes . . ." she sighed.

She felt his hand go between their bodies. "Come for me, baby. I want to feel you come like this."

He started in with a wicked, licking touch while keeping up with the slow pump. Within moments, lightning gathered in her core and exploded, blasting out all over her, the orgasm locking her onto him in a series of contractions.

"Oh . . . yeah," he said hoarsely. "Grab onto me. That's what I like . . . *shit*."

When she finally went limp, she opened her eyes in a daze and found him looking at her with total awe . . . and more than a little concern.

"Was that all right?" he asked.

"Amazing." The relief that bled into his face made her chest ache. And then she realized something. "Wait . . . what about you?"

He swallowed hard. "I would love to finish in you."

"Then do it."

"It's not going to take me long," he said under his breath.

As he began to move again, she went motionless and just absorbed the feel of him.

"Baby?" he said roughly. "This okay? You're so still."

"I want to know what your part is like."

"Heaven," he said into her ear. "With you, it's heaven."

He dropped down off his arms, his body hard and heavy as it began to churn above hers. She opened her legs as wide as they could go, her head moving up and down on the pillow from how he was pumping into her. God, he was strong.

With luscious propriety, she ran her hands across his bunched shoulders, then down his surging spine to the place that was hinging against her. She knew just when it was getting to be time for him. His rhythm became urgent, the distance of the thrusts getting tighter, the speed increasing. His whole body grew rigid within its range of movement, surging back and forth, no chance of stopping now.

Breath shot out of his mouth and brushed over her shoulder and the sweat beading on his skin wiped off onto hers. When his hand grabbed her hair and squeezed into a fist, she felt a lick of pain and didn't care. Especially as his face lifted up and his eyes squeezed shut as if he were in exquisite agony.

Then he stopped breathing altogether. The veins popped at the sides of his neck as he threw his head back and roared. Deep inside, she felt his erection kicking, felt hot liquid shoot into her in spasms that shook his whole body.

He collapsed onto her, damp, overheated, gasping. His muscles twitching all over.

She wrapped her arms around him, her legs, too, and held him within her, cradling him.

How beautiful he was, she thought. How beautiful . . . all this was.

THIRTY-SIX

Marissa came awake to the sounds of the shutters lifting for the night and the feel of hands stroking over her stomach, her breasts, her neck. She was on her side, with Butch tucked in tight against her back . . . and his hard planes of muscle were rocking in an erotic rhythm.

His erection was hot and it was searching her out, probing at the crease of her buttocks, wanting in. She reached behind and dug her fingers into his flank, urging him on, and he took the cue. Wordlessly, he rolled on top of her back, his body pushing her facefirst into the pillows. She shoved them out of the way so she could breathe as he split her legs open with his knees.

She moaned. Which evidently woke him up.

He jerked back as if he'd punched his arms into the bed. "Marissa . . . I . . . ah, I didn't mean to . . ."

When he retreated, she rose onto her knees, trying to keep contact with him. "Don't stop."

There was a moment of pause. "You must be sore."

"Not at all. Come back on me. Please."

His voice went all gravel and rasp. "Jesus . . . I'd hoped you'd want to do this again. And I'll go easy, I swear."

God, that rough sound was nice first thing in the evening.

His broad hand smoothed down her spine, and his mouth brushed the top of her hip, then her tailbone, then went lower, to the skin of her bottom. "You look so beautiful like this. I want to have you like this."

Her eyes flared. "You can do that?"

"Oh, yeah. I'll go deeper. You want to try?"

"Yes . . ."

He pulled her hips up farther and settled her weight on all fours, the bed creaking while he repositioned their bodies. As he came in behind her, she looked through her legs. All she saw was his thick thighs and his heavy, hanging sack and his straining arousal. Her core went utterly wet, as if her body knew exactly what was coming.

His chest eased down over her back, and one of his hands appeared beside her head, planting into the mattress as a fist. His forearm flexed and the veins in it thickened as he leaned to the side and brought the head of his erection to the tender skin between her legs. With a little teasing brush, he worked himself back and forth along the outside of her and she knew he was looking at her sex while he did it.

Going by the way he started to shake, he really liked what he saw.

"Marissa . . . I want to—" He cut himself off with an indistinct curse.

"What?" She twisted a little so she could look up at him around her shoulder.

As he stared down at her, his eyes had that hard, intense gleam he seemed to get when he was serious about sex, but there was something else in them, a glowing need that had nothing to do with their bodies. Instead of explaining himself, he planted his other hand into the bed, eased onto her back and pushed his hips in tight without penetrating her. With a gasp, she dropped her head and watched his arousal shoot straight up through her legs. The tip stretched almost to her belly button.

God, now she knew why he liked to look. Because . . . yes, she liked the sight of him all aroused, too.

"What were you going to say?" she groaned.

"Baby . . ." His breath was hot on her neck, his voice a dark, driving demand in her ear. "Ah, shit, I can't ask you like this."

His mouth locked onto her shoulder, his teeth pressing into her skin. As she cried out, her elbows went lax, but he caught her before she fell into the mattress, holding her up with an arm between her breasts.

"Ask me . . ." she panted.

"I would . . . if I could stop this . . . but oh, God . . ."

He pulled back, then entered her, going just as deep as he'd said he would, the powerful surge making her arch her back and call out his name. He started in with that rhythm that drove her wild, but he was still gentle, moving with so much less power than she sensed he could.

She was loving the feel of him, that fullness, that stretching and gliding back, when it dawned on her that they were going to go to work on his body within the hour.

What if this was their last time?

Tears pooled. Matted her lashes. Blinded her. And when he twisted her chin around so he could kiss her, he saw them.

"Don't think about it," he whispered against her mouth. "Stay with me in this moment. Stay right here with me."

Remember this moment. Remember him here . . .

He pulled out, turned her over, and joined them face-to-face, brushing at her cheeks and kissing her as he kept up with the sex. They peaked at the same time, the pleasure so great, his head went loose on his neck as if he couldn't hold it up any longer.

Afterward, he rolled onto his side and gathered her against his chest. As she listened to the thumping of his heart, she prayed the thing was as strong as it sounded.

"What were you going to say?" she whispered in the dimness.

"Will you be my wife?"

She lifted her head. His hazel eyes were dead serious and she had the feeling he was thinking the same thing she was: Why hadn't they been mated sooner?

The single word left her on a sigh. "Yes . . ."

He kissed her softly. "I want to do it both ways. Your way and in a Catholic church. Would that be all right?"

She touched the cross he wore. "Absolutely."

"I wish there was time to—"

The alarm clock started to go off. With a vicious move, he slapped it into silence.

"I guess we need to get up," she said, moving away a little.

She didn't get far. He pulled her back down to the bed, pinned her with his body, and slipped his hand between her legs.

"Butch—"

He kissed her full on and then said against her mouth, "Once more for you. Once more, Marissa."

His gliding, talented fingers left her liquid, her skin and bones melting into him as his mouth went to her breast and he pulled her nipple between his lips. He drove her quickly out of control until she was flushed and gasping, arching into him, enthralled.

Urgent, electric pressure built up and then snapped free in a blaze of current. With loving attention, he helped her ride out the orgasm as she skipped like a flat stone over water, hitting the surface of the pleasure and flying again, only to land and ricochet once more.

The whole time he was above her, watching her with hazel eyes that would haunt her for the rest of her life.

He was going to die tonight. She knew it with total certainty.

*   *   *

John sat in the back of the empty classroom, taking up space in the far corner at his regular, by-his-lonesome table. Training usually started at four, but Zsadist had sent out an e-mail saying classes would begin three hours later tonight. Which was fine. John had had the chance to watch Wrath in action longer.

As the clock ticked closer to seven, the other trainees filed in. Blaylock was last. He was still moving slowly, but he was talking more easily with the guys, kind of like he was getting used to himself. He took a seat up front, shuffling his long legs around to fit.

Abruptly, John realized someone was missing. Where was Lash? Good God . . . what if he'd died? But no— somebody would have passed that news along.

Down in front, Blaylock laughed at one of the other trainees, then bent over to put his backpack on the floor. As he came back to level, his eyes met John's across the room.

John flushed and looked away.

"Hey, John," Blaylock said, "you want to come sit with me?"

The whole class went quiet. John glanced up.

"View's better from here." Blaylock nodded to the blackboard.

Silence followed. The kind where the *Jeopardy!* theme plays in everyone's head.

Not knowing what else to do, John grabbed his books, walked down the aisle, and slid into the empty seat. As he parked it, conversation sprang up again while more books landed on the tables and papers rustled.

The clock overhead clicked, the hands showing seven on the dot. As there was still no Zsadist, the talk got even louder in the room, the guys yanking around in earnest now.

John ran his pen in circles on a blank page, feeling awkward as all get-out and wondering what the hell he was doing up front. Maybe it was a practical joke on him? Shit, he should have stayed—

"Thank you," Blaylock said quietly. "For throwing down for me yesterday."

Whoa . . . maybe this wasn't a joke.

John surreptitiously slid his notebook over so Blaylock could see it. Then he wrote, *I didn't mean to take it that far*.

"I know. And you won't have to do it again. I mean, I can handle him."

John eyed his classmate. *No doubt,* he wrote.

From over on the left, one of the guys started humming the *Star Trek* theme, for God only knew what reason. Others chimed in. Someone lit off with a William Shatner: "I don't know . . . why I have to . . . talk like this, Spock . . ."

In the midst of the chaos, the sound of heavy boots coming down the hall drifted into the room. God, it was like there was an army out in the corridor. With a frown, John looked up to see Wrath walking past the door to the classroom. Then Butch and Marissa went by next. Then Vishous.

What were they all so grim about? he wondered.

Blaylock cleared his throat. "So, John, you want to hang with me and Qhuinn tonight? We were going to chill at my house. Bang some beers. Nothing special."

John whipped his head around, then tried to came his surprise. But wow. First time any of them had suggested meeting up after class.

Cool, John wrote as Zsadist finally came in and shut the door.

Downtown at the Caldwell police station, Van Dean smiled at the badge in front of him, making sure his face was showing a whole lot of No Big Deal. "I'm an old friend of Brian O'Neal's, that's who I am."

Homicide detective José de la Cruz measured him with smart brown eyes. "What did you say your name is?"

"Bob. Bobby O'Connor. I grew up in Southie with Brian. He moved away. I did, too. Then I came back east recently and someone told me he was working as a cop in Caldwell so I figured I'd drop by. But when I call the CPD main line? No Brian O'Neal. And all I got was the he-doesn't-work-here runaround."

"What makes you think showing up in person will change the answer?"

"I was hoping someone could tell me what happened to him. I called his parents in Southie. His father said he hadn't talked to Brian in a long time, but last he knew his son was still working as a cop. Look, man, I've got no ulterior motive here. I just want some answers."

De la Cruz took a long drink out of his black coffee mug. "O'Neal was put on administrative leave back in July. He did not return to the force."

"That's it?"

"Why don't you give me a telephone number? If I remember anything else, I'll call you."

"Sure thing." Van recited some random numbers, which de la Cruz wrote down. "Thanks, and I'd appreciate a call. Hey, you were his partner, right?"

The other man shook his head. "No. I wasn't."

"Oh, that's what the guy at Dispatch said."

De la Cruz picked up a file from his paper-ridden desk and opened it. "We're done here."

Van smiled a little. "Sure thing. Thanks again, detective."

He was almost out the door when de la Cruz said, "By the way, I know you're full of shit."

"Excuse me?"

"If you were a friend of his, you'd have asked for him by the name Butch. Now gitcha ass out of my office and pray that I'm too busy to follow up on you."

Shit. Busted. "Names change, detective."

"Not his. Good-bye, Bobby O'Connor. Or whoever you are."

Van left the office, knowing he was damn lucky you couldn't get arrested just for asking questions about someone. Because sure as hell, de la Cruz would have cuffed him if the guy could have.

Bullshit, those two hadn't been partners. Van had read about them in an article in the *Caldwell Courier Journal*. But it was obvious that if de la Cruz knew what had become of Brian . . . Butch . . . whatever O'Neal, the detective was a dead end on the info trail for Van. And then some.

Van beelined it out of the police station into a nasty March drizzle and jogged over to the minivan. Thanks to his legwork, he had a pretty clear idea of what had happened to O'Neal in the last nine months. Guy's last known address was a one-bedroom in a who-cares apartment building a couple blocks over. Manager had said that when the mail piled up and rent wasn't paid on time, they'd gone in there. The place had been full of furniture and stuff, but it had been clear no one had been keeping house for a while. What little food there was had rotted, and the cable and phone had been turned off for nonpayment. It was like O'Neal had just walked out one morning all business as usual . . . and never come back.

Because he'd fallen into the vampire world.

Must be kind of like joining the Lessening Society, Van thought as he fired up the Town & Country. Once you were in, you cut all your ties. And never went back.

Except the guy was still in Caldwell.

And that meant sooner or later, O'Neal was going to get popped, and Van wanted to be the one to do it. It was time for an inaugural kill and that ex-cop would fit the bill as well as anything else with a heartbeat would.

Just like Mr. X had said. Find the guy. Take him out.

As Van came up to a stoplight, he frowned, thinking that drive to murder probably should have bothered him. Except ever since he'd been inducted into the Society, he seemed to have lost some of his . . . humanity. And more was getting up to go every day. He didn't even miss his brother anymore.

That should have bothered him, too, right? But it didn't.

Because he could feel a dark kind of power growing inside of him, taking up the space left by his soul's departure. Every day he was getting more . . . powerful.

THIRTY-SEVEN

Butch walked across the bright blue mats of the gym, his destination a steel door on the far side marked EQUIPMENT ROOM. Along the way, as he followed Wrath and V, he held on to Marissa's cold hand. He wanted to give her some kind of pep talk, but she was too smart for that old *it's-gonna-to-be-okay* thing. Bottom line was, no one knew what was going to happen, and trying to falsely reassure her was like training a floodlight on the free fall he was about to take.

At the end of the mats, V unlocked the reinforced door and they filed into a jungle of workout gear and caged weapons, heading back to the physical therapy/first aid suite. V let them in and hit the lights, fluorescent tubes flickering on in a chorus of hums.

The place was right out of an episode of *ER*, all white tiles and glass-front stainless-steel cabinets filled with vials and medical supplies. In the corner there was a whirlpool tub, a massage table, and a cardiac crash cart, but none of that registered much. Butch was primarily interested in the center of the room, where showtime was going to happen: Sitting like a stage waiting for Shakespeare, there was a gurney with some kind of a high-tech chandelier hanging over it. And underneath . . . a drain in the floor.

He tried to imagine himself up on that table under those lights. And felt like he was drowning.

As Wrath shut the door, Marissa said in a flat voice, "We should be doing this at Havers's clinic."

V shook his head. "No offense, but I wouldn't take

Butch to your brother for a paper cut. And the fewer people who know about this, the better." He went over to the gurney and checked that the brake was engaged. "Besides, I'm a damn good medic. Butch, ditch the clothes and let's do this."

Butch stripped to his boxers, his skin goose-bumping all over. "Can we do something about the temperature in this meat locker?"

"Yup." V walked over to the wall. "We want it warm in here for the first part. Then I'm going to throw the air-conditioning on hard-core and you'll love me for it."

Butch went to the gurney and popped his body up on the thing. As a hiss and a rush of toasty air came from overhead, he held his arms out for Marissa. After closing her eyes briefly, she came to him, and he took refuge in her body heat, hugging her hard. Her tears were slow and silent, and when he tried to talk to her, she just shook her head.

"Would you choose to be mated this day?"

Everyone in the room jerked around.

A diminutive figure in black robes had appeared in the corner out of nowhere. *The Scribe Virgin.*

Butch's heart jackhammered. He'd seen her only once before, at Wrath and Beth's mating ceremony, and she was now as she had been then: a presence to respect and fear, power incarnate, a force of nature.

Then he realized what she'd asked. "I would, yes . . . Marissa?"

Marissa's hands went down as if she were about to pick up the skirting of a gown she wasn't wearing. Then she dropped her arms awkwardly, but still curtsied low and with grace. As she held the pose, she said, "If it would not offend, we would be honored beyond measure to be joined by Your Holiness."

The Scribe Virgin came forward, her deep chuckle filling the room. As she laid her glowing hand on Marissa's bowed head, she said, "Such manners, child. Your line has always had such perfect manners. Now come to your height and lift thine eyes unto me." Marissa came out of the curtsy and looked up. As she did, Butch could have sworn the Scribe Virgin sighed a little. "Beautiful. Just beautiful. You are so exquisitely formed."

Then the Scribe Virgin looked at Butch. Though there was an opaque black veil over her face, the impact of her stare made his skin tingle all over in warning. Like he was standing in the path of an impending lightning strike.

"What is your father's name, human?"

"Eddie. Edward. O'Neal. But if you don't mind, I'd rather not bring him into this, okay?"

Everyone in the room stiffened and V muttered, "Take it easy with the inquiry, cop. *Really* easy."

"And why is that, human?" the Scribe Virgin asked. The word *human* was pronounced like the phrase *piece of shit*.

Butch shrugged. "He's nothing to me."

"Are humans always so dismissive of their lines?"

"My father and I have nothing to do with each other, that's all."

"Therefore blood ties mean little to you, yes?"

No, Butch thought, glancing over at Wrath. Blood ties were *everything*.

Butch looked back at the Scribe Virgin. "Do you have any idea how relieved—"

As Marissa gasped, V stepped in and slapped his gloved hand over Butch's mouth, yanking him backward by the head and hissing in his ear, "Do you want to get fried like an egg here, buddy? No questions—"

"Ease from him, warrior," the Scribe Virgin snapped. "This I wish to hear."

V's grip slid off his face. "Watch it."

"Sorry about the question thing," Butch said to the black robes. "But I just . . . I'm glad I know what's in my veins. And honestly, if I die today, I'm grateful I finally know what I am." He took Marissa's hand. "And who I love. If this is where my life took me after all those years of being lost, I'd say my time here wasn't wasted."

There was a long silence. Then the Scribe Virgin said, "Do you regret that you leave behind your human family?"

"Nope. This is my family. Here with me now and elsewhere in the compound. Why would I need anything else?" The cursing in the room told him he'd thrown another question out there. "Yeah . . . ah, sorry—"

A soft feminine laugh came from under the robes. "You are rather fearless, human."

"Or you could call it stupid." As Wrath's mouth fell open, Butch rubbed his face. "You know, I'm trying here. I really am. You know, to be respectful."

"Your hand, human."

He offered her his left, the one that was free.

"Palm up," Wrath barked.

He flipped his hand over.

"Tell me, human," the Scribe Virgin said, "if I asked for the one you hold this female with, would you offer it to me?"

"Yeah. I'd just reach over to her with the other guy." As that little laugh came again, he said, "You know, you sound like birds when you do that chuckle thing. It's nice."

Over to the left, Vishous put his head in his hands.

There was a long silence.

Butch took a deep breath. "Guess I'm not allowed to say that."

The Scribe Virgin reached up and slowly lifted the robes from her face.

Jesus . . . Christ . . . Butch squeezed Marissa's hand hard at what was revealed.

"You're an angel," he whispered.

Perfect lips lifted in a smile. "No. I am Myself."

"You're beautiful."

"I know." Her voice became authoritative again. "Your right palm, Butch O'Neal, descended of Wrath son of Wrath."

Butch let go of Marissa, regripped her with his left hand, and reached forward. When the Scribe Virgin touched him, he flinched. Though his bones weren't crushed, the awesome strength in her was merely shelved potential. She could grind him to powder on a whim.

The Scribe Virgin turned to Marissa. "Child, give me yours now."

The instant that connection was made, a warm current flooded Butch's body. At first he assumed it was because the heating system in the room was really cooking, but then he realized the rush was under his skin.

"Ah, yes. This is a very good mating," the Scribe Virgin pronounced. "And you have my permission to join for however long you have together." She dropped their hands and looked at Wrath. "The presentation to me is complete. If he lives, you shall finish the ceremony as soon as he is well enough."

The king bowed his head. "So be it."

The Scribe Virgin turned back to Butch. "Now, we shall see how strong you are."

"Wait," Butch said, thinking about the *glymera*. "Marissa's mated now, right? I mean, even if I die, she will have had a mate, right?"

"Death wish," V said under his breath. "Fucking Death Wish Boy we got over here."

The Scribe Virgin seemed flat-out amazed. "I should kill you now."

"I'm sorry, but this *matters*. I don't want her falling under that whole *sehclusion* thing. I want her to be my widow so she doesn't have to worry about anyone else leading her life."

"Human, you are *astoundingly* arrogant," the Scribe Virgin snapped. But then she smiled. "And totally unrepentant, aren't you."

"I don't mean to be rude, I swear. I just need to know she's taken care of."

"Have you had use of her body? Have you taken her as a male does?"

"Yeah." As Marissa turned bright pink, Butch tucked her face into his shoulder. "And it was . . . you know, with love."

As he whispered something soothing to Marissa, the Scribe Virgin seemed touched, her voice turning almost kind. "Then she shall be as you say, your widow, and not fall under any provisions affecting unmated females."

Butch sighed in relief and stroked Marissa's back. "Thank God."

"You know, human, if you learned some manners, you would fare well with me."

"If I promise to work at it, will you help me live through what's coming?"

The Scribe Virgin's head fell back as she laughed in a loud burst. "No, I will not help you. But I find myself wishing you very well, human. Very well indeed." Abruptly, she glared at Wrath, who was smiling and shaking his head. "Do not assume such leeway with etiquette applies to others who seek me out."

Wrath ditched the grin. "I am well aware of what is proper, as are my brothers."

"Good." The robes shifted back into place, lifting up and going over her head without the help of hands. Just before her face was covered, she said, "You will wish to bring the queen to this room before you commence."

And then the Scribe Virgin disappeared.

Vishous whistled between his teeth and wiped his brow with his forearm. "Butch, man, you are *so* lucky she liked you, true?"

Wrath flipped open his cell phone and started dialing. "Shit, I thought we were going to lose you before we even started— Beth? Hey, my *leelan*, could you come to the gym?"

Vishous grabbed a stainless-steel tray stand and wheeled it over to a cabinet. As he started putting things in sterile wraps on top, Butch shifted his legs around and stretched out on the gurney.

He stared up at Marissa. "Things don't work out, I'll wait for you in the Fade," he said, not because he believed it but because he wanted to reassure her.

She bent down and kissed him, then stayed with her cheek against his until V quietly cleared his throat. As Marissa stepped back, she began to speak in the Old Language, a soft rush of desperate words, a prayer that was more breath than voice.

V brought the tray stand up to the gurney, then went to Butch's feet. As the brother moved around, he had something in his hand, but he wasn't showing what it was, keeping his arm always out of sight. There was a metallic clank and the far end of the table tilted up. In the heat of the room, Butch felt the blood rush to his head.

"You ready?" V asked.

Butch stared at Marissa. "I feel like this is happening so fast, all of a sudden."

The door opened and Beth walked in. She said a soft hello and went to Wrath, who put his arms around her and drew her close.

Butch glanced back at Marissa, whose prayers had increased in speed until they were a blur of words. "I love you," he said. Then he looked at V. "Do it."

Vishous lifted his hand. There was a scalpel in it, and before Butch could track the movement, the blade cut into one of his wrists deeply. Twice. Blood welled, a bright, glistening red, and he grew nauseous as he watched it drip down his forearm.

An identical pair of burning cuts were made in his other wrist.

"Oh . . . Jesus." As his heart rate shot through the roof, the blood ran faster.

Fear came on him hard and he had to open his mouth so he could breathe.

Off in the distance, he heard voices, but he couldn't track them. And the room seemed to be receding. As reality warped and twisted, his eyes latched on to Marissa's face and pale blue eyes and white-blond hair.

He did his best to swallow the panic so he didn't scare her. "It's okay," he said. "It's okay . . . it's okay, I'm okay . . ."

Someone grabbed his ankles and he jerked in surprise . . . but it was just Wrath. And the king held him as V tilted the table even more so the blood ran out even faster. Then Vishous came around and gently eased Butch's arms off the table so they were hanging down. Closer to the drain.

"V?" Butch said. "Don't leave, okay?"

"Never." V brushed Butch's hair back with a gesture so tender it was out of place coming from a male.

Somehow everything got frightening. On some kind of survival reflex, Butch started to struggle, but V leaned on his shoulders, keeping him in place.

"Easy, cop. We're all right here with you. Just relax if you can . . ."

Time stretched out. Time . . . God, time was passing,

wasn't it? People kept talking to him, but Marissa's uneven voice was all he really heard . . . though as she was praying, he didn't know what she was saying.

He lifted his head and looked down, but he couldn't see his wrists anymore to track what was—

All of a sudden he started to shiver uncontrollably. "I'm c-cold."

V nodded. "I know. Beth, turn the heat up some more, okay?"

Butch looked at Marissa, feeling helpless. "I'm getting c-colder."

Her prayers stopped. "Can you feel my hand on your arm?" He nodded. "You feel how warm it is? Good . . . imagine it all over your body. I'm holding you . . . I'm hugging you. You're against me. I'm against you."

He smiled. He liked that.

But then his eyes fluttered, the sight of her flickering like she was a movie on a screen, and the projector was broken.

"Cold . . . turn heat up." His skin prickled all over. His stomach felt like a lead balloon. His heart seemed to be twinkling in his chest, not beating anymore.

"Cold . . ." His teeth chattered, so very loud in his ears, but then he couldn't hear anything. "Love . . . you . . ."

Marissa watched as the pool of Butch's brilliant red blood grew bigger and bigger around the drain until she was standing in some of it. Oh, God . . . all his color had left him, his skin going paper white. He didn't seem to be breathing anymore.

V came forward with a stethoscope and put it on Butch's chest. "He's close now. Beth, get over here. I need you." He handed the stethoscope to the queen. "You listen to that heart of his. I want you to tell me when you don't hear anything for ten seconds or more." He pointed at the clock on the wall. "Track it by that third hand up there. Marissa, you come hold your boy's ankles, true? Wrath is about to get busy."

When she hesitated, V shook his head. "We need someone to keep him on the table and Wrath and I have to go to work. You're still going to be with him, you can talk to him from there."

She leaned down, kissed Butch's lips and told him she loved him. Then she replaced Wrath, taking over the job of keeping Butch's heavy body from sliding off the gurney onto the floor.

"Butch?" she said. "I'm right here, *nallum*. Can you feel me?" She squeezed the cold skin of his ankles. "I'm right here."

She kept talking to him calmly, though she was terrified about what was going to happen next. Especially when Vishous brought over the cardiac crash cart.

"You ready, Wrath?" the Brother asked.

"Where you want me?"

"Right here next to his chest." Vishous picked up a long. thin, sterile pack and ripped it open. The needle inside was about six inches in length and seemed thick as a pen. "How we doing with that heart rate, Beth?"

"Slowing down. God, it's so faint."

"Marissa? I'm going to ask you to get quiet so she can hear better, okay?"

Marissa shut her mouth and resumed praying in her head.

In the minutes that passed, they became a frozen tableau around Butch. The only thing that moved in the room was his blood as it dripped out of those deep wounds in his wrists and flowed down the drain. The soft *glug, glug, glug* in the floor made Marissa want to scream.

"It's still beating," Beth whispered.

"Here's what's going to happen," Vishous said, looking back and forth across Butch's body. "When Beth gives me the signal, I'm going to pop the table upright. While I work on Wrath, I want you two to seal up Butch's wrists. Seconds count. You need to close those wounds quick, we clear?"

They both nodded.

"Slower," Beth said. Her dark blue eyes narrowed on the clock and she lifted a hand to press one of the stethoscope's earpieces in tighter. "Slower . . ."

Seconds suddenly stretched out into infinity, and Marissa flipped into some kind of autopilot, her fear and panic buried under a powerful focus that came out of nowhere.

Beth frowned. Bent down closer, as if that would help. "Now!"

V set the table to level and Marissa ran around to one of Butch's wrists as Beth dropped to the other one. While they sucked the wounds closed, V shoved that thick needle right into the crook of Wrath's arm.

"Everyone back away," V barked when he withdrew it from the king's vein.

He shifted his grip on the syringe so he was holding it in his fist and leaned over Butch. With hurried movements, he felt around the sternum with his fingertips. Then he slammed that needle right into Butch's heart.

Marissa stumbled back as the plunger was depressed. Someone caught her. Wrath.

V extracted the syringe and tossed it on the table. Then he picked up the paddles of the crash cart and there was a juicing-up noise from the machine.

"Clear!" V shouted. And slapped the metal pads on Butch's chest.

Butch's torso jerked and V put his fingers to the male's jugular.

"Clear!" He hit Butch again.

Marissa sagged in Wrath's arms as Vishous threw the paddles onto the crash cart, pinched Butch's nostrils, and blew into his mouth twice. Then the Brother started chest compressions. As he performed CPR, he growled, his fangs bared as if he were pissed off at Butch.

Whose skin was now turning gray.

" . . . three . . . four . . . five . . ."

As V continued to count, Marissa struggled free. "Butch? Butch . . . don't leave . . . stay with us. Stay with me."

" . . . nine . . . ten." V pulled back, blew two breaths into Butch's mouth, then put his finger to the male's throat.

"Please, Butch," she begged.

V went for the stethoscope. Moved the disk around, searching. "Nothing. *Fuck*."

THIRTY-EIGHT

Two minutes later, Marissa grabbed V's shoulder when the Brother stopped CPR. "You can't quit!"

"I'm not. Give me your arm." When she did, Vishous cut through the skin of her wrist. "Over his mouth. *Now.*"

Marissa rushed to Butch's head, pushed his lips and teeth apart and put the slice right to him as Vishous resumed chest compressions. She held her breath, praying that Butch would start to drink, hoping that some of her was getting into him and helping.

But, no . . . he was dead . . . Butch was dead . . . *Butch was dead—*

Someone was moaning. Her. Yes, she was making that noise.

Vishous paused and felt Butch's neck. Then fumbled for the stethoscope. He was putting the disk down when Marissa thought she saw Butch's chest move. Or maybe not.

"Butch?" she said.

"I got something." Vishous repositioned the disk. "Yeah . . . I got something—"

Butch's ribs expanded as he sucked a breath in through his nose. Then his mouth moved against her wrist.

She repositioned her arm so the wound fit better over his lips. "Butch?"

His chest inflated more deeply, his mouth backing off her vein as he drew air down into his lungs. There was a pause and then another breath. Deeper still . . .

"Butch? Can you—"

413

Butch's eyes popped open. And she went cold to the core.

The male she loved was not in that stare. There was nothing in it. Just blank hunger.

With a roar, he grabbed her arm, his grip so powerful she gasped. There was no escape as he latched on with his mouth and started drinking in ferocious pulls. Twisting on the table, he savaged her wrist, his eyes fixated, animalistic as he breathed through his nose and swallowed in great yanks.

Through the pain, she felt total, abject fear.

Tell me you're still in there, she thought. *Tell me you are still with us . . .*

It wasn't long before she became light-headed.

"He's taking too much," Vishous said, all urgent.

Before she could respond, she became aware of a scent in the room, a dark . . . yes, a bonding scent. Wrath's. Except why would he feel the need to establish his mating territory here and now?

She swayed and Vishous's hard fingers grabbed her upper arm. "Marissa, you're done."

But Butch was starving, mad from hunger. "No! No—"

"Let me take over."

Marissa's eyes shot to Beth . . . then focused on Wrath. Standing at his *shellan's* side, Wrath's face was set in violent lines, his body coiled as if he were about to fight something.

"Marissa? Will you let me feed him?" Beth said.

Marissa looked at the queen. God, those words, those same words that had been spoken back in July . . . when Wrath's body had balanced on the edge of life and Marissa's vein had been what was needed.

"Will you, Marissa?"

As she nodded her head numbly, Wrath started to growl;

414

his lips peeling off fangs that had elongated into white knives.

Oh, Lord, this was a very dangerous situation. Fully bonded males did not share. *Ever.* In fact, they would fight to the death before they let another male anywhere near their females when it came to feeding.

Beth looked up at her *hellren.* Before she said anything, Wrath bit out, "V, get your ass over here and hold me back."

As Vishous approached the king, he wished Rhage was with him.

Shit . . . this was a bad idea. A pure-blooded, bonded male vampire about to watch his *shellan* feed someone else. Holy hell, when the Scribe Virgin had suggested Beth come down, V had assumed it was for ceremonial purposes, not so she could be a vein. But what was the choice? Butch was going to suck Marissa dry and not have enough and there wasn't another female in the house who could do the job: Mary was still human and Bella was pregnant.

Besides, like dealing with Rhage or Z would be any easier? For the beast, they'd need a tranq gun the size of a cannon and Z . . . well, *shit.*

Beth reached up and stroked her *hellren*'s face. "Maybe you shouldn't watch."

Wrath grabbed her by the throat and kissed her hard. Then he brought up her wrist and scored her flesh, opening her vein.

"Go to him. Now." He pushed her away, then slammed his body back against the wall. "Vishous, you better fucking hold me. Or this is going to get ugly."

Wrath's awesome body was trembling, his muscles tensed up, his skin breaking out in a sweat. From behind his wraparounds, his eyes glowed with a light so fierce you could see it plainly.

V hurled himself at his king and met instant, straining resistance. Dear God, this was going to be like holding back a bull.

"Why don't . . . you leave?" V grunted as he worked to keep Wrath's body in place.

"Would have to . . . get past them . . . to get to the door. No . . . way."

V twisted his head and looked at the table.

Man, Marissa was going to be on the floor if she didn't get free of Butch. And the cop was going to fight like hell if that source of blood left his mouth.

"Beth!" V shouted as he and Wrath struggled. "Pinch the cop's nostrils. Pinch them hard and hold his forehead down. That's the only way you'll get him to release her."

When Beth grabbed Butch's nose, the cop made an inhuman noise, as if he knew what was coming. And his body jackknifed on the table like he was prepared to fight whoever was going to take his food away.

Oh, Christ, please don't let him attack Beth, V thought. Wrath was so lit he was liable to break free and kill the guy. *Please—*

The females handled it beautifully. Marissa yanked her wrist away and nailed Butch in the shoulders, punching into him, holding him down as Beth brought her wrist to his mouth. As that fresh vein came to him, Butch took to the new blood like a babe and moaned at the taste.

Which naturally caused Wrath to go apeshit.

The king's body lurched toward the table, Vishous getting dragged along.

"Marissa!" V shifted his grip so he was around Wrath's waist like a sash. "I need help over here!"

She looked over at Wrath . . . and she was good—damn, the female was good.

She undoubtedly wanted to be by Butch's side. Instead, she flashed over and rammed her body against the Wrath tangle that was about to unravel. The king stumbled back under the force of impact and V repositioned himself, his head torqued at a bad angle but his arms right where they needed to be, one up Wrath's back and locked on his neck, one around the waist. For kicks and giggles, V wrapped a leg through Wrath's thighs so if the male lunged forward again he would trip first.

As if on cue, Marissa did the same, entwining one of her legs with Wrath's and running an arm up the front of his chest.

Oh . . . shit. She was bleeding hard from that wrist of hers.

"Marissa . . . move your arm toward me . . ." V breathed deeply, muscles straining. "Marissa . . ."

She didn't appear to hear him. Was too busy watching what was happening on that gurney.

"*Marissa* . . . you're bleeding out. Lower your damn wrist."

She shifted her elbow and her arm dropped, but she really wasn't focused on herself.

Until V put his lips to her skin. Then she gasped and looked down.

Their eyes met. Hers were wide.

"Just to keep you from bleeding," he said against her wrist.

As Butch made a noise, she turned back to her mate.

And suddenly, time stopped for V in spite of the load he was holding back. He stared at Marissa's perfect profile as he licked the chewed mess of her wrist, sealing the wounds, easing the pain of them, starting the healing process. Compelled by something he didn't want to name, he ran his tongue over her skin again and again, tasting both her blood and . . . Butch's mouth.

Vishous repeated the licking more times than he had to. And on the last swipe, when he knew that he had to stop because he'd gone over the line already . . . when he knew he was going to lose control of Wrath unless he paid attention . . . on the last swipe, he looked out at Butch. And pressed his lips against the skin at his mouth in a kiss.

He had the strangest feeling he was saying good-bye to his roommate.

Butch woke up in a maelstrom. A whirlpool. A . . . blender.

There was a roaring throughout his body, something that sent every one of his muscles into contraction. He was . . . drinking something. Something so good it brought tears to his eyes . . . something thick and lovely against the tongue, a dark wine. As he swallowed again and again, he thought dimly that he'd tasted something like it before. Not this exact vintage but—

His eyes flipped open and he nearly passed out.

Holy shit, he was *alive* and on the other side and . . .

Wait, this wasn't Marissa. There was black hair hanging down over his face.

He jerked his mouth out of the way. *"Marissa?"*

When he heard her reply, he looked to the sound of her voice. Only to recoil.

Good . . . God. Not exactly what he expected to see and not a welcome wagon to his new life, either. Not by a long shot.

Wrath was right out of a Saturday-night movie, a hulking, snarling vampire monster, fangs bared, eyes glowing. And he wanted at Butch.

The good news was that he was being held back by Vishous and Marissa. The bad news was that they seemed to be on the verge of losing control of him.

Butch looked up at Beth, who was sucking the wound at her wrist shut. "Oh . . . shit." He'd drunk a lot from her, hadn't he? Oh . . . *shit*.

He let his head fall back against the table. Wrath was going to kill him. Absolutely. When they let that boy go, the king was going to wipe the floor with him.

Butch was cursing and measuring the distance to the door as Beth walked up to the trio.

"Wrath?" In a lower voice she said, "Keep holding him."

Butch turned on his side and met Marissa's eyes, praying he wasn't about to lose his life now. And he was impatient to get close to his female, but this was one situation that needed to be diffused with care.

"Wrath?" Beth repeated.

Wrath's instincts were so fired up, she had to talk at him for a while to get him focused on her instead of Butch.

"It's over, okay?" She touched his face. "It's done, it's over."

With a moan of desperation, Wrath pressed his lips to her palm, then squeezed his eyes shut in agony. "Tell them . . . tell them to let go slowly. And Beth . . . Beth, I'm going to come at you. I can't . . . stop that. But it'll be better than killing him . . ."

"Yeah . . . much better," Butch agreed.

Beth stepped back and braced herself. "Let him go."

It was like turning a tiger loose. Marissa ducked and scrambled out of the way while Wrath threw Vishous off with such force the brother slammed into a cabinet.

In one coordinated launch, the king went for Beth and bit her on the throat. As she gasped and fell back in ecstasy, Wrath wheeled around and nailed Butch with pure murder in his eyes. It was obvious the king drank now not for sustenance but to mark, and his bonding scent was a screaming warning that filled the room. As soon as he felt his point had been made, he picked his *shellan* up in his arms and left. There was no question where they were headed: nearest room with a door so he could get inside of her.

Butch reached out for Marissa, and she came to him in the manner of hope to the disaffected: an illuminating warmth, a promise of a future worth living, a loving benediction. As she bent over him and held on tight, he kissed her softly and spoke a whole lot of nonsense, the words leaving him in an uncontrolled, un-thought-out rush.

When they separated a little to breathe, he looked at Vishous. The brother was standing awkwardly next to the open door and staring down at the floor, his big body trembling ever so slightly.

"V?"

V's diamond eyes lifted and he blinked quick. "Hey, man." As Butch reached out a hand, Vishous shook his head. "Glad you're back, cop."

"Fuck you, come here. V . . . gitcha ass over here."

V shoved his hands in his pockets and slowly walked to the gurney. Marissa was the one who linked them, drawing Vishous's arm up and out so Butch could reach the brother's palm.

"You all right?" Butch asked, squeezing.

For a split second, his grip was returned. Then V stomped one of his shitkickers like a horse and broke the contact. "Yeah. Fine."

"Thank you."

"Yeah."

V was so twitchy, Butch took pity on him and changed the subject. "So is it over? Is that it?"

V stroked his goatee and glanced at the clock. Then looked at Butch's body. "Let's wait another ten minutes."

Okay, fine. Butch passed the time running his hands up and down Marissa's arms. And shoulders. And face. And hair.

Eventually, V murmured, "I guess it is done."

Even though there was a curious disappointment in the brother's voice, Butch grinned. "Well, that wasn't too bad. Except for the dying part, of course. That wasn't . . ." He let the sentence drift and frowned.

"What is it?" Marissa said.

"I don't know. I—" Something was happening . . . something in his gut . . .

Vishous came over to the table. "What's going on, cop?"

"I . . ." The vast wave of pain came over him like a shroud of nails, wrapping around his body, cutting into him from every angle possible. He gasped under the onslaught, his vision conking out, then coming back. "Oh, *shit. I'm dying . . .*"

Vishous's face appeared in front of his. And the bastard was smiling . . . a big, fat Cheshire cat grin. "This is the change, my friend. Now . . . now you're turning."

"What the f—" He didn't get the word out. Red-hot agony became all he knew and he receded deep within himself, getting lost in the swirling torture. As it intensified even further, he hoped to pass out. No such luck.

After a hundred and fifty light-years of suffering, the popping started: The bones in his thighs were the first to snap and he howled, but there was no time to dwell on it because his upper arms were next. Then his shoulders. His spine . . . his lower legs . . . hands . . . feet . . . his skull screamed and his jaw ached. He rolled over . . . spit out two teeth . . .

Through the hurricane of the change, Marissa was with him, talking to him. He held on to her voice and the image of her in his head, the only thing steady in his world of suffering.

THIRTY-NINE

Way across town, in a very nice, very secluded house, John finished his first beer. And then his second. And his third. He was surprised his stomach could handle them, but they went down smooth and stayed that way.

Blaylock and Qhuinn were on the floor in front of the bed, locked in on a plasma-screen TV playing *sKillerz*, that kick-ass game that was every where. By some freak of nature, John had beaten them both, so they were battling for second place.

As John lounged back on Blaylock's comforter, he tipped the Corona bottle to his mouth, realized it was empty, and looked at the clock. Fritz would be picking him up in about twenty minutes and that might be a problem. He was buzzing. Hard.

It was really nice.

Blaylock laughed and keeled over onto the floor. "I can't believe you beat me, you bastard."

Qhuinn picked up his beer and gave Blay a little knock in the leg with the thing. "Sorry, big guy. But you suck."

John propped his head up on his hand, relishing the feel of being all pleasantly out of it and mellow. He'd been so pissed off for so long, he hadn't been able to remember what relaxed felt like.

Blay glanced over at him with a grin. "Of course, strong/silent up there is the real ass-kicker. I hate you, you know that?"

John smiled and flipped the guy off. As the two on the floor laughed, a BlackBerry sounded.

Qhuinn answered it. Did a lot of *Uh-huh*. Hung up. "Shit . . . Lash ain't coming back for a while. Seems like you"—the guy looked at John—"scared the shit out of him."

"Man, that kid always was an asshole," Blay said.

"Straight up."

They were quiet for a while, just listening to Too Short's "Nasty." Then Qhuinn got this intense look on his face.

His eyes, one blue, one green, narrowed. "Yo, Blay . . . so what was it like?"

Blay's stare shot quickly to the ceiling. "Losing at *sKillerz* to you? A real buzz kill, thank you very much."

"You know that's not what I'm talking about."

With a curse, Blay reached over to a little refrigerator, took out another beer, and cracked it open. The guy had had seven and seemed sober as ever. Of course, he'd also eaten four McDonald's Big Macs, two things of large fries, a chocolate milk shake, and two cherry pies. Plus a bag of Ruffles.

"Blay? Come on . . . what happened?"

Blaylock took a slug from the bottle and swallowed hard. "Nothing."

"Fuck. You."

"Okay, *fine*." Blay took another draw. "I . . . ah, I wanted to die, okay. Was convinced I would. Then I . . . you know . . ." He cleared his throat. "I . . . ah, took her vein. And it got worse after that. A helluva lot worse."

"Whose vein was it?"

"Jasim's."

"Whoa. She's hot."

"Whatever." Blay leaned to the side, grabbed a sweat-shirt, and pulled it over his hips. Like he had something worth covering up there.

Qhuinn tracked the movement. So did John.

"Did you have her, Blay?"

"No! Believe me, when the transition hits, sex is *not* on your mind."

"But I've heard afterward—"

"No, I did not do it with her."

"Okay, that's cool." But clearly Qhuinn thought his buddy was nuts. "So what about the change? What did it feel like?"

"I . . . I broke apart and came back together." Blay drank deeply. "That's it."

Qhuinn flexed his little hands, then curled them into fists. "Do you feel different?"

"Yeah."

"How?"

"Christ, Qhuinn—"

"What do you have to hide? We're all going to go through it. I mean . . . shit, John, you've got to want to know, right?"

John looked at Blay and nodded, hoping like hell the two would keep talking.

In the quiet that followed, Blaylock stretched out his legs. Through the new blue jeans he had on, his heavy thigh muscles bunched and relaxed.

"So what do you feel like now?" Qhuinn prompted.

"Myself. Only . . . I don't know, so much stronger."

"Niiiiiice." Qhuinn laughed. "I can't wait."

Blaylock's eyes shifted over. "It's not something to look forward to. Trust me."

Qhuinn shook his head. "You are so wrong about that." There was a pause. "Do you get hard a lot now?"

Blay turned the color of a barn. *"What?"*

"Come on, you had to know that one was coming. So do you?" Silence stretched out. "Hello? Blay? Answer the question. Do you?"

Blay rubbed his face. "Um . . . yeah."

"Often?"

"Yeah."

"You work it, right? I mean . . . you must. So what's that like?"

"Are you out of your fucking mind? I'm not—"

"Just tell us once. We won't ask you again. Swear. Right, John?"

John nodded slowly, aware he was holding his breath. He'd had dreams, erotic dreams, but that wasn't the same as it actually happening. Or getting to hear about it firsthand.

Unfortunately, Blaylock seemed to have clammed up.

"Christ, Blay . . . what's it like? *Please.* All my life I've been waiting for what you have. I can't ask anyone else . . . I mean, like I'm going to my father with this shit? Just spit it out. What does it feel like to come?"

Blay picked at the label on his beer. "Powerful. That's what it's like. It's just this . . . powerful rush that builds up and then . . . you explode and drift."

Qhuinn's eyes closed. "Man, I want that. I want to be male."

God, that was exactly what John hungered for.

Blay chugged his Corona, then wiped his mouth. "Of course, now . . . now I want to do it with someone."

Qhuinn cracked one of his half smiles. "What about Jasim?"

"Nah. Not my type. And we're done with this. Conversation's over."

John glanced at the clock, then shuffled to the edge of the bed. With a quick scribble, he wrote on his pad and flashed it. Blay and Qhuinn both nodded.

"Good deal," Blay said.

426

"You up for hanging tomorrow night?" Qhuinn asked.

John nodded and stood up—only to stumble and have to catch himself on the mattress.

Qhuinn laughed. "Look at you, punk. You're faced."

John just shrugged and concentrated on getting himself to the door. As he opened it, Blay said, "Yo, J?"

John glanced over his shoulder and cocked an eyebrow.

"Where can we learn that sign language thing?"

Qhuinn nodded and popped open another beer. "Yeah, where?"

John blinked. Then wrote on his pad, *The Internet. Search for American Sign Language.*

"Good deal. And you can help us, right?"

John nodded.

The two went back to the TV and fired up another game. As John shut the door, he heard them laughing and he started to smile. Only to feel the sting of disgrace.

Tohr and Wellsie were dead, he thought. He shouldn't be . . . enjoying stuff. A real man wouldn't get distracted from his goal, from his enemies . . . for nothing more than the company of friends.

John weaved down the hall, throwing one arm out to balance.

Trouble was . . . it felt so good to just be one of the guys. He had always wanted to have friends. Not a big group or anything. But a few, solid, strong . . . friends.

The kind you could rely on 'til death. Like brothers.

Marissa did not understand how Butch survived what happened to his body. It just seemed impossible. Except this was, evidently, what males went through, particularly warriors. And as he was of Wrath's line, he definitely had that thick blood in him.

When it was over, hours later, Butch lay on the table in the now frigid room, just breathing. His skin was waxy and covered with sweat like he'd run twelve marathons. His feet hung off the far edge of the gurney. His shoulders were nearly twice as big, and his boxers were stretched tight over his thighs.

His face comforted her, though. It was the same as it had been before, proportional with his new body, but the same. And when his eyes opened, they were the hazel she knew so well, with the spirit inside them that was his alone.

He was too dazed to speak, but he shivered, so she brought him a blanket and spread it over him. As the soft weight landed, he flinched as if his skin were too tender, but then he mouthed the words *I love you* and slid away into sleep.

Abruptly, she became more tired than she'd ever been in her life.

Vishous finished cleaning up the blood on the floor with a spray nozzle and said, "Let's eat."

"I don't want to leave him."

"I know. I asked Fritz to bring something to us and he left it just outside."

Marissa followed the Brother out into the Equipment Room and they each sat down on double-sized benches built out from the wall. They ate Fritz's little picnic munchies in the midst of racks of nunchakus and training daggers and swords and guns. The sandwiches were good and so were the apple juice and the oatmeal cookies.

After a while, Vishous lit a hand-rolled and leaned back. "He's going to be fine, you know."

"I can't see how he got through it."

"Mine was like that."

She stopped with a second ham sandwich on the way to her mouth. "Really?"

"Worse, actually. I was smaller than him when it happened."

"He's the same on the inside, though, isn't he?"

"Yup, he's still your boy."

When she finished the sandwich, she put both her legs up on the bench and eased back against the wall. "Thank you."

"For what?"

"Sealing me up." She held out her wrist.

His diamond gaze shifted away. "No problem."

In the quiet, her eyelids drooped and she shook herself to wake up.

"Nah, let yourself go," Vishous murmured. "I'll watch him and as soon as he comes around, I'll let you know. Go on . . . lie down."

She stretched out, then curled on her side. She didn't expect to sleep, but shut her eyes anyway.

"Lift your head," Vishous said. When she did, he slid a rolled-up towel under her ear. "This is better for your neck."

"You're very kind."

"You kidding? Cop would kick my ass for letting you be uncomfortable."

She could have sworn Vishous brushed his hand down her hair, but then figured it was in her mind.

"What about you?" she said softly as he sat on the other bench. God, he had to be as tired as she was.

His smile was remote. "You don't worry about me, female. Just sleep."

Surprisingly, she did.

V watched Marissa pass out from exhaustion. Then he tilted his head and looked into the PT/first aid suite.

From this angle he could see the soles of the cop's much larger feet. Man . . . Butch really was one of them now. A card-carrying, fanged-up, warrior male who looked like he was going to stand at about six-six, maybe six-seven. Wrath's bloodline was definitely in that boy— and V wondered if they were ever going to find out why.

The door to the Equipment Room swung open and Z walked in, with Phury right behind him.

"What happened?" the two of them asked in unison.

"Shhh." V nodded at Marissa. Then in a quiet voice he said, "See for yourself. He's in there."

The two went to the doorway. "Holy shit . . ." Phury breathed.

"That's a big one," Z muttered. Then he sniffed the air. "Why is Wrath's bonding scent all over this place—or is it me?"

V stood up. "Come outside to the gym, I don't want to wake either of them."

The three walked onto the blue mats and V shut the door most of the way behind them.

"So where is Wrath?" Phury asked as they sat down. "I thought he was here to witness the whole thing."

"He's busy." No doubt.

Z stared at the door. "That cop's big, V. That cop is really big."

"I know." V laid himself out flat on his back and took a drag. As he exhaled, he refused to look at his brothers.

"V, he's *really* big."

"Don't even go there. It's too early to know what he's going to be like."

Z rubbed over his skull trim. "I'm just saying. He's—"

"I know."

"And he's got Wrath's blood in him."

"*I know*. But look, it's too soon, Z. It's just too soon. Besides, his mother isn't a Chosen."

Z's yellow eyes grew annoyed. "Stupid fucking rule if you ask me."

FORTY

Butch woke up on the gurney in the midst of taking a deep breath in through his nose. He was . . . smelling something. Something that pleased him greatly. Something that made him hum with power. *Mine*, a voice said in his head.

He tried to shake the word off, but it just got louder. With every breath he took, the single syllable repeated in his brain until it was like the beat of his heart: Involuntary. The source of his very life. The seat of his soul.

With a groan, he sat up on the table, only to lurch off balance and nearly fall onto the floor. As he caught himself, he looked down at his arms. What the—no, this was wrong. These were not his arms—or . . . shit, his legs either. His thighs were *huge*.

This is not me, he thought.

Mine, came the voice again.

He looked around. God, everything in the clinical room was crystal clear, like his eyes were windows that had been wiped clean. And his ears . . . he looked up at the fluorescent lights. He could actually hear the electricity going through the tubes.

Mine.

He inhaled again. Marissa. That scent was Marissa. She was close by—

His mouth opened of its own accord, and he let out a deep, rhythmic purr that ended in a growled word: *Mine*.

His heart pounded as he realized the control tower in his head had been completely overtaken. No longer logical, he was being ruled by a possessive instinct that made what he'd felt toward Marissa before look like a passing fancy.

Mine!

He glanced down at his hips and got a load of what was doing in his now way-too-small boxers. His cock had grown along with the rest of him, and it was punching out at the stretched-thin cotton. The thing twitched as he looked at it as if to get his attention.

Oh . . . God. His body wanted to mate. With Marissa. *Now.*

As if he'd called her name, she appeared in the doorway. "Butch?"

With no warning, he became a torpedo, his body aiming itself at her and shooting across the room. He took her down to the floor and kissed her hard, mounting her while he grabbed the front of her slacks and wrenched the zipper down. Grunting, straining, he peeled her pants off her smooth legs, spread her thighs roughly, and buried his face in her core.

As if he were a split personality, he watched himself act from a distance, seeing his hands shove her shirt up and capture her breasts while he tongued her. Then he was surging forward, baring fangs he somehow knew how to use and biting through the front of her bra. He kept trying to get himself to stop, but he was caught in some kind of centrifugal force, and Marissa . . . she was the axis he whirled around.

From the maelstrom, he groaned, "I'm sorry . . . oh, God . . . *I can't stop* . . ."

She grabbed on to his face . . . and stilled him completely. It was unbelievable and he didn't know how she did it, it was just . . . his body came to a total halt. Which made him realize she had the oddest control over him. If she said no, he would stop. On a dime. Period.

Except she wasn't putting the brakes on. Her eyes glowed with an erotic light. "Take me. Make me your female."

She tilted her hips to him, and his body shot right back into the frenzy. Rearing up, he ripped apart the waistband of his boxers and slammed into her with the things hanging open. He penetrated her so deep, stretched her so wide, he felt like she gloved every inch of him.

As she cried out and sank her nails into his ass, he went for it hard and fast. And while the sex raged, he felt the two halves of himself knitting together. While he pumped wildly, the voice he'd always known to be him and this new one that was talking at him became one.

He was looking into her face as he started to orgasm, and the ejaculations were like nothing he'd ever known. Sharper, more powerful, and they went on forever, as if he had an infinite supply of what he was filling her up with. And she was loving it, kicking her head back on the tile in pleasure, her legs tight around his hips, her core eating up everything he gave her.

When it was over, Butch collapsed, panting, sweating, dizzy. It was only then that he noticed they fit together differently; his head was higher up on her, his hips demanded more room between her legs, his hands were bigger next to her face.

She kissed his shoulder. Licked at his skin. "Mmmm . . . and you smell good, too."

Yeah, he did. The dark spice that had come out of him before was now a vibrant scent in the room. And the marking was all over Marissa's skin and hair . . . and it was inside of her, too.

Which was *right*. She was *his*.

He rolled off her. "Baby . . . I'm not sure why I had to do that." Well, half of him wasn't sure. The other half just wanted to do it to her again.

"I'm glad you did." The smile she gave him was radiant. As brilliant as the noonday sun.

And the sight of it made him realize with satisfaction that he was also her man: It was a two-way street here. They belonged to each other.

"I love you, baby."

She repeated the words, but then her smile slipped. "I was so afraid you would die."

"But I didn't. It's over and done with and I'm on the other side. I'm with you on the other side."

"I can't go through that again."

"You won't have to."

She relaxed some and stroked his face. Then frowned. "It's a little cold in here, isn't it?"

"Let's get you dressed and back to the main house." He reached out to bring her shirt down . . . and his eyes latched on to her breasts with their perfect pink nipples.

He grew hard again. Full to bursting. Desperate for another release.

That smile of hers reappeared. "Come back up on me, *nallum*. Let my body ease yours."

She didn't have to ask twice.

Outside the Equipment Room, V, Phury, and Zsadist stopped talking and listened. Going by the muted sounds, Butch was up and awake and . . . busy. As the brothers laughed, V shut the door all the way, thinking that he was very happy for that pair in there. Very . . . happy.

He and the twins continued to shoot the shit, with V lighting up on occasion and ashing into an Aquafine bottle. An hour later, the door opened and Marissa and Butch appeared. Marissa was dressed in a martial-arts *ji*, Butch had a towel around his hips, and the bonding scent was all over them. They looked well used and very, very sated.

"Um . . . hey, guys," the cop said, blushing. He looked good, but he wasn't moving too well. In fact, he was using his female as a crutch.

V cracked a smile. "You look taller."

"Yeah, I . . . ah, I'm not getting around so good. Is that normal?"

Phury nodded. "Definitely. Took me a long time to get used to the new body. You'll have some control over it in a couple of days, but it's going to be weird for a while."

As the pair came forward, Marissa looked as if she was struggling under the weight of her male and Butch seemed wobbly, like he was trying not to lean on her as much as he really needed to.

V stood up. "You want help on the way back to the Pit?"

Butch nodded. "That'd be great. I'm about to fall on her."

V got in at Butch's side and propped the cop up. "Home, Jarvis?"

"God, yes. I would love a shower."

Butch took Marissa's hand, and the three of them headed slowly to the Pit.

The trip through the tunnel was silent except for Butch's shuffling feet. And as they went along, V remembered coming out of his own transition, waking up tattooed with warnings all over his face and his hand and his private areas. At least Butch was safe, and he had people to protect him while his strength gathered.

V had been taken out and left for dead in the woods beyond a warrior camp.

Butch also had another thing going for him: a female of worth who loved him. Marissa was positively glowing at his side and V tried not to look at her too much . . . except he couldn't stop. So warm, the way she stared at Butch. So very warm.

V had to wonder what that was like.

When they stepped into the Pit, Butch let out a ragged sigh. Clearly his energy had flagged completely by now, sweat breaking out across his forehead as he struggled to remain upright.

"How about your bed?" V said.

"No . . . shower. I need a shower."

"Are you hungry?" Marissa asked.

"Yeah . . . oh, God, yeah. I want . . . bacon. Bacon and . . ."

"Chocolate," V said wryly as he muscled the cop down to the guy's suite.

"Oh . . . chocolate. Fuck, I would kill for that." Butch frowned. "Except I don't like chocolate."

"You do now." V kicked the bathroom door open and Marissa ducked into the shower and turned the water on.

"Anything else?" she asked.

"Pancakes. And waffles with syrup and butter. And eggs . . ."

V shot the female a look. "Just bring anything edible. He'd eat his own shoes at this point."

". . . and ice cream and turkey with stuffing . . ."

Marissa kissed Butch on the lips. "I'll be right b—"

Butch grabbed her by the head and held her to his mouth with a moan. As a fresh flood of the bonding scent came out of him, he maneuvered her against the wall and pinned her with his body, hands traveling, hips pushing forward.

Ah, yes, V thought. *The newly transitioned male.* Butch was going to be throwing wood every fifteen minutes for a while.

Marissa laughed, utterly delighted with her mate. "Later. Food first."

Butch settled back immediately, like she'd called his

lust to a heel and it behaved because it wanted to be a good boy. As she left, the cop's eyes followed her with rank hunger and adoration.

V shook his head. "You are a total sap."

"Man, if I thought I loved her before . . ."

"The bonded male biz is some powerful shit." V stripped Butch of his towel and shoved him under the water. "Or so I've heard."

"Ow." Butch glared up at the showerhead. "I don't like this."

"Skin's going to be extra sensitive for a week or so. Holler if you need me."

V was halfway down the hall when he heard a yelp. He hightailed it back, barging through the door. "What? What's—"

"I'm going bald!"

V whipped back the shower curtain and frowned. "What are you talking about? You've still got your hair—"

"Not my head! My body, you idiot! I'm going bald!"

Vishous glanced down. Butch's torso and legs were shedding, a rush of dark brown fuzz pooling around the drain.

V started laughing. "Think of it this way. At least you won't have to worry about shaving your back as you get old, true? No manscaping for you."

He was not surprised when a bar of soap came firing at him.

FORTY-ONE

It was a week later that Van learned something important about himself.

His humanity was gone.

As a moan echoed through the empty basement, he glanced at the civilian vampire who was strapped on a table. Mr. X was working the thing over and Van was watching. Like this was nothing more than someone getting a haircut.

He should have thought it was wrong. In all his years as a fighter, he'd inflicted a lot of pain on opponents, but he'd avoided hurting the innocent and had despised people who went after the weak. Now? His sole reaction to this base cruelty was annoyance . . . because it wasn't working. The only thing they'd learned about O'Neal was that a human fitting the man's description had been seen among males suspected to be Brothers in some of the clubs downtown—Screamer's and ZeroSum in particular. But they'd known all that already.

He was beginning to suspect the *Fore-lesser* was working out his frustrations at this point. Which was such a waste of time. Van wanted to go after vampires, not play armchair quarterback at a scene like this.

Except, shit, it wasn't like he'd had a shot at killing one of those bloodsuckers yet. Thanks to Mr. X keeping him off the field, all he'd taken out since joining the Lessening Society were other frickin' *lessers*. Every day, Mr. X lined him up against another one. And every day, Van beat his opponent into submission, then stabbed the guy.

And every day, Mr. X got more and more wound up. It was like Van was letting the *Fore-lesser* down, although with a seven and oh record, it was hard to figure out precisely how.

As gurgling sounds drifted over on the blood-scented air, Van cursed under his breath.

"Am I boring you over there?" Mr. X snapped.

"Not at all. This is *really* great to watch."

There was a short silence. Then a disgusted hiss. "Don't be such a lightweight."

"Whatever. I'm a fighter, man. I'm not into this captive-beating shit, especially when it's not leading to anything."

Those flat, pale eyes burned. "Go patrol with some of the others, then. Because if I have to look at you any longer, you're going to find yourself on this table."

"Finally." Van headed for the stairs.

As his combat boot hit the first step, Mr. X spat, "Your weak stomach is such a disgrace."

"My guts aren't the problem here, trust me." Van kept going.

Butch stepped off the treadmill in the gym and wiped the sweat off his face with his shirt. He'd just run eleven miles. In fifty minutes. Which would be a sustained pace of about a five-minute mile. Holy . . . shit.

"How you feel?" V asked from the bench press.

"Like Lee fucking Majors."

There was a clang as nearly seven hundred pounds came to rest on the stand. "*Six Million Dollar Man* reference dates you, cop."

"I grew up in the seventies. Sue me." Butch sucked back some water, then looked to the doorway in a flash. His breath caught, and a split second later Marissa walked in.

God, she was gorgeous in black slacks and a cream jacket—businesslike yet feminine. And her pale eyes sparkled across the room.

"Thought I'd come by before I left for the night," she said.

"Glad you did, baby." He did the best he could to towel himself off as he went over to her, but she didn't seem to mind him hot and sweaty. At all. Her palm cupped his chin as he bent down and said a hello against her mouth.

"You look good," she whispered, running her hand down his neck and over his bare pecs. She traced his cross with light fingers. "Very good."

"Do I." He smiled as he hardened in his running shorts, remembering how an hour and a half ago he'd woken her up from the inside out. "Well, I'm not as good as you."

"I could debate that." He hissed as she stepped up against him.

With a growl, he ran through the layout of the training center in his mind, trying to figure out where they could disappear for ten minutes. Um . . . yeah, there was a classroom nearby with a good lock on the door. Perfect.

He glanced over at V, about to throw his roommate an *I'll be right back*, when he was surprised to find the brother staring at the two of them, lids low, expression unreadable. Vishous looked away quickly.

"So, I have to go," Marissa said, stepping back. "Big night."

"You can't stay for just a little longer? Five minutes, maybe?"

"I would love to, but . . . no."

Wait a minute, he thought. There was something different about the way she was staring at him. In fact, her eyes were locked on the side of his neck and her mouth was slightly open. Then her tongue made a quick sweep of her lower lip, as if she were tasting something good. Or maybe wanting to taste something.

A bolt of mad lust shot through him.

"Baby?" he said roughly. "You need something from me?"

"Yes . . ." She stood up on her tiptoes and spoke into his ear. "I gave you so much when you were going through the transition that I'm a little weak. I need your vein."

Holy shit . . . what he'd been waiting for all along. *The chance to feed her.*

Butch grabbed her around the waist, popped her feet off the floor, and carried her toward the door like the weight room was on fire.

"Not yet, Butch." She laughed. "Put me down. You're barely a week out."

"No."

"Butch, put me down."

His body obeyed the command, even though his mind wanted to argue. "How much longer?"

"Soon."

"I'm strong now."

"I can wait a couple of days. And it's better if we do."

She kissed him and looked at her watch. The one she wore was his favorite from his collection, the Patek Philippe with the black alligator band. He loved the idea that she had it with her wherever she went.

"I'll be at Safe Place all night," she said. "We have a new female and two youngs arriving, and I want to be there when they check in. I'm also calling my first staff meeting. Mary's coming and we're going to do it together. So I probably won't be back until dawn."

"I'll be here." He caught her as she turned away and spun her back into his arms. "Be careful out there."

"I will."

He kissed her deep, wrapping his arms around her slender body. Man, he couldn't wait until she came back. And missed her the moment she left.

"I am a total sap," he said as the door closed.

"Told you." V got up off the bench press and picked up a pair of stacked one-hander weights. "Bonded males are a thing."

Butch shook his head and tried to refocus on what else he wanted to accomplish in the gym tonight. For the past seven days, while Marissa went off to her new job, he stayed at the compound and worked on how to handle this new body of his. The learning curve was steep. In the beginning, he'd had to figure out the most simple functions, like how to eat and how to write. Now, he was trying to get a sense of his physical limits to see when . . . if . . . he would break. The good news was, so far, everything worked. Well, almost everything. One of his hands was a little messed up, though not in any serious way.

And the fangs were fabulous.

As were the strength and endurance he now had. No matter how far or how hard he pushed himself in the gym, his body took the punishment and responded with growth. At meals, he ate like Rhage and Z, sucking back some five thousand calories every twenty-four hours . . . and even still, he was always hungry. Which made sense. He was packing on muscle like he was shooting 'roids.

Two open questions remained. Could he dematerialize? And could he handle sunlight? V had suggested holding off on both of those for a month or so, and that was fine. There was enough to worry about in the meantime.

"You're not quitting, right?" V asked as he looked up from the bicep curls he was doing. The weight in each of his hands was probably two seventy-five.

Butch could pull them that heavy now, too.

"Nah, I still got juice." He went over to an elliptical machine and got on to stretch his legs out.

Man, on the topic of juice . . . he was totally and completely sexed out. All the time. Marissa had moved into his bedroom at the Pit and he couldn't keep his hands off her. He felt so bad about it, and he tried to hide the need, but invariably she knew when he wanted her and she never turned him away, even if it was only to finish him.

She really seemed to relish the sexual control she had over him. And so did he.

God, he was hardening again now. All he had to do was think of her and he was ready even if he'd already gone four, five times that day. And the thing was, what made his sex drive such a pleasure was that it wasn't just about needing a release. It was all about her. He wanted to be with her, inside of her, all around her: not sex for sex's sake, but . . . well . . . making love. To her.

Man, he was a total frickin' sap.

But, hell, why should he front? This had been the best week of his whole miserable life. He and Marissa were so good together—and not just in the sack. Aside from training himself in the gym, he'd spent a lot of time helping her with the social services project, and the common purpose had brought them even closer together.

The Safe Place, as she'd named the house, was ready to start running now. V had wired the Colonial up but good, and though there was still a lot to do, at least they could begin accepting folks in earnest. Right now there was just the mother and the child with the leg in a cast, but it sounded like there would be a lot more.

Man, throughout everything, all the changes, all the new things, all the challenges, Marissa was amazing. Smart. Capable. Compassionate. He'd decided his vampire nature, that previously buried part of him, had chosen his female very wisely.

Although he still had some guilt over mating her. He kept thinking about everything she'd walked away from— her brother, her old life, all that fancy *glymera* shit. He'd always felt like an orphan after leaving both his family and where he'd grown up behind, and he didn't want that for her. But he wasn't going to let her go.

Hopefully, they could finish the mating ceremony soon. V had said it wouldn't be a good idea cutting into him during the first week, which was fine, but they were going to do the carving ASAP. And then he and Marissa were going to walk down the aisle, too.

Funny, he'd started going to weekly midnight Mass all regularlike. Wearing his Sox cap, and keeping his head down, he sat in the back of Our Lady and stayed to himself as he reconnected with God and the Church. The services eased him immeasurably, in a way nothing else could.

Because the darkness was in him still. He was not alone in his skin.

Inside of him there was a shadow, something that lurked between the spaces of his ribs and the disks of his spine. He sensed it there always, shifting around, pacing, watching. Sometimes it actually looked out of his eyes, and that was when he feared himself the most.

But going to church helped. He liked to think the goodness in the air there seeped into him. Liked to believe that God listened to him. Needed to know that there was a strength outside of himself that would help him stay connected to his humanity and his soul. Because without that he would be dead though his heart still beat.

"Hey, cop?"

Without losing a stride on the elliptical, Butch looked over to the weight room's door. Phury was standing in it, that amazing hair of his shining red, yellow, and brown under the fluorescent lights.

"What up, Phury?"

The brother came in, his limp hardly noticeable. "Wrath wants you to come to our meeting tonight before we go out."

Butch glanced at V. Who was studiously lifting and keeping his eyes on the mats. "What for?"

"Just wants you there."

"Okay."

After Phury left, he said, "V, you know what's doing about this?"

His roommate shrugged. "Just come to the meetings."

"Meeting-*s*? Like every night?"

Vishous kept pumping, his biceps veining up hard-core under all the weight. "Yeah. Every night."

Three hours later, Butch and Rhage headed out in the Escalade . . . and Butch wondered what the hell had happened. He was fully strapped in a black leather jacket with a Glock under each arm and an eight-inch hunting knife on his hip.

He was going in tonight as a fighter.

It was just a trial and he had to talk to Marissa, but he wanted this to work out. He wanted . . . yeah, he wanted to fight. And the brothers wanted him to as well. The bunch of them had talked it all through, especially the shit about his dark side. The bottom line was he was capable and he wanted to kill *lessers* and the Brotherhood needed more bodies on their side of the war. So they were going to give it a shot.

As Rhage drove them downtown, Butch looked out the window and wished V wasn't off for the night. He would have liked his roommate to be with him for this maiden-voyage stuff, although at least Vishous was sitting it out because it was his turn to on the rotation schedule, not because he was losing it. Hell, V seemed to be doing much better with the dreams; there hadn't been any more screams in the middle of the day.

"You ready for the field?" Rhage asked.

"Yeah." In fact, his body was roaring to be used, and used specifically like this, in battle.

About fifteen minutes later, Rhage parked behind Screamer's. As they got out and walked toward Tenth Street, Butch halted halfway down the alley and turned to the side of the building.

"Butch?"

Struck by a sense of his own history, he reached out and touched once again the blackened bomb burst pattern where Darius's car had blown up. Yeah . . . it had all started here last summer . . . at this place. And yet as he felt the scratchy, damp bricks under his palm, he knew the real beginning was right now. His true nature was uncovered now. He was who he needed to be . . . now.

"You okay, my man?"

"Full circle, Hollywood." He turned to his buddy. "Full circle." As the brother gave him a *Huh, what?* Butch smiled and started walking again.

"So how's this usually go down?" he said, as they came out on Tenth.

"On an average night, we cover a twenty-five-block radius twice. This is trolling, really. *Lessers* are looking for us, we're looking for them. We fight as soon as we—"

Butch stopped and his head swiveled around all by itself, his upper lip curling off his fancy new fangs.

"Rhage," he said softly.

The brother let out a low laugh of satisfaction. "Where are they, cop?"

Butch started gunning toward the signal he'd picked up on, and as he went along, he felt the raw force of his body. The damn thing was like a car with a performance engine in it, no longer a Ford but a Ferrari. And he let loose as he pounded down the dark street with Rhage on his tail, the two of them moving in harmony.

The two of them moving like killers.

Six blocks away they found three *lessers* confabbing it at the throat of an alleyway. As a unit, the slayers' heads turned and the second Butch locked eyes with them, he felt that horrible recognition flare. The linkup was immutable, marked by dread on his side and confusion on theirs: They seemed to recognize he was both one of them and a vampire.

In the dark, grungy alley, the battle bloomed like a summer thunderstorm, the violence coalescing, then exploding out in punches and kicks. Butch took head shots and body shots and ignored them all. Nothing hurt bad enough to care about, as if his skin were armor and his muscles were steel.

Eventually, he slammed one of the slayers on the ground, straddled the thing, and reached for the knife at his hip. But then he stopped, overcome by a need he couldn't fight. Leaving the blade where it was, he leaned down, got face-to-face, and took control with his stare. The *lesser*'s eyes popped in terror as Butch's mouth opened.

Rhage's voice came at him from a vast distance. "Butch? What are you doing? I got the other two, so all you need to do is stab that thing. Butch? *Stab him.*"

Butch just hovered over the *lesser*'s lips, feeling a surge of power that had nothing to do with his body and everything to do with the dark part in him. It started so slowly, the inhale almost gentle . . . and the breath went on forever, one steady draw that grew in strength until the blackness passed out of the *lesser* and into him, the transfer of the true essence of evil, the Omega's very nature. As Butch swallowed the vile black rush and felt it settle into his blood and bones, the *lesser* dissolved into a gray mist.

"*What the fuck?*" Rhage breathed.

Van stopped running at the entrance of the alley and followed an instinct that told him to melt into the shadows. He'd come prepared to fight, called in by a slayer who said some hand-to-hand with two Brothers was going down. But as he arrived now, he saw something he just knew wasn't right.

A tremendous vampire was on top of a *lesser*, the two locked stare to stare as he . . . shit, sucked the slayer into nothingness.

As a fall of ash floated down onto the dirty pavement, the blond Brother at the scene said, "What the fuck?"

At that moment, the vampire who'd done the consuming lifted his head and looked down the alley directly at Van, even though the darkness should have hidden his presence.

Holy shit . . . it was the one they were looking for. The cop. Van had seen the guy's picture on the Internet in those articles from the *CCJ*. Except he'd been human then and he sure as fuck wasn't now.

"There's another one," the vampire said in a hoarse, ragged voice. His arm lifted weakly and he pointed at Van. "Right there."

Van took off running, not about to get smoked up.

It was *so* time to find Mr. X about this.

FORTY-TWO

About a half mile away, in his penthouse overlooking the river, Vishous picked up a fresh bottle of Grey Goose and cracked the thing open. As he poured himself another glass of hooch, he looked at the pair of empty one-liters that were on the bar.

They were going to get another friend. Real soon.

As rap music pounded, he took his crystal glass and the newly opened Goose and weaved his way over to the sliding glass door. With his mind, he willed the lock free and pushed the thing wide.

A cold blast hit him and he laughed at the sting as he stepped outside, surveyed the night sky, and drank deeply.

Such a good liar he was. Such a good one.

Everyone thought he was fine because he'd camo'd his little problems. He wore a Sox hat to hide the eye twitch. Set his wristwatch to go off every half hour to beat back the dream. Ate though he wasn't hungry. Laughed though he found nothing funny.

And he'd always smoked like a chimney.

He'd even gone so far as to flat-out front to Wrath. When the king had asked how he was doing, V had looked the brother right in the face and told him, in a thoughtful, reflective voice, that although he continued to "struggle" with falling to sleep, the nightmare was "gone" and he felt much more "stable."

Bullshit. He was a pane of glass with a million cracks in it. All he needed was one soft tap and he was going to shatter.

The fracture potential wasn't just about his lack of visions or his twelve-gauge dream. Sure, all that shit made it worse, but he knew he would be where he was even without that overlay.

Watching Butch with Marissa was killing him.

Hell, V didn't begrudge them their happiness or anything. He was damn glad it had worked out for the pair, and he was even starting to like Marissa a little. It just hurt to be around them.

The thing was . . . although it was totally inappropriate and creeped him out, he thought of Butch as . . . *his*. He'd brought that man into the world. He'd lived with him for months. He'd gone out to get the guy after the *lessers* had done their business all over him. And he'd healed him.

And it had been his hands that had turned him.

With a curse, Vishous weaved his way over to the four-foot-high wall that ran all the way around the penthouse's terrace. The Goose bottle made a little scraping noise as he put it down, and he swayed as he brought his glass up to his mouth. Oh . . . wait, he needed another refill. He palmed the vodka and spilled a little as he poured. Again with the quiet scraping noise as he set the Goose back on the ledge.

He drank the stuff down, then bent over and looked at the street thirty floors below. Vertigo grabbed him by the head and shook him until the world spun and from out of the twirling mess, he found the term for his particular brand of suffering. He was brokenhearted.

Shit . . . what a mess.

With a total absence of mirth, he laughed at himself, the hard sound getting sucked away by the gusting, bitter March wind.

He put a bare foot up on the cold stone. As he reached

out to steady himself, he glanced down at his ungloved hand. And froze with terror.

"Oh . . . Jesus . . . *no* . . ."

Mr. X stared at Van. Then shook his head slowly. "What did you say?"

The two of them were standing in a wedge of shadow at the corner of Commerce and Fourth Street, and Mr. X was very glad they were alone. Because he couldn't believe what he was hearing and didn't want to look too stunned in front of any of the others.

Van shrugged. "He's a vampire. Looked like one. Acted like one. And recognized me immediately, although how he saw me I have no idea. But the slayer he took out? See, that was the weird thing. The guy just . . . vaporized. Not at all like what happens when you stab one of us. And the blond Brother was totally shocked. So does any of this kind of thing happen often?"

None of it happened often. Especially the part about a guy who had been a human but now apparently had fangs. That shit just went against nature, and so did the inhalation routine.

"And they just let you go?" Mr. X said.

"The blond was all worried about his buddy."

Loyalty. Christ. Always loyalty with those Brothers. "Did you notice anything about O'Neal? Other than that he seemed to have gone through the change?"

Maybe Van was just mistaken—

"Um . . . his hand was fucked up. Something's wrong with it."

Mr. X felt a tingle go through him, like his body was a bell that had been struck. He kept his voice deliberately calm. "What exactly was wrong?"

Van brought up his hand and curled the pinkie in tight

452

to the palm. "It's kind of bent like this. The little finger's all stiff and curled up, like he can't move it."

"Which hand?"

"Ah . . . the right. Yeah, the right one."

In a daze, Mr. X leaned back against the side of the Valu-rite Dry Cleaners building. And the prophecy came to him:

> *There shall be one to bring the end before the master,*
> *a fighter of modern time found in the seventh of the twenty-*
> * first,*
> *and he shall be known in the numbers he bears:*
> *One more than the compass he apperceives,*
> *Though mere four points to make at his right,*
> *Three lives has he,*
> *Two scores on his fore,*
> *and with a single black eye, in one well will he be birthed*
> * and die.*

Mr. X's skin tightened all over. Shit. *Shit.*

If O'Neal could sense *lessers*, maybe that was the one more than the compass he apperceived. And the hand thing fit if he couldn't point using his pinkie. But what about the extra scar—wait . . . the entry way where the Omega had put a part of himself into O'Neal . . . including his belly button that would be two scores. And maybe the black mark that had been left behind was the eye the Scrolls had mentioned. As for the born and die, O'Neal had been birthed in Caldwell as a vampire and would probably find his death here at some point, too.

The equation added up, but the real kicker was not the math. It was that no one, but no one, had ever heard of a *lesser* being offed like that.

Mr. X focused on Van, realization sliding into place and realigning everything. "You are not the one."

"You should have left me," Butch said as he and Rhage pulled up outside of V's building. "Left me and gone after that other *lesser*."

"Yeah, right. You were looking like roadkill, and there were more slayers on the way, I guarantee it." Rhage shook his head as they both got out. "You want me to walk you up? You're still sporting that special dead-squirrel glow."

"Yeah, whatever. Go back out and fight those fuckers."

"I love it when you get all hard-core on me." Rhage smiled a little, then grew serious. "Listen, about what hap—"

"That's why I'm going to talk to V."

"Good. V knows everything." Rhage put the Escalade's keys in Butch's hand and gave him a squeeze on the shoulder. "Call me if you need me."

After the brother disappeared into thin air, Butch went into the lobby, waved at the security guard, and grabbed an elevator. The ride up the building took forever and he passed the time feeling the evil in his veins. His blood was black again. He knew it. And he fucking *reeked* of baby powder.

When he stepped out, feeling like a leper, he heard music thumping. Ludacris's *Chicken N Beer* was all over the place.

He pounded on the door. "V?"

No answer. Hell. He'd already barged in on the brother once—

For some reason, the door clicked and eased open half an inch. Butch pushed it wider, every cop instinct in him screaming while the rap grew louder.

"Vishous?" As he stepped inside, a cold breeze shot

454

through the penthouse, barrelling in through an open sliding glass door. "Yo . . . V?"

Butch glanced at the bar. There were two empty bottles of Goose and three caps on the marble counter. Binge time.

Heading for the terrace, he expected to find V passed out on a lounger.

Instead, Butch walked into a whole lot of *heaven-help-us*: Vishous was up on the wall that ran around the building, naked, swaying in the wind and . . . glowing all over.

"Jesus Christ . . . V."

The brother wheeled around, then stretched his radiant arms wide. With a crazed smile, he slowly turned in a circle. "Nice, huh? It's all over me." He lifted a bottle of Goose to his lips and swallowed good and hard. "Hey, do you think they'll want to tie me down and tattoo every inch of my skin now?"

Butch slowly crossed the terrace. "V, man . . . how 'bout we get you down from there?"

"Why? I bet I'm smart enough to fly." V glanced behind himself at the thirty-story drop. As he weaved back and forth in the wind, his illuminated body was startlingly beautiful. "Yeah, I'm so fucking smart I bet I can beat gravity. Wanna watch?"

"V . . ." *Shit*. "V, buddy, come down from there."

Vishous looked over and abruptly seemed to sober up, his brows meeting in the middle. "You smell like a *lesser*, roommate."

"I know."

"Why's that?"

"I'll tell you if you come down."

"Bribes, bribes . . ." V took another pull on the Goose. "I don't want to come down, Butch. I want to fly . . . fly away." He tilted his head back to the sky and lurched . . . then caught himself by swinging the bottle. "Oops. Almost fell."

"Vishous . . . *Jesus Christ*—"

"So, cop . . . the Omega's in you again. And your blood's black inside your veins." V pushed his hair out of his eyes, and the tats on his temple showed, all backlit by the glow under his skin. "And yet you're not intrinsically evil. How did she put it? Ah . . . yes . . . the seat of evil is in the soul. And you . . . you, Butch O'Neal, have a good soul. Better than what's in me."

"Vishous, come down. Right now—"

"I liked you, cop. From the moment I met you. No . . . not the first moment. I wanted to kill you when I first met you. But then I liked you. A lot." God, V's expression was nothing Butch had ever seen before. Sad . . . affectionate . . . but most of all . . . yearning. "I watched you with her, Butch. I watched you . . . making love to her."

"What?"

"Marissa. I saw you, on top of her, in the clinic." V whipped his incandescent hand back and forth through the air. "It was wrong, I know, and I'm very sorry . . . but I couldn't look away. You two were so beautiful together and I wanted that . . . shit, whatever it was. I wanted to feel that. Yeah, just once . . . I wanted to know what it was like to have sex normally, to care about the person you were coming with." He laughed in a horrible burst. "Well, what I want isn't exactly normal, is it? Will you forgive me my perversion? Forgive me my embarrassing and shameful deprivation? Fuck . . . how I degrade us both . . ."

Butch was prepared to say absolutely anything to get his friend off that ledge, but he truly had the sense that V was horrified with himself. Which was so unnecessary. You couldn't help the way you felt, and Butch wasn't threatened by the revelation. He somehow wasn't surprised, either.

"V, buddy, we're cool. You and me . . . we're cool."

V lost that longing expression, his face turning into a cold mask that was utterly frightening given the situation. "You were the only friend I had." More with that god-awful laugh. "Even though I had my brothers, you were the only one I was close to. I don't do relationships well, you know. You were different, though."

"V, it's the same for me. But can we get you—"

"And you weren't like those others, you never cared I was different. The others . . . they hated me because I was different. Not that it matters. They're all dead now. Dead, dead . . ."

Butch had no idea what the hell V was talking about, but the content didn't matter. The past tense being used was the problem.

"I am still your friend. Always your friend."

"Always . . . funny word, always." V started to bend at the knees, just barely keeping his balance as he sank into a crouch.

Butch moved forward.

"No, you don't, cop. You stop right there." V put the bottle of vodka down and traced his fingertips lightly over the neck of the thing. "This shit's taken good care of me."

"Why don't we share some?"

"Nah. But you can have what's left." Vishous's diamond eyes lifted up and the left one started to expand until it ate up all the white part. There was a long pause, then V laughed. "You know, I can't see anything . . . even when I open myself up, even when I volunteer for it, I'm blind. I'm future-impaired." He glanced at his body. "But I'm still a fucking nightlight. I'm like one of those goose lamps, you know, the kind you plug into the wall that glow?"

"V—"

"You're a good Irishman, right?" When Butch nodded, V said, "Irish, Irish . . . let me think. Yeah . . ." Vishous's eyes sobered, and in a voice that cracked, he said, "May the road rise to meet you. May the wind always be at your back. May the sun shine warm upon your face and the rains fall soft upon your fields. And . . . my dearest friend . . . until we meet again may the Lord hold you in the palm of His hand."

In one powerful surge, V sprang backward off the ledge into thin air.

FORTY-THREE

"John, I need to talk to you."

John looked up from Tohr's chair as Wrath came into the study and shut the door. Going by how grim the king looked, this was very serious, whatever it was.

Putting aside his lesson on the Old Language, John braced himself. Oh, God, what if it was the news he'd dreaded hearing every day for the last three months?

Wrath came around the desk and moved the throne so it faced John. Then he sat down and took a deep breath.

Yeah, this is it. Tohr's dead and they've found the body.

Wrath frowned. "I can smell your fear and sadness, son. And I can understand both, given the situation. The funeral is going to be in three days."

John swallowed and wrapped his arms around his shoulders, feeling a black whirlwind spin around him and take the world away.

"Your classmate's family has asked that all the trainees be present."

John jerked his head up. *What?* he mouthed.

"Your classmate, Hhurt. He didn't make it through his change. He died last night."

So Tohr wasn't dead?

John scrambled to pull himself back from one brink, only to find himself looking over the edge of another. One of the trainees had *died* from the change?

"I thought you'd heard already."

John shook his head and pictured Hhurt. He hadn't known the guy well at all, but still.

"Sometimes it happens, John. But I don't want you to worry about it. We're going to take good care of you."

Someone had *died* during the transition? *Shit . . .*

There was a long silence. Then Wrath propped his elbows on his knees and leaned forward. As his glossy black hair slipped over his shoulder, it brushed his leather-clad thighs. "Listen, John, we need to start thinking about who'll be there for you when you go through the change. You know, who will feed you."

John thought of Sarelle, who the *lessers* had taken along with Wellsie. His heart clenched. She was supposed to have been the one he used.

"We can play this one of two ways, son. We can try to line someone up on the outside. Bella knows some families who have daughters and one of them . . . hell, one of them might even make a good mate for you." As John's body got tight, Wrath said, "I've got to be honest, though—I'm not really into that solution. It could be hard to get an outsider to you in time. Fritz would have to pick her up, and minutes count when the change comes. But if you want—"

John put his hand on Wrath's tattooed forearm and shook his head. He didn't know what his other option was, but he was damn sure he didn't want to get near an available female. Without thinking, he signed, *No mate. What's my other choice?*

"We could have you use a member of the Chosen."

John cocked his head to the side.

"They're the Scribe Virgin's inner circle of females and they live on the other side. Rhage uses one, Layla, to feed from because he can't live off Mary's blood. Layla's safe and we can have her here in the blink of an eye."

John tapped Wrath's forearm and nodded his head.

"You want to use her?"

Yeah, whoever she was.

"Okay. Good. Good deal, son. Her blood is very pure and that will help."

John eased back into Tohr's chair, dimly hearing the old leather creak. He thought of Blaylock and Butch, who had both survived the change . . . thought of Butch especially. The cop was so happy now. And big. And strong.

The transition was worth the risk, John told himself. Besides . . . like he had a choice?

Wrath went on, "I'll go ask the directrix of the Chosen, but that's just a formality. Funny, this is the way it used to be, warriors being brought into their power by those females. Shit, they're going to be thrilled." Wrath drew a hand through his hair, pushing it back from his widow's peak. "You'll want to meet her, of course."

John nodded. Then got nervous.

"Oh, don't worry. Layla will like you. Hell, afterward, she'll even let you take her if you want to. The Chosen can be very good at initiating males like that. Some of them, like Layla, are trained for it."

John felt a stupid expression slap itself onto his face. Wrath wasn't talking about sex, was he?

"Yeah, sex. Depending on how hard the change is for you, you may end up wanting it right away." Wrath let out a wry chuckle. "Just ask Butch."

In response, John could only stare at the king and blink like a lighthouse.

"So there we have it." Wrath stood up and moved the massive throne back to the desk with no effort at all. Then he frowned. "What did you think I was coming to talk to you about?"

John dropped his head and absently stroked the arm of Tohr's chair.

"Did you think it was about Tohrment?"

The sound of the name made John's eyes burn and he refused to look up as Wrath sighed.

"You thought I was coming to tell you he was dead?"

John shrugged.

"Well . . . I don't believe he's gone unto the Fade."

John's stare shot up to those wraparounds.

"I can still feel this echo in my blood and it's him. When we lost Darius? I couldn't feel him anymore in my veins. So, yeah, I believe Tohr lives."

John felt a shot of relief, but then went back to smoothing the chair's arm.

"You think he doesn't care about you because he hasn't called or come back?"

John nodded.

"Look, son, when a bonded male loses his mate . . . he loses himself. It's the hardest separation you can imagine—harder, I've heard, than losing a young for a male. Your mate is your life. Beth's mine. If anything happened to her . . . yeah, as I said to Tohr once, I can't even go there in the hypothetical." Wrath reached out and put his hand on John's shoulder. "I'll tell you something. If Tohr comes back, it will be because of you. He felt as though you were his kid. Maybe he could walk away from the Brotherhood, but he won't be able to leave you behind. You have my word."

John's eyes welled, but he was not going to cry in front of the king. As he set his spine along with his teeth, the tears dried in place, and Wrath nodded as if he approved of the effort.

"You are a male of worth, John, and you will make him proud. Now, I'm going to go see about Layla."

The king went to the door, then looked back over his shoulder. "Z tells me the two of you go out every night. Good. I want you to keep that up."

When Wrath left, John leaned back in the chair. God,

those walks with Z were so strange. Nothing being said, just the two of them dressed in parkas, traipsing through the woods right before dawn came. He was still waiting for the Brother to ask questions, to poke and prod, to try and dig around the inside of his head. But there had been nothing like that yet. All it had been was the two of them, walking in silence beneath tall pines.

Funny, though . . . he'd come to rely on those little forays. And after this talk of Tohr, he was really going to need one tonight.

Butch was screaming his lungs raw as he raced across the terrace for the ledge. He threw himself at the lip and looked down, but couldn't see anything because he was so far up and there were no lights on this side of the building. As for the sound of a body drop? God knew he was hollering loud enough to drown out that kind of distant *thunch*.

"Vishous!"

Oh, God . . . maybe if he got down there fast enough, he could . . . shit, get V to Havers—or something . . . *anything*. He wheeled around, ready to run to the elevator—

Vishous appeared before him as a glowing ghost, a perfect reflection of what the brother had been, an ethereal vision of Butch's one true friend.

Butch stumbled, a pathetic wail coming out of his mouth. "V . . ."

"I couldn't do it," the ghost said.

Butch frowned. "V?"

"As much as I hate myself . . . I don't want to die."

Butch went cold. Then ran as white-hot as his room-mate's body.

"You fucking bastard!" Butch shot forward without thinking and grabbed Vishous by the throat. "You fucking . . . *bastard*! You scared the shit out of me!"

He hauled his arm back and cold-cocked V right in the face, his fist cracking against jawbone. As he braced himself for a return shot, he was absolutely livid. Instead of fighting back, though, V locked his arms around Butch, put his head down, and just . . . crumpled. Shook all over. Trembled to the point of frailty.

Cursing the brother to hell and back, Butch absorbed Vishous's weight, holding the guy's naked, glowing body tight while the cold wind whirled around them both.

When he ran out of swear words, he said into V's ear, "You ever pull a stunt like that again, I'll kill you myself. We clear?"

"I'm losing my mind," V said against Butch's neck. "The one thing that's always saved me and I'm losing it . . . I've lost it . . . I'm gone. It's the only thing that's saved me and now I have nothing . . ."

As Butch squeezed harder, he became aware of an easing inside of himself, a sensation of relief and healing. Except he didn't think much about it because something hot and wet seeped into his collar. He had a feeling it was tears, but he didn't want to draw attention to what was doing. V was no doubt totally horrified by the show of weakness, assuming the guy was crying.

Butch put his hand on his roommate's nape and murmured, "I'll do the saving until you get your head back, how about that? I'll keep you safe."

When Vishous finally nodded, something dawned on Butch. Shit . . . he was up against the glow, a whole lot of the glow . . . but he wasn't on fire or in pain. In fact . . . yeah, he could feel the blackness in him seeping out of his skin and bones, leaching into the white light that was Vishous: That was the relief he'd noticed just now.

Except why wasn't he burning up?

From out of nowhere, a female voice said, "Because this

is what shall be, the light and the dark together, two halves making a whole."

Butch and V yanked their heads around. The Scribe Virgin was floating above the terrace, her black robes unstirred despite the frigid gusts that blew all around.

"That is why you are not consumed," she said. "And that is why he saw you from the start." She smiled a little, though he didn't know how he knew it. "This is the reason destiny brought you to us, Butch, descended of Wrath son of Wrath. The Destroyer has arrived and you are he.

"Now the new era in the war begins."

FORTY-FOUR

Marissa nodded as she shifted her cell phone to her other ear and reviewed the order list on her desk. "That's right. We need an industrial range, six burners minimum."

Sensing someone in her doorway, she looked up. Only to have her mind go completely blank. "May I . . . ah, may I call you back?" She didn't wait for a reply, just hit the END button. "Havers. How did you find us?"

Her brother bowed his head. He was dressed as usual, in a Burberry sport coat, gray slacks, and a bow tie. His hornrimmed glasses were different from the ones she was used to seeing on him. And yet the same, too.

"My nursing staff told me where you were."

She rose from her chair and crossed her arms over her chest. "And you have come here why?"

Instead of answering, he looked around and she could imagine he wasn't impressed. Her office was nothing more than a desk, a chair, a laptop computer, and a whole lot of hardwood floor. Well . . . and a thousand pieces of paper, each with something she needed to do on it. Havers's study, on the other hand, was an Old World den of learning and distinction, the floors covered by Aubusson rugs, the walls hung with his diplomas from Harvard Medical School as well as a fraction of his Hudson River School landscape collection.

"Havers?"

"You have done great things at this facility."

"We're just getting started, and it's a home, not a facility. Now why are you here?"

He cleared his throat. "I have come at the *Princeps* Council's request. We are voting on the *sehclusion* motion at the next meeting and the *leahdyre* said he's been trying to reach you for the last week. You haven't returned the calls."

"I am busy, as you can see."

"But they cannot vote unless all of the membership is in the room."

"So they should remove me. In fact, I'm surprised they haven't figured out how to already."

"You are of the six founding bloodlines. You cannot be removed nor excused as things stand now."

"Ah, well, how inconvenient for them. You'll understand, however, if I'm not available that evening."

"I haven't told you a date."

"As I said, I'm unavailable."

"Marissa, if you disagree with the motion, you can make your stance clear during the testimony phase of the meeting. You can be heard."

"So all of you with voting rights are in favor?"

"It's important to keep females safe."

Marissa went cold. "And yet you turned me out of the only home I had thirty minutes before dawn. Does that mean you've changed your commitment to my sex? Or is it that you don't see me as female?"

He had the grace to flush. "I was highly emotional at the time."

"You seemed very calm to me."

"Marissa, I'm sorry—"

She cut him off with a slice of her hand. "Stop. I don't want to hear it."

"So be it. But you shouldn't impede the council just to get back at me."

As he fiddled with his bow tie, she caught a glimpse

of the family's signet ring on his pinkie. God . . . how had they ended up like this? She could remember when Havers was born and she'd looked at him in their mother's arms. Such a sweet baby. Such a—

Marissa stiffened as something occurred to her. Then she quickly covered the shock that surely showed on her face. "All right. I'll go to the meeting."

Havers's shoulders eased and he told her the when and where. "Thank you. Thank you for this."

She smiled coolly. "You are so very welcome."

There was a long silence during which he eyed her pants and sweater and her desk of papers. "You seem very different."

"I am."

And she knew by the tight, awkward expression on his face that he had remained the same. He would have so preferred her in the mold of the *glymera*: a female of grace presiding over a home of distinction. Well, tough luck. She was all about rule number one now: Right or wrong, she made the choices in her life. No one else did.

She picked up her phone. "Now, if you'll excuse me—"

"I would offer my services to you. The clinic's, I mean. Free of charge." He pushed his glasses up higher on his straight nose. "The females and their young who stay here will need medical care."

"Thank you. Thank you . . . for that."

"I will also tell the nursing staff to be on the lookout for signs of abuse. We will refer to you any cases we find."

"That would be most appreciated."

He inclined his head. "We are pleased to be of service."

As her cell phone went off, she said, "Good-bye, Havers."

His eyes widened and she realized it was the first time she'd ever dismissed him.

468

But then change was good . . . and he'd better get used to the new world order.

The phone rang again. "Shut the door behind you, if you don't mind."

After he left, she glance at her cell's caller ID and sighed in relief: Butch, and thank God for it. She so needed to hear his voice.

"Hi," she said. "You'll never believe who just—"

"Can you come home? Right now?"

Her hand closed tight on the phone. "What's wrong? Are you hurt—"

"I'm fine." His voice was way too level. Nothing but false calm. "Except I need you to come home. Now."

"I'm leaving this moment."

She grabbed her coat, shoved her phone into her pocket, and went looking for her one and only staff member.

When she found the older female *doggen*, she said, "I have to go."

"Mistress, you seem upset. Is there anything I can do?"

"No, thank you. And I'll be back."

"I shall take care of everything in your stead."

She squeezed the female's hand and then hurried outside. Standing on the front lawn in the raw spring night, she struggled to calm herself enough to dematerialize. When it didn't work immediately, she thought she was going to have to call Fritz for a pickup: She was not only worried, she needed to feed, so it was possible she wasn't going to be able to do it.

But then she felt herself go. As soon as she materialized in front of the Pit, she barged into the vestibule. Its inner lock sprang free before she even put her face in front of the camera, and Wrath was on the other side of the heavy panels of wood and steel.

"Where's Butch?" she demanded.

"I'm right here." Butch stepped into her line of sight, but didn't come near her.

In the stark silence that followed, Marissa walked in slowly, feeling as though the air had turned into a slush she had to fight her way through. Numbly, she heard Wrath shut the door, and from the corner of her eye she saw Vishous rise to his feet from behind his computers. As V walked around the desk, the three males traded looks.

Butch held out his hand. "Come here, Marissa."

When she took his palm, he led her to the computers and pointed to one of the monitors. Up on the screen was . . . text. A whole lot of dense text. Actually, there were two sections of documents, the field split down the middle.

"What is this?" she asked.

Butch gently sat her in the chair and stood behind her, resting his hands on her shoulders. "Read the passage in italics."

"Which side?"

"Either. They're identical."

She frowned and ran her eyes over something that seemed almost a poem:

There shall be one to bring the end before the master,
a fighter of modern time found in the seventh of the twenty-first,
and he shall be known in the numbers he bears:
One more than the compass he apperceives,
Though mere four points to make at his right,
Three lives has he,
Two scores on his fore,
and with a single black eye, in one well will he be birthed and die.

Confused, she scanned what was around it, only to have horrible phrases jump out at her: "Lessening Society," "Induction," "Master." She looked up to the title on the page and shuddered.

"Dear God . . . this is about . . . *lessers*."

As Butch heard the icy panic in her voice, he sank down on his knees beside her. "Marissa—"

"What the hell am I reading about here?"

Yeah, how to answer that one. He was still having a hard time coming to terms with it all himself. "It seems as though . . . I am this." He tapped the smooth screen and then looked at his deformed pinkie, the one that was shriveled up tight to his palm . . . the one he couldn't straighten . . . or point with.

Marissa shifted away from him warily. "And *this* is . . . what?"

Thank God V spoke up. "What you're looking at is two different translations of the Lessening Society's Scrolls. One we had from before. One is from a laptop that I confiscated from the slayers about ten days ago. The Scrolls are the handbook of the Society and the section you're looking at is what we call the Destroyer Prophecy. We've known about it for generations, ever since the first copy of the Scrolls fell into our possession."

As Marissa's hand went to her throat, she was obviously getting the gist of where they were headed. She started shaking her head. "But it's all riddles. Surely—"

"Butch has all the markers." V lit up a hand-rolled and exhaled. "He can sense *lessers*, so that's one more than north, south, east, or west he apperceives. His pinkie is misshapen from the transition, so he has only four fingers he can point with. He's had three lives, childhood, adulthood, and now as a vampire, and you could argue he was birthed here in Caldwell when we turned him. But the real tell-tale is that scar on his belly. It's the black eye and one of two scores on his forefront. Assuming you count his belly button as the first."

She looked at Wrath. "So what does this mean?"

The king took a deep breath. "It means Butch is our very best weapon in the war."

"How . . ." Marissa's voice drifted.

"He can shortcut a *lesser*'s return to the Omega. See, during the induction, the Omega shares a part of himself with each slayer and that piece comes back to the master when the *lesser* is killed. As the Omega is a finite being, this return is critical. He needs to get back what he puts in them if he's to continue to populate his fighters." Wrath nodded toward Butch. "The cop breaks that part of the cycle. So the more *lessers* Butch consumes, the weaker the Omega will become until there is, literally, nothing left of him. It's like chipping away at a boulder."

Marissa's eyes slid back to Butch. "Consume exactly how?"

Oh, man, she wasn't going to like this part. "I just . . . inhale them. Take them into me."

The terror in her eyes killed him, it really did. "Won't you become one, then? What stops you from being taken over?"

"I don't know." Butch settled back on his heels, terrified that she would bolt. Not that he'd blame her. "But Vishous helps me. In the way he healed me with his hand before."

"How many times have you done . . . whatever to them?"

"Three. Including the one tonight."

Her eyes squeezed shut. "And when did you first do it?"

"About two weeks ago."

"So none of you know the long-term effects, do you?"

"But I'm okay—"

Marissa burst up from the chair and walked out from behind the desk, her eyes on the floor, her arms wrapped around herself. When she stopped in front of Wrath, it was to glare at him. "And you want to use him?"

"This is about the race's very survival."

"What about his?"

Butch got to his feet. "I want to be used, Marissa."

She looked over at him with hard eyes. "May I remind you, you almost died from the Omega's contamination?"

"That was different."

"Was it? If you're talking about putting more and more of that evil in your system again, exactly how is it different?"

"I told you, V helps me process it. It doesn't stay with me." He got no reply to that. She just stood stock-still in the middle of the room, so self-contained he didn't know how to reach her. "Marissa . . . we're talking about purpose. My purpose."

"Funny, you told me in bed this morning that I was your life."

"You are. But this is different."

"Ah, yes, everything is different when you want it to be." She shook her head. "You couldn't save your sister, but now . . . now you have a shot at saving thousands of vampires. Your hero complex must be thrilled."

Butch bit down hard, jaw flexing. "That is a cheap shot."

"But true." Abruptly, she grew weary. "You know, I am really sick and tired of violence. And fighting. And people getting hurt. And you told me you weren't going to get involved with this war."

"I was human then—"

473

"Oh, please—"

"Marissa, you've seen what those *lessers* can do. You've been at your brother's clinic when the bodies have been brought in. How can I not fight?"

"But you're not just talking about hand-to-hand combat. You're taking it to a whole different level. *Consuming* slayers. How can you be sure you won't turn into one?"

From out of nowhere, fear sliced through him, and as her eyes narrowed on his face, he knew he didn't hide the anxiety fast enough.

She shook her head. "You're worried about that, too, aren't you? You're not certain you won't turn into one of them."

"Not true. I won't lose myself. I know it."

"Oh, really. Then why are you holding on to your cross like that, Butch?"

He glanced down. Shit, his hand was locked on the crucifix so tight his knuckles were white and his shirt was all bunched up. He forced himself to drop his arm.

Wrath's voice cut in. "We need him, Marissa. The race needs him."

"*What about his safety?*" She let out a sob, but then quickly smothered it. "I'm sorry, but I—I can't smile and say Go get 'em. I spent days under quarantine watching him—" She wheeled toward Butch. "Watching *you* nearly die. It almost killed me. And the thing is, back then it wasn't your choice, but this . . . this is a choice, Butch."

She had a point. But he couldn't back down. He was what he was, and he had to believe he was strong enough not to fall into the darkness. "I don't want to be a kept pet, Marissa. I want a purpose—"

"You have a pur—"

"—and that purpose is *not* going to be sitting at home waiting for you to get back from your life. I'm a man, not

474

a piece of furniture." When she just stared at him, he said, "I can't sit on my hands when I know there's something I can do to help the race—*my* race." He went over to her. "Marissa—"

"I can't . . . I can't do this." She put her hands out of his reach and backed up. "I've seen you almost die too many times. I won't . . . I can't do this, Butch. I can't live like that. I'm sorry, but you're on your own. I will not sit back and watch you destroy yourself."

She turned and walked out of the Pit.

Up at the main house, John waited in the library, feeling like he was about to jump out of his skin. As the clock chimed, he looked down at his little chest and the tie that was hanging off of his neck. He'd wanted to look nice, but the getup probably came across like he was posing for a school picture.

When he heard fast footsteps, he glanced up at the open double doors. Marissa walked by, heading for the staircase and looking desolate. Butch was tight on her heels, looking worse.

Oh, no . . . He hoped they would be okay. He liked them both so much.

When a door shut with a bang upstairs, he walked over to the diamond-pane windows and stared outside. As he put his hand up to the glass, he thought about what Wrath had said—that Tohr was alive, somewhere.

He so wanted to believe that.

"Sire?" When he turned at the sound of Fritz's voice, the old man smiled. "Your guest has arrived. Shall I show her in?"

John swallowed. Twice. Then nodded. Fritz disappeared and a moment later a woman appeared in the doorway. Without looking at John, she bowed to him and stayed parallel to the floor in supplication. She seemed to be about six feet tall and was wearing something like a white toga. Her blond hair was coiled on top of her head, and though he couldn't see her face now, the split-second eyeball he'd gotten of it stuck with him.

She was beyond beautiful. Straight into angel territory.

There was a long silence, during which all he could do was stare.

"Your grace," she said softly. "May I meet thine eyes?"

He opened his mouth. Then started to nod frantically.

Except she just stayed as she was. Well, duh, she couldn't see him. Shit.

"Your grace?" Now her voice wavered a little. "Perhaps . . . you would care for another of us?"

John went over to her and lifted his hand to touch her lightly. Um, where, though? That toga thing was low-cut and slit up the sleeves as well as down the front of the skirt . . . God, she smelled good.

He tapped her awkwardly on the shoulder, and she inhaled as if he'd surprised her.

"Your grace?"

With a little pressure on her arm, he brought her upright. *Whoa* . . . her eyes were really green. Like summer grapes. Or the inside of a lime.

He gestured to his throat and then made a cutting motion with his hand.

Her perfect face tilted to the side. "You do not speak, your grace?"

He shook his head, a little surprised Wrath hadn't mentioned it. Then again, the king had a lot of other things on his mind.

In response, Layla's eyes positively glowed, and as she smiled, she knocked him out. Her teeth were perfect and her fangs were . . . incredibly lovely. "Your grace, the vow of silence is to be commended. Such self-discipline. You shall be a warrior of great power, you who have been bred from Darius son of Marklon's line."

Good Lord. She was seriously impressed by him. And hell, if she wanted to think he'd taken a vow, that was fine. No reason to tell her he had a defect.

"Perhaps you would like to have knowledge of me?" she said. "So that you are assured you shall have what you want when you are in need?"

He nodded and glanced over at the couch, thinking he was glad he'd brought a pad with him. Maybe they could sit there for a while and get to know one another—

When he looked back she was gloriously naked, the toga thing in a pool at her feet.

John felt his eyes bug out. Holy . . . *shit.*

"Do you approve, your grace?"

Jesus, Mary, and Joseph . . . Even if he'd had a voice box, he still would have been speechless.

"Your grace?"

As John started to nod, he thought, man, wait until he told Blaylock and Qhuinn about this.

FORTY-FIVE

The following evening, Marissa emerged from the base-ment rooms of Safe Place and tried to pretend that her world hadn't crashed and burned.

"Mastimon wants to talk to you," a little voice said.

Marissa turned around and saw the young with the leg cast. Forcing a smile, she crouched down and got eye to eye with the stuffed tiger. "Does he?"

"Yes. He says that you are not to be sad, because he is here to protect us. And he wants to hug you."

Marissa took the ratty toy and cradled it tight to her neck. "He is both fierce and kind."

"True. And you should keep him with you for now." The young's expression was all business. "I have to help *mahmen* prepare First Meal."

"I'll be careful of him."

With a solemn nod the young was off, pegging her half-pint crutches into the floor.

As Marissa held on to the tiger, she thought about what it had been like to pack up her few things and leave the Pit the night before. Butch had tried to talk her out of going, but the decision he'd made was in his eyes, so the words he'd spoken had made no difference.

The reality was, her love had not cured his death wish or his risk-taking personality. And as painful as the separation was, if she stayed with him, it would be untenable: nothing but night after night of waiting for the call to come that he was dead. Or even more tragic, that he had turned into something evil.

Plus, the more she thought about it, the more she didn't trust him to keep safe. Not after his suicide attempt in the clinic. And the regression he'd volunteered for. And the transition he'd put himself through. And now the battling—the consuming of *lessers*. Yes, the outcomes had been positive so far, but the trend wasn't good: All she had to go on was a consistent pattern of self-abuse that she knew damn well sooner or later he was going to get seriously damaged by.

She loved him too much to watch him kill himself.

As tears came to her eyes, she wiped them away and stared into space. After a while, some kind of flickering thought, like an echo, flashed through the back of her mind. But whatever it was faded quickly.

Forcing herself to stand up, she was momentarily lost. She literally couldn't remember what she was doing or why she was in the hall. In the end, she headed for her office because there was always something waiting for her to do there.

One thing about being a former cop was you never lost your idiot radar.

Butch paused in the alley next to ZeroSum. Down the way, loitering at the club's emergency exit, was that half-pint, Eurotrash, flash-in-the-pan blond kid who'd made such a stink at the waitress last week. Next to him was one of his steakheads and the pair were lighting cigarettes.

Although why they were smoking it up out here in the cold didn't make a lot of sense.

Butch hung back and watched. Which of course gave him time to think. Which sucked, as usual. Man, anytime things got quiet, all he could see was Marissa getting into Fritz's Mercedes and that S600 disappearing through the gates.

With a curse, Butch rubbed the center of his chest and hoped like hell he found a *lesser*. He needed to fight something to take the edge off this perma-ache. Like *now*.

From off Trade Street, a car turned into the alley and came forward at a fast clip. As it flew past and stopped short at the club's side door, the black Infiniti was spinning enough chrome to qualify as a frickin' disco ball. And what do you know, Little Blond Dickhead sauntered over like this was an arranged meet-and-greet.

As the kid and the driver gum-flapped and palm-slapped, Butch couldn't tell exactly what was doing, but he was damn sure they weren't comparing cookie recipes.

When the Infiniti reversed it out, Butch stepped from the shadows, figuring there was one way of knowing if his hunch was correct: Assume and see what came back at him. "Tell me you aren't going to deal that shit inside? The Reverend hates freelancers."

The little blond guy wheeled around, all righteous pissed. "Who the fuck are—" His words dried up. "Wait, I've seen you before . . . except . . ."

"Yeah, I got my chassis overhauled. I run better now. Lot better. So what are you—" Butch froze as he felt his instincts fire up.

Lessers. Close by. Shit.

"Boys," he said calmly. "You need to take off now. And you can't reenter through that door."

Dickhead's attitude came back online. "Who do you think you are?"

"Trust me on this and get your groove on. *Now*."

"Fuck you, we can stand out here all night if we—" The punk froze, then blanched as a sweet smell rode down to them on a breeze. "Oh, my God . . ."

Hmmm, so Little Blond Dickhead was a pre-trans, not human. "Yeah, like I said. Get gone, kid."

The pair took off, but they weren't fast enough: A trio of *lessers* appeared at the open end of the alley, blocking their way.

Great. Just terrific.

Butch activated his newest wristwatch, sending out a beacon and coordinates. Within moments, V and Rhage materialized by his side.

"Use the strategy we agreed on," Butch muttered. "I'll sweep up."

The two nodded their heads as the *lessers* closed in.

Rehvenge stood up from his desk and pulled on his sable coat. "Gotta bounce, Xhex. *Princeps* Council meeting. I'm dematerializing, so I don't need the car, and I hope to be back in an hour. But before I go, what's the status of that newest OD?"

"Off to the Saint Francis ER. He's probably going to live."

"And that rogue dealer?"

Xhex opened his door for him, like she was encouraging him to leave. "Still haven't found him."

Rehv cursed, reached for his cane, and headed over to her. "I am *not* happy about this sitch."

"No kidding," she muttered. "And here I thought you were down with it."

He pegged her with a hard stare. "Don't fuck around with me."

"I'm not, boss," she snapped back. "We're doing everything we can. Do you think I *like* calling nine-one-one for these fools?"

He took a deep breath and tried to chill his temper. Man, it had been a bad week at the club. Both of them were on short fuses, and the rest of the staff at ZeroSum were about to hang themselves in the bathroom from the tension.

"Sorry," he said. "I'm wound."

She ran a hand over her man's haircut. "Yeah . . . me, too."

"What's doing on your end?"

He didn't expect her to answer. But she did. "You hear about the human? O'Neal?"

"Yeah. One of us. Who'd've thought, huh." Rehv had yet to see the guy up close and personal, but Vishous had called with a heads-up on the miracle that had gone down.

Rehv honestly wished the cop well. He liked that bigmouthed man—er, male. But he was also very aware that his feeding days with Marissa had come to an end and so had any hope of mating her. The shit stung, it really did, even though linking up with her would have been a really bad idea.

"Is it true?" Xhex asked. "About him and Marissa?"

"Yeah, he's not a free agent."

The oddest expression filtered through Xhex's features . . . sadness? Yeah, looked like it.

He frowned. "I didn't know you were that into him."

Instantly, she was back to herself, eyes sharp, face showing nothing but hard-ass. "Just because I liked banging him doesn't mean I wanted him as a mate."

"Fine, sure. Whatever."

Her upper lip peeled off her fangs. "Do I look like the type who needs a male?"

"Nope, and thank God. The idea of you going soft violates the natural world order. Besides, you're the only one I can feed from, so I need you unattached." He passed by her. "I'll see you in two hours, tops."

"Rehvenge." When he glanced back, she said, "I need you to stay single, too."

Their stares locked. God, they were quite a pair, weren't

they. Two liars living among Normals . . . two snakes in the grass.

"Don't worry," he murmured. "I'm never taking a *shellan*. Marissa was . . . a flavor I wanted to taste. Never would have worked out long term."

After Xhex nodded, as if they'd resealed their deal, Rehv left.

As he walked through the VIP section, he stuck to the shadows. He didn't like to be seen with his cane, and if he had to use it, he wanted people to think it was a vanity thing, so he tried not to rely on it too much. Which was a little dangerous considering his lack of balance.

He got to the side door, worked some mind magic with the alarm system, then popped the bar release. He stepped out, thinking he—

Holy Christ! There was a frickin' melee in the alley. *Lessers*. Brothers. Two civilians crouched and quivering in the middle. And big bad Butch O'Neal.

As the door clicked shut behind Rehv, he widened his stance and wondered why the hell the security cameras hadn't—oh, *mhis*. They were surrounded by *mhis*. Nice touch.

Standing on the sideline, he watched the fight, listening to the dull thuds of bodies hitting bodies, hearing the grunts and the shifting of metal, smelling the sweat and the blood of his race mixing with the baby powder sweetness of the slayers.

Damn, he wanted to play, too. And he couldn't see why he shouldn't.

When a *lesser* stumbled his way, he caught the bastard, slammed it up against the bricks, and smiled while looking into a pair of pale eyes. It had been so long since Rehv had killed something and the flip side of him missed the experience. Craved it. Man, the snuffing out of life was something the bad in him yearned for.

And he was going to feed his beast. Right here. Right now.

In spite of the dopamine in his system, Rehv's *symphath* abilities came at his beckoning, riding the crest of his aggression, suffusing his vision with the color red. Baring his fangs in a smile, he gave in to his sinister half with the ecstatic pleasure of an addict long deprived.

With invisible hands, he tunneled into the *lesser*'s brain, rooted around, and triggered all kinds of fun memories. It was like popping lids off soda bottles, and what bubbled out debilitated his prey, scrambling the *lesser* so badly it was rendered defenseless. God, such ugliness inside the bastard's head—this particular slayer had had a real sadistic streak, and as every single one of his nasty deeds and dirty abuses clouded his mind's eye, he started to scream, clapping his hands to his ears and falling to the ground.

Rehv brought up his cane and whipped off its outer casing, revealing a lethal length of steel, the blade red as his twodimensional sight. But when he got ready to stab, Butch grabbed his arm.

"This is where I come in."

Rehv glared at the guy. "Fuck that, this is my kill—"

"No, it isn't." Butch went down to his knees beside the *lesser* and . . .

Rehv clamped his mouth shut and stared with fascination as Butch leaned over and started to suck something out of the slayer. Except there wasn't time to enjoy the *Twilight Zone* episode. Another *lesser* came gunning for Butch, and Rehv had to leap back as Rhage took the thing down in a tackle.

Rehv heard more footsteps and faced off at yet another *lesser*. Good. This one *he* would handle, he thought with a hard grin.

Man, *symphaths* loved to fight, they really did. And he was no exception to his nature.

Mr. X pounded down the alley where the brawl was happening. Though he couldn't see or hear anything, he sensed the buffering around the scene, so he knew this was the right place.

Van cursed from behind him. "What the hell is this? I can feel the fight—"

"We're about to penetrate the *mhis*. Get ready."

The two kept running and hit what felt like a wall of cold water. As they burst through the barrier, the fight was revealed: Two Brothers. Six slayers. A couple of cowering civilians. A very large male in a full-length fur coat . . . and Butch O'Neal.

The former cop was just lifting himself up from the ground, looking sick as a dog and positively glowing with the master's footprint. As Mr. X met O'Neal's eyes, the *Fore-lesser* skidded to a halt, overcome by a sense of accord.

And irony of ironies, at that very instant when the connection was made, at that precise moment when there was an exchange of recognition, the Omega called from the other side.

Coincidence? Who cared. Mr. X pushed off the demand, ignoring the itching in his skin. "Van," he said softly, "it's time for you to show your stuff. Go get O'Neal."

"About fucking time." Van bolted for the newly born vampire, and the two of them squared off, circling each other in the manner of fighters. At least until Van stopped moving, becoming nothing more than a breathing statue.

Because Mr. X had willed it so.

Man, he had to smile as he caught the panicked expression on Van's face. Yeah, losing control of all your large-muscle groups certainly did freak a guy out, didn't it.

And O'Neal was surprised as well. He closed in with care, wary but obviously ready to take advantage of the freeze-frame Mr. X was imposing on his subordinate. The takedown happened fast. In a quick move, O'Neal put an armlock around Van's neck, flipped him over, and pinned him down to the ground.

Mr. X didn't give a shit about sacrificing an asset like Van. He needed to know what happened when—*holy shit!*

O'Neal . . . O'Neal had opened his mouth and was inhaling and . . . Van Dean was just sucked into nothingness, absorbed, swallowed, owned. Unto dust.

Relief flooded into Mr. X. Yes . . . *yes*, the prophecy was fulfilled. The prophecy had been realized in the skin of an Irishman who had been turned. *Thank you, God.*

Mr. X took a halting, desperate step forward. Now . . . now would be the peace he sought, his loophole realized, his freedom ensured. *O'Neal was the one.*

Except Mr. X was suddenly intercepted by a Brother who had a goatee and tattoos on his face. The big bastard came out of nowhere like a boulder, hitting X so hard his legs buckled. They started to fight, but X was terrified he'd be stabbed instead of consumed by O'Neal. So when another slayer jumped into the fray and grabbed the Brother, Mr. X disengaged and disappeared into the periphery.

The Omega's call was a screaming demand now, that godawful tickling a roar across Mr. X's flesh, but he wasn't answering. He was going to get himself killed tonight. But only in the right way.

Butch lifted his head from his latest victim's ash pile and began to retch in horrid, full-torso heaves. His body felt as it had back when he'd just woken up in the clinic however long ago. Contaminated. Stained. Dirty beyond bleaching.

God . . . what if he'd taken in too much? What if he'd reached the point of no return?

As he vomited, he felt, though did not see, V come over. Forcing his head up, Butch groaned, "Help me . . ."

"I'm going to, *trahyner*. Give me your hand." As Butch held his palm up in despair, Vishous whipped off his glove and grabbed on good and hard. V's energy, that beautiful, white light, poured down Butch's arm and ripped through him in a blast, cleansing, renewing.

United by their clasped hands, they became again the two halves, the light and the dark. The Destroyer and the Savior. A whole.

Butch took all V had to give. And when it was over, he didn't want to let go, afraid if the connection was broken the evil would somehow come back.

"You okay?" V said softly.

"I am now." God, his voice was hoarse as hell from the inhaling. Maybe also from the gratitude.

V gave a yank and Butch shot upright to his feet. As he let himself fall back against the alley's brick wall, he discovered the fighting was over.

"Nice work for a civilian," Rhage said.

Butch glanced to the left, thinking the brother was talking to him, but then he saw Rehvenge. The male was slowly bending over and picking up a sheath from the ground. With an elegant move, he took the red-bladed sword in his hand and slid it home to the pummel. Ah . . . that cane was also a weapon.

"Thanks," Rehv replied. Then his amethyst eyes shifted over to Butch.

As the two of them stared at each other, Butch realized they hadn't really met up since the night Marissa had fed.

"Hey, man," Butch said, putting his palm out.

Rehvenge walked over, leaning heavily on his cane. As the two of them shook, everyone took a deep breath.

"So, cop," Rehv said, "mind if I ask what you were doing to those slayers?"

A whimpering sound cut off any reply, causing them all to look at the Dumpster across the way.

"You can come out, boys," Rhage said, "Place is clear."

The hotshot blond pre-trans and his rented meat shuffled into the light. Both of them looked like they'd been put through a dishwasher: they were damp with sweat in spite of the cold, their hair and clothes all messed up.

Rehvenge's hard face registered surprise. "Lash, why aren't you in training now? Your father's going to have a shit fit that you were down here instead of—"

"He's taking a hiatus from classes," Rhage muttered dryly.

"To deal drugs," Butch added. "Check his pockets."

Rhage went in for some frisk action, and Lash was too shocked out to protest. The result was a wad of cash as big as the kid's head and a handful of little cellophane packets.

Rehv's eyes glowed with angry purple light. "Give that shit to me, Hollywood—the powder, not the green." When Rhage handed the stuff over, Rehv cracked one of the packets, licked his pinkie, and stuck it inside. After he put his finger on his tongue, he grimaced and spat. Then he jabbed his cane at the kid. "You're not welcome here anymore."

That little news flash seemed to shake Lash out of his stupor. "Why not? It's a free country."

"First of all, this is *my* house, that's why. Second, not that I need any other reason, the shit in those bags is contaminated and I'm willing to bet you're responsible for the rash of ODs we've had lately. So like I said, you're not welcome here anymore. I won't have punks like you spoiling my stream of commerce." Rehv stuffed the baggies in his coat pocket and glanced at Rhage. "What are you going to do with him?"

"Drive him home."

Rehv smiled coldly. "How convenient for us all."

Abruptly, Lash fell into whimper mode. "But we're not going to tell my father—"

"Everything," Rehvenge snapped. "Trust me, your daddy's going to know fucking *everything*."

Lash's knees wobbled. And then the BMOC passed out cold.

Marissa walked into the *Princeps* Council meeting, not caring that for once everyone looked at her.

Then again, they'd never seen her in pants or with her hair pulled back in a ponytail. So surprise, surprise.

She took a seat, opened up her brand-new briefcase, and started going through applications for residence monitors. Although . . . she wasn't really seeing anything. She was exhausted, not just from the work or the stress but because she really had to feed. Soon.

Oh, God. The idea of it made her sick with sadness, and she sank into thoughts of Butch. As she pictured him, that persistent, foggy echo in the back of her head returned. The thing was like a little bell chiming, reminding her of . . . what?

A hand landed on her shoulder. As she jumped, Rehv sat down next to her.

"Just me." His amethyst eyes passed over her face and her hair. "It's good to see you."

"You, too." She smiled a little, then glanced away, wondering whethe she would have to go back to using his vein. Ah . . . hell. Of course she would.

"What's doing, *tahlly*? You okay?" he asked smoothly. The question was so casual, she got the eerie sense he knew exactly how upset she was and somehow knew the cause. He'd always read her so well for some reason.

As she opened her mouth, the council *leahdyre*'s gavel pounded down at the other end of the glossy table. "I'd like to bring the meeting to order."

The voices in the library dried up fast, and Rehv leaned back in his chair, a bored expression suffusing his hard face. With elegant, powerful hands, he folded his sable coat around his legs, overlapping the thing as if the room were thirty below, not a balmy seventy.

Marissa shut her briefcase and settled in, realizing that she'd assumed a similar pose to his, just without all the fur. *Good heavens*, she thought. *How times have changed.* Once she'd been terrified of these vampires. Utterly intimidated. Now, as she looked around at the exquisitely gowned females and the formally dressed males, she was just . . . bored by it all. Tonight, the *glymera* and the *Princeps* Council seemed like nothing more than an antiquated social nightmare no longer relevant to her life. Thank God.

The *leahdyre* smiled and nodded to a *doggen* who stepped forward. In the servant's hands was a sheet of parchment stretched over an ebony board. Long streamers of silk ribbon hung from the document, the various colors reflecting each of the six originating families. Marissa's line was pale blue.

The *leahdyre* looked around the table, his eyes studiously skipping over Marissa. "Now that we have the full council here, I would like to entertain the first order of business, said business to concern the passage of the recommendation to the king on the matter of mandatory *sehclusion* for all unmated females. First, as per the rules of procedure, we will give leave for commentary from the nonvoting members herein this room."

There was quick assent from everyone . . . except for Rehvenge. Who was very clear about how he felt.

In the pause following his terse rejection of the motion, Marissa could feel Havers's stare on her. She kept her mouth shut.

"Well done, council," the *leahdyre* said. "I shall now call the roll of the six voting *princeps*." As each name was read, the corresponding *princeps* rose, gave the consent of his or her bloodline and affixed the seal of the family's ring upon the parchment. This happened without a glitch five times. And then the last name was spoken. "Havers, blooded son of Wallen, blooded grandson of . . ."

As her brother rose from his chair, Marissa rapped her knuckles sharply on the table. All eyes shot to her. "Wrong name."

The *leahdyre*'s eyes went so wide she was quite sure he could see behind himself. And he was so aghast at her interruption, he was speechless as she smiled a little and glanced at Havers. "You may sit down, physician," she said.

"I *beg* your pardon," the *leahdyre* stammered.

Marissa got to her feet. "It's been so long since we've done one of these votes . . . not since Wrath's father died." She leaned forward on her hands as she pegged the *leahdyre*'s face with a level stare. "And back then, centuries ago, my father lived and cast our family's vote. So obviously that is why you are confused."

The *leahdyre* looked at Havers in a panic. "Perhaps you will inform your sister she is out of order—"

Marissa cut in. "I'm not his sister anymore, or so he's told me. Though I believe we can all agree that blood lineage is immutable. As is the order of birth." She smiled coolly. "It so happens that I was born eleven years before Havers. Which makes me older than he is. Which means he can sit down because as the eldest surviving member of my family, the vote from our bloodline is mine to cast. Or not. And in this case, it is most definitely . . . *not*."

Chaos broke out. Absolute pandemonium.

In the midst of which, Rehv laughed and clapped his palms together. "Hot damn, girl. You are *so* the shit."

Marissa took little joy in the power play, feeling more relieved than anything else. The vote had to be unanimous or that stupid motion was going nowhere. And thanks to her that was a big fat *nowhere*.

"Oh . . . my God," someone said.

As if a drain opened in the center of the floor, all the noise was sucked out of the room. Marissa turned around.

Rhage was in the doorway of the library holding a pre-transition male by the scruff of the neck. Behind him were Vishous . . . and Butch.

FORTY-SIX

Standing in the library's archway, Butch did his best not to flat-out stare at Marissa, but it was tough. Especially because she was sitting next to Rehvenge.

He tried to distract himself by looking around. The meeting she was in was full of highfliers. Christ, looked like a political summit, except for the fact that they were all dressed to the nines, especially the females. Man, Elizabeth Taylor's jewelry box had nothing on these chicks.

And then the drama bomb went off.

The guy at the head of the table looked over, saw Lash, and went corpse-white. Rising slowly, he seemed to have lost his voice. As had everyone else in the room.

"We need to talk, sire," Rhage said while giving Lash a shake. "About your boy's extracurricular activities."

Rehvenge stood up. "We sure as hell do."

This broke up the meeting like an axe to an ice block. Lash's dad whipped out of the library and hurried Rhage, Rehvenge, and the kid into a sitting room. Like he was utterly mortified. Meanwhile, the fancy types got up from the table and started to mill around. None of them looked happy, and most of them shot hard looks in Marissa's direction.

Which made Butch want to teach them how to show some respect. Until they were bleeding from the lesson.

As his fists cranked tight, his nostrils flared and he sifted through the air, finding Marissa's scent and absorbing it into every pore he had. Naturally, his body went apeshit being so near her, the damn thing heating up, getting urgent. Shit, it was all he could do to get his arms and legs to stay put. Especially as he felt her look at him.

When a cool breeze tunneled into the house, Butch realized the huge front door was still open from their arrival with the kid. As he looked out into the night, he knew it was better for him to go. Cleaner. Neater. Less dangerous, too, given how badly he wanted to grind these snobs for treating Marissa with coldness.

He walked out of the house and took a meander across the front lawn, strolling over the muddy spring ground for a while before doubling back toward the house. He stopped as he came up to the Escalade because he knew he was no longer alone.

Marissa stepped from behind the SUV. "Hello, Butch."

Jesus, she was so beautiful. Especially up close like this.

"Hey, Marissa." He put his hands in the pockets of his leather coat. And thought about how he missed her. Wanted her. Craved her. And not just for sex.

"Butch . . . I—"

Abruptly, he tensed, his eyes picking up on something that was coming across the lawn. A man . . . a white-haired man . . . a *lesser*.

"*Shit,*" Butch hissed. In a rush, he grabbed Marissa and started hauling her back toward the house.

"What are you doing—" As soon as she saw the *lesser,* she stopped fighting him.

"Run," he commanded. "Run and tell Rhage and V to get their asses out here. And lock that fucking door." He gave her a shove and wheeled around, not taking a breath until he heard a heavy slam and then bolts being pushed home.

Well, what do you know. It was the *Fore-lesser* coming up the lawn.

494

Man, he wished he didn't have an audience. Because before he killed the guy, he really wanted to tear him apart as payback. Eye for an eye, so to speak.

As the bastard got closer, the slayer lifted his hands in surrender, but Butch didn't buy the act. Or the one-man gig. He let his instincts roam around, expecting to find a whole legion of slayers on the grounds. Surprisingly, there were none.

Still, he felt safer as V and Rhage materialized behind him, their bodies displacing the cold air.

"I think it's just him," Butch murmured, his body primed for a fight. "And I don't need to tell you this . . . but he's *mine*."

As the slayer came closer, Butch got ready to spring, but then shit got weird. Holy hell—he had to be seeing things. The *lesser* couldn't have tears flowing down his face, could he?

In an anguished voice, it said, "You, the cop. Take me . . . finish me. Please . . ."

"Don't trust this," Rhage said from the left.

The *lesser*'s eyes shifted to the brother and then returned to Butch. "I just want this over. I'm trapped . . . Please, kill me. It has to be you, though. Not them."

"My fucking pleasure," Butch muttered.

He lunged at the guy, expecting all manner of fight to come back at him, but the bastard put up no resistance at all, just landed on his back like a bag of sand.

"Thank you . . . thank you . . ." The freaky-ass gratitude ran out of the *lesser*'s mouth, a stream without end, marked with aching relief.

As Butch felt the urge to inhale come over him, he held on to the *Fore-lesser*'s throat and opened his mouth, acutely aware of the eyes of the *glymera* staring out from the Tudor mansion. Right as he started to draw, all he could think of was Marissa. He didn't want her to see what was going to happen next.

Except . . . nothing did. There was no exchange. Some kind of block was preventing the evil from being transferred.

The *Fore-lesser*'s eyes cracked wide in panic. "It worked . . . with the others. It worked! I saw you . . ."

Butch kept inhaling until it was clear that for whatever reason, this was one he couldn't consume. Maybe because it was the *Fore-lesser*? Who the fuck cared.

"With the others . . ." the *lesser* was babbling. "With the others, it worked . . ."

"Not with you apparently." Butch reached to his hip and unsheathed his knife. "Good thing there's another way." He hauled back, lifting the blade over his head.

The *lesser* screamed and started to flail. "No! He'll torture me! Noooooooooo—"

The hollering died right off as the slayer popped and fizzled.

Butch sighed in relief, glad he'd done the deed—

Only to have a wave of malice shoot through him, burning like the extremes of cold and heat combined. As he gasped, nasty laughter bubbled up from out of nowhere and weaved through the night, the kind of disembodied sound that made a man think about his own coffin.

The Omega.

Butch grabbed for his cross through his shirt and sprang to his feet just as a static-filled apparition of the Evil appeared before him. Butch's body rebelled, but he didn't step back. Dimly, he felt Rhage and V close in tight with him, flanking him, protecting him.

"What is, cop?" V murmured. "What are you looking at?"

Shit, they couldn't see the Omega.

Before Butch could explain, the distinctive, echoing voice of the Evil weaved in and out of the wind, in and out of his head. "So you are the one, are you not? My . . . son, as it were."

"Never."

"Butch? Who are you talking to?" V said.

"Did I not sire you, then?" The Omega laughed some more. "Did I not give you part of me, then? Yes, I did. And you know what they say about me, don't you?"

"I don't want to know."

"You should." The Omega reached out a ghostly hand, and though it closed no distance between them, Butch felt it on his face. "I always claim what is *mine*. Son."

"Sorry, my Father position is already filled."

Butch dragged his cross out and let it dangle from its chain. Dimly, he thought he heard V curse, as if the brother had figured out what was going on, but his attention was only on what was in front of him.

The Omega looked at the heavy piece of gold. Then flicked his glance over Rhage and V and the house behind. "Trinkets don't impress me. Neither do the Brothers. Nor the sturdiest locks and doors."

"But I do."

The Omega's head whipped around.

The Scribe Virgin materialized behind him, totally unrobed and glowing like a supernova.

The Omega instantly changed shape, becoming a wormhole in the fabric of reality, no longer an apparition but a smoky black pit.

"Oh, shit," V barked, as if he and Rhage were now able to see everything.

The Omega's voice emerged from its dark depths. "Sister, how fare thee this night?"

"I command thee back to *Dhunhd*. Go thou, now." The

497

glow of her intensified until it began to encase the Omega's sinkhole.

A nasty growl drifted free. "Think you that banishment cures my presence? How simple you are."

"Go thou, now." A stream of words flowed from her into the night, neither the Old Language nor any other tongue Butch had ever heard.

Just before the Omega disappeared, Butch felt the eyes of the Evil bore into him as that horrible voice echoed out, "Lo, how you inspire me, my son. And may I say you would be wise to search for your blood. Families should congregate."

Then the Omega disappeared in a flare of white. As did the Scribe Virgin.

Gone. Both of them. Nothing remaining except a bitterly cold wind that cleared the clouds from the sky like curtains ripped away by a savage hand.

Rhage cleared his throat. "Okay . . . I'm not sleeping for the next week and a half. How about you two?"

"You all right?" V asked Butch.

"Yeah." No.

Jesus Christ . . . he was not the Omega's son. Was he?

"No," V said. "You're not. He just wants to believe you are. And he wants you to think you are. But that doesn't make it true."

There was a long silence. Then Rhage's hand landed on Butch's shoulder. "Besides, you don't look a thing like him. I mean . . . hello? You're this beefy Irish white boy. He's like . . . bus exhaust or some shit."

Butch glanced over at Hollywood. "You're sick, you know that?"

"Yeah, but you love me, right? Come on. I know you feel me."

Butch was the first to start chuckling. Then the other

two joined in, the weight of the heavy-duty, high-powered weirdout that had just happened draining away a little.

But as their laughter faded, Butch's hand went to his stomach.

Twisting around, he looked to the mansion, searching the pale, frightened faces on the other side of the leaded windows. Marissa was right in front, her brilliant blond hair reflected in the moonlight.

He closed his eyes and turned away. "I want to take the Escalade back. By myself." If he didn't get some time alone, he was going to scream. "But first, do we need to do anything about the *glymera* and everything they saw?"

"Wrath will definitely hear about this from them," V muttered. "But as far as I'm concerned they're on their own. Besides, they can pay their therapists to work through this shit. Not our biz to calm them out."

After Rhage and V dematerialized back to the compound, Butch started for the Escalade. As he deactivated the SUV's security alarm, he heard someone running across the ground.

"Butch! Wait!"

He glanced over his shoulder. Marissa was jogging down toward him, and when she stopped, she was so close he could hear the blood in the chambers of her heart.

"Are you hurt?" she asked, running her eyes all over him.

"No."

"Are you sure?"

"Yes."

"Was that the Omega?"

"Yes."

She took a deep breath, like she wanted to probe but knew he wasn't going to talk about what had happened with the Evil. Not with the way things were between them. "Ah, before it came, I saw you kill that slayer. Is that . . . that burst of light, is that what you—"

"No."

"Oh." She dropped her eyes to his hands. No . . . she was looking at the dagger on his hip. "You were out fighting, before you came here."

"Yeah."

"And you saved that boy . . . Lash, didn't you?"

He glanced at the SUV. Knew he was a thin inch away from throwing himself at her, hugging her hard, and begging her to come home with him. Like a total fucking idiot. "Look, I'm going to leave, Marissa. Take . . . care."

He walked around to the driver's side and got in. When she followed, he shut the door on her, but he didn't start the engine.

Shit, through the glass and steel of the Escalade, he could feel her as vividly as if she were against his chest.

"Butch . . ." The sound of his name was muffled. "I want to apologize for something I said to you."

He gripped the steering wheel and started out the front wind-shield. Then like the sap he was, his hand popped the door and he pushed it open. "Why?"

"I'm sorry I brought the whole rescuing-your-sister thing into it. You know, back at the Pit. That was cruel."

"I . . . Shit, you had a good point. I have been trying to save people all my life because of Janie. So don't feel bad."

There was a long pause, and he sensed something strong coming out of her, something—ah, yes, her need to feed. She was starving for a vein.

And naturally, his body wanted to give her every single one he had. Natch.

To keep himself in the damn Escalade, he put his seat belt on, then took one last look at her face. It was taut with strain and . . . hunger. She was really fighting her need, trying to hide it so they could talk.

"I gotta go," he said. Like *now*.

"Yes . . . me, too." She flushed and stepped back, her eyes meeting his briefly and skirting away. "Anyway, I'll see you. Around."

She turned away and started walking quickly back up to the house. And guess who appeared in the doorway to meet her: Rehvenge.

Rehv . . . so strong . . . so powerful . . . so completely able to feed her.

Marissa didn't make it another yard.

Butch shot out of the SUV, grabbed her around the waist, and dragged her back to the car. Although it wasn't as if she fought him. In the slightest.

He popped the rear door of the Escalade and all but threw her inside. As he started to get in, he looked at Rehvenge. The guy's violet stare was glowing, like he had half a mind to get involved, but Butch nailed the male right in the eye and pointed at the guy's chest, the universal signal for *you-stay-right-there-buddy-and-you-get-to-keep-your-teeth*. Rehv's lips moved in a curse, but then he bowed his head and dematerialized.

Butch leaped into the back of the SUV, slammed the hatch, and was on top of Marissa before the ceiling light dimmed. It was crowded in the rear, his legs twisted at odd angles, his shoulder shoved against something, probably the back of a seat, whatever. He couldn't have cared less and neither did she. Marissa was all over him, wrapping her legs around his hips and opening her mouth to him as he brutally kissed her.

Butch flipped them over so she was on top, fisted a bunch of her hair, and yanked her right down to his throat. *"Bite!"* he snarled.

Holy fuck, did she ever.

He felt a searing pain as her fangs sliced into him, and as he was penetrated, his body jerked wildly, causing his flesh to tear even more. Oh, but it was good. So good. She was taking deep draws from his vein and the satisfaction of feeding her was a buzzing rush.

He pushed a palm between their bodies and cupped the heat at the center of her, rubbing at her core. As she let out a crazy moan, he shoved up her shirt with his other hand. God bless her, she broke the contact with his neck long enough to whip off her blouse and ditch her bra.

"The pants," he said hoarsely. "Lose your pants."

As she stripped awkwardly in the confined space, he undid his zipper and sprang his erection free. He didn't dare touch the thing, he was so close to orgasm.

She mounted him fully naked, her pale blue eyes glowing, positively afire in the darkness. The red stain of his blood was on her lips and he rose up to kiss her mouth, then angled himself so as she sat down she hit his body just right. He kicked his head back as they joined and she pierced his neck on the other side. As his hips started going hard, she eased up on her knees so she was stable as she drank.

The orgasm shattered him.

But the moment it was over, he was ready to go again. And he did.

FORTY-SEVEN

When Marissa had taken all she needed, she eased off Butch and lay next to him. He was on his back, staring up at the Escalade's ceiling, one hand resting on his chest. He breathed raggedly, his clothes all rumpled and misaligned, his shirt up around his pecs. His sex lay glistening and spent on his hard stomach, and his neck wounds were raw even after she'd licked them.

She'd used him with a savagery she hadn't thought she had in her, her needs driving them both into an absolute, primal frenzy. And now, in the aftermath, she could feel her body going to work on what he'd given her, her eyelids drooping a little.

So good. He'd been so good.

"Will you use me again?" Butch's voice, always full of gravel, was nearly gone.

Marissa closed her eyes, her chest hurting so badly she had trouble breathing.

"Because I want it to be me instead of him," he said.

Oh . . . so this was about an act of aggression directed toward Rehvenge, not about feeding her. She should have known. She'd seen the look Butch had given Rehv just before getting into the car. He obviously still held a grudge from before.

"Never mind," Butch said, putting himself back into his pants and zipping up. "None of my business."

She had no reply for him, but he didn't seem to expect one. He handed her her clothes, didn't look at her as she dressed, and the second her nakedness was covered, he opened the back door.

Cold air rushed in . . . and that was when she realized something. The inside of the car smelled of passion and feeding—thick, heady fragrances that were enticing. But there was not one hint of the bonding scent. Not one hint.

She couldn't bear to glance back at him as she walked away.

It was close to dawn when Butch finally pulled into the compound's courtyard. After parking the Escalade between Rhage's deep purple GTO and Beth's Audi station wagon, he walked over to the Pit.

After he and Marissa had parted, he'd driven around the city for hours, following the paths of meaningless streets, passing by nonexistent houses, stopping at traffic lights when he remembered to. He'd come home only because daylight was going to flash over the land very soon and it just seemed like the thing to do.

He looked to the east, where the barest hint of radiance showed.

Walking out to the center of the courtyard, he sat on the edge of the fountain's marble pool and watched as the shutters came down over the windows of the main house and the Pit. He blinked a little at the glow in the sky. Then blinked a lot.

As his eyes started to burn, he thought about Marissa and remembered every single thing about her, from the shape of her face to the fall of her hair to the sound of her voice and the scent of her skin. Here in privacy, he let his feelings out, giving in to the aching love and the hateful yearning that refused to leave him be.

And what do you know, the bonding scent made an appearance once again. He'd somehow managed to

504

withhold it when he'd been around her, feeling as though marking her wasn't fair. But here? Alone? No reason to hide.

As the sunrise gathered momentum, his cheeks flared with pain, like he had a sunburn, and his body twitched with alarm. He forced himself to stay because he needed to see the sun, but his thighs trembled from the urge to run, and he wasn't going to be able to hold them for long.

Shit . . . he was never going to catch daylight again, was he? And with Marissa out of his life, there would be no kind of sunshine for him. Ever.

The darkness owned him, didn't it.

He released the lock on himself because he had no choice, and the instant he did, his legs raced across the courtyard. Hurling his body through the Pit's vestibule, he slammed the innermost door and breathed roughly.

There was no rap music playing, but V's leather jacket was tossed on the chair behind the computers, so he was around. Probably still at the big house doing a postgame wrap-up with Wrath.

As Butch stood by himself in the living room, the familiar urge to drink hit hard, and he could see no good reason not to give in. Dumping his coat and his weapons, he headed for the Scotch, poured himself a long/tall, and brought the bottle out with him from the kitchen. Going over to his favorite couch, he lifted the glass to his lips and while he swallowed, his eyes fell on the newest issue of *Sports Illustrated*. There was a picture of a baseball player on the cover and next to the guy's head, in big yellow print, was a single word: *HERO*.

Marissa was right. He did have a hero complex. But it wasn't about some kind of an ego trip. It was because maybe if he saved enough people he could be . . . forgiven.

That's what he was truly after: absolution.

Flashbacks from his younger years started to play like pay-per-view, except sure as shit this wasn't a movie he'd choose to order. And in the midst of the show, his eyes slid to the phone. There was only one person who could ease him about this stuff, and he doubted she would. But damn, if he could reach out and have his mother say, just once, that she forgave him for letting Janie get into that car . . .

Butch sat down on the leather sofa and put his Scotch aside.

He waited there for hours, until the clock said nine. And then he picked up the phone and dialed a number that started with the area code 617. His father answered.

The conversation was just as awful as Butch had thought it might be. The only thing worse? The news from home.

As he ended the call on the cordless, he saw that the total elapsed time, counting the six rings at the beginning, was one minute thirty-four seconds. And it was, he knew, likely the last time he would talk to Eddie O'Neal.

"What's doing, cop?"

He jumped and looked up at Vishous. Saw no reason to lie. "My mother's sick. For the past two years, apparently. Has Alzheimer's. Bad. Of course, no one thought to tell me. And I would never have known if I hadn't just called."

"Shit . . ." V came over and sat down. "You want to go see her?"

"Nope." Butch shook his head and picked up his Scotch. "Got no reason to. Those people aren't my business anymore."

FORTY-EIGHT

The following evening, Marissa shook the hand of her new residence director. The female was perfect for the position. Smart. Kind. Soft of voice. Trained in public health at NYU—the night school, of course.

"When would you like me to start?" the female said.

"How's tonight sound?" Marissa replied wryly. When she got an enthusiastic nod in response, she smiled a little. "Great . . . Why don't I show you to your office."

When Marissa got back from the upstairs bedroom she'd assigned the director, she went to her laptop, logged in to Caldwell's multiple listing service, and started looking at some other properties for sale within the community.

It wasn't long before she saw nothing at all. Butch was a constant pressure on her chest, an invisible weight that made it hard to breathe. And if she wasn't busy, memories of him consumed her.

"Mistress?"

She looked up at Safe Place's *doggen*. "Yes, Phillipa?"

"Havers has referred a case to us. The female and her son are going to be driven here tomorrow after the young is stabilized, but the case history taken by the clinic's nurse is going to be e-mailed over to you within the hour."

"Thank you. Will you get a room ready for them downstairs?"

"Yes, mistress." The *doggen* bowed and left.

So, Havers was keeping his word, wasn't he.

Marissa frowned, that now perennial sense that she was missing something coming back to her. For some reason, an image of Havers came to mind and wouldn't leave . . . and that's what brought the shadowed thought to light.

From out of nowhere, she heard her own voice when she'd been talking to Butch: *I will not sit back and watch you destroy yourself.*

Good God. The exact words her brother had said to her when he'd kicked her out of the house. Oh, sweet Virgin Scribe, she was doing to Butch precisely what Havers had done to her: banishing him under the noble guise of prudent disapproval. Except wasn't the point really about saving herself from feeling scared and out of control because she loved him?

But what about his death wish?

The sight of him facing off against that *lesser* on the *leahdyre*'s front lawn came to her: Butch had been cautious in that situation. Careful. Not reckless. And he'd moved with skill, not a berserker's messy flailing.

Oh . . . hell, she thought. What if she'd been wrong? What if Butch could fight? What if he *should* fight?

Except what about the Evil? The Omega?

Well, the Scribe Virgin had interceded to protect Butch. And he had still been . . . Butch after the Omega had vanished. What if—

A knock sounded and she jumped to her feet. "My queen!"

Beth smiled from the doorway, lifting a hand. "Hi."

All tangled in her head, Marissa fell into a curtsy, which made Beth shake her head with a chuckle.

"Am I ever going to get you to cut that out?"

"Likely not . . . It's the burden of my upbringing." Marissa tried to concentrate. "Have you . . . ah, have you come to see what we've done here in the last—"

Bella and Mary appeared behind the queen.

"We want to talk with you," Beth said. "It's about Butch."

Butch stirred in his bed. Cracked open an eye. Cursed as he saw the clock. He'd overslept, probably because of how hard he'd gone the night before. Were three *lessers* too much in one night? Or maybe it had been feeding—

Oh, hell, no. He was *so* not thinking of that. Not remembering that.

He rolled over onto his back—

And jacked right off the mattress. "Oh . . . *fuck*!"

Five figures in black hooded robes surrounded his bed.

Wrath's voice came first in the Old Language, then in English: "There is no going back from the question that shall be posed to you this night. You shall be given it only once, and your answer will stand for the rest of the life you lead. Are you prepared to be asked?"

The Brotherhood. Holy Mary, Mother of God.

"Yes," Butch breathed, grabbing his cross.

"Then I shall say unto you now, Butch O'Neal descendant of mine own blood, and the blood of mine father, will you join us?"

Oh . . . shit. Was this real? A dream?

He looked at each one of the hooded figures. "Yes. Yes, I will join you."

A black robe was thrown at him. "Tender this to your skin, raising the hood unto your head. At all times, you shall say nothing unless spoken to. You shall keep your eyes on the ground. Your hands shall be clasped at the small of your back. Your bravery and the honor of the bloodline we share shall be measured in every action you take."

Butch stood up and pulled on the robe. Wished briefly he could hit the bathroom—

"You will be permitted to empty your body. Do it now."

When Butch came out, he made sure his head was down and his hands were linked behind him.

As a heavy hand landed on his shoulder, he knew it was Rhage's. No one else's palm weighed so much.

"Come with us now," Wrath said.

Butch was led out of the Pit and right into the Escalade, the SUV parked practically in the vestibule, as if they didn't want anyone to know what was happening.

After Butch slid into the back, the Escalade's engine turned over and many doors were shut. With a lurch, they slowly progressed through what he assumed was the courtyard until they started to bump along like they were heading over the back lawn and into the woods. No one said a thing, and in the silence he couldn't help wondering what the hell they were going to do to him. For sure this was not going to be a cakewalk.

Eventually the SUV stopped and everyone got out. Trying to follow the rules, Butch stepped to the side and stared at the ground, waiting for someone to lead him. Someone did while the Escalade was driven away.

As Butch shuffled forward he was able to see moonlight on the ground, but then the source of light was abruptly cut off and it became utterly dark. Were they in a cave? Yes . . . they were. The smell of damp earth filled his nose and beneath his bare feet he could feel small stones taking bites out of his soles.

Some forty steps later he was jerked to a stop. There was a whispering sound and then more walking, now on a downward slope. Another stop. More quiet noises as if a well-oiled gate was being retracted.

Then warmth and light. A polished floor of . . . marble. Glossy black marble. As they continued along, he had the sense that they were processing through some high-ceilinged place because what little sounds they made reverberated upward and echoed. There was another pause, followed by lots of shifting of fabric . . . the brothers disrobing, he thought.

A hand clamped on the back of his neck and the deep growl of Wrath's voice shot into his ear. "You are unworthy to enter herein as you stand now. Nod your head."

Butch nodded.

"Say that you are unworthy."

"I am unworthy."

The Brotherhood's voices suddenly let out a loud, hard shout in the Old Language, as if in protest.

Wrath continued: "Though you are not worthy, you desire to become as such this night. Nod your head."

He nodded.

"Say that you wish to become worthy."

"I wish to become worthy."

Another shout in the Old Language, this time a cheer of support.

Wrath went on: "There is only one way to become worthy and it is the right and proper way. Flesh of our flesh. Nod your head."

He nodded.

"Say that you wish to become flesh of our flesh."

"I wish to become flesh of your flesh."

A low chanting started up, and Butch had the impression that a line had formed in front of and behind him. Without warning, they started to move, the back and forth surging motion mirrored by the cadence of powerful male voices. Butch struggled to get into the rhythm, bumping forward into what he suspected was Phury by the subtle scent of red smoke, then getting bumped from behind by what he knew was Vishous just because he knew. Shit, he was making a mess of the whole thing—

And then it happened. His body found the groove and he was moving with them . . . yes, they were all as one with the chanting and the movement, back . . . forth . . . swaying left . . . then right . . . the voices, not the muscles of their thighs, carrying their feet forward.

Suddenly, there was an acoustic explosion, the sounds of the chanting fracturing and re-forming in a thousand different directions: They had entered a vast space.

A hand on his shoulder told him when to halt.

The chanting stopped as if unplugged, the sounds ricocheting for a while, then floating away.

He was taken by the arm and led forward.

At his side, Vishous said in a low voice, "Stairs."

Butch stumbled a little, then took the steps. When he got to a plateau, he was positioned by V, his body put . . . wherever it needed to be. As he settled into his stance, he had the sense he was right in front of something big, his toes up against what seemed to be a wall.

In the silence that followed, a bead of sweat dripped off his nose and landed right between his feet on the glossy floor.

V squeezed his shoulder as if in reassurance. Then stepped away.

"Who proposes this male?" the Scribe Virgin demanded.

"I, Vishous, son of the Black Dagger warrior known as the Bloodletter, do."

"Who rejects this male?" There was quiet. Thank God.

Now the Scribe Virgin's voice took on epic proportions, filling the space around them and every inch between Butch's ears until all he knew was the sound of the words she spoke. "On the basis of testimony from Wrath son of Wrath, and upon the proposal by Vishous, son of the Black Dagger warrior known as the Bloodletter, I find this male before me, Butch O'Neal, descended of Wrath son of

Wrath, an appropriate nomination unto the Black Dagger Brotherhood. As it is within my power and discretion to do so, and as it is suitable for the protection of the race, I have waived the requirement of the maternal line in this case. You may begin."

Wrath spoke. "Turn him. Unveil him."

Butch was repositioned so he faced out, and Vishous removed the black robe. Then the brother slipped the gold cross around so it hung down Butch's back, and walked away.

"Lift thine eyes," Wrath ordered.

Butch's breath sucked in as he looked up.

He was standing on a black marble dais, staring out at a subterranean cave lit by hundreds of black candles. In front of him there was an altar made of a huge stone lintel balanced on two squat posts . . . on top of which was an ancient skull. Beyond that, lined up before him, was the Brotherhood in all their glory, five males whose faces were solemn and whose bodies were strong.

Wrath broke ranks and came up to stand at the altar. "Step back against the wall and hold on to the pegs."

Butch did as he was told, feeling smooth, cool stone against his shoulders and his ass as his hands fell onto two sturdy grips.

Wrath brought up his hand and it was . . . shit, it was covered by an antique silver glove that sported barbs at the knuckles. Inside the fist he was making was the handle of a black dagger.

Extending his arm, the king scored himself down the wrist and held the wound over the skull, the dome of which had a silver cup mounted in it. What flowed from Wrath's vein was caught and held, a glossy red pool that captured the candlelight.

"My flesh," Wrath said. Then he licked his wound closed, put the blade down, and approached Butch.

Butch swallowed hard.

Wrath clapped his palm on Butch's jaw, shoved his head back and bit him in the neck, hard. Butch's whole body spasmed and he gritted his teeth to keep from yelling out, his hands squeezing at the pegs until his wrists felt like they were going to snap. Then Wrath stepped back and wiped his mouth.

He smiled fiercely. "Your flesh."

The king curled up a fist within the silver glove, hauled back his arm, and nailed Butch in the chest. The barbs sunk into his skin as air exploded out of his lungs, the raw sound leaping and bounding throughout the cave.

As he caught his breath, Rhage came up and took the glove. The brother performed the ritual just as Wrath had: cutting his wrist, holding it over the skull, speaking the same two words. After he sealed up his wound, he approached Butch. The next two words were mouthed and then Rhage's hard-core fangs were piercing Butch's throat, the bite positioned below Wrath's. Rhage's punch was fast and solid, right where Wrath had thrown his, on the left pec.

Next it was Phury. Followed by Zsadist.

By the time they were done, Butch's neck felt so loose he was convinced his head was going to roll off his shoulders and bounce down the steps. And he was dizzy from the poundings on his chest, blood running down his stomach onto his thighs from the wound.

Then it was V's turn.

Vishous came up onto the dais, his eyes down. He accepted the silver glove from Z and slipped it over the black leather he already wore on his hand. Then he scored himself with a quick flash of the black blade and stared at the skull as his blood dripped down into the basin, joining the others'.

"My flesh," he whispered.

He seemed to hesitate before turning to Butch. Then he pivoted and their eyes met. As candlelight flickered over V's hard face and got caught in his diamond irises, Butch felt his breath get tight: At that moment, his room-mate looked as powerful as a god . . . and maybe even as beautiful.

Vishous stepped in close and slid his hand from Butch's shoulder to the back of his neck. "Your flesh," V breathed. Then he paused, as if asking for something.

Without thinking, Butch tilted his chin up, aware that he was offering himself, aware that he . . . oh, fuck. He stopped his thoughts, completely weirded out by the vibe that had sprung up from God only knew where.

In slow motion Vishous's dark head dropped down and there was a silken brush as his goatee moved against Butch's throat. With delicious precision, V's fangs pressed against the vein that ran up from Butch's heart, then slowly, inexorably, punched through skin. Their chests merged.

Butch closed his eyes and absorbed the feel of it all, the warmth of their bodies so close, the way V's hair felt soft on his jaw, the slide of a powerful male arm as it slipped around his waist. On their own accord, Butch's hands left the pegs and came to rest on V's hips, squeezing that hard flesh, bringing them together from head to foot. A tremor went through one of them. Or maybe . . . shit, it was more like they both shuddered.

And then it was done. Over with. Never to happen again.

Neither of them looked at the other as V broke away . . . and the parting was complete and irrevocable. A path that would not be walked. Ever.

V's hand snapped back and then connected with Butch's chest, the impact harder than all the others, even Rhage's.

As Butch choked from the force of the punch, Vishous turned away and rejoined the Brotherhood's lineup.

After a moment, Wrath walked forward to the altar and picked up the skull, lifting it high, presenting it to the brothers. "This is the first of us. Hail to him, the warrior who birthed the Brotherhood."

As the brothers let out a war cry that filled the cave, Wrath turned to Butch.

"Drink and join us."

Butch went for it with gusto, grabbing the skull, tilting his head back, pouring the blood right down his throat. The brothers chanted as he drank, their voices getting louder and louder, ringing out. He tasted each one of them. The raw power and majesty of Wrath. The vast strength of Rhage. The burning, protective loyalty of Phury. The cold savagery of Zsadist. The sharp cunning of Vishous.

The skull was taken from his hands and he was pushed back against the wall.

Wrath's lips lifted darkly. "Better hold on to those pegs."

Butch gripped them just as a wave of churning energy slammed into him. He bit down to keep from letting out a howl and was dimly aware of the brothers growling in approval. As the roar increased, his body began to buck against the pegs like he'd front-loaded his nose with a kilo of blow. Then everything whacked out on him, every neuron in his brain firing, every blood vessel and capillary filling. With heart pounding, head swimming, body straining, he—

Butch woke up on the altar, naked and curled on his side. There was a burning sensation on his chest, and when he put his hand to it, he felt something grainy. Salt?

As he blinked and looked around, he realized he was

in front of a black marble wall etched with what must have been names in the Old Language. God, there were hundreds of them. Stunned by the sight, he sat up and pushed himself to his feet. When he stumbled forward, he somehow caught his balance before he would have touched what he knew was sacred.

Staring at the names, he was certain they had all been carved by the same hand, each one of them, because every symbol was of identical and loving quality.

Vishous had done this. Butch didn't know how he knew—no, he did. There were these echoes in his head now . . . echoes of the lives of his . . . brothers? Yes . . . and all these males whose names he read were his . . . brothers. He somehow knew each of them now.

With wide eyes, he followed the columns of writing until . . . there . . . there it was, down on the right. The one at the bottom of the line. The last one. Was it his?

He heard clapping and looked over his shoulder. The brothers were back in their robes, but the hoods were down. And they were beaming, positively beaming, even Z.

"That's you," Wrath said. "You shall be called the Black Dagger warrior *Dhestroyer*, descended of Wrath son of Wrath."

"But you'll always be Butch to us," Rhage cut in. "As well as hard-ass. Smart-ass. Royal pain in the ass. You know, whatever the situation calls for. I think as long as there's an *ass* in there, it'll be accurate."

"How about b*ass*tard?" Z suggested.

"Nice. I feel that."

They all started laughing and Butch's robe appeared in front of him, held by Vishous's gloved hand.

V did not meet his eyes as he said, "Here."

Butch took the robe, but he didn't want his roommate to run. He said with quiet urgency, "V?" Vishous's brows arched, but his eyes stayed away. "Vishous? Come on, man. You're going to have to look at me sometime. V . . . ?"

Vishous's chest expanded . . . and his diamond stare slowly swung to Butch. There was a heartbeat of intensity. Then V reached out and repositioned the cross so it once again hung over Butch's heart. "You did well, cop. Congratulations, true?"

"Thanks for putting me up for it . . . *trahyner*." As V's eyes flared, Butch said, "Yeah, I looked up what the word meant. 'Beloved friend' fits you perfect as far as I'm concerned."

V flushed. Cleared his throat. "Good deal, cop. Good . . . deal."

As Vishous walked off, Butch drew the robe on and looked down at his chest. The circular scar over his left pec was burned into his skin, a permanent marking, just like the one each of the brothers had. A symbol of the bond they shared.

He ran his fingertip over the sealed-up scar and salt granules fell free to the glossy floor. Then he looked to the wall and went over there. Crouching down, he touched the air above his name. His new name.

Now I am truly born, he thought. *Dhestroyer, descended of Wrath son of Wrath*.

His vision got blurry and he blinked fast, but his lids couldn't keep up. As the tears rolled down his cheeks, he quickly brushed them aside on his sleeve. And that was when he felt the hands on his shoulders. The brothers—*his* brothers—had surrounded him and he could feel them now, could actually . . . sense them.

Flesh of his flesh. As he was flesh of theirs.

Wrath cleared his throat, but still, the king's voice was slightly hoarse. "You are the first inductee in seventy-five years. And you . . . you are worthy of the blood you and I share, Butch of mine blooded line."

Butch let his head fall loose on his shoulders and he wept openly . . . though not out of happiness, as they must have assumed.

He wept at the hollowness he felt.

Because however wonderful this all was, it seemed empty to him.

Without his mate to share his life with, he was but a screen for events and circumstance to pass through. He was not even empty, for he was no vessel to hold even the thinnest of air.

He lived, though was not truly alive.

FORTY-NINE

On the way back to the mansion, everyone was full of energy and talking it up in the Escalade: Rhage was popping shit as usual. Wrath was laughing at him. Then V got to throwing back, and before long everyone was taking potshots at each other. As brothers do.

Butch settled himself deep in the bucket seat, aware that this homecoming, like the ceremony beforehand, was of such great joy for the Brotherhood. And even if he couldn't feel that, he was truly glad for them.

They parked in front of the mansion, and when Butch got out, the big house's vestibule doors swung wide and the Brotherhood formed an open circle behind him. The chanting started again, and they processed into the rainbow-colored foyer to great applause: The *doggen* were there waiting, all twenty of them, and in front of the servants were the three females of the compound dressed in breathtaking gowns. Beth was wearing the bloodred one she'd been married in, Mary was dressed in royal blue, and Bella was in shimmering silver.

Butch wanted Marissa there so badly, he couldn't stand to look at the *shellans* from the ache in his chest. He was about to make a desperate, pansy break for the Pit when the sea of bodies parted and . . .

Marissa was revealed in a gown of vibrant peach, the color so lovely and vivid he wondered if sunshine hadn't condensed in her very form. And the chanting stopped as she came forward.

Confused, unable to understand the why of her appearance, Butch nonetheless reached for her.

Except she went down to her knees in front of him, the gown pooling all around her in great waves of satin.

Her voice was husky with emotion as she ducked her head. "I would offer you, warrior, this pledge of luck when you fight." She lifted her hands up and in her palms was a thick braid of her hair tied on either end with pale blue ribbon. "It would be my pride to have you keep this on you in battle. It would be my pride to have my . . . *hellren* serve our race. If you still . . . would have me."

Completely wiped out by the gesture, Butch eased down to the floor and lifted up her trembling chin. As he thumbed away her tears, he took the braid from her and cradled it to his heart.

"Of course I would have you," he whispered. "But what's changed?"

She glanced back at the three females of the house in their majestic dress. Then in an equally quiet voice, she said, "I talked to some friends. Or rather, they talked to me."

"Marissa . . ." It was all he could say.

As his voice seemed to have dried up, he kissed her, and while they embraced, a great cheer rose up into the vast foyer.

"I'm so sorry I was weak," she whispered in his ear. "Beth and Mary and Bella came to see me. I'm never going to be at peace with the danger you face as a member of the Brotherhood. I'm going to worry every night. But they trust their males to be careful, and I . . . I believe you love me. I believe you wouldn't leave me if you could help it. I . . . I believe you will be careful with yourself and that you will stop if the evil threatens to overwhelm you. If they can handle the fear of loss, so can I."

He squeezed her even tighter. "I'll be careful, I swear I *swear*."

They stayed on the floor, locked together, for a while Then Butch lifted his head and looked at Wrath, who had taken Beth into his arms.

"So, brother," Butch said. "You got a knife and some salt? Time to finish a certain mating, you feel me?"

"We've got you covered, my man."

Fritz came forward with the same pitcher and bowl of Morton's best that had been used at Wrath and Beth's ceremony. And Rhage and Mary's. And Zsadist and Bella's.

As Butch looked into his *shellan*'s pale blue eyes, he murmured, "Darkness will never take me . . . because I have you. Light of my life, Marissa. That's what you are."

FIFTY

The following evening, Marissa smiled as she looked up from her desk. Butch filled her office's doorway, his body so very big.

God, even though his neck was still healing from his induction, good Lord, he looked good. Strong. Powerful. Her mate.

"Hi," he said, flashing that chipped front tooth of his. As well as his fangs.

She smiled. "You're early."

"Couldn't stay away a moment longer." He came in and shut the door . . . and as he subtly turned the lock into place, her body heated up.

He walked around her desk and swiveled her chair to face him, then knelt down onto the floor. As he spread her thighs, he nestled in close, his bonding scent filling the air as he nuzzled her collarbone. With a sigh, she wrapped her arms around his heavy shoulders and kissed the soft skin behind his ear.

"How fare you, *hellren*?"

"Better now, wife."

While she held on to him, she shifted her eyes to her desk. There, amidst the papers and folders and pens, was a little white figurine. The exquisitely carved piece was a marble sculpture of a female sitting cross-legged with a double-bladed dagger in the palm of one hand, an owl on her opposite wrist.

Beth had had them made. One for Mary. One for Bella. One for Marissa. And the queen had kept one for herself.

The dagger's significance was obvious. The white owl was a link to the Scribe Virgin, a symbol of prayers spoken for the safekeeping of their warrior mates.

The Brotherhood was strong, a unit, a powerful force in their world for good. And so too were the females. Strong. A unit. A powerful force for good in their world.

Banded together as tightly together as their warriors.

Butch lifted his head and looked up at her in total adoration. With the mating ceremony completed, and her name in his back, she had dominion over his body by both law and instinct, a control he willingly surrendered to her, lovingly surrendered to her. He was hers to command and it was, as the *glymera* had always said, beautiful to be truly mated.

Only thing those fools ever got right.

"Marissa, I want to take you to meet someone, okay?"

"Of course. Now?"

"No, tomorrow at nightfall."

"All right. Who—"

He kissed her. "You'll see."

Looking deeply into his hazel eyes, she stroked back his thick, dark hair. Then traced his eyebrows with her thumbs. Ran a fingertip down his bumpy, broken-too-many-times nose. Tapped lightly on his chipped tooth.

"Kind of battle-worn, aren't I?" he said. "But you know with some plastic surgery and a couple caps, I could be a highflier just like Rhage."

Marissa glanced back at the figurine and thought about her life. And Butch's.

She shook her head slowly and leaned in to kiss him. "I wouldn't change a thing about you. Not one single thing."

EPILOGUE

Joyce O'Neal Rafferty was in a rush and thoroughly bitched out as she headed into the nursing home. Baby Sean had spent all night throwing up and it had taken three hours of waiting at the pediatrician's before the doctor could squeeze them in. Then Mike had left a message that he was working late, so he didn't have time to go to the supermarket on the way home.

Goddamn it, they had nothing in the refrigerator or the cupboards for dinner.

Joyce hitched Sean up on her hip and raced down the corridor, dodging meal carts and a gang of wheelchairs. At least Sean was asleep now and hadn't thrown up for hours. Dealing with a fussy, sick baby as well as her mother was more than Joyce could handle at once. Especially after a day like today.

She knocked on the door to her mother's room, then went right in. Odell was sitting up in bed, leafing through a *Reader's Digest*.

"Hey, Mom, how're you feeling?" Joyce went over to the Naugahyde-covered wing chair by the window. As she sat down, the cushion squeaked. And so did Sean as he woke up.

"I'm good." Odell's smile was pleasant. Her eyes vacant as dark marbles.

Joyce checked her watch. She'd stay ten minutes, then hit Star Market on the way home.

"I had a visitor last night."

"Did you, Mom?" And without a doubt, she was going to buy enough for a week straight. "Who was it?"

"Your brother."

"Teddy was here?"

"Butch."

Joyce froze. Then decided her mother was hallucinating. "That's nice, Mom."

"He came when no one was around. After dark. He brought his wife. She's so pretty. He said they're getting married in a church. I mean, they're already husband and wife, but it was in her religion. Funny . . . I never figured out what she was. Maybe a Lutheran?"

Definitely hallucinating. "That's good."

"He looks like his father now."

"Oh, yeah? I thought he was the only one who didn't take after Daddy."

"His father. Not yours."

Joyce frowned. "I'm sorry?"

Her mother assumed a dreamy expression and looked out the window. "Did I ever tell you about the blizzard of '69?"

"Mom, go back to Butch—"

"We all got stuck at the hospital, us nurses along with the doctors. No one could come or go. I was there for two days. God, your father was so upset about having to care for the kids without me." Abruptly, Odell seemed years younger and sharp as a tack, her eyes clearing. "There was a surgeon there. Oh, he was just so . . . different from everyone else. He was the chief of surgery. He was very important. He was . . . beautiful and different and very important. Frightening, too. His eyes, I see them still in my dreams." Just as suddenly, all that enthusiasm evaporated and her mother deflated. "I was bad. I was a bad, bad wife."

"Mom . . ." Joyce shook her head. "What are you saying?"

Tears started to fall down Odell's lined face. "I went to confession when I got home. I prayed. I prayed so hard. But God punished me for my sins. Even the labor . . . the labor was terrible with Butch. I nearly died, I bled so badly. All my other births were fine. Not Butch's . . ."

Joyce squeezed Sean so hard, he started to wriggle in protest. As she loosened her hold and tried to soothe him, she whispered, "Go on. Mom . . . keep talking."

"Janie's death was my punishment for being unfaithful and carrying another man's child."

As Sean let out a wail, Joyce's head spun with a horrible, terrible suspicion that this was . . .

Oh, come on, what the hell was she thinking? Her mother was crazy. Not right in the head.

Too bad she looked really frickin' lucid right now.

Odell started nodding as if responding to a question someone had asked. "Oh, yes, I love Butch. Actually, I love him more than any of the rest of my children because he's special. Could never let that show, though. Their father bore too much of what I'd done. To favor Butch in any way would be an insult to Eddie and I couldn't . . . I won't embarrass my husband like that. Not after he stayed with me."

"Dad knows . . . ?" In the silence that followed, things started falling into place, an ugly puzzle coming together. Shit . . . this was for real. *Of course Dad knew. That was why he hated Butch.*

Her mother grew wistful. "Butch looked so happy with his wife. And oh sweet Mary, she's beautiful. They are perfect for each other. She's special like his father was. Like Butch is. They're all so special. It was a shame they couldn't stay. He said . . . he said he'd come to say good-bye."

As Odell teared up, Joyce reached out and grabbed her mother's arm. "Mom, where did Butch go?"

Her mother glanced down at the hand that touched her. Then frowned a little. "I want a saltine. May I have a saltine?"

"Mom, look at me. Where did he go?" Although why that suddenly seemed important she wasn't sure.

Vacant eyes shifted over. "With cheese. I would like a saltine. With cheese."

"We were talking about Butch . . . Mom, concentrate."

God, the whole thing was all such a shock and yet no shock at all. Butch had always been different, hadn't he?

"Mom, where is Butch?"

"Butch? Oh, thank you for asking. He's doing so well . . . he looked so happy. I'm so glad he got married." Her mother blinked. "Who are you, by the way? Are you a nurse? I used to be a nurse . . ."

For a moment, Joyce almost pressed the issue.

But instead, as her mother kept babbling, she looked out the window and took a deep breath. Odell's mindless prattle suddenly seemed comforting. Yes . . . the whole thing was all nonsense. Only nonsense.

Let it go, Joyce told herself. *Just let it go*.

As Sean stopped crying and settled against her, Joyce hugged his warm little body. Amidst the nonsensical ramblings coming from the bed, she thought of how much she loved her baby boy. And always would.

She kissed his soft head. Family, after all, was the staff of life.

The very staff of life.

LOVER AWAKENED

In the shadows of the night in New York, a secret band
of brothers exists like no other – six vampire warriors,
defenders of their race. Of these, Zsadist is the most
terrifying member of the Black Dagger Brotherhood.

A former blood slave, the vampire Zsadist still bears the
scars from a past filled with suffering and humiliation.
Renowned for his unquenchable fury and sinister deeds,
he is a savage feared by humans and vampires alike.
Anger is his only companion, and terror is his only
passion – until he rescues a beautiful aristocrat from
the evil Lessening Society.

Bella is instantly entranced by the seething power
Zsadist possesses. But even as their desire for one
another begins to overtake them both, Zsadist's thirst
for vengeance against Bella's tormentors drives him
to the brink of madness. Now, Bella must help her
lover overcome the wounds of his tortured past,
and find a future with her.

978-0-7499-3823-9

LOVER UNBOUND

Dr Jane Whitcomb, leader of a cardiac trauma team, is about to leave the medical centre for the night when an emergency is brought in — a man with a gunshot wound to the heart. As she examines him, however, she begins to suspect that her dangerously sexy new patient is not entirely human.

One night, while he's still in recovery, this tattooed stranger reaches out to her. He seems soothed by her presence. And she is oddly captivated by his.

She will soon learn that he is Vishous — V for short — the smartest vampire in the Black Dagger Brotherhood. But his tortured past has left him avoiding intimacy. It is against V's nature to let anyone see his vulnerable side. Except Jane. He has the oddest sense that she understands . . .

978-0-7499-3848-2

LOVER ENSHRINED

Phury, Zsadist's twin brother and a vampire in the Black Dagger Brotherhood, makes the ultimate sacrifice and stands in for a fellow brother to become the chosen – one who will save the brotherhood's bloodlines.

Tormented by the love he has for his twin's mate, he devotes his passion to the higher good of his race and forbids himself from being distracted by a romantic relationship.

The war with the Lessening society is graver than ever, and the brothers need the few warriors they have to fight. Phury is resigned never to divert himself with love or put his brothers in jeopardy, until he comes face to face with the only woman who can tempt his heart and make him question his chosen destiny . . .

978-0-7499-3903-8